Jackie Kabler is an a[...]e psychological thrillers ha[...]n the UK and Canada and[...]t. Her novels have been tra[...]

Before becoming a writer Jackie spent twenty years as a news reporter for GMTV, BBC and ITV news, covering major stories around the world including the Kosovo crisis, the Asian tsunami, famine in Ethiopia, the Soham murders and the disappearance of Madeleine McCann. She now combines writing with her job as a presenter on TV shopping channel QVC; she is also an ultramarathon runner and keen gardener.

Born in Coventry but spending much of her childhood in Ireland, Jackie lives in Gloucestershire with her husband.

www.jackiekabler.com

 x.com/jackiekabler

 instagram.com/officialjackiekabler

Also by Jackie Kabler

Am I Guilty?

The Perfect Couple

The Happy Family

The Murder List

The Vanishing of Class 3B

THE LIFE SENTENCE

JACKIE KABLER

One More Chapter
a division of HarperCollins*Publishers*
1 London Bridge Street
London SE1 9GF
www.harpercollins.co.uk
HarperCollins*Publishers*
Macken House, 39/40 Mayor Street Upper,
Dublin 1, D01 C9W8, Ireland

This paperback edition 2024
1
First published in Great Britain by
HarperCollins*Publishers* 2024

A catalogue record of this book is available from the British Library

ISBN: 978-0-00-854457-7

This novel is entirely a work of fiction. The names, characters and incidents portrayed in it are the work of the author's imagination. Any resemblance to actual persons, living or dead, events or localities is entirely coincidental.

Printed and bound in the UK using 100% Renewable Electricity
by CPI Group (UK) Ltd

For Míceál Murphy
(Buff!)

ONE

Heather

You don't expect your life to change in a bookshop. Books may be among the best things in the world, and maybe *reading* can change your life, but that's a whole other conversation. What I mean is that when you're in a bookshop listening to a talk by one of your favourite authors, you don't expect the stranger sitting beside you to effectively throw a bomb into your safe little world and blow it all to smithereens. You don't expect her to steal your handbag, either. But I'm jumping ahead now, so let's start from the beginning.

My name is Heather Harris and I'm a bookseller at a gorgeous shop in Chiswick, west London. But today is Wednesday, one of my days off, so I hop on a Tube to Richmond upon Thames, just a few miles away. I've been a fan of crime writer Lydia Cornish for years, and when I heard she was doing a talk and a signing at Words on the Street, the big high-street bookstore, I knew I couldn't miss it. It's the sort of thing I often do on a day off, the sort of thing that makes my friends roll their eyes and mutter words like 'obsessed' under their breath, although it's all done with affection, or at least I hope so. Sometimes, they follow the muttering with the 'helpful' suggestion that I should try signing up to a dating app because I've been on my own too long now, and I need to 'live a little'. I nod and grin and make vague gestures that imply I might take up the suggestion, one day soon. I won't though. Not yet. My last proper relationship ended nearly two years ago and… well, let's just say it put me off a bit. Dating doesn't interest me right now. My life is full; I'm content just the way I am. But I digress, again.

So, the Lydia Cornish event. I love this bookstore; Words on the Street is probably five times bigger than the shop I work in, but somehow they manage to keep the atmosphere cosy, like an old library. There are squishy armchairs and a coffee bar at the back, the smell of cinnamon and caramel mingling with the scent of ink and paper so deliciously that sometimes I wonder if they actually pump it in through the air conditioning, just to create the perfect ambience. I've spent many a happy afternoon here, browsing the shelves and sipping cappuccinos, squirrelling away ideas to take back to my boss, Kwee, for our little place.

Anyway, today I queue up to get my book signed – Lydia is lovely, as I'd hoped she'd be – and now it's time for the talk. I'm sitting in the third row from the back, my handbag tucked under my chair, my phone still in my hand so I can take some photos for Instagram. When the woman sits down next to me, I don't pay her much attention at first; I turn to look at her as she stoops to put her own bag on the floor, and she gives me a shy smile, so I smile back. But then I see Lydia making her way across the shop floor and get distracted, snapping some pictures and then listening, fascinated, as she describes her writing process and the inspiration behind some of her bestselling novels. Engrossed as I am though, every now and again I find myself glancing at the woman sitting beside me because, well, there's just something… odd about her; something *off*, about the way she's behaving. For a start, she doesn't seem to be listening to Lydia at all. And, even more maddeningly, she doesn't seem to be able to keep still, constantly crossing and uncrossing her legs, picking at her nails, and pulling jerkily at a loose thread on the side seam of her jeans. There's a big clock on the wall in the children's book section over to the right, a clock with a cat in the number 12 position and white mice at 3, 6, and 9, and every few minutes she stares at it, frowning, as if willing the hands to move faster.

Is she just killing time, maybe, because she's early for an appointment or something? I'm puzzled and slightly irritated. Why come to something like this if you've no interest in it, and then just sit there, fidgeting?

She's a thin woman, probably about my age – early thirties – fine blonde hair pulled into a tight little bun at the back of her head. Her face is pretty, with high cheekbones and pale, freckled skin, but her expression is tight and anxious, and just sitting next to her is starting to make me feel uncomfortable. I look around, scanning the rows of seats for an empty chair, wondering if I should move, but the talk seems to be wrapping up, Lydia asking if anyone has any questions before she has to head off to another event in central London. And so I sit there, trying to concentrate, trying to focus on the conversation and not on my growing feeling of resentment towards this stranger, who's definitely somewhat spoiled what should have been a very pleasant hour.

She's probably just having a bad day, I tell myself, as the room erupts into applause, and Lydia stands up to leave.

Remember, you never know what people are going through…

Be kind…

I turn, intending to swallow my annoyance and ask her if she enjoyed the talk, but she's bending down, reaching for her bag, and then standing up abruptly. Without looking at me again, she marches away, camel trench coat swinging, black leather handbag clutched under her arm. Moments later, she's disappeared into the throng of customers. I stare after her, still perplexed by her peculiar behaviour, then sigh and pick up my own bag. It's nearly four o'clock, and if I hang around too much longer I'll get caught up in the evening rush hour, so I leave the store and hurry to the Tube station, the sky a stony grey on this early March afternoon, the threat of rain hanging in the damp air. As I approach the entrance, I reach into my bag for my wallet, and…

'What the—?'

I splutter the words out loud as I slip the black leather strap from my shoulder and stare at my bag. It *looks* like my bag… it *is* my bag. Or is it? It's the same make, the same colour, the same style, but this bag looks newer than mine, somehow. And the contents… the contents are definitely *not* mine. My precious signed copy of Lydia Cornish's new book isn't there, for a start. Nor is my wallet, or my house keys, or my make-up bag. Instead, there's a wodge of crumpled tissue paper, two apples – *apples?* – and a piece of white card, with something written on it. I pull it out and stare at it.

There are thirteen words, followed by a mobile phone number.

IF YOU WANT YOUR BAG AND ALL YOUR STUFF BACK, CALL ME.

NOW.

TWO

Heather

Thankfully, my phone is still in my coat pocket, where I'd shoved it as I left Words on the Street. I move away from the Tube station entrance as a man pushing a buggy containing a small crying child rushes past me, glaring and tutting at me for daring to block his path. I realise my heart is pounding and the hand clutching the phone trembles a little, although my predominant emotion is anger.

What the hell *is going on?*

It's that bloody woman who sat next to me! It must be, I think furiously, as I tap in the phone number from the card and wait for the call to connect. Who else could have taken my bag – swopped my bag – for an almost identical one? It was with me the whole time until I put it under my seat for the talk. But why on earth…? And now I have to call her to get my own bag back? This is ridiculous!

'Hello?'

The voice is female, quiet, nervous.

'What's going on? Have you stolen my bag? What's *wrong* with you?'

I spit the words into the phone, more loudly than I intended, and an elderly woman who's just emerged from the station looks at me with a startled expression and walks away with impressive speed, leaving a trail of lavender perfume in her wake.

'I'm sorry. I didn't steal it, not really. I'm going to return it. I just needed to get your attention, and I couldn't speak to you in such a public place. I know this all sounds very weird but… can you come and meet me, now? I'm in the little café at the far end of Lake Street. It's just around the corner from the Tube station—'

'Oh, for God's sake!' I interrupt her, infuriated. This isn't just *weird*, it's outrageous.

'It's you who was sitting next to me just now, isn't it? Who *are* you?'

There's a pause, and then she speaks again, a quiver in her voice.

'My name's Felicity. Felicity Dixon. *Please*, Heather. Please, come and meet me. I'll explain everything, and I'll give you all your stuff back. I'm so sorry, but it'll make sense when we speak, I promise. I'm here now, in a booth at the back. *Please*.'

'How do you know my name? Oh shit. *Fine*. I think I know the place you mean. I'll be there in two minutes, OK? But this had better be good.'

This is fast becoming one of the most bizarre events of my life, I think, as I stomp down the road, barely apologising as I barge into people on the busy pavement, my thoughts tumbling over each other in my head.

She called me Heather, so she clearly knows who I am. But how? I'm pretty sure I've never seen her before. What could she possibly want to talk to me about? And why do something so *crazy*?

I look down at my bag – or the bag that *isn't* actually my bag at all – still feeling astonished. I bought it at Marks & Spencer, from their leather essentials collection, so it wouldn't be too hard for someone to find the same one, but it seems like such an extreme length to go to, just to speak to someone. Why didn't she just message me on social media if she wanted to speak to me privately? How did she know where I'd be today? How did she know what my bag looks like, in order to buy herself the same one? And how did she know I'd be carrying it with me today? It's not the only bag I have, although I have been using it almost daily for weeks now. But still... And why has it got *apples* in it?

Unexpectedly, I find myself grinning. This is so surreal it's becoming almost funny.

This Felicity, *whoever she is, had better have a good explanation, that's all I can say.*

I push open the café door. I've been here once before, and it's nice; a small, always busy deli and coffee shop, with a selection of mismatched tables and chairs and a row of booths, upholstered in blue leather, along one wall. I see Felicity immediately, leaning out of the booth at the very back and raising a hand briefly in greeting before sliding back into her seat. I weave my way between the tables, dodging a waiter carrying a tray laden with teacups and what look like slabs of carrot cake, and plonk myself down opposite her. I wriggle out of my coat and dump it on the seat beside me.

'Right. Who are you, what do you want, and can I please have my bag back now?' I say loudly, and she visibly flinches.

'Please, *please* be quiet,' she hisses. 'I think we're OK in here, but I'm just trying to be *so* careful…'

She glances furtively around the café and then turns back to face me, as I stare at her, feeling more confused and exasperated than ever.

'For goodness' sake, are you going to tell me what's going on here or not?' I snap, but I make an effort to lower my voice. She looks scared, I suddenly realise.

'And I'll have my bag now, too,' I add. It's sitting on the table, and I grab it and rummage through the contents. Everything's still there – my signed book, my wallet, my make-up bag. Everything.

I look up.

'Well?' I say. 'Here's yours by the way. Why the heck has it got *apples* in it?'

I push the other bag across the polished wood of the tabletop and see a tiny smile lift the corners of her mouth.

'For weight,' she says. 'Look – let me try to explain. I needed to speak to you, OK? I'll explain why in a minute. I've been following you on Instagram for a while, your bookseller account. But I didn't want to just message you, because I don't trust social media, you know? It can be hacked, and I didn't want any written proof of any communication between us. Anyway, I was going to come and visit you in Meadow Bookshop, where you work? But again, I thought that might be too risky, too close to home. So I thought no, wait 'til she's out somewhere, on neutral ground. Then you posted about the Lydia Cornish event, and it seemed perfect—'

'OK. So why not just talk to me there, about whatever it is?'

I can't help myself interrupting her – this is all getting madder by the minute. Is this woman suffering from some sort of paranoia?

'You sat *next* to me. We could easily have chatted. Why do all the mad bag swopping?'

She sighs.

'I know it seems a bit extreme, but I knew there'd be loads of people around, and they have CCTV cameras in that bookstore – the big places always do – and I just didn't want...'

She hesitates.

'This just feels safer. They don't have any cameras here – I've checked. I came in last week and told them I thought I'd had my purse stolen here the day before, and asked if they had any security camera footage I could look at, and they said they don't have CCTV. I just didn't want any record of... of this conversation. And if I'd sat down next to you at the talk, and suddenly asked you if you'd go for coffee with me, a total stranger, you wouldn't have come, would you?'

I shrug.

'Probably not,' I admit.

She nods.

'So, the bag thing, well, it was a bit of a risk, but you post lots of pictures of yourself, and for the past couple of months that's the only bag you seem to have used. I spotted it in M&S when I was out shopping, and thought it might just work. I mean, we all panic when we lose our handbag, don't we? I guessed you'd come and meet me here if you thought I had yours. The paper's just the stuffing that was in it when I bought it and, as I said, the apples were for... well, *weight*.

They were the first heavy-ish thing that came to hand this morning. I thought if you picked it up and it felt suspiciously light you'd realise it wasn't yours too soon, before I'd left the shop, and you'd cause a fuss and... well, it could easily have gone horribly wrong. And luckily, you still had your phone in your hand when I picked up your bag and left. Otherwise you'd have had to borrow one to call me...'

Her voice tails off, and she sighs, then looks at me with a contrite expression.

'You seem a bit gobsmacked,' she says. 'Sorry.'

I *feel* gobsmacked. I can't quite believe what I'm hearing – the *lengths* this woman has gone to, just to speak to me in private. *Why?* What can be so important she's swopping handbags and checking out the security camera status of cafés?

'Well, I'm certainly going to rethink some of my Instagram posts,' I say. 'I suppose you don't realise quite how much you're giving away sometimes.'

Felicity nods.

'Lots of people do it,' she says. 'It kind of amazes me. They say exactly where they're going, at exactly what time, they post pictures before they go showing exactly what they're wearing... It's a stalker's dream.'

I raise an eyebrow and she leans across the table, eyes wide.

'*I'm* not a stalker,' she adds. 'I promise you. That was a one-off... Oh, hi!'

She turns quickly as a waiter, a young man wearing a black T-shirt and sporting a neatly trimmed beard appears beside us, waving a small notebook.

'Hi again,' he says, with a friendly smile. 'Ready to order, now your friend's here?'

Felicity nods, reaching for the menu that's propped up against a small vase of white primroses at the end of the table.

'Just a latte for me, please,' she says, and holds the menu out towards me.

I wave it away.

'Same for me, thanks,' I say.

'Two lattes, coming up.'

The waiter grins and walks quickly away again, and I wait until he's out of earshot before turning back to Felicity.

'OK, there's nobody in the booth next to ours or anywhere close enough to overhear,' I say. 'So, shoot. Before I expire from curiosity.'

She nods slowly, tucking a loose strand of blonde hair behind her ear.

'OK, well, it's about your friend, Amber. Amber Ryan. Your friend who's currently serving a life sentence in prison.'

I feel my mouth fall open, and my breath catches in my throat. *What?* This is about… *Amber*?

'Are… are you OK, Heather?' asks Felicity hesitantly.

She reaches a hand across the table and rests it briefly on my wrist, her skin cool against mine. It's a sweet gesture, caring even, but I snatch my arm away so forcefully that she jerks backwards in her seat.

No. This is not happening, I think. *No, no, no.*

I take a deep breath and look Felicity straight in the eye.

'Amber Ryan is *not* my friend,' I say.

THREE

Heather

Amber Ryan.

I try not to think about her, but sometimes the memories creep back anyway. The memories of how close we once were, and how it all went wrong; of what she did next, and where she is now.

We met when we were fifteen, at school, back home in Gloucestershire. Her family had moved down from Manchester because of her dad's job, and Amber joined my year at Bayshill School at the beginning of the spring term. I thought she was beautiful – eyes a soft green that reminded me of wasabi, and hair a mass of deep red waves. By the time the summer holidays began, we were best friends, and for the next ten years or so we were inseparable. We went through it all together: the ecstasy and agony of first boyfriends and first break-ups, the stress of exams and the jubilation when we finally made it to university, the wild nights out and the dreadful hangovers, the celebrations when we both managed to land our first proper jobs in London within weeks of each other. It meant we could move here together, just as we'd always dreamed. We'd shared a flat at uni, always with a couple of others to keep the rent down, but in London it was just us and even though we didn't have much money for the first couple of years, we had an absolute ball. And then, slowly, things began to change.

We were about twenty-five by then, and Amber, who'd been working in marketing for an events company, had started dating a new guy she'd met on a job. I normally liked her boyfriends well enough, but Theodore... Well, even the *name*, right? Theodore was a bit of a dick, or at least I thought so. He was a director for a videography company that filmed trade exhibitions, fashion shows, and conferences. It wasn't exactly Hollywood, but Theodore acted as if he was overseeing the latest Tom Cruise movie, pontificating endlessly about storyboarding and graphics and dubbing and blah, blah, blah. Even his voice – an inflectionless drone – annoyed me, as he prattled on and on, sprawling on the sofa in our little flat in Maida Vale, drinking our wine, and constantly brushing his long, dark fringe back off his forehead, a habit so irritating I had to sit on my hands to stop myself slapping him. I couldn't fathom what Amber saw in him and, in true Heather fashion, I couldn't stop myself from telling her that, vehemently and regularly.

I should have kept my mouth shut; I've always had a problem with being too forthright with my opinions. And this time, I should have realised that Amber was besotted, and that for the very first time, if it came to a choice between me and a guy, the guy might just win. And, to cut a long story short, that's exactly what happened. We fell out, big time, over

Theodore. I told her she was wasting her time on a dullard like him, and she told me I was jealous and needed to get a life.

'You hardly ever date. You're too damn fussy, that's your problem. You think you're something special, Heather, and you're *not*. You're a jealous, superior little *cow*!' she spat at me, during one particularly heated exchange.

So stupid, in retrospect, throwing away so many years of friendship over a *man*. We'd argued before – many times over the years, in fact. Despite being so close, we were very different people. I'm feisty and fiery; Amber's more sensitive and easily hurt. They'd always been brief spats before, but this time was different. Maybe she was right. Maybe I *was* a bit jealous. Maybe I *should* have made more effort to get out there and find someone for myself, and butted out of her love life. Anyway, we just couldn't seem to get past it, and in the end we were arguing so much that living together simply stopped working. Amber decided to move out of our shabby little two-bed, and into Theodore's only slightly less shabby one-bed in Hammersmith, and that was that.

We saw each other a handful of times over the next few months, but the damage had been done, and the meetings slowly fizzled out. Then, about a year later, Amber emailed me to say she and Theodore had parted ways, and that she'd found a job in Liverpool and would be leaving London. She wished me well, but she didn't ask if we could meet up again before she went. I cried for hours, surprised by how hurt I felt, but what could I do? Our friendship was over, reduced to the occasional text on birthdays and at Christmas, and so we both just got on with our lives. After reading English literature at university, I'd started my career in publishing, working as an editorial assistant, aiming one day to become an editor of bestselling crime novels. But my job wasn't well paid, and when Amber left I couldn't afford the rent on our flat alone. I had to move, ending up in a grotty little studio and feeling, for a while, utterly miserable.

Then my aunt – my dad's sister who'd never married or had children and who'd always treated me like a surrogate daughter – died quite suddenly and left me her house in Nottingham. With my parents' blessing, I sold it, and suddenly for the first time in my life I had money in the bank – enough to buy a one-bedroom flat in Chiswick outright. Mortgage-free, I quickly realised that although my heart lay in the book world, what I really wanted to do was talk about them and sell them, not help to create them. And so, on the day I turned twenty-nine, I quit my publishing job and started working in the beautiful bookshop just a short walk from my new home.

For a while, everything was great. I had a solid group of friends. I finally *truly* loved my job. I even dated. Amber had been right; I *was* too fussy, always seeking a perfection I'd never been able to find, and so I chilled out a bit, took some chances, and had some fun. And then—

Well, for now I'm going to gloss over this bit. I met a guy called Jack Shannon, and for a while I actually thought he might be the mythical 'one', the one I'd been waiting for. *Christ!* How wrong can you be? Suffice it to say we dated for a while, it got freaky – and 'freaky', I can assure you, is an understatement – and I got out, fast. It took me a long time to get my head straight and then, out of the blue, Amber got in touch again. She was moving back to London, and she wanted to see me – and my heart leapt in my chest.

By then we were both thirty-two, and it had been more than six years since we'd last been in a room together. My chest felt tight as I walked into our old favourite bar that night, but it was… OK. Nice, even. A little strained, a bit awkward, the conversation a tad stilted as we shared a bottle of wine and, both too nervous to eat much, a few tapas, but *nice*. And I think we both felt the same as we gave each other a hesitant hug on the street outside before heading home: that this friendship *could* be resurrected; that we'd been foolish to let it drift; that we should never have let it fall apart in the first place. It might take some time, a period of getting to know each other again, but we could get it back. We could get *us* back.

Except, we didn't. What actually happened, in an incredible twist of fate, was that just three days later Amber was out with her new work mates and she met a man. A man called Jack Shannon. Yes, *that* Jack Shannon. My ex. By the time she got round to telling me about it, she'd already been on four dates with him, and she was besotted, *again*.

It was like history repeating itself. When she told me, when I heard his name and saw his photo on her phone and realised it really was the same Jack, I tried to warn her. I tried *so hard*. Tried to tell her what he was really like. And she lost it. She told me to keep my bloody nose out of her life. She told me it was like Theodore all over again and that she must have been mad to think we might be able to rekindle our friendship.

'I'm sorry I'm seeing your ex, Heather, but I didn't know he was your ex, did I, when I got together with him? And it's not like you dated for long. But here you go again, single and jealous. I give up. Piss off, OK?'

And that's it; a potted history of me and Amber.

Although there's a postscript, of course. I tried to forget about her after that final row, all hope of rebuilding our friendship dashed. And then, a few months later, she popped up again, but this time on the news. Amber had done something so extraordinary, and so out of character, that at first I couldn't believe it. And then I was forced to accept that it was true, and that was when I *really* started trying to forget about her. It all hurt too much to even think about. Did I ever really know her at all? And now, this total stranger sitting across the table from me wants to *talk* about it? About *Amber*?

No. Just no.

'She is *not* my friend,' I say again. 'And I have absolutely no desire to discuss her with you. What are you, a reporter or something? I'm out of here.'

I stand up, reaching for my coat with one hand and picking up my bag with the other. The expression on Felicity's face turns from concern to alarm.

'No! Please, I'm not a reporter. This is so important. Please, *please* hear me out. Just give me five minutes, and if I can't convince you, then fine, go. But I'm begging you, Heather. It's life or death. Literally.'

'Two lattes! Here you go, ladies.'

The waiter's back, carrying two tall glass mugs of coffee on a tray.

'Thanks,' I say, and he smiles and nods and deposits the drinks on the table then bustles off. I wait until he's far enough away to be out of earshot again then sit back down and turn to Felicity. She looks as if she might be about to burst into tears. Her hands are clasped so tightly together the knuckles are white.

'Fine. Five minutes,' I say. 'Go.'

She shifts in her seat.

'Thank you *so* much. OK, well, it's about Amber Ryan, as I said. About her, and about Jack Shannon, and what really happened—'

'We all *know* what happened.'

I interrupt her sharply, and she winces, and then shakes her head.

'That's just it. I believe – I'm almost certain – that it didn't play out like that at all. Just let me explain. You dated Jack first, right? You *know* what he's like.'

'Yes, I do. I dated him, then I left him, then Amber dated him, and we fell out, and then she did what she did and went to prison. Look, I don't care anymore, OK? This is nothing to do with me. I want nothing to do with either of them. This is pointless. I don't get what you want from me.'

I half rise from my seat again, but Felicity reaches across the table and grabs my wrist.

'Please, *please*. Maybe you don't care about Amber anymore, but you did once, right? And I know she still cares about you.'

I shrug her hand off and sit down again, glaring at her, but my stomach flips.

'How would you know that?' I ask.

'Through my brother, Nathan. He knows Jack, and he met Amber several times. They got on, you know? And she talked about you. She told him how much she missed you. How she wished you were still friends.'

'Humph. She was the one who told *me* to piss off. All I was trying to do was help her,' I say. I'm aware I sound like a sulky teenager, so I sigh and add: 'OK. Go on. You said this is "life or death"?'

'I need you to speak to Nathan,' she says. 'He can explain properly. He believes – we both do – that nothing was what it seemed, with Amber and Jack. With what happened. And it's *Nathan's* life that's potentially in danger, and his little girl's. He's moved away – he lives in Spain now – but I can arrange a phone call? Because we think you're the only one who might be able to help. To expose the truth. To clear Amber's name.'

I frown, not understanding. *What's she talking about?*

'What do you mean, expose the truth? Felicity, the jury was unanimous. Amber never even tried to *appeal* the guilty verdict. You're not making any sense.'

Felicity's gaze flits around the café for a few seconds, then she leans towards me again.

'No,' she says. Her tone is low but her voice is steady and there's a steely, determined look in her eyes.

'You're wrong. The jury got it wrong. The *police* got it wrong. We believe Amber Ryan is innocent. And she's not just in prison for a crime she didn't commit, Heather. She's in prison for a crime that never even happened.'

FOUR

Amber

Prisoner number A6868RX. That's my name nowadays. Well, it's not really, obviously. I'm still Amber Ryan, somewhere deep inside. But A6868RX is the number that was assigned to me when I first arrived here at HM Prison Downhall, and it's how I prefer to think of myself now, most of the time. It's easier, somehow. The person I once was, reduced to a string of numbers and letters. Dehumanised. That's how I feel here; not quite human anymore. A shadow. A ghost.

I've been inside for nearly nine months now. *Inside.* The word almost makes me smile. I don't think I'd ever heard it outside TV dramas until I came here.

'E's inside, ain't 'e? Banged up.

Nine months. Three on remand in another prison while I waited for my trial, and six months 'banged up' here. I got a life sentence, with a minimum term of fifteen years to serve before I'll be eligible for parole. Me, Amber Ryan. *How?* It all seems like a bad dream now, that final day in court; a blurred sequence of one horrendous event after another, my sense of shock and disbelief and terror at what was happening rendering me almost zombie-like.

I remember it in flashes – pictures, sounds, sensations. The cold, hard steel of the handcuffs around my wrists; the smell of sweat and stale clothing in the van to Downhall; the roughness of the hands that searched my body in a hot little room, a flickering strip light overhead making my skin look green.

My early weeks here are a blur too: the noise; the rigid daily timetable of cell unlocking, meals, and activities; the first excruciating visit from my mother, white-faced and tight-lipped, dissolving into tears every few minutes as she sat across from me, hands clasped so tightly together her carefully painted fingernails dug into her skin.

'I can't believe I'm having to do this… I can't believe you're here…' she whispered, over and over again.

I can't believe I'm here either. But then, I hear so many of the women saying the very same thing.

I didn't do it.

They've got the wrong girl.

I was framed…

I scream it internally, every single day. But I don't say it out loud, not anymore. What's the point? Nobody believes me, not even my own legal team. Not my mother, nor any of my friends. Nobody. And how can I blame them? I'm not even certain myself. *Did* I do what they said I did, in some sort of temporary psychotic state, a moment of previously undiagnosed madness or mental illness? And yet, that makes no sense either, because apparently most of what I did was planned – planned for weeks, *months.* Planned meticulously. It's gone round and round in my head for so long now that sometimes I don't know what's real anymore. There are days when I feel so confused I barely remember my own name. I always remember my number though. A6868RX.

'A'right, Ambs?'

Lost in thought, I jump as my cellmate, Stacey, walks into the room and flings herself onto her bed, a narrow bunk along the wall opposite. She's been down in Education, doing her computer course, this afternoon. I've just got back from my current prison job as library orderly, and I'm lying on my bed too, staring at the peeling paint on the ceiling. In a few minutes, at five o'clock, it'll be time for our evening meal. On the outside, I never used to eat until at least eight, but I've got used to it. I've got used to all of it, because I have to. This is my life now, for years to come.

'I'm OK, Stace. How was it today?' I reply, and she grunts something non-committal, pulling her hairband off to release her high ponytail and running her fingers through her long, dark hair. She's OK, Stacey Lottes.

'Quite appropriate, my name. Did Lottes of bad shit back in the day, but I'm nice really,' she said when we first met.

She's been in and out of prison since her teens, but now she's here for what they call 'aggravated vehicle taking'. She got fourteen years for stealing a car while drunk, and driving it into a shop front, badly injuring a passer-by who died two weeks later. But she *is* nice; a reformed character, I think. We're very different people, but we rub along pretty well. She's relentlessly perky, which lifts me up when I'm having a bad day, and even though I snap at her sometimes, she never seems to take offence.

'Chill, Ambs. Could be worse,' is one of her frequent

responses, and even though I'm not sure how much worse it could possibly be than this, her attitude is a good one, I think, and so I always apologise, and she shrugs and grins.

'Water off a duck's back, mate,' she always says, then adds: 'Don't do it again, mind,' and winks.

I spend a lot of time wishing I'd said and done things differently.

I should never have got involved with Jack Shannon.

I should have listened to Heather, when she tried to warn me about him.

I should have reached out to her when it all happened.

Hindsight is a wonderful thing; that's a saying, isn't it? And 'you regret the things you don't do in life far more than the things you do'. That's true too. And now it's too late. I didn't do the things I should have done, and I did the things I shouldn't have done. And now I'm here, and there's absolutely nothing I can do about it.

FIVE

Heather

It's Thursday evening, and I've just got home from work in a state of… apprehension? Anticipation? I'm not sure what it is, but I feel wobbly and I can't seem to stop checking the time and the volume on my phone, fearful of missing Felicity's brother Nathan's call. It's just after six-thirty, and he's due to call me at seven. I have time to eat something, but I don't seem to have an appetite, so I pour a glass of white wine from the half-drunk bottle in the fridge and sip it slowly, putting it down every now and again to straighten a cushion or wipe a speck of dust from a vase. The place is already immaculate, just as I like it, but I'm trying not to think too much, and the tidying distracts me.

It's big, my flat, for a one-bed; one of the benefits of buying a period conversion instead of a purpose-built apartment. I have the ground floor of an Edwardian semi on a quiet side street not far from Chiswick High Road. There are just two of us in the building; I share a spacious hallway and the small rear garden with Johnny, my sixty-six-year-old upstairs neighbour, who grows flowers and vegetables in beautifully maintained beds and is quite happy to share them with me, even though my only contribution to garden maintenance is wandering around with a watering can when he goes on holiday. We get on great, Johnny and I, with many a happy summer's evening spent drinking cocktails on the little patio as the sun goes down. It's nice, having a neighbour who's become a good friend. Sometimes we're joined by his on–off Spanish boyfriend, Carlos, or one of my friends; sometimes it's just us. In the winter, we sit indoors instead, upstairs in the huge, comfortable armchairs in the big bay window of his lounge, or downstairs on the sofa in front of my fireplace, snug in the light of the extremely realistic-looking flickering flames of the electric faux fire.

Johnny's away this week though, and so the house is quiet. No gentle thuds from above or footsteps on the stairs, just me and, right now, my racing mind and restless legs. I take another sip of wine then cross to the mirror on the wall, rubbing a finger across a smear and making it worse. I sigh and stare at my reflection for a moment, aware that I'm frowning, and that I look tense and nervous.

'Come on, Nathan, *call* me,' I murmur. 'Let's get this over with.'

I run a hand over my jet-black bob – I'm naturally brunette, but I dye it darker – smoothing the blunt fringe, then dab at the corner of my mouth where my trademark red lipstick has bled a little into the crease. I think again about Felicity Dixon, and the extraordinary lengths she went to to get me to sit down in a café with her and persuade me to speak to her brother. She certainly knows how to leave things on a cliffhanger, I'll give her that.

That line, my *God*!

She's not just in prison for a crime she didn't commit, she's in prison for a crime that never even happened…

I stared at her, open-mouthed, for a full five seconds when she said that. Then I asked her what the hell she was talking about.

'That makes *no* sense, Felicity,' I spluttered. 'Of *course* it happened!'

But she'd shaken her head, mouth set in a tight line, and told me that Nathan would explain everything. And so here I am, beyond intrigued but at the same time experiencing a mixture of emotions I can't seem to identify.

Amber Ryan. Somehow, back in my life again, I think, then jump violently as my phone, sitting on the arm of the sofa behind me, finally rings. I grab it.

'Hello?'

There's a moment of silence, then a deep, male voice says: 'Hello? Is this Heather? Heather Harris?'

'Yes. Nathan?'

'Yes. Hi. Thanks so much for agreeing to speak to me. I hope you have a few minutes? This might take some time,' he says, and I'm almost sure I can hear a wry smile in his voice. For some reason this instantly makes me feel calmer.

'I have no plans for the evening, and a glass of wine in my hand,' I reply, and I find myself smiling too. I reach for the glass and sit down. 'So, shoot. What on earth is all this about? Your sister certainly pulled out all the stops to get my attention.'

'She told me,' he says. 'The girl did good. Might have gone just a *bit* over the top though.'

'You're not kidding!' I say, and hear him laugh. 'So much subterfuge. I still don't get why she was *so* paranoid about using social media to send me a message, and about CCTV? I'm hoping you're going to explain?'

'Oh, she has her reasons, trust me,' Nathan replies. 'I mean, she's always been the anxious sort, even when we were kids. But it's definitely got worse recently, especially since we embarked on this... well, this thing I'm about to fill you in on. I'm pretty twitchy, but she's properly scared, and she's trying to protect *me* by being super security conscious. That bookshop thing, well, she just wanted to play it really safe, and not have any possible record of her contact with you.'

He pauses.

'Yes, she said something about life and death. I'm sorry, but I just don't understand,' I say.

Nathan sighs.

'OK, so... this is all very complicated, and I'm going to get through as much of it as I can, although there's been a slight last-minute hitch in that I'm actually at work now. The factory night manager's gone off sick, so I'm covering— Sorry, I don't know if Felicity explained? I live in Spain, just outside Valencia. I work for a furniture manufacturer. Anyway, I'm in my office right now but I'm a bit worried I might be called away – there's a lot going on this evening – so let me just try and tell you as much as I can, in broad terms, and then I can fill you in with more details if you think you can help. It's pretty intense stuff, I'm warning you.'

I swallow a mouthful of wine and put my glass down.

'OK. Well, I'm certainly making no promises about being able to help with anything. I'm totally confused. So, unconfuse me,' I say, and there's another little laugh at the other end of the line, then he clears his throat.

'Right. So, I believe you dated Jack Shannon about two years ago, correct? Just for a few months?'

'Correct. For four months. That was long enough.'

'I'm sure. I joined his company just a few weeks before you split up, I think, in early May of that year. And I really admired him, at first. The business is mega-successful, as you know, and we kind of got on. He took me on to run the daytime side of things after the previous guy retired, because Jack prefers to work nights – again, as you know…'

His voice tails off, and I think maybe he's expecting me to respond in some way, but I say nothing, and after a couple of seconds he continues.

'Anyway, I suppose we sort of became friends. I'm a single dad – my wife died of cancer a year after Lacey, my daughter, was born.'

'Oh no! I'm so sorry,' I say.

'Thanks. It was tough, but… we're OK,' he replies. 'So, you know, I didn't go out much and when he was between girlfriends – they never lasted long – Jack would invite us both round for movie nights, pizza nights, stuff like that. I'd bring Lacey and we'd put her down to sleep in one of the spare bedrooms and just hang out. I mean, we'd mainly talk business, but we'd have a laugh too. Obviously, I knew even then he was… well, odd. He has issues. But, if you can get past all that, he's an entertaining guy, charming, funny… Again, I don't need to tell you that.'

'When you first meet him, maybe,' I say, a little more sharply than I intend to, and Nathan agrees.

'Yes. Anyway… Oh bugger. Hang on. Sorry Heather…'

There's another voice in the background, a man speaking in Spanish, and I hear Nathan replying, also in Spanish, and then he's back.

'I was afraid this might happen. There's something I have to go and sort out, and it might take a while. I've told him five minutes, so I'll just have to give you a quick outline, OK? And then maybe we can speak again in a day or so?'

'Sure, OK…' I say, but he's still talking, more quickly now.

'So, in a nutshell I now believe Jack Shannon is a very dangerous man. As I said, we sort of became friends, and I suppose he became quite relaxed around me. Anyway, in February of last year he started dating Amber, and I liked her, you know? I only met her a few times, but we had some nice chats, and I was pleased for Jack, that he'd found someone like her. I'd heard about you before, from Jack, but she told me about you too, how you'd been friends. And then one night while I was round there, just me and Jack – it was late March by then – I found out about something. I'll explain *how* I found out later, but it was about something he did, to a woman called Rose. Rose Campbell, who he dated quite a while ago – not long before you actually. Basically, what happened was that she finished with him, and for various reasons he couldn't handle it, and so he… Rose died, Heather. I'm not saying he *killed* her, *murdered* her, but he *caused* her death, if that makes any sense. What he did to her resulted in her losing her life. And my God, that night, the night in March I mentioned, when I was round at his, and found out about it…'

He pauses, then continues.

'He was drunk, very drunk actually. And when I confronted him, he just… admitted it all. He *bragged* about it. He was like a different person. It was *creepy*. He just started *ranting*. He told me he'd had enough of women rejecting him, that it had happened once too often, that Rose deserved to die, and he wasn't going to let anyone else get away with it ever again. He said if anyone else did it, he'd be carrying out a similar punishment. That's what he called it, a *punishment*. He even told me he'd already planned his next punishment. How fucking mad is that? Sorry…'

He hesitates again, clearly concerned I'll be offended by his language.

'Anyway, he said he'd already planned it down to the last detail, making it "much, much better" than what he did to Rose. Then he went on to describe exactly *how* he'd do it when he did it the next time—'

'What?'

I've been listening with increasing horror and disbelief, and I can't keep quiet any longer.

'Nathan, are you serious? This can't be—'

'Oh, there's more,' he says. 'A lot more. But making a long story short and, very foolishly in retrospect, I told him it was all completely unacceptable and threatened to go to the police. I knew that would probably lose me my job, even saying it, but I couldn't just let it go, you know? What he told me – it was *horrendous*. And then he lost it, totally lost it. He told me that if I did, if I told *anyone*, he'd make sure I died too. And Lacey. He threatened my *daughter*. She's five years old, Heather, and he said she'd *die*.'

He pauses, and I gasp. I'm suddenly aware that my throat feels tight, my skin clammy. I'm not sure what I was expecting from this conversation, but it certainly wasn't this. Jack's not *normal*, sure. That's why I finished with him. In the end, there were too many things about him that deeply disturbed me. But all this? All these allegations? *Killing* people, or threatening to? 'Punishing' women who reject him? *Seriously?* I mean, *I* rejected him, didn't I? I walked away from our brief relationship, and he never 'punished' me. Is this guy for real? I open my mouth to say something, but Nathan's already started talking again.

'And then, to make matters worse, Jack told me his late father was a senior cop. I'm sure you already know that, but apparently Jack makes regular fat donations in his memory to some police charity. I totally got the implication – that he's well in with the Metropolitan Police. Very cosy. And I had no *real* evidence he'd done anything wrong, just what I'd seen and heard in his house. No real physical evidence I could actually lay my hands on, even though I know it's there. I just don't know exactly where… Again, I need to explain this properly, and I just don't have time now. I'm so sorry…'

'*Christ!* You really do need to explain properly,' I say. 'I'm struggling to take this in, Nathan. What evidence? And what does any of it have to do with Amber, or with me?'

'I know, I know it sounds mad, and I'm getting to the Amber bit. Hang on. OK, so ultimately, I decided I couldn't take the risk – of doing anything about Jack, I mean. I was scared to go to the police, I was even scared to try to warn Amber. They were close at that point. They'd only been dating a couple of months, and she seemed really happy, and I thought if I said anything, she'd be bound to tell Jack, and I just couldn't take the chance. I'd already lost my wife, and if anything happened to Lacey…'

I hear him swallow, as if he has a lump in his throat.

'… So I quit my job. I just left. I packed up everything and moved over here,' he continues. 'It's nearly a year ago now. I just tried to forget about it all, you know? I made a fresh start. I tried to stop feeling guilty about not doing anything about it. I told myself I had to put Lacey first. And then, I'd only been here a couple of months, and the Amber thing kicked off. And it was just like he told me, Heather. What happened, the *way* it happened, what he said she did, it was just as he'd described to me, all those months before. She must have tried to leave him, and he punished her, exactly as he'd planned. There was never a crime committed, Heather. He staged the entire thing. I'm sure of it. Amber didn't *die*, like Rose did. But she went to prison for life for a crime that *never happened*.'

'Oh, come *on*!'

This is just too much. My shock is turning into incredulity. OK, so when I first heard about what Amber did, I was dumbfounded. But the evidence? Rock solid. I read every article about the court case. Pored over every detail. And the photos, the injuries… Of *course* the crime happened. It was laughable to suggest it didn't.

'I'm sorry, Nathan, but I just don't believe this,' I say.

There's a soft groan on the other end of the line.

'This is so hard over the phone. Look, I promise you, I honestly believe it was all fabricated, all fake. What Amber was convicted of, it *was* a crime that didn't happen. It was just made to *look* like it happened. Jack must have laid a brilliant false evidence trail, because he totally convinced the police investigation. He must have had help too. I have an inkling about one person who may have been involved, and I'll share that with you if you— Anyway, he must have started laying the groundwork in advance, long before Amber actually ended their relationship, just in case. I think that's why, even though she pleaded not guilty, she had so little to back that up. I think she just sort of gave up. She knew the jury wouldn't believe her, and she was right. The guilty verdict was unanimous, as I'm sure you know. But what I'm almost a hundred per cent certain of, is that *she* didn't do anything wrong. Amber's totally innocent of any crime – I'm convinced of it. There *was* no crime. There was certainly wrong-doing, but it was all Jack. His perverse, twisted way of getting revenge.'

I'm silent for a few moments, trying to take all of this in, still incredulous. It's *mad*, all of it.

Then I say: 'But *I* finished with Jack too, Nathan. *I* left him. If what you say is true, he did something terrible to this Rose, the woman *before* me, and then something nearly as bad to Amber, who came *after* me. Why am *I* still walking around alive and well and not in prison?'

There's a pause on the line so long that I wonder if we've been cut off.

Then: 'You're his unfinished business,' Nathan says.

Another pause.

'That's one of the reasons I had to talk to you. Oh shit. Hang on…'

His what? *His 'unfinished business'*?

I hear the Spanish voice in the background once more and

Nathan's brusque reply, and I feel a prickling sensation on my scalp.

What does that mean?

I lick my lips and find my mouth is dry. I pick up my wine and take a couple of sips, noticing that my hand is shaking slightly as I put the glass down again. This is... surreal. Do I believe a single word this stranger is saying? And yet... there's something in the *way* he's saying it, the tone of his voice, the urgency. He sounds genuine; his story sounds true. Yet how can it be?

'Heather? Are you still there?'

He's back.

'I'm still here,' I say. 'What do you mean, "unfinished business"?'

Even I can hear the tremor in my voice.

'I'm so sorry. I didn't mean to frighten you,' he says. 'Look, I'm going to have to go in a minute. We've got a major problem with a piece of broken machinery downstairs. What I meant was that that's what he called you. Unfinished business. He was working on a huge foreign deal around the time you split up and it distracted him – that's what he told me. He talked about you a lot, for a while; you were special, he said, and he thought you felt the same. When you ended it, it came as a shock, but because he was so busy, he let it go, and I think that's played on his mind. He said once that he'd thought about "going after" you, but he's never done it, for some reason. That's why I think—'

'Shit, Nathan. If you're trying to make me feel better, it's not working,' I say, interrupting him. 'That's why you think *what*?'

'That's why I think you're the one who can expose him,' he says.

'Expose him? What…? *What?*' I splutter.

'Expose him. Expose what he's done. All of it. We both think you could, Felicity and I,' he replies, and there's a hint of desperation in his voice now.

'I told her about you, how you were Jack's ex and also Amber's friend, and then we started following you on Instagram, and after a while we both agreed. *You* could do this. We can't think of anyone else, or any other way. He'd take you back, I know he would. You're the one who got away. If you could get back in there, Heather, back into that house, into his life, I think we could bring him down. We could prove what he did to Rose, and to Amber. Get him locked up, make me and my daughter feel safe again. The evidence is there, I know it is, and I could help you, but—'

'No way! Absolutely *no way*,' I say, leaping to my feet.

Is he insane?

'You think I'd go back there? To Jack?' I snarl. 'Especially after what you've just told me? Are you *crazy*? I'm still not even sure I believe a word of it, to be honest. But if even a *tenth* of what you've said is true, how could you seriously expect me to go back to him and put myself in danger? You don't even know me. I don't know you. Why would I do something like that on your say-so? What's in it for me? I never knew Rose. Amber and I haven't been friends for a long time.'

My stomach lurches painfully as I say those words, but I plough on, furious now.

'And I work in a *bookshop*, for God's sake! I'm not a private detective. Hire one, if you're so keen to expose Jack. Get someone else to do your dirty work!'

I'm livid now and my heart is racing as I pace up and down the room. I'm tempted to just cut off the call.

In fact, my finger's hovering over the button but then I hear him say, 'Shit. I've done this all wrong, haven't I? I get it, I really do. But I honestly don't think he'd physically hurt you, Heather. He's threatened *me*, yes, but he didn't lay a hand on either Rose or Amber, did he? That's not his style. And he *needs* to be stopped. The police just aren't an option – there's no way they'll investigate him without any new evidence, especially not with his connections. And as for a private detective, I reckon he'd suss that straight away. He's too clever, Heather. If we don't do this, he'll do it again, and again, I know he will. And if I'm being honest, I'm still terrified. I'm terrified he'll come after me and my little girl. I'm scared that I'm the only person he's told about all this, and that one day he'll come after me to make sure I never tell anyone else. I'm surprised he hasn't yet, to be honest. Maybe he just thinks I'm *so* scared I'll keep my mouth shut forever. And yes, you might work in a bookshop, but crime's your thing, isn't it? And you're smart, and you could get back in there. I know you could. I've tried, I promise you. I've thought about it non-stop since Amber went to prison but I genuinely can't think of any other way that has even half a chance of working. Look, *please* don't dismiss it out of hand. Could you at least *think* about it? Amber told me you were once so close, like sisters. If you have *any* feelings left for her, could you reconnect maybe? Go and visit her in prison, or at least speak to her on the phone? See what *she* has to say?'

I hesitate, still breathing heavily. And then Amber's face

flashes into my mind, an image I saw in a newspaper on the day she was sentenced, her face tear-streaked, a haunted look in her eyes, and all my resolve suddenly crumbles.

'Oh, bloody hell,' I say. 'OK. I can't promise anything, not now. But I'll think about it. Call me again at the weekend.'

'Thank you. Thank you so much,' he replies, and I can hear the relief in his voice. 'And yes, I will. OK. Bye for now.'

The line goes dead, and I stagger to the sofa, my legs unsteady. I sit for a long time, staring blankly into space, everything Nathan's just told me rocketing around my brain.

Then, slowly, I reach for my phone. I wonder if what I'm about to do might just be the biggest mistake of my life, but I know I'm going to do it anyway. I have to, don't I? If I don't, I'll never know the truth, and suddenly, quite unexpectedly, that seems really important.

I open Google, and type: *how to book a prison visit.*

SIX

Heather

'Nice new selection for the crime section. Happy to sort these out, Heather? Heather? You awake?'

There's a thud as a box of books is deposited on the counter beside me, and I turn to see Kwee with a quizzical expression on her face.

'Sorry. Off in my own little world for a minute. No problem,' I say quickly, and she grins and gives me a thumbs-up.

'Cheers. I'm just heading upstairs. Milly's floating around somewhere but it's pretty quiet this morning so you should be OK for a bit.'

'Course we will. See you later,' I reply. She smiles again and heads off towards the back of the shop and the door to the stairs leading to her cosy little office. I watch her go, realising she's had her hair done. It's freshly cropped almost to the scalp at the sides, her trademark dark brown curls on the top of her head looking even bouncier than usual in contrast. I hadn't even noticed until now, and I'm usually excellent at spotting even the smallest change in someone's appearance.

Am I that distracted?

Obviously I am…

It's been nearly two weeks since my first phone call with Nathan Dixon. And tomorrow, I'll be visiting Amber in prison. Every time I think about it, I feel a little frisson of nerves and anxiety.

It took a while to organise. A prisoner, it turns out, has to add you to their visitor list before you can start the process, so I had to phone the prison and ask them to pass on my request, following which I spent a sleepless night worrying she'd refuse to see me and at the same time half hoping that she would, so I could walk away from this whole farcical business. But then I got a message saying she'd agreed to let me come, and so now it's all arranged. Tomorrow I'll be walking into HMP Downhall, a women's closed category prison in Surrey. I've never been to a prison before – why would I have? – and I have no idea what to expect, which is only adding to my trepidation, so for now I'm focussing on what I *can* control. The journey, for a start, is already carefully planned; approximately half an hour on the London Underground from Chiswick to Victoria, then an hour's train ride.

'It'll be fine,' I whisper as I take the new books carefully out of the box Kwee left and stack them neatly on my trolley. 'Just visiting an old friend. Reconnecting, building bridges, having a chat. Nothing to worry about…'

My little self-directed pep talk isn't working though, and as I make my way across the shop floor to the crime section –

usually my happy place – my stomach flutters. It's just after ten, and I'd normally have a coffee and maybe one of the delicious flapjacks from the bakery down the road around now, but hunger seems to have deserted me.

I've thought, more than once, about trying to visit Amber in prison since she was convicted last year. But I'd always come to the same conclusion: she wouldn't want me to. Our final argument had been *so* bitter; so many nasty things were said. It really had felt as if our friendship was absolutely, irrevocably over. She hadn't reached out to me either – not when she was arrested and charged, nor at any time during her trial. And yet now, I've been told by this brother and sister duo who've suddenly invaded my life, that Amber does still think about me, and wishes we'd never fallen out. Quite frankly, the whole thing is doing my head in.

'OK, Heather?'

I'm adding the new books to a display almost robotically, my hand moving automatically from trolley to table-top and back again, and I jump as Milly sweeps past, a customer scuttling behind her. She winks at me, clearly amused she's startled me, and I clutch my chest theatrically as she beams and heads off round the corner into non-fiction, her perfume, a scent of peaches with a hint of vanilla, still lingering in the air around me as she vanishes.

I love Kwee and Milly. They own the store together; they do everything together, really. They bought the beautiful Meadow Bookshop a year before I joined them. They married two years ago in the most wonderful ceremony at Old Marylebone Town Hall, the rock-and-roll register office which in the past has seen the likes of Paul McCartney and Liam Gallagher tie the knot. Kwee is Irish, and her real name is Caoimhe, which apparently is pronounced "Kwee-va", but which virtually nobody can ever get right.

'I gave up ages ago. Kwee is grand,' she told me when she interviewed me. I liked her immediately, and I *loved* her look: her cool hair, her dark yet somehow intensely sparkly eyes, her signature striped cotton shirts teamed with paper-bag trousers, braces, and leather brogues. Milly, a born and bred Londoner, couldn't look more different, with her short, sassy blonde hair that always looks windswept even indoors, and a penchant for floaty, floral dresses and ankle boots. Together they're a formidable team – we won Independent Bookshop of the Year last year, against stiff competition from all over the UK – and I count myself extremely lucky to have them both as true friends now, as well as employers.

As for this shop, well, as well as being award-winning, it's just generally fabulous. It's one of the oldest in Chiswick, housed in a beautiful eighteenth-century bow-fronted building, its exterior painted deep red. In the summer, we put some of our favourite books on trestle tables outside on the pavement to entice passing trade; in winter, we give away free hot chocolate on Friday afternoons, whisked up by Milly in the tiny kitchen upstairs. It's great, all of it. But now the simple pleasure of doing a job I love with people I adore is being tarnished by the nagging worry of what Felicity and Nathan Dixon have told me, and what they want me to do. I spoke to Nathan a second time after my visit to Amber was confirmed, and the conversation left me dazed because he finally filled me in on all the details about precisely what he believes Jack did and, more importantly, *how* he thinks he did it. Although he made it sound plausible, by the time we ended the call my head was spinning.

This is way out of my comfort zone, way out of my league. It's like walking into the pages of one of my favourite thrillers – but a bookseller-turned-undercover-detective? Nobody would write that. It's too contrived, too unbelievable…

And yet here I am, the first step underway, and tomorrow I'll be off to a prison to meet a convicted criminal. Will I take the *next* step, once I've spoken to Amber? I don't know, I really don't. I did do some research on Rose Campbell, though. She was the girlfriend before me, the one who called time on her relationship with Jack three years ago and ended up dead. When I googled her, not much came up; any social media accounts she might have had must have been closed after her death. But there *was* still a profile on LinkedIn, describing her as a senior accountant at Shannon Medical, Jack's company. And then, the bleak newspaper report of her death.

> Rose Campbell, who was thirty-two at the time, died when her car careered across the M4 from the outside lane to the hard shoulder at high speed and then overturned, sliding along the tarmac for nearly 100 metres before spinning back into the inside lane, slamming into two other vehicles and injuring three other people. It happened shortly after 2am on a wet Thursday. Rose, who died at the scene before the police and ambulance arrived, was said to have had a blood

alcohol level of more than three times the legal limit for driving.

It appeared, on the surface, to be a straightforward case of a drunk driver reaping what she'd sown, but what Nathan told me about what really happened made me shiver. And on this one he's adamant. Nathan had already left the country when the Amber thing began, so on some elements of that he's making what he calls 'educated and highly informed guesses', based on what he claims Jack told him about his future plans. But as for Rose...

'I've seen some of the evidence with my own eyes, Heather,' he said, his voice husky with emotion, even though Rose was a woman he'd never actually met. 'And it made me feel sick. And the rest Jack just told me himself that night when he was off his face. He may not have been in the car with her, but he killed her – or as good as. She'd still be alive if it wasn't for him, that's for sure.'

I stared at her photo in the newspaper article for a long time. Rose – her mother Jamaican, her father Chinese – was stunning, with long black hair and a glorious smile, her teeth white and even, her lips full and glossy. She looked so happy in the picture, and I felt tears prick my eyes as I tried to make sense of what Nathan had told me. I know Jack Shannon. But *this*? Reacting *that* strongly to being dumped by a girlfriend? *Why?* It all sounds so extreme, so *improbable*. I'm sceptical by nature, and I've started to wonder if Nathan might have some ulterior motive here. Was he fired by Jack, for instance, and didn't really quit his job as he claims? Could this all be some sort of attempt at payback?

And yet…

'Excuse me? Where's the children's section, please? And do you have the new Malorie Blackman? I wrote down the name of it but now I can't read my own writing. What's it called? My daughter's going to a birthday party after school today and I totally forgot to get a present and now I'm running around like a blue-arsed fly.'

I turn abruptly to see a tall woman with a frazzled expression standing behind me, waving a piece of paper with something scrawled on it in black ink.

'Sorry,' she says apologetically. 'Did I make you jump?'

'My fault. Daydreaming,' I say.

I find the book quickly and she hurries off, calling her thanks over her denim-jacket-clad shoulder. I wave and shout that I hope her day gets easier. Then, slowly, I make my way back to the crime section, my head still full of Nathan and Rose and Amber and Jack *bastard* Shannon.

If all Nathan says is true – and so much depends on what happens when I see Amber tomorrow – then I *have* to help, don't I? But a speculative conversation with a stranger is one thing. If this becomes real…

An image of Jack's face floats into my head, and I shudder violently, as if an icy finger has slipped under my clothes and is slowly stroking my spine.

Can I really do it?

My head swims. I lean on the table in front of me for support. I blink, trying to force myself to take long, slow breaths, and to focus on the new books in front of me. I try to take in their bright covers, the seductive images I normally find irresistible, that make me want to flip through their pages and discover what lies within. But today, even the books aren't enough, and the thought intrudes again. My stomach clenches.

If I do this, it means going back.

Back somewhere I never thought I'd go. Somewhere I don't know if I *can* go.

It means going back to the dark.

SEVEN

Heather

'Hi, you.'

She's here, lowering herself onto the chair on the opposite side of the small table I've been sitting at self-consciously for the past three minutes, fiddling with my hair and repeatedly wiping my damp palms on my jeans, unable to keep still.

It's Amber. She's *here*.

It's been a while, admittedly, but she looks very different. Thinner. Older. Her hair is loose around her shoulders, the ends scraggy and in need of a trim. Although she's always been pale, today her skin looks ghostly white, almost translucent. She's wearing a bright green prison bib over a blue sweatshirt, and has no make-up on. I immediately feel overdressed and over-made-up in my navy blazer and red lipstick. I wriggle uncomfortably in my seat as she settles herself in hers, pulling it a little closer to the table and clasping her hands loosely in front of her.

For a few moments we just stare at each other.

This is nuts.

I can't believe I'm here, in a shabby, noisy prison visitor hall with a woman I've known since childhood; a woman I grew up with, lived with, loved like a sister. How does she cope in this place? How do any of them cope? There are hundreds of women locked up here and it's *horrible,* even for visitors. Just to get as far as this room I've had to have a pat-down search, been sniffed by a drugs dog, been made to put my bag into a locker and been marked on the hand with an ultra-violet stamp ('Just so we know you're a real visitor, and not one of that lot pretending to be one and trying to walk out,' I was told when I asked why, although I can't imagine how often *that* happens – there seem to be guards *everywhere*). But at least I *can* walk out again, and we only have an hour to talk before I do – if we can manage that without another row. So, here goes. I clear my throat.

'Thanks for seeing me. How… how are you? What's it like in here?' I say hesitantly.

She shrugs and gives me a hint of a smile.

'Not great,' she says. 'I never shower without flip-flops, my mattress is about as thick as a yoga mat, and I've never eaten so many potatoes in my life. On the plus side, I've got a job in the library and I probably read more books than you do now.'

'Yeah, yeah,' I say. Her smile widens a little, and something inside me shifts.

She's still there, I think. *The old Amber. Maybe this will be OK after all…*

'So, why? Why now? After… everything. Why are you here?' she asks.

I glance around the room, seeing dozens of green bibs now.

The low buzz of conversation gets steadily louder, but nobody seems to be looking at us. There's a guard sitting on a small platform against the far wall, and two more walk slowly up and down, one winking as he passes a wide-eyed little boy at the table closest to ours. The child – he looks about three years old – is sitting on a young woman's knee, a man in a grey tracksuit opposite them. The man's clearly trying to get the little boy's attention, making faces at him across the table, but the child seems more interested in the pacing prison officers and the small play area at the other end of the room where there's a rainbow painted on the wall above a checkerboard mat with a few toys scattered across it.

'There, Mummy. *There*,' he says, squirming in her lap and pointing. I turn back to Amber.

'Where do I even start?' I say quietly. 'OK, so… I met someone. A woman called Felicity Dixon. I think you know her brother, Nathan? He worked for Jack.'

'Nathan?'

She frowns, then nods.

'Yeah, I met him a few times. He was nice. But what's he got to do with anything?'

'I'll tell you, but… Oh, Amber! Look, I know we fell out, but I'm so sorry I didn't get in touch, you know, when you were arrested and everything…'

She's shaking her head.

'*I* should have called *you*. You warned me about Jack, and I wouldn't listen, and then… I don't know, I just felt so *stupid*, and ashamed of the things I said to you. You were right. I should never have gone there, and now I'm stuck in this *nightmare*.'

Her eyes fill with tears, and I automatically stretch a hand across the table, reaching for hers.

'No touching!' one of the guards barks at me from across the room, and I snatch my hand back.

'Shit. This is awful. Amber, don't cry, please. I'm here now. It's OK,' I whisper, and she nods, wiping her eyes with the backs of her hands.

'Thank you,' she whispers back.

We lock eyes for a few seconds, and something unspoken seems to pass between us. For some reason we both smile.

'Before I tell you about Felicity and Nathan, can you just tell me what happened? What *really* happened?' I ask. 'I know what the court heard. But, is that really how it went down? Because it seemed so… It sounded like there was just *so* much evidence against you. But you pleaded not guilty. So did it really happen like they said it did?'

She shrugs.

'I don't know,' she says. 'I know that doesn't make sense, but I just… I don't know. Sometimes I think it *was* me, you know? Because all that evidence, all that *stuff* the police found… That can't lie, can it? Maybe I did do it, or some of it? Maybe I was ill? Maybe I had some sort of breakdown? But honestly, Heather…'

She pauses, and the desperate look in her eyes makes my heart twist. She looks broken, defeated, so different from the strong, vibrant woman I remember.

'… I don't think I did it. Any of it,' she says quietly. 'I told them that. I told everyone that. My mum, my lawyers, everyone. But I couldn't make them believe me. My legal team told me the prosecution case was too strong, and that I'd have to plead guilty if I was to have any chance of a more lenient sentence. And I actually thought about doing that for a while, because I was so scared, you know? I was just so terrified of being locked up. I thought I'd *die*. But in the end, I couldn't. I refused. I insisted on pleading *not* guilty and they weren't happy about that at all. But the whole time, I just kept thinking *something* would happen. That somebody would appear and save me, you know? I thought someone would suddenly realise it was all a terrible misunderstanding. I thought the person who'd really done it would be found. But they weren't, and it's gone round and round in my head so many times now and I *still* don't know. I can't understand. I mean, I was there that night, but I just don't know *how*...'

The tears have returned, and I ache to reach over to her again and hold her hand. She sounds so distressed. So sincere.

'Please don't cry. Amber, it's going to be all right. Look, who knows you better than anyone? Better than your mother, even? Me, right? So, listen to me,' I say gently. 'Shall I get us a coffee? And some biscuits? And then we'll talk?'

She nods and rubs her damp cheeks with her thin hands, the nails short, the cuticles ragged.

'Chocolate, please,' she says, and I roll my eyes.

'Well, obviously,' I reply, as I stand up. 'Once a chocoholic, always a chocoholic.'

I'm rewarded with the ghost of a smile.

Surprised to find that my legs feel a little rubbery, I head towards the counter just inside the door, at which a small queue of visitors has formed. There's a coffee machine and a tea urn and baskets stacked with a dozen or so different varieties of biscuits and chocolate bars. As I wait my turn I glance back at Amber, but she's not looking in my direction. Her gaze is fixed on her hands which are clasped in front of her now, and her shoulders are slumped. My head is buzzing. This place, seeing her again in such an emotional state…

What am I getting myself into?

And yet… it's Amber. My best friend for so many years. I can't just leave her here to rot. Not if there's a chance, any chance at all…

The queue is moving slowly and I shuffle forwards a few steps and then stop again, my mind drifting back to my conversations with Nathan and Felicity, that crazy line still bouncing around my brain.

A crime that never even happened…

Over the past couple of weeks, I've spent hours online rereading the newspaper articles about Amber, trying to make sense of it all. All the papers covered the story, each headline more lurid than the last. The words danced before my eyes as I tried to replace the stark facts presented to the jury with Nathan's version of events. I'm still struggling to make it fit.

Amber Ryan, the woman who stole a valuable jewellery collection from her wealthy businessman boyfriend and then viciously attacked him when he discovered her crime, was jailed for life today…

That was *The Mirror,* and the comments below it were full of vitriol.

Money-grabbing bitch, said one.

Absolute sicko, said another. *What's wrong with women nowadays? Poor guy gives her everything and she does that to him?*

I couldn't blame them for thinking like that, not really. It was exactly how Jack and Amber's relationship had been portrayed by the prosecution: the generous, loving man who'd showered his partner with gifts and given her the run of his stunning riverside home, only to be bitterly betrayed.

'I know you say the crime never happened, but it was all there, all the *proof*,' I said to Nathan. 'The huge jewellery theft, that horrific assault. All the details of her plans to take the jewellery and sell it on. How she pulled out a knife and stabbed him, multiple times. We all saw the stab wounds, the photos—'

'Yes, we did,' he said, interrupting me. 'And I'm not saying nothing illegal happened here. Jack was obviously stabbed. I'm just saying that what Amber's been convicted of never happened. It's fake.'

'So what *are* you saying? Who stabbed him then? You're surely not implying Jack did that to *himself*? Who stabs *themselves*?'

'Or he got someone else to do it,' Nathan replied. 'To frame her. He *paid* someone to attack him. Think about that.'

I did. I did think about it, and about everything else he told me, but I also thought about the court case. The facts seemed so clear. The jury was told that Amber had stolen over half a million pounds' worth of jewellery from Jack, beautiful pieces he'd inherited from his late mother. Then, in a confrontation in his home office, she carried out a frenzied attack, stabbing him in the stomach, the arm and the right hand before making her escape. None of the injuries had been life-threatening, but the wound to his hand had been serious, damaging a tendon and nerves and leaving him with partial paralysis despite several surgeries. Would anyone really inflict that sort of injury on *himself*?

The news reports said that Amber had appeared shell-shocked in the dock, sometimes white-faced and silent, sometimes bursting into tears. She didn't give evidence herself; clearly, her legal team had persuaded her against that, at least. But on the final day of the trial, she broke down as the verdict was read out, screaming that she was innocent, that this was all a terrible mistake.

And then, of course, came the horror of her life sentence. She was convicted of both the jewellery theft and of grievous bodily harm with intent. Even if she's released at some point many years into the future, she'll remain on licence for the rest of her life, and if it's ever thought she's of any risk to the public she'll be immediately recalled to prison, even if she never commits another offence. Although she was of previous good character with no criminal record, the judge said her crimes showed a significant degree of premeditation and planning, and that she'd clearly gone to Jack's home that night intending to attack him.

The knife has never been found, and nor has the jewellery – Amber's denial of any wrongdoing and therefore her refusal to say what she'd done with these things further contributed to the severity of her sentence. But even without these crucial exhibits, the combination of Jack's testimony, his injuries and all the other evidence presented by the prosecution quickly sealed her fate. There were dozens of emails sent and then deleted from her account, discussing the jewellery with potential buyers. There was her arrival at and hurried departure from his home on the night of the attack, captured on CCTV. There was his blood on her clothes and hands and in her car. It was all so convincing, so impossible to argue against. The jury reached a guilty verdict in less than a day of deliberations.

I'm still thinking about it as I sit down opposite her again, sliding a cardboard mug of milky coffee and two mini-packs of chocolate digestives across the table.

'Thanks,' she says, and immediately rips open one of the packets, snapping off a piece of biscuit and popping it into her mouth.

'It's the little things in here,' she mumbles, then swallows. 'Chocolate never tasted so good. So, go on. While I stuff my face, hit me. I'm intrigued.'

I can see she's perked up a little, and there's a spark of interest in her eyes now.

And so, I tell her.

In a hushed voice, and falling silent every time a guard passes, I describe my curious first meeting with Felicity and subsequent shocking chats with her brother. I run through what he's told me about what he believes really happened to her, and about Rose too, and she listens with rapt attention, her coffee cooling on the table. Even the biscuits are temporarily forgotten. She's silent throughout, her eyes wide, as if she can't quite take in what she's hearing. But when I get to the bit about me potentially trying to help, which would mean getting involved with Jack again, she gasps.

'Are you serious? You'd consider doing *that*? For me? After everything? Heather, are you sure?'

I hesitate.

'That's why I'm here,' I say. 'Nathan was convincing, but I

need to hear your side of it. If Jack really has done the things Nathan says he has, then *somebody* has to do something. But… honestly, I'm not sure yet if that's going to be me. That's all I can say for now.'

She nods, her eyes shiny with unshed tears.

'That's enough. Just the fact that you've come here. It's been *so* awful, Heather. When I was arrested, the trial… I mean, a few friends write the odd letter, but most of them don't want to know me anymore. If I had a sister, or a brother, maybe that would have helped, but I don't of course, and since Dad died…'

She takes in a shuddery breath, and I feel another sharp pang of sympathy. Amber and her dad had been close, but he'd passed away not long after we first moved to London together. She and her mum had always had a more volatile relationship. Mrs Ryan is a peevish, prickly woman who was by and large civil with me as her daughter's best friend but who I'd by no means describe as warm or supportive. She's the sort of person who worries constantly about what the neighbours think, and about 'making a good impression'. I can only imagine her reaction to her only child being sentenced to life in prison.

'Mum does come to see me, but not often,' Amber says. 'And she just tells me it's time I face up to what I've done. I'd given up, you know? Stopped hoping I might one day get out of here. What's the point? And so this… this is like some sort of crazy miracle.'

Yet again, tears are rolling down her pale cheeks.

'Well, let's not jump the gun,' I say hastily. 'I need to hear it all from you first, OK?'

'Sorry. Of course.'

She picks up her cup and takes a sip of coffee, grimacing as she puts it down again.

'Cold,' she says. 'Never mind. Right, so… I get confused sometimes, that's the only thing. Jack… well, you know. He messes with your head. But OK. I'll start at the beginning.'

Now it's my turn to sit and stare, by turns bemused and astonished as she relates her version of the events of last summer. With my handbag sitting in a locker outside the visitor room, I don't have a notebook and pen with me, or any other way of taking notes, but I have a good memory and I'm making a mental list, filing it all away in my head.

It doesn't add up. Not all of it. Her recollection of the stabbing is particularly hazy. Even so, her story is mostly convincing, and when she's finished, I lean back in my seat and exhale heavily.

'Wow,' I say. 'If it's all true, what is *wrong* with Jack Shannon? He's an absolute fruitcake. Sick, sick bastard.'

'I think we both knew that anyway, right?' she replies, and I roll my eyes and nod.

'So what do you think?' she says, and I can hear fear in her voice. 'Can you… Do you want to…? Will you…?'

I tap my forehead.

'Give me a day or so to think about it. But it's not a no. Right now, it's a definite maybe.'

EIGHT

Heather

I settle myself at the kitchen table, open my laptop, and check the time. Twelve minutes past eight. It's three minutes until my Zoom call is due to start, and nervousness is twisting my stomach. When I got back from seeing Amber yesterday, I paid my neighbour, Johnny, a quick visit, came back down to my flat and paced up and down for a while, then messaged Nathan to say I'd pretty much made my decision. But if I'm going to do this – which, despite grave misgivings and waves of queasiness every time I think about the reality of it, I'm almost certain I am, now – I'm going to need help. *Lots* of help.

My chat with Johnny confirmed what I'd already been thinking as I travelled back from HMP Downhall. Johnny is an ex-cop; he was a detective inspector for West Midlands Police in Birmingham until he retired six years ago. I think our shared interest in crime is one of the reasons we get on so well, even if *my* experience of it so far has largely been limited to reading about it in novels. Without giving any real detail, I ran past him what I said was a 'hypothetical scenario', asking him what it would take to get a closed case re-investigated, after someone had already been found guilty and sent to prison.

He raised an eyebrow, clearly curious, but he didn't press me for more information.

'It wouldn't be easy,' he said. 'It would have to be something like an error in the trial proceedings possibly. Or new evidence, of course. A new testimony that wasn't available at the time of the original trial. New witnesses, new documents. If the defendant pleaded guilty to the crime you can't request a case reopening, though. Does that help?'

It does, and now I tap my laptop keyboard to wake up the screen and log on. A minute or so later, there they are, two faces, smiling at me. On the right is Felicity, looking very similar to how she looked when I met her at Words on the Street, her blonde hair pulled tightly back from her face in a little bun or ponytail, I can't tell which. And on the left is her brother, Nathan. I had, out of interest, looked him up online after our first phone call, but the photos I found don't do him justice. He's *gorgeous* – blond like his sister and broad-shouldered with muscular arms shown off by the sleeves of his white T-shirt pulling tight over his biceps.

Nice, I think, then instantly reprimand myself. *Really,* really *not the time.*

'Hi,' I say. 'Good to see you again, Felicity. And to finally see your face, Nathan.'

'Lovely to see you too,' they both say at exactly the same time. As we all laugh, my heaving stomach calms a little, the tension in my body easing.

'Sorry. We do that a lot. Weird brother-sister thing,' Felicity says. 'We lost both our parents quite young, so we're pretty close. But it's great to see you, and to hear you want to go ahead. I know it all sounds mad, but if we can get some sort of justice and show everyone who Jack Shannon really is… And we *can* do it if we work together, Heather. I honestly believe that.'

'So do I,' says Nathan. 'Thank you so much, Heather. You don't know what this means, to me and to Lacey too.'

'That's OK, but…' I hesitate. 'Look, I'm almost a hundred per cent certain I'm going to give it a go. Not all of Amber's story is totally convincing, partly because she doesn't seem to be able to remember much detail about the night of the stabbing. Trauma, maybe? But on the whole, I think I do believe her. And I think you're both right – I don't think there's any official way of doing it, of getting the police to investigate him, without something to show them first. I've spoken to a friend who's a former police detective – don't worry, I didn't tell him anything – and he agrees. The police won't reopen the case unless there's new evidence, or a new witness who didn't come forward at the time. I mean, that witness would be you, obviously, Nathan, but if you think it's too risky for you, without new evidence to back you up, that's fair enough. So that leaves us with *finding* that new evidence, which is where I'm going to have to come in. I'm just glad Amber stuck to her not-guilty plea, because if she hadn't, that would have scuppered everything, apparently. So, yes, if you really, *really* don't think a private detective's an option, and there's no one else who can do this…?'

'We don't,' Nathan says quickly. 'Jack doesn't let many people get close, you know? And as I said, you're the one who got away. I'll be honest – I don't know whether he'll want you back because there's real feelings there, or just because he'll want to, you know… try to punish you in some way, because he didn't do that last time. But either way, I genuinely don't think he'll need much persuasion to go on a date with you again. And once you're back in there…'

He shrugs.

'And you won't have to be there for long,' he rushes to add. 'We'll get you in and out as quickly as possible. Felicity and I will be on call day and night for you. We'll help as much as we can. And if he does start anything weird, we'll be one step ahead of him this time, won't we? We know what he's capable of. There's no way he'll be able to do to you what he did to Rose and Amber. We can outsmart him. Knowledge is power, right?'

'I really hope so,' says Felicity quietly.

'Can we just not go there for now?' I say. 'I'm hoping it'll be *very* quick. A couple of weeks max. Hopefully he won't have *time* to start any funny business. And you know what? If he really wanted to punish me, as you put it, he's clever enough to have done that from a distance, don't you think? And he hasn't. So, I just don't want to think about it. If I do, I'll chicken out.'

Felicity nods vehemently.

'Right, let's talk tactics then. Was your break-up a bad one?' A frown furrows her brow. 'That's worrying me a bit. I know you think it'll be easy, Nathan, but if it was me, and some guy dumped me and then two years later he starts calling me again saying he made a mistake, I don't think I'd be too impressed.'

'It wasn't *too* bad,' I say. 'It was more of a slow drift. I'd been thinking of ending it for a few weeks, but I was scared about how he might react, so I kept putting it off. I kind of did it gradually in the end. I cancelled on dates a few times, then I finally plucked up the courage to tell him I was just too busy for anything committed and I didn't really see a future for us. Thankfully, because he was so engrossed with work, he just sort of said fine, whatever, and that was that. There was no massive row, no big falling-out or anything. That's why I'm hoping it might be OK—'

'Of course it'll be OK. Men are different when it comes to stuff like this, especially men like Jack,' Nathan says, interrupting me. 'If there's a beautiful woman he once very much had feelings for who wants to keep him company again, it won't take much to get over his ego, even if it is for vindictive reasons. I'd bet my house on it.'

A beautiful woman? I can feel blood rushing to my cheeks at the compliment and hope fervently that the picture quality on our video call isn't good enough to make the sudden colour change too obvious. I clear my throat.

'Right, well. I suppose I'm in then,' I say, and I feel my throat tighten. 'For better or for worse. I still have his mobile number, assuming he hasn't changed it. So I guess I'll just drop him a text? Say something like I've been thinking about him recently and wondering if he'd like to go out for a drink? What if he's dating someone else, though?'

'He's not. I've checked,' says Nathan. 'I keep in touch with a couple of my former colleagues and I gave one of them a buzz the other day just for a catch-up. I managed to steer the conversation round to Jack and casually asked how he was and if he was seeing anyone. He's been single since Amber, apparently. The rumour at the office is he's still too "traumatised" by what happened to date anyone.'

He draws air quotes with his forefingers as he speaks, rolling his eyes, and then turns suddenly as a small figure appears behind him.

'Lacey!' he says. 'What are you doing out of bed?'

It's a small girl, dressed in pink pyjamas with tousled fair hair.

'I need a drink,' she says, and he slips an arm around her.

'Daddy's just chatting to Auntie Felicity and our friend Heather,' he says, pointing at his screen. Lacey peers at us, grinning widely and waving as she recognises her aunt. She's adorable. Nathan tells her to go back to bed, saying he'll bring her some water in two minutes, and she nods and skips away. I think about Nathan's claims that Jack threatened not just his life but this child's too and feel a rush of loathing. How *could* he?

Nathan turns back to his webcam.

'Yes, text him,' he says. 'I'm sure that'll work. And once you get back into his house, I suggest you try to stay over as much as possible, if you can bear to. Easter's coming up; maybe you can use the holiday weekend as a chance to hang out, if you're not working? We need you to be there alone, when he goes off to work or when he's asleep, so you can do some snooping. I'm going to email you a comprehensive list of exactly what to look for, OK? There's also at least one other person we might need to approach, but we're going to have to tread very carefully. And if you feel threatened or scared in any way, just get yourself out of there immediately, OK? It's not worth anyone else getting hurt, or… well, or worse…'

His voice trails off, and the knot of anxiety in my stomach tightens again. Then Amber's face flashes into my head, and I lick my dry lips.

'It's fine. I'll be fine. Send me that email, OK? And I'll text Jack this evening to get the ball rolling. I'll keep you both posted.'

'Thank you so much,' Felicity and Nathan say, again simultaneously, and we all smile.

This time we have the upper hand, not Jack, I think. *It'll be fine. And if I can pull it off, and expose all this… wow. Just wow.*

'Right, I need to run,' Nathan says. 'Fliss, I'll speak to you over the weekend. And Heather… good luck, OK?'

NINE

Amber

'Friday night. What'll we do, Ambs? Fancy a few late cocktails down Soho?'

Stacey grins at me. She's lying on her bunk, still fully clothed apart from her trainers. I smile back.

'Sounds good. Then a club, what do you think? Dance 'til dawn?' I say.

'You're on, mate. Just gotta choose something to wear. Grey trackies or this sexy little black number?'

She wiggles her hips suggestively, running her hands down the jersey fabric clinging tightly to her thighs, then snorts with laughter, and I can't help laughing with her. In reality, this Friday evening has been spent like every other at Downhall: an early dinner, some TV time, and now locked down for the night in this eight-square-metre room. Sometimes we play cards, or read, but often I just want to sleep, permanently exhausted for no reason I can understand. I think it's partly the sensory overload in this place; it overwhelms me at times, the constant nature of it. The noise. The *smells*.

The noise is bad. There's no quiet time here, not even in the dead of night. Shouting, banging doors, screaming, particularly if someone hasn't had their methadone or other medication. Sometimes I want to clamp my hands over my ears and scream too, but I'm scared that if I do that, I might never stop. And so I breathe instead. I take deep, calming breaths, trying to tune it all out, trying to go somewhere a long way inside myself, to a happy place, somewhere where the sun shines and a soft breeze blows and all I can hear is birds singing in a blue sky high above me. It works, briefly, but I can't do the deep breathing for too long because of the smells. They're almost worse than the noise. Food, cigarette smoke, sweat, industrial cleaning products, weed. It really surprised me, the weed. In a *prison*? And not just weed; other drugs too. And in astounding quantities, somehow skilfully smuggled in, passed around, sold. I wonder sometimes if the prison officers turn a blind eye to most of it because drugged-up prisoners are probably happier and easier to manage. Or maybe they're not paid enough to try too hard to stop it. Maybe the job gets too much for them at times. I can understand that.

At least *my* job in the library gives me some small sense of normality. If you ignore the bars on the windows, it feels almost like a library in the real world. It's a place of respite, a quiet oasis in a loud, panicky, stressful desert, and I'm not sure I'd be quite as sane as I currently am without it.

But now, suddenly, there's Heather too, and her astonishing visit, and the incredible thing she's offering to do for me. I still can't quite believe it; I keep having to stop what I'm doing to inhale slowly, to focus my thoughts. Because if she can pull this off, I have a chance of returning to *full* sanity, *full* normality. Is that possible, really? I don't know, but the process is about to begin. She called me tonight to tell me that she's meeting up with him tomorrow evening. Heather and Jack, face to face again after all this time. She texted him last night after she had an online meeting with Nathan and his sister, Felicity, and he got back to her within an hour, she said. He was surprised to hear from her, a little reticent in his reply, but kept her waiting for an answer for just a further ten minutes when she asked him if he'd like to get together for a drink this weekend. She feels a little queasy, she said, at the prospect, but she's doing it.

I cried on the phone then. I told her I'll be grateful to her for the rest of my life for coming to see me, for coming back to me, after everything. She told me not to be so silly, her tone turning all business-like and efficient, as it always does when she's feeling a little emotional, and that made me cry even more. But we have a plan now. Nathan and Felicity are going to help as much as they can from the outside, and I am too, if there's anything I can do from here. It's on. It's happening. I put the phone down with a shiver of hope and excitement.

We had to have the conversation in a sort of code, of course. We worked it out in whispers on Wednesday when she visited, anxious not to be overheard by the guards, swiftly changing the subject to something innocuous each time one wandered past. Prison phone calls are all recorded and, I believe, listened to at random, or selected to be listened to if staff have any concerns, so we have to be careful, very careful. What Heather's going to do may not be strictly legal, we think. Hence, tonight she told me everything she needed to tell me without sounding suspicious at all: just two old friends chatting about other friends and about starting things up again with an ex. Talking about it is the easy bit. It's Heather who's taking all the risks here, Heather who's doing the unthinkable, and going back to… to *that*.

'Game of Spades?'

I jump, lost in thought, and see Stacey leaning on one elbow over on her bunk, waving a pack of cards at me. Spades is an American card game, popular in US jails, one I'd never heard of until I came to Downhall. I don't love cards, but I definitely need the distraction tonight.

'Sure,' I say, and she grins and sits up, patting the blanket beside her to indicate that I should come and sit next to her. I do, and she begins to shuffle the deck. I watch her, my mind drifting again to Heather, and to Jack, and I feel a tremor run through me, a little ripple of fear this time.

Good luck, my old friend.

Because, my God, you're going to need it.

TEN

Heather

So let me tell you about Jack Shannon. I'm in a cab, heading for Barnes, which is just a ten-minute drive or so from home. Barnes is lovely, a London suburb that feels like an English country village. It has green spaces and a bird reserve and historic eighteenth- and nineteenth-century architecture, and even a duck pond. It's also where Jack lives, in a magnificent four-storey house on the banks of the Thames. We're meeting in The Bridge Arms, a quaint, traditional place with open fires on cold nights, and fantastic food, although I don't know how I'll be able to eat anything this evening. My armpits feel damp, my mouth dry. I've been on edge all day, unable to concentrate at work, so much so that Kwee, noticing I'd put a Patricia Cornwell book the wrong side of a Harlan Coben on the shelf (we arrange books in precise alphabetical order), pulled me aside to gently ask what was wrong. I fobbed her off with some excuse about not sleeping very well last night – not a lie – and she let it go, but I eventually asked if I could leave an hour early, pretending to have a bad headache. I needed extra time to get ready. To prepare myself for the evening ahead. And now, it's ten minutes. Ten minutes until I see him again.

Holy crap. What am I doing?

We're due to meet at eight. Sunset was just before 6.30pm today, so I suggested the meet-up time knowing it would be properly dark outside by then. Because that's something you have to take into consideration, you see, when you're hanging out with Jack Shannon. The daylight, and the darkness.

There are more things, but this is the one you discover first, when you start to get to know him: Jack does not go out in daylight. Yes, you're reading that correctly. He exists in the dark. He works, and plays, and exercises and *lives* only between sunset and sunrise.

He's like a vampire, I thought with shock when he first told me; when I first understood what this lifestyle choice would mean for me, as his girlfriend. And then, as I tend to do, I looked up vampires online and realised that Jack is even more extreme than they are. Most vampires, if they were to actually exist, are only affected by direct sunlight, so they're OK outdoors in daytime if they stick to shady spots. Dracula, the archetypal vampire, walked the streets of London and Yorkshire six times a day, although the daylight did diminish his powers. But Jack… Jack shies away from daylight completely.

It was something that, remarkably, he managed to hide from me for quite some time when we were first together. We met in a bar in early February, and at that time of year in the UK, of course, it's getting dark around 5pm. The first thing that struck me when he approached me and began chatting was his looks – Jack is exquisite to look at – but I quickly realised there was a lot more to him than piercing green eyes and incredibly kissable lips. He's fiercely intelligent, an art lover, and – something that's very important to me – extremely well read. When he started talking about how important he thought a novel's setting was, I was intrigued; by the time we'd got into the difference between story and plot, I was hooked. Our first few dates were all at night, as dates often are for two people with full-time jobs, at bars, restaurants, clubs. I didn't even twig the first time we slept together, which was about a month after we met. We went back to my place after a Sunday night meal at an Italian bistro in Chiswick – I think it was our fourth date, and I simply couldn't resist him any longer. The sex was mind-blowing, and I was very much hoping for round two the next morning but Jack apologised profusely and told me he had to leave very early, citing a work breakfast meeting. He kissed me goodbye just before 6am, well before sunrise – disappointing, but not too unusual. Work is work, after all. So far, so unextraordinary. It wasn't until he asked me to come back to *his* for the night for the first time, six weeks or so into our relationship, that the truth finally emerged.

By then it was late March and the clocks had changed, so the sun was coming up shortly before seven. It was a day off for me, a Wednesday, and we'd been out until after one, so I treated myself to a lie-in in Jack's luxurious superking bed with its deep, plush mattress and silky high-thread-count sheets. When the alarm on my phone went off at 8.30, Jack rolled over in bed and reached for me; the sex was delicious – slow and sleepy and sensual. I finally dragged myself out of his arms an hour later, desperate for a pee, and when I returned from the bathroom to find he'd fallen asleep again, I crept across to the huge window that I knew overlooked the Thames, keen to see the view my new boyfriend woke up to every day. I quietly pulled back the heavy charcoal-grey velvet curtains and found a blackout blind underneath. I spotted a switch to the left-hand side of the window frame so I pressed it and a soft whirring noise began as the blind began to move smoothly upwards. The early morning light streamed into the room, the river glinting and shimmering in the sunshine just metres away.

'NOOOOOOOO!'

A sudden roar from the bed made me jump violently, and I whirled around to see Jack dragging the duvet over his head, his face contorted with fury.

'Shut the *bastard* blind!' he screamed and, my heart thumping, I fumbled for the switch. The blind lowered again, plunging the room back into darkness.

'I'm… I'm sorry! I didn't mean to wake you. Are you OK?' I stuttered, taken aback by the ferocity of his anger.

'*Fuck!*' he said viciously, from under the duvet.

I stared in his direction for a few moments, letting my eyes adjust to the gloom. My initial panic began to subside, to be replaced by indignation.

What an aggressive, over-the-top reaction, I thought. Up until then – although, to be fair, we'd only seen each other half a dozen times – Jack had been the perfect new partner. He was sweet and attentive and calm by nature, and this was suddenly a whole new side of him, one I wasn't sure I liked.

'Well, I'm sorry,' I said again, crossing the room to sit down on the bed. 'But wow, Jack. Did you have to yell like that?'

He sighed, and emerged from under the duvet, his hair ruffled. He reached for my hand.

'No, *I'm* sorry,' he said quietly. 'I should have explained, before you opened the curtains. I was planning to, but I fell asleep, and then I overreacted. I shouldn't have shouted.'

And then he told me the astounding truth. Told me that for years now – *years!* – he'd shied away from daylight, going out only after dark and sleeping during the day. Last night was one of his occasional exceptions.

'New girlfriend and all that. Didn't want to put you off me too soon, you know? I normally work at night and go to bed in the morning,' he said. 'Look... something happened to me, a long time ago, on a bright sunny day. It... it traumatised me, I suppose. I don't want to talk about it, Heather, not now. I'll tell you one day, OK? But... Anyway, this... this thing, this way of life, I suppose it came on gradually. At first I started staying indoors in summer, and then... I don't know. But the last few years... I just prefer it. I think of it as being on permanent nightshifts, you know? Sleep during the day, do everything else at night. It works for the company too, with so much of our business being abroad now. Much easier to arrange online meetings with New York or Tokyo or Hong Kong, stuff like that. It's just how it is. You'll get used to it.'

He smiled at me then, but I was gaping at him, unable to take it in. A hundred different questions and scenarios were running through my brain.

'But... what about holidays? What about shopping? How do you—?'

Then I thought about his body, his muscular torso, the caramel colour of his skin against white sheets.

'And... and you're so fit, and you're *tanned*, Jack! You have a *suntan*! How...?'

He laughed loudly, releasing my hand and leaning back on his pillows.

'OK, one thing at a time! Holidays, I don't bother. Haven't for years. I'm too busy anyway. Shopping isn't hard. I don't really like having staff in the house, but needs must; I have a live-in housekeeper who mostly keeps the same hours as me but also does anything that requires going out in daylight, so that works. She generally does the food shops too, but if I fancy anything random that isn't in the kitchen, well, we live in the UK, Heather. Twenty-four-hour supermarkets? The rest I do online. Clothes, all that stuff. It's not hard, come on. And I'll show you round the house in a bit. I have everything I need here. A gym, a sun bed. Yes, I know, I know. Who uses sun beds anymore? But I'm careful. And I take Vitamin D too. It's fine. It works.'

I was still staring at him, my thoughts racing.

But if we get married? What about the wedding? The honeymoon? Even though I knew it was ridiculous to be wondering about something like that when I'd known this man for only a matter of weeks, my mind was still forging ahead. *Picnics in the park, Sunday afternoon walks, long, lazy lunches? None of it; he can't do any of it. This is insane. How can anyone live like this?*

'But... Jack, this is awful. We can get you help if it's got this bad. It's just a phobia, that's all. *I'll* help you. *I'll* find someone—'

'NO!'

He growled the word so fiercely I jumped again, scuttling backwards and almost falling off the bed.

'No,' he said again, a little more quietly, and he reached for my hand once more, gripping it tightly. 'Thank you, but no. This is *not* a phobia, Heather. It's a lifestyle choice now, OK? I *can* go out in daylight, if I want to. I just choose not to. And as I said, you'll get used to it. Things are quieter at night. London traffic is lighter. You can do everything faster and easier. Trust me, you might even start to enjoy it. Now, come here.'

He leaned forwards and kissed me then, his tongue slipping into my mouth, both hands moving to my hair, pulling me close. For a few moments, still reeling from the shock of what I'd just heard, I resisted, my body rigid. But... well, this is one of the things that *is* good about Jack Shannon. He's so good in the sack it's almost absurd. Within seconds, and despite having so recently left his bed, I felt yet again as though my insides were melting, my desire for him obliterating all rational thought.

Well, it's certainly different... I remember thinking, as he pushed me back onto the duvet, his body hard and hot against mine.

In retrospect, of course, I know I should have walked out that morning and never gone back. I should have questioned him more; demanded to know exactly what had triggered his bizarre way of life; told him it was completely incompatible with mine, incompatible with that of *any* normal person. But, for some reason, Jack already had me a little fixated. It had been so long since I'd met anyone who turned me on like he did, who fascinated me like he did.

So what if he lives a little differently? I told myself. *Normal is boring, right?*

And so I decided to stay. As it turned out, not for very long. We dated for just those four months, in the end, because there were other things I soon discovered about Jack Shannon that were even darker than his strange nocturnal lifestyle – no pun intended. If only I'd known then that the hours he keeps is possibly the *least* disturbing thing about him. But his other… *eccentricities*, let's call them for now, took a little longer to reveal themselves. And even when they did, he had ways of making me doubt myself, of making me wonder if it was *me* who had the problem, *me* who was acting oddly. I got out eventually, but I stayed with him way, way longer than I should have.

And now I'm going back.

As my taxi drives away, I feel a moment of sheer panic.

Oh shit, shit, shit…

I wipe my clammy palms on the smooth ponte fabric of my figure-hugging black dress and feel a swirl of nausea in the pit of my stomach.

But I have to do this, don't I?

The commitment's been made. They're all depending on me now, Amber and Nathan and Felicity. And, as I keep reminding myself, I'm not alone in this. I have them, my invisible army, my back-up. And I know what to expect, this time. I *know* Jack. I know how he behaves, and what he does, and who he is. I can handle it. It's OK. It's going to be fine.

Breathe, Heather. Breathe.

I inhale deeply, once, twice. I take in the cool night air, centring myself. And then I proceed the few short steps to the front porch of the inn and push the door open. The warmth and light and noise envelop me instantly and I pause, taking it in, this traditional British pub on a Saturday night, full of families and friends and couples all out eating and drinking and laughing and chatting. Surely nothing bad can happen here, in this big, lively establishment where everyone's simply out to have a good time, to celebrate getting through another week, to mark a birthday or anniversary maybe. Well, maybe not everyone's here to party. My eyes flit from face to face: to a group of young women laughing raucously as they clink prosecco glasses, and then to an elderly man sitting alone at a corner table, raising a half-empty pint to his mouth, his eyes sad. I watch him for a moment, wondering what his story is, and then suddenly I feel a prickle on the back of my neck, and I know he's here. Jack. He's here, and *he's* watching *me*.

I turn my head to the right, and there he is.

He looks… incredible. Even from this far away, I can see his intense cat-like eyes, fixed on mine. He has a new smattering of stubble, a neat beard of sorts, and his thick, dark hair with its streak of grey at the front is swept back from his lightly tanned forehead. He's wearing a dark jacket with a white T-shirt visible underneath it.

I smile.

He doesn't smile back.

Instead he nods, and then my feet are somehow moving towards him, my heart rate climbing as I wind my way between the drinkers. My head swims.

Still the most attractive man I've ever met, I think, and immediately berate myself. And yet even in those final days before I walked away the first time, my desire for his touch never quite evaporated. I hated that. How could I still want a man like him to touch me? And yet now, even though Jack might be a hundred, a *thousand,* times worse than I ever dreamed back then, I can already feel it. As I reach his table and he stands up to brush my cheek with his lips, I breathe in the spicy, familiar scent of him and I feel that little fizz of desire somewhere deep in my belly. I hate myself all over again.

Get a grip, woman, I think fiercely as I slide into the chair opposite him. *You're here to do a job, to play a part. Get a grip.*

'Hi Jack,' I say. 'It's so nice to see you.'

He regards me coolly for a couple of seconds, his eyes roving from my hair to my breasts, then, finally, meeting mine again.

'As I said when you messaged, it was a bit of a surprise to hear from you,' he says. 'It's been a while.'

I nod.

'Nearly two years,' I say. 'Jack, I'm so sorry, about the way it ended. I suppose I just wasn't in the right headspace for a relationship back then. But I've often thought about you. This might sound cheesy, but I sort of feel you were... well, you were the one that got away. Unfinished business, if you like.'

I can feel my heart thumping in my chest as I say the words I've been rehearsing all day, using the same phrase Nathan used when he talked about me and Jack. Will it work? Will a man like Jack *really* let me back in again? He's staring at me intently, and my scalp prickles. Which way is this going to go?

'So, thanks for coming,' I add. 'And you look *hot,* by the way.'

I give him a cheeky grin, the one he always used to say he loved. For a moment he just continues to stare, expressionlessly, and then suddenly his face relaxes into a broad smile.

'You are a little minx,' he says. 'But you look hot too, so yes, I forgive you. Everyone deserves a second chance. I took the liberty of ordering champagne. Drink?'

I hadn't even noticed the bottle sitting in an ice bucket, two glasses beside it. I grin again and nod.

'Never been known to refuse champagne,' I say, and as he pours I try to quell the mixture of unease and elation that's rushing through me.

It's worked. Step one. You've done it, I think, as I accept the glass of amber bubbles and clink it against his. It's only then that I notice his hand. He's holding the glass in his left, the same hand he used to pour the champagne. His right hand is resting on the table, a jagged scar across the back of it, the fingers oddly twisted. I want to look at it properly, but I tear my gaze from it, and meet his eyes instead.

'Cheers,' I say.

He's scrutinising me again. His smile is gone, his expression intense. I stare back, feeling a strange tingle in my chest.

God, he's handsome.

Is this desire, reignited? Or something else? Trepidation? Fear?

Why is he looking at me like this?

'Cheers, Heather,' he says.

There are a few moments of silence, and my chest tightens. I wonder if he can see the tension in my body, the wariness in my eyes. Then his lips curve upwards, into just a hint of a smile.

'Oh,' he adds. 'And welcome back.'

ELEVEN

Heather

Of course I wake up in his bed.

I'm not stupid; I knew he'd expect me to sleep with him, but I could have held off for a few days at least. I could have simply had drinks and dinner with him last night and then gone home. I could have taken this fake revival of our relationship at a slightly more leisurely pace. But seeing him again, feeling the effect he had on me – desire tinged with terror – made me realise I need to act *fast*. I need this to be over as quickly as possible. Jack, after his initial coolness, seemed to revert to how he was when we first met: charismatic, interesting, interested in me. And so I put on the performance of my life. I forced myself to relax, made myself drink the champagne and eat the food and chat just as if it was a normal date. We caught up, I told him what I'd been up to since we last met, and I listened to his stories of his ever-expanding business. And later, when the second bottle of bubbly was opened, the alcohol anaesthetising my anxieties, I let his knee touch mine under the table. I felt his hand reach for mine and stroke it, his fingers running sensuously over my skin. It's been a long time since I had a date, and I even let myself enjoy it a little, sitting in a pub with such a devastatingly good-looking man, seeing the longing looks from other women – and, indeed, men – who walked past us with undisguised admiration in their eyes.

Throughout though, the same thoughts kept running through my head: this is dangerous; Jack is dangerous; I can't let my guard down, at any point; I don't want to prolong this or be in his company for any longer than I have to; I *cannot* get sucked in, not even for a moment. And yet for this to work, I have to convince him that it *is* real, that I want to be back in his life. And I have to hope, with everything I've got, that I'm his 'unfinished business' in a good way. If there's the slightest hint he's going to try to destroy me like he did Rose and Amber, I'm out of here. But in the meantime, I need to be everything he wants me to be. And so, when he paid the bill and then leant towards me, his voice husky, and said, 'Come home with me', my breathing quickened and I nodded.

'I'd like that,' I whispered, and I saw the glint of satisfaction in his eyes. He waited until we were just inside his front door before he kissed me, and despite myself, despite everything that happened before and everything I know now, it was as if my body had a mind of its own. My lips parted, my hands ran up the firm muscles of his back and the delicious sensation of his mouth on mine extinguished all my fears, just for a few seconds. Then, thankfully, I came to my senses and gently pulled away.

'Can we take it slowly, for now?' I said. 'I'm so happy to see you again, and I want to stay with you tonight, but…'

He nodded.

'Of course, no pressure,' he replied. 'It'll be worth waiting for, eh?'

He grinned and gave me such an exaggerated, lascivious wink that I genuinely laughed.

'Idiot,' I said. 'But yes, it will be.'

And so we climbed into bed together, both keeping our underwear on, and just kissed. His right hand, I quickly realised, does have *some* movement; it's not entirely paralysed, but it's clumsy, and he definitely favours the left now. He has a thin scar across his abdomen too, and another on his right bicep – the other knife wounds allegedly inflicted by Amber. I ran my hand gently across them, murmuring that I was so sorry this had happened to him, and he nodded, thanking me, but adding that he preferred not to talk about it.

'I know she was once a friend of yours,' he said, nuzzling my ear and then gently biting the lobe, teasing it with his tongue, making my breath come in little gasps. 'And obviously she's not anymore, but I just want to forget it, if you don't mind. I'm fine. I've moved on. I assume you're no longer in contact?'

'Absolutely not. The woman's clearly a psycho,' I replied. He nodded and rolled on top of me, slowly kissing his way up my neck. I sighed with pleasure, and then found myself questioning everything again.

Having now seen Jack's injuries with my own eyes, does Nathan really have this right? Would any sane man actually attack *himself* with a knife, or pay someone else to do that, just to punish a woman for leaving him? It seems inconceivable, ludicrous. But then, I have to remember that Jack isn't sane. Not really, is he…?

Good Lord, though – his skill in the bedroom certainly hasn't been impaired. But although my body was aching for more, the smoothness of his skin and the smell of his hair turning me on far, far more than I wanted to admit, even to myself, somehow after a few minutes I managed to plead tiredness and turned away. Sleep didn't come quickly though, and I lay there in the dark, trying to order my thoughts and plan my next move. I guessed Jack would do what he almost always did when I spent the night, and I was right. He dozed for an hour or so, sleeping off the booze, and then slipped out of bed, heading for his office down the corridor. It might have been two in the morning, but it was essentially the afternoon of Jack's working day, and even on a Sunday he had business to attend to, plans to make for the week ahead. It's his real sleeping time during the day that I'm counting on. I need him to be happy for me to hang around in his home, free to do what I need to do while he's asleep.

Now, I roll over and stretch, my limbs sliding across the soft sheets. I wonder what time he'll come back to bed. It's usually around 11am, and it's nearly 10 now, but I don't dare ask him if I can stay today and wait for him to get up this evening; it's too soon, and I don't want him to get suspicious. But maybe I'll suggest meeting up again on Tuesday night, ahead of my day off on Wednesday. I'll have to have sex with him at some point, I know that – and soon, too. My feelings around that are too complicated to process right now, so I decide to stop lying here thinking and get up, shower, say goodbye to Jack and then head home and call Nathan and Felicity.

I pull my black dress back on and realise the walk of shame beckons. I'm already imagining the sardonic smile I'm sure I'll see on the face of my cab driver when I leave this house at ten-thirty in the morning, very clearly wearing the clothes I was out in last night, when the bedroom door opens suddenly. I turn, expecting to see Jack standing there, but to my surprise it's a woman wearing a navy tabard over a white T-shirt and jeans and holding a duster.

'Oh! Hello!' I say.

She nods unsmilingly, dark brown eyes flitting from my still damp hair to my bare feet, as if sizing me up.

Then she says: 'Good morning. I'm Rhona. Rhona MacDonald. Mr Shannon's housekeeper. Sorry to disturb. I didn't know he had company.'

Her accent is Scottish, and she looks a little older than me but ten times fitter. She's broad-shouldered with muscular arms and hair as dark as her eyes scraped back from her face.

'Hi, Rhona.'

I look around for my shoes, feeling a little awkward. She's still standing in the doorway, silently watching me. Is she waiting to clean the room? Where are my wretched shoes?

'Erm... I'm Heather,' I say, turning back to her. 'I'm... well, I suppose I'm an old friend of Jack's. Mr Shannon's. We knew each other a couple of years ago and we've just sort of... got back together. Have you worked for him long?'

I suddenly spy the shoes, over by the still curtained window, and go to pick them up. Rhona just stands there, motionless, and I feel my face reddening. Is she going to completely ignore my question?

Clutching the black stilettos, I turn back to look at her as she says: 'Just been here a week. It's a bit different, but it suits me. You know, working at night. I've just finished my shift.'

Her face still bears no hint of a smile, and so I do what I always do when I feel uncomfortable: I keep talking.

'Oh, not long then! You're right, it must be a bit different here. From other places you've worked, I mean. Or... well, I suppose it depends where you've worked! But I don't think many people live like Jack, you know... Anyway, have a good sleep...'

My voice tails off. Rhona's eyes have a look of vague amusement in them now, but maybe I'm imagining that, because her mouth is still set in a stern line.

'Thanks. Bye.'

She nods curtly and leaves the room, closing the door firmly behind her. I sit down on the bed to pull on my shoes, feeling a little disconcerted.

Another new one, I think. During the four months I dated Jack, he went through two housekeepers – Veronica and Elaine... or was it Ellen? I can't remember, but it's no real surprise they change so regularly. It's not a bad gig, conditions-wise; a big house to look after, but one which is always pretty spotless, with Jack living alone in it, and a small but perfectly formed basement apartment that comes with the job. The downside for most people, of course, is the working hours. As he told me that first night I stayed over, Jack's housekeeper mostly has to live like he does: at night. They prepare his lunch at one in the morning, his dinner at 7am, and, in-between the kitchen stints, they clean his home while he works then disappear during the day while he sleeps. I've always thought how odd it must be for him, when he goes out as he did last night, to drink alcohol or eat steak at what is normally his breakfast time, but he doesn't seem to mind that once or twice a week, which is fortunate. Most of the housekeepers can't handle the whole peculiar situation for long though, and I find myself hoping that Rhona might soon find it doesn't suit her so well after all, and leave. In my conversations with Nathan and Felicity, for some reason I'd forgotten about the housekeepers – I think maybe Nathan had too. It's going to make what I have to do here harder – having someone else in the building, even if she is sleeping in her apartment downstairs while I'm poking around.

I reach for my mobile and book an Uber. I need to get out of here now. I need to get into the daylight and out of this artificially lit house with all its blinds and curtains blocking out the sunshine. But before I go, I need to arrange that second date. The next time I'm in this house, in just a few days' time perhaps, I can begin.

I leave the bedroom and head down the long corridor to Jack's office.

First step, tick.

And now… game on.

TWELVE

Heather

'Wow, Heather. Are you sure that's a good idea?'

I'm at work on Monday morning, rain beating against the windows of the bookshop and, in reply to a question from Kwee about what I did on Saturday night, I've just told my boss that I went on a date with Jack Shannon. First time around, I didn't go into much detail about why I ended things; I think I felt too ashamed that I'd allowed myself to get involved with a man like him, that I hadn't got out sooner. But I'd told Kwee and Milly enough about his oddness for them to be glad I was no longer with him. Now, if Kwee raises her eyebrows much further they're going to disappear into the curls that dip onto her forehead.

'I mean, all the living at night bollocks,' she says. 'Why would you want to go back to *that*?'

I shrug, trying to appear nonchalant.

'I know,' I say. 'But it's just a casual thing this time. I'm single, he's single... We're just keeping each other company a bit, nothing serious. And he's *gorgeous*, Kwee.'

Kwee sighs.

'Ahh, fair enough. He's a looker, I'll give you that.'

I stare at her, surprised.

'You never met him, last time, did you?'

She frowns, hesitating as if thinking, then rolls her eyes.

'No. But you showed me photos. Don't you remember, on our Easter night out that year? When you were… slightly drunk?'

I nod slowly. I don't remember actually, but there's every possibility that happened. I was drinking a lot more back then. I'd needed it, to cope with Jack.

'Anyway, be careful, OK? Now, can I leave you to sort the posters for the Geoff Spoonly event? I need to lock myself away and do some ordering. Milly will be in shortly – she's just at the dentist. Check-up, nothing nasty.'

'Of course. See you later.'

Kwee heads off, squeezing my arm in what I take to be a supportive gesture as she goes, and for the next couple of hours I force myself to focus on work. First, I make a couple of reels for Instagram, which I've somewhat neglected recently, to let my followers know about some of the fabulous new books that have arrived this week. And then, the event. Geoff Spoonly, the young adult fiction writer, is launching his new novel here, and making the promotional posters for the window and to dot around the store is a good diversion. Milly arrives not long after Kwee goes up to her office, and she's happy to deal with the customers this morning, so I sit quietly at the computer behind the cash desk, making the posters as eye-catching as I can, then printing them out and pinning them up.

At noon, Milly tells me to take the early lunch break, so I head upstairs to our little kitchen, make a cup of coffee and settle myself into one of the two chairs by the window, notebook on my knee. Outside, it's still pouring, and down on the street umbrellas bob as pedestrians dodge puddles on the pavement, the leaves of the plane tree opposite the shop drooping under the weight of the raindrops. We're lucky in Chiswick, to have so many trees; I love them all year round, their leafy joyfulness in spring and summer, their fiery glory in autumn, their bare, sculptural beauty in winter. I nibble on the chicken and avocado sandwich I made at home this morning, idly people-watching, then sip my coffee slowly. Finally, with just ten minutes left of my break, I reluctantly open my notebook. I need to get everything straight in my head before I see Jack again tomorrow night, and I start by reading through the details Nathan gave me about what he believes happened to Rose and Amber, now neatly bullet-pointed by me. Using paper and ink is something I still like to do, old-fashioned though that sounds; it helps make everything real, somehow, and I can't afford to make any mistakes with what I'm about to do. I already have a loose plan, and as I read Rose and Amber's stories once more, my anger intensifies. If Nathan has this right, what sort of monster is Jack Shannon?

I start with Rose, and as I look at the photo of her, laughing and happy, that I've now printed out and stapled to a page of my notebook, I feel a rush of sadness. Nathan says she began dating Jack three years ago, not long after she began working for him. It had, apparently, gone quite well for a while, or at least that's what Jack told Nathan. But then, presumably, it all became a bit too much for poor Rose, and so she ended the relationship. Nathan doesn't know why Jack took this particular dumping so badly – 'Maybe it had been building for a while, and he finally snapped', he said – but what he claims Jack did next is this.

First, he bragged to Nathan, he hacked Rose's email and somehow accessed her bank account too, leaving a trail of evidence to make it appear that she'd stolen over a hundred thousand pounds from Shannon Medical. He transferred the cash gradually, in a number of small transactions, to a new offshore account he'd set up in her name.

'She was a senior accountant, so she had access to all the company accounts, of course, which would have made it easier,' Nathan said. 'But, although Jack's a clever guy, he's no IT genius. While I worked there he was always calling the twenty-four-hour tech team in the middle of the night if even the slightest thing went wrong with his computer. He had no idea how to fix it on his own, so he must have had help from someone else to hack into Rose's accounts. I think I know who that was, and I'm working on getting his details for you. We'll figure out how to approach him further down the line. But this is the thing: I'm a hundred per cent sure there'll be hard copies of those emails somewhere. There's a paper trail, Heather, I'd bet my apartment on it. Jack's odd like that. He *always* printed and kept hard copies of important documents. He backed them up to the cloud too, but he liked to print. He liked to hold them in his hand. And when it comes to personal documents, he doesn't trust banks or safety deposit boxes. He'll use them for company stuff, obviously. But anything personal, I'd always see him printing off and putting in his briefcase. I have no idea where he keeps them, but if we can find them, that's freaking gold dust.'

'Are you sure? You really think he's stashing something that important at *home*?' I said, deeply sceptical. It seemed so… basic. 'This is really what you want me to do? Physically search his house?'

Nathan was insistent.

'I do. His home is the only place he really feels safe, I think. He doesn't trust many people. Believe me, Heather, everything we need is in that house, I'm sure of it. It's what the police would do, if they could be persuaded to investigate him. But as they currently have no grounds for that, other than our – well, *my* – say so, we're just going to have to do it ourselves. Well, *you* are. For which I thank you again, from the bottom of my heart.'

'Hmm. Don't thank me yet,' I said darkly.

'I have every faith in you. You've got this,' he replied.

Nathan went on to describe how after the so-called crime was discovered by another of the company's accountants, who'd noticed financial discrepancies, Rose had been reported to the police, arrested, charged, and released on bail. That night, Jack had invited her round to his house, initially feigning shock and sympathy for his ex-girlfriend about the allegations against her, telling her there must be some mistake, and that he was sure it could be cleared up. She'd cried on his shoulder, and they'd drunk a bottle of wine together, and then a second, Jack making sure Rose had drunk most of it. And then he'd shown his true colours. He'd admitted it was actually him who'd been behind it all, him who'd accessed her accounts and carried out the money transfers. He'd told her he'd made sure the evidence against her was utterly compelling, with a trail of emails and documents that would make it appear that she, and she alone, was responsible. He'd stressed that this had been done so cleverly that all traces of the hacking of her accounts had been erased and that nobody would ever suspect anyone else had had a hand in it. And he'd told her, with great relish, that her future was now in ruins, that she was facing prison and the end of her career; that this was the punishment she so richly deserved for the way she'd treated him by walking out on their relationship. The revelations had left Rose first speechless with horror, and then in hysterics, screaming and crying and begging Jack not to do this, but he'd simply laughed at her. And Nathan knows all this – what Jack said and Rose's reaction – because he's seen it with his own eyes and heard it with his own ears. Not because he was there – Nathan didn't even start working for Jack until six months after Rose died – but because Jack recorded the entire encounter.

'He *videoed* it, Heather,' Nathan told me. 'He sat there in his living room with that poor, broken woman, filming the whole conversation on some sort of hidden camera. And that night, the night I found out about it all, I walked in and found him there, pissed, rewatching that video and laughing. *Laughing*. He was getting off on it. Reliving it. And I know he had that footage on a DVD, because I watched him eject it from his machine. You know how he still likes to watch his old DVDs? Still has a DVD player under his TV? Old school. I mean, most people watch back security camera footage on their phones, nowadays, don't they? But he'd made a hard copy of it, like he does with his documents. And he still has that somewhere too, I'd swear to it.'

I nodded at that. The hidden camera doesn't surprise me. I've had my own experiences of Jack's fondness for recording things. I remembered too his huge collection of old movies, all on DVD, perfectly organised by release date and genre. He loves DVDs. But this footage of Rose? To keep it, and rewatch it, and *laugh* at it? When the woman is dead? My God!

'Rose died later that night,' Nathan continued. 'She was so drunk and in such a state when she left his place that she got in her car and she drove onto the M4 and she had that accident and she died. He could have at least stopped her doing that, you know? He could have at least sent her home in a fucking taxi, and not let her get behind the wheel. But he didn't. Her death is down to him, no doubt about that. The case of the stolen money was obviously closed when Rose passed away. Maybe they got the money back from that off-shore account after her death, I don't know. Anyway, nobody ever looked at it again. But we have to clear Rose's name, even if it is posthumously. Her family, her friends… Jack told me they all knew what she'd been charged with, and some of them think she took her own life on that motorway because she was so scared of what might happen to her. They deserve to know the truth. If we can find that DVD, and proof that Jack was behind the theft of the money… well, the police would *have* to do something, wouldn't they?'

I feel a little sick now as I read through the details of Rose's story again, my lunchtime sandwich lying heavy in my stomach. I take another sip of my coffee and turn the page, then put the mug down and inhale deeply, bracing myself to revisit my notes on Amber.

Nathan told me how Jack had seemed to relish telling him in detail about his idea for revenge on any future girlfriend, should she treat him like Rose had.

'He said that next time, one of his plans was to make it look as if she'd stolen a load of valuable jewellery from him,' Nathan said. 'He said he'd already made a list of buyers he could send emails to from the woman's account. The prosecution claimed Amber must have squirrelled the jewellery away somewhere, but it's still in his house, I know it is. We *need* to find that too. And then the main event. He said this time he was going to throw in a little extra, to make the allegations against her even more serious. He didn't tell me any more about that, but it *must* have been a reference to the stabbing, and we need to find out how that happened. He *could* have done it himself, but I think that would have been really difficult, given the nature of his injuries.'

'It's the bit that's still bothering me,' I said. 'The prosecution said Amber went to the house armed with a knife, because that's what Jack claimed; she told me she *does* remember holding a knife in her hand, but she says it was Jack's and that she doesn't remember using it. She thinks someone else must have been there, but there's no evidence of that, and of course Jack told the police it was her knife and her who stabbed him, so everything *she* said was written off as lies.'

'Yep. My feeling is someone else *was* there, although I don't know who. Maybe they accidentally went a bit too far, because that hand injury was pretty serious. It's probably hard to stab someone accurately. There *are* a lot of questions: no one other than Amber was seen arriving or leaving his house on that final night, for one, so how did this accomplice get in and out? Only Amber was captured on his security cameras and that was another nail in her coffin. The knife was never found, but I suppose that's gone forever. In the river, I suspect, seeing as it's right outside his house. So don't worry about that. There's one other thing though, which came up at the trial. There was a phone call, allegedly made by Amber to a potential buyer, confirming she'd soon be in possession of the jewellery and fixing a time to go and show it to him. It was definitely a woman who made that call, so does Jack have a *female* accomplice? I have no idea who that might be, and I'll try and come up with some ideas, but it's just something else to look out for, Heather.'

'No pressure, then,' I muttered. How was I supposed to track down all of this *stuff*? Hidden documents and DVDs and jewellery and now accomplices, too? Once again, I had the surreal feeling that I'd somehow stepped into the pages of a novel, and it really wasn't anywhere near as much fun as I might have thought it would be.

'I know. It's a lot. He seriously upped his game with Amber,' Nathan said. 'But imagine if he filmed what happened with her too, to play back later? Imagine if there's a DVD that shows what really happened that night? That would be *dynamite*.'

I bombarded Nathan with questions after that. I was astounded that nobody else had come forward at the time of either Rose's death or Amber's trial; that nobody seemed to be suspicious.

'I mean, first Jack has a girlfriend who allegedly steals money from him, and then dies, and then he has a girlfriend who steals jewellery from him and stabs him? That's a bit of a coincidence, isn't it? And neither of them had ever committed a crime before, had they? Or at least, I know Amber hadn't, and I haven't seen anything online that implies Rose was anything other than a clean-living accountant.'

'Agreed. But the police, well, I think there was a lot of misogyny around both of those cases. Jack painted the women as gold-diggers, dating him for his money and out for what they could get.'

'OK, but what about their friends or families? Not one person had any suspicions about Jack, or about them being framed by somebody?'

There was a pause on the line, then Nathan replied calmly: 'Well, *you* didn't, did you? You knew Jack, and you even went as far as trying to warn Amber not to date him. But when she ended up in court, *you* didn't come forward, did you?'

I gasped at that, the truth of his words stinging like a sharp slap to the face. My cheeks flood with colour as I remember how it felt to hear Nathan's words. He was right. When I heard about what Amber had allegedly done, I was appalled, and horrified at how far Jack must have pushed her to make her do something so drastic. But for some reason, even though I knew that Jack was objectionable in so many ways, it simply never occurred to me that it could have been *him* behind it all. I, like the police and the jury, saw the damning evidence unfolding and only came to one conclusion: that Amber was the guilty party.

And so here I am, trying to make amends. I look at my list

again, at the five crucial pieces of evidence I need to find so we can take this to the police and force them to look at Jack's involvement, no matter how 'cosy' he might be with the Met. If I find anything else along the way, that's a bonus. But these are the important things.

1. Hard copies of emails / other documents relating to both crimes.
2. DVDs made from his security camera recordings.
3. The jewellery Amber's alleged to have stolen.
4. Who helped Jack hack their email / bank accounts?
5. Who is / are Jack's possible accomplice / s who made the phone call and stabbed him? A woman? More than one person?

I glance at my watch. Lunch break over. I need to get back downstairs to relieve Milly, and I need to spend the rest of today and tomorrow trying to concentrate on work and pretending to my friends that my reunion with Jack is simply a bit of fun. As I head back to the shop floor, I make a silent vow.

I will not fail.

I'm going to do everything in my power to bring Jack Shannon down.

I just have to find five little things. And tomorrow night, I begin.

THIRTEEN

Heather

I had sex with Jack last night.

Shit.

I'm lying in bed with him now, just after eight on Wednesday morning, feeling such a jumble of emotions I'm surprised he hasn't noticed something's wrong. We're lying on our sides, his body curled around mine from behind, the fingers of his good hand running languorously up and down my leg, his breath warm against my neck. I can feel my heart drumming, my breathing more rapid than it should be, and I don't know if it's from the physical desire for him that still shocks and appals me, or from the shame and confusion of it all. I'm pretty sure it's the latter right now. I wanted him last night, though. There's no doubt about that, even though it makes me feel ill to admit it. But… *Jesus*. The way he dropped tiny, featherlight kisses along my shoulder, the way his hands gripped my buttocks, his groin grinding against mine… Whatever this man has done, however evil he may truly be, raw lust simply took over. When we'd finished, when Jack had done his usual Jack thing and gone back to work in his office down the hallway shortly after 2am, I lay awake for hours, disgusted at myself. And yet, I had to do it, didn't I? I need access to this house, and I need to keep him sweet, keep him happy. And so here I am, prostituting myself. Twice, so far, because we also had sex this morning, when Jack climbed back into bed beside me. It was unusually early for him, just before seven. I mean, seriously. *Twice?* I'm sure Nathan and Felicity won't ask me, but if they do, I'm definitely not telling them I shagged him *twice* in less than twelve hours.

'You OK?'

He whispers the words, but I'm so lost in thought that I jump, and he laughs and pulls me closer, his hand moving lower on my stomach.

'Sorry – half asleep,' I say.

'I'm pretty knackered too,' he says. 'You've worn me out, Harris. It's a bit too early for me to go to bed but I'm staying here now. Make yourself at home until you need to leave, OK?'

He sighs, kisses my ear, and rolls away from me, pulling the duvet over his shoulders.

'Thanks. I might use the gym, if that's all right? I brought my gear, just in case.'

'Knock yourself out. I'll call you later. Have a good day.'

'Sleep well,' I say softly, but there's no reply, his breathing already slowing. Jack has always had an uncanny knack of falling asleep almost instantly, which I used to find most annoying but right now am delighted by.

Sleep well, and sleep deeply, I think. *That's a good Jack.*

I wait for another minute, then slip out of bed and head for the en suite, grabbing my holdall on the way. This time, he asked me in advance to stay over; I told him I had an author event in Piccadilly at midday – the truth, as it happens – and asked if it was OK if I hung out here until eleven or so, rather than going home. I *did* bring my gym gear, but I have no intention of actually working out; instead, I now have a couple of hours to devote to the task in hand, presuming that Rhona will be off to bed shortly too. She'd been buzzing around when we got in last night – we went for dinner at a lovely Greek place in Soho – and she gave me the same, unsettling look she'd given me the first time we met. It was as if she was assessing me in some way, mentally giving me marks out of ten. I don't like Rhona, I've decided. She makes me feel uneasy. Those dark, dark eyes… There's something about them and the way she stares at me, as if she's gazing through pools of murky water, unknown horrors lurking in their depths. Her eyes freak me out a little. Although maybe it's good, in some ways, to have someone else in the house at times; last night, for example.

We were sipping decaf coffees in the lounge, classical music playing through the speakers concealed in the ceiling. It's a stunning room, made even more so at night because that's when Jack flings the curtains open, revealing the breathtaking arc of the River Thames, its depths inky black but with a thousand lights glittering on its surface, the moving, swelling, watery heart of London. The room has floor-to-ceiling bow windows and a huge marble fireplace; the sofas are cream linen, the floor polished oak. The house is a six-bedroom Georgian masterpiece and, to his credit, Jack has turned it into a home with every modern convenience while still preserving every one of its exquisite period features. There may be a high-tech sound system in the living areas, and a state-of-the-art gym, but every piece of coving, panelling and decorative stonework has been lovingly protected or restored, the ultra-contemporary and the centuries-old happily sitting side by side.

I was sitting there last night, my cup warm in my hand, mesmerised by the view of the river, when Jack suddenly broke the silence.

'Take off your clothes,' he said quietly.

My heart practically leapt into my throat.

No. I can't. Not here, I thought frantically.

I took another sip of coffee, playing for time.

Then I said: 'Shall we just go to the bedroom instead?'

I looked at him meaningfully, raising a suggestive eyebrow, but he shook his head slowly, his eyes roaming my body from his seat on the sofa opposite.

'I want to look at you now. Here,' he said, and my stomach rolled.

'Jack, I—'

And then, suddenly, the door opened and Rhona walked briskly in, carrying a basket of cleaning products. She stopped abruptly, eyes widening, as she realised the room was occupied.

'Oh!' she said. 'I'm so sorry. I thought you'd gone to— I didn't think anyone was in here. I was just about to do this room, but that's OK, I can—'

'It's fine, Rhona,' I said quickly. 'We were just going to head off to bed, weren't we, Jack?'

He hesitated for a moment, then stood up.

'We were. Work away, Rhona. Thanks.'

I felt a flood of relief, and as we left the room I gave Rhona a small smile. She simply nodded, pulling a can of furniture polish from her basket. She was clearly not interested in me, but I gave her a silent thank-you as I left her to her cleaning. It was almost midnight, but of course that was late morning for her in this job, wasn't it? Mad, all of it. As I followed Jack to his bedroom, I wondered how Rhona would react if she knew what I know: the reason I didn't want to take off my clothes in the living room is that if I did, every second would be filmed and recorded. As was everything Rhona was doing in that room too, of course. It was one of the other things I'd discovered about Jack, the last time we dated.

Cameras.

Jack doesn't just have security cameras on the outside of his property to deter would-be burglars, like most people do. Not just those that captured Amber arriving and leaving the night he was attacked. He has them *everywhere*. Although Nathan obviously knew Jack had filmed his encounter with Rose, he hadn't been aware of the full extent of Jack's camera obsession until I told him, and he'd been horrified.

'But how… how are we…? How are you going to get round that? Shit, Heather. It's impossible, then—'

'It's not. I have a plan. Don't worry,' I told him, although I *was* worried, of course. I still am. But I'm here now, so…

Anyway, back then, I discovered the living-room camera first. There are bookcases on either side of the fireplace, their shelves lined with beautiful hardbacks. Some are very rare, some are first-editions – a collection that must be worth a fortune. I was alone in the room one day, waiting for Jack to change to go out for dinner. I'd been idly running my fingers across the books' spines, admiring them and wondering if I'd ever be able to afford even one such treasure myself one day, when I suddenly noticed something strange. What was that, on that book with the black leather cover? I stared at it for another few seconds, then moved away, trying to act normally, even though my heart had begun to pound.

I knew exactly what I'd just seen. I'd been talking to Johnny upstairs about the subject only a week or so previously, after seeing a news story about a bed-and-breakfast owner in Edinburgh who'd fitted a spy camera into a smoke alarm directly over the bed in one of his rooms.

'They're tiny, these days,' Johnny had told me. 'Smoke alarms, electrical sockets, air vents, picture frames, books – you name it, they can pop one in and nobody's any the wiser.'

A camera. There was a *camera* in the spine of that book. A tiny hole, barely bigger than the head of a pencil, with a hint of reflective glass inside it. Shit. *Shit.* Maybe it *was* just for security, to protect these extremely valuable books, but still. Cameras don't discriminate, do they? They record everything. So, Jack was recording me? Recording *us*, and what we did together? My legs had suddenly felt weak. Thankfully, at that point all we'd done in the living room was kiss and have a quick fumble, but I shuddered at the thought of what we could have done. I should have called him out on it immediately, I know that. I should have told him it made me horribly uncomfortable. I should have asked him to turn the cameras off when I was in the house.

But for some reason, I didn't. Jack clearly had major issues – with the daylight thing, for example – and I convinced myself this was just another way he made himself feel safe.

What I did do, though, was tell Johnny about it, then pick his brains about how best to locate other potential cameras in the house. As always, he kept his thoughts about how wise I might be to continue in this relationship to himself, and simply gave me the advice I needed. There were a number of ways of finding cameras, I learned, but if I didn't want Jack to see what I was up to, I needed to be subtle about it, so Johnny got me an amazing little gadget. It's a tiny palm-sized hidden camera detector, a device that looks like a small phone but which can locate camera lenses, infra-red systems, and radio frequencies simply from a quick scan of a room. It flashes up any suspicious finds on its screen.

Johnny showed me how to use it discreetly, walking slowly around a room with the detector in my hand, as if I was reading something on my mobile. I spend a lot of time on my phone anyway, updating my Instagram feed and responding to messages, so I agreed that this probably wouldn't arouse Jack's suspicions. I spent the next couple of weeks gradually checking out each room of the house, and what I found horrified me. There appeared to be no cameras in Jack's private spaces – his office or, thankfully, his bedroom or en suite bathroom. But they were pretty much everywhere else. In corridors, the kitchen, the gym, tiny hidden cameras recorded every movement and every word. It's one of many reasons I've decided not to tell Johnny that I'm back with Jack and back in this house. Not yet anyway. He'd think I'm cuckoo.

During my prison visit, Amber told me that Jack had said many things to her during the confrontation in his office on that last fateful night, one being the revelation that he had multiple videos of her, stripping for him in various rooms, naked and vulnerable, videos he said he would make public. To her enormous relief, to date he hasn't done that ('Maybe me getting a life sentence was enough for him,' she said drily). I haven't told Felicity or Nathan about it – I don't want to make Felicity even more anxious than she already is – but it makes me wonder how many other women have fallen victim to Jack's spying; how many other such videos could be hidden somewhere in this elegant home. Maybe – and my fists clench at the thought – maybe, despite my careful noting of the positions of every camera in the house back then, maybe I missed some; maybe I feature too.

But I can't dwell on that now. It's time to start searching. Safe in Jack's bathroom, I open my bag and get dressed. Rhona should be finishing her shift soon; Jack normally only keeps his housekeeper around in the daytime if he needs her to run a vital errand, or let a plumber or electrician in to do a repair, things like that. But, as Rhona seemed to be working all night, that's unlikely today, and if she *is* still around, I can just stay in the gym until she's out of the way. My leggings have pockets, and I push the detector into one just in case. Who knows – he may have fitted new cameras in the past two years. My phone goes into a pocket on the other side, then I pull my hair back into a ponytail. I look in the mirror and nod at my reflection.

'Right. Let's go,' I whisper.

I open the door slowly, and hear tiny snores emanating from the bed. Jack's body is a motionless mound under the quilt.

Good.

I slip out of the room and walk briskly down the corridor towards his office.

FOURTEEN

Heather

The corridor is empty – no sign of Rhona. It's almost eight-thirty, and I'm very much hoping she *is* down in her apartment by now, because although I was greatly relieved when she walked into the room last night, I do *not* want to have her walk in on me this morning. What I'll be doing would be tricky to explain away, and it'll be hard enough trying to avoid the cameras. I can do without a living, moving pair of human eyes as well.

If Jack sees me entering his office, though – I have no idea how often he checks or plays back his video footage – then I have my cover story. The first time we dated, there were a few occasions when I stayed over and forgot to bring my mobile phone charger, and he told me to use the one permanently plugged in in his office. Last night, I told him I'd done it again, making a show of groaning over my rapidly depleting battery and bemoaning the fact that I'd need my phone in the morning to update Instagram before I headed off to my event. He'd rolled his eyes.

'You know where my charger is. Same place as always. Feel free,' he said.

So I have an excuse now for going into that room alone, and I confidently stride along the dim landing, knowing I'm being recorded as I go. The cameras are in the ceiling in this part of the house, I recall. Jack's office is at the back of the building, which means no river view, but it's still a lovely space, quiet and calm, with white walls and a huge 1950s desk with a bottle-green leather top. The room overlooks the large paved rear courtyard with its olive trees and palms in big terracotta pots; it's somewhere I've enjoyed sitting with a morning coffee in the past, a peaceful, Mediterranean-style sanctuary in busy south London. But there's no time for that this morning, and anyway the blinds are closed, of course; Jack might have them open at night, but now, with the sun bright in the sky outside, the office is dim and quiet as I push the door open and flick on the overhead light.

I look around. Everything is neat and orderly. No piles of paperwork sit on the uncluttered desktop and the small bin in the corner is empty. I pull out my security camera detector and wander slowly around the room, looking down at it in my cupped hand and tapping it occasionally, as if I'm checking emails on my phone. Actually I'm waiting for that notification to pop up, butterflies fluttering in my stomach.

Phew. Still nothing.

If Jack did fit a camera in here to record his encounter with Amber, he clearly removed it again afterwards, and while I know these detectors aren't a hundred per cent accurate, this is as good as I can get, so I stuff it back into my pocket. I spot the phone charger and plug my phone into it, just for show. If Jack does check his corridor footage, and asks me why I spent so long in here simply putting my phone on charge, I'm planning to tell him I sat down and updated my social media as the battery was topping up. I think that's believable enough, especially as I'll make sure I actually *do* post something this morning. I have a few preprepared stories and posts in my drafts, ready to upload, because although Jack doesn't use Instagram himself, he could still check my page. Even so, I don't want to be in this room for too long. Something tells me that if Jack *is* hiding hard copies of incriminating documents and videos, his own office is the last place they're likely to be – far too obvious. But I still need to be thorough, so I begin working my way around the room, opening every drawer and flicking through every file. Nothing is locked, and after ten minutes all I've seen are endless boring invoices and other correspondence, all obviously related to Shannon Medical.

Jack's company manufactures and sells medical products, providing everything from surgical instruments to pharmaceuticals for hospitals, dentists, and general practitioners. The company is big, and getting bigger, and I wonder yet again why someone so successful lives such a limited life, never travelling, never truly enjoying the rewards of so much hard work. He never did tell me about the event that triggered his rejection of daylight, and I finally gave up asking.

'It is what it is, Heather. It's me, and that's that. Take me or leave me,' he'd said firmly.

Eventually, of course, I'd chosen the latter course of action, but I know now that he never explained to Amber either, or to Nathan, and I wonder if anyone else knows. If not any of his current friends or colleagues, there must be *someone*, from his past possibly, who could shed some light on it?

Shed some light. I allow myself a smirk at the unintended irony, then sigh and look around the room, thinking. OK, nothing in plain sight, which is no surprise. Where else in this room could Jack have stashed something he didn't want anyone to find?

That was something else I'd run past Johnny the other day. I asked him where a savvy person would hide something really important if they don't want to use a bank safety deposit box or anything like that. If they want to make sure something valuable is securely locked away in their own home, where would they put it?

'What are you up to, Heather?' he asked, then immediately held up a hand.

'No, no, don't tell me. I don't want to know. But you're worrying me a bit with these questions recently, young lady. OK, fine. I'd say the key thing is to avoid the most likely places. You know, your bedroom, wardrobe, desk drawers, jewellery box. Thieves will always look there first. Filing cabinets are really easy to open, so not there either. And a locked box is pointless – they'll just take it and open it later. If it's documents then inside or in between books, or in a floor safe. A normal wall safe isn't as secure as people think. You can literally cut them out of the wall and take them away – they're not even particularly heavy. But floor safes are harder to access, and you can hide them under rugs and carpets. Cellars and attics are good too. If it was me, I'd stick important stuff in a box and write "Christmas decorations" or something like that on it and shove a load of tinsel in the top. Also, kitchen cupboards for small valuables, stuff like jewellery. I'd wrap them and hide them in cereal boxes or big jars of rice or pasta. Who's going to start emptying out food?'

He carried on listing potential hiding places for a further two minutes, as I scribbled notes, astounded by the ingenuity of some of the suggestions. But as I quickly work my way around Jack's office, I can't see any plausible locations at all. The room is minimalist in style; other than the desk, chair, filing cabinet and one set of shelves, there's little in here. The floor is the original pine, sanded and bare, with no sign of a floor safe, and there are just two pictures on the wall, one a rural landscape and the other an oil portrait of what Jack calls 'a Georgian gentleman'. In other rooms, he has collections of striking modern art, but these two pieces are antiques. I look closely at them, remembering what Johnny told me about picture frames.

'Hiding things behind pictures is really popular in TV dramas but it doesn't work so well in real life. It makes the frames look oddly thick – it's pretty easy to spot.'

These frames look normal to me, and a quick check behind each painting confirms that neither is concealing a wall safe. I simply can't see any other possible hiding places.

Dammit, I think. But at least that's one room ticked off the list. *Where now?*

The gym. I unplug my phone and slip it back into my pocket, then leave the office. As I head down the corridor again, I wonder if there's anywhere in any of these hallways and landings that I should be searching, but again the floors are wooden and uncarpeted and the walls aren't panelled but painted, the finish smooth and unblemished. I could be wrong, but I don't think there's anything here. I think Johnny's right about Jack's bedroom too, and his bathroom – too risky, when he has girlfriends sleeping over – and I very much doubt he'd hide anything in a guest bedroom or other bathroom either, for the same reason. For now, I plan to focus on the more probable spots, and the gym's as good as any. I pause when I reach the door. Rhona looks super-fit, and I know Jack lets his housekeepers use his gym as a perk of the job. Admittedly, even though he often used to tell me how he wished he didn't need their help, and could live alone, he does treat them pretty well. But there's no sound coming from within, and I slip inside gratefully, fumbling for the light switch. Empty.

I'm not majorly into pumping iron – I'm more of a walker, and I don't mind a bit of yoga or Pilates – but even with my limited experience of such places, I've always been impressed by Jack's home gym. There's a treadmill, a cross trainer, a rowing machine, a bike, a punch bag, various scary-looking weights machines and benches, and even a small trampoline in the corner. Off to the side, another door leads into a smaller room where his sunbed lives. There are no windows, but the ceiling is dotted with bright spotlights and a graffiti-style mural, featuring a host of athletic-looking characters sprinting and leaping along a neon-lit city street, has been painted across the entire back wall.

I stand by the door, reacquainting myself with the layout. Last time, I'd located the single camera in here easily. There's a floor-standing water dispenser in the corner, a stack of paper cups on a small table beside it next to a pile of handtowels. The camera was concealed in the centre front of the dispenser, just above the tap; its position, I assume, gives it a perfect view of the entire gym. I pull my detector from my pocket and stroll around the room, again tapping the device in my hand as if I'm checking emails or texts on my phone. When I get to the water cooler, the screen lights up, but as I finish my circuit there's no indication of any new cameras, and my head swims with relief.

I assume that Jack controls his security system from his phone, but I know that even if I stole it, and was able to hack into it, it would be far, far too risky to disable the cameras – he'd be bound to notice. So, I'm going to have to foil them by another method, and this is my first chance to try out the very simple way I'm hoping to do that. I slip the detector back into the thigh pocket in my leggings and then, casually, making sure not to look anywhere near the spot where I know the camera is hidden, I wriggle out of my grey hoodie and toss it over the cooler.

Bingo. It's just long enough, and it's landed in the perfect position. That's quite normal, isn't it, to take off your outer layer and hang it somewhere when you're about to do a workout?

Heather one, camera nil, I think, with a smile.

Next, I pull my phone out and in a few taps I've connected to the gym's Bluetooth speakers and selected a workout playlist. As the first track begins, I turn the volume up – Jack obviously records sound as well as pictures, and I need some noise to cover the fact that I'm rooting around in here instead of working up a sweat. Then I start searching.

I don't really think this room is going to offer me any rewards. I know that, as well as the housekeepers, Jack lets his very occasional guests use his gym too, so it's probably not somewhere he's going to store his dirty little secrets. I go through the motions anyway, but it doesn't take long. There's absolutely nowhere to secrete anything, and once I've done the main room I slip into the sunbed annexe. There was no camera in here previously – presumably because Jack uses it naked, as his perfect full-body tan very much suggests – but I pull out my detector again to double-check.

Safe.

Good.

A quick whizz around later, I decide I'm done. There's nothing in here but the sunbed, a white towelling robe hanging from a coat stand and a small basket of body lotions and goggles on a side-table. The floor, like that of the main room, is smooth, non-slip rubber and there are no nooks or crannies, no alcoves, no hiding places at all that I can see. I check the time and realise it's almost ten, and that I'm going to have to get a move on if I'm going to have time to get showered and changed and travel into town for midday.

One more room? I turn the music off, lift my camera-covering hoodie from the water dispenser and head downstairs. I haven't had breakfast yet – not even a coffee – but the kitchen is going to take time to search, and the camera in there, if it's still where it was before, isn't going to be so easy to obstruct. Shall I just call it a day, have some breakfast, and leave?

I run through a mental checklist. Still discounting all the bedrooms and bathrooms, I have yet to search the lounge, the snug, the main dining room, the kitchen and its casual dining area, plus the big walk-in 'pantry slash utility room', and what about the cinema room? I ponder on that for a few moments, then discount that too. It's small, just four huge, comfortable reclining chairs, a small bar area and a big screen. The floor, again, is wooden and it's one of the rooms most regularly used by Jack's visitors; my gut feeling is that it's just too well frequented for him to use it to hide anything important.

Then there's the cellar and attic. A nervous knot begins to form in my stomach as I imagine having to creep around in a cobwebby, confined space, not sure if I'm being watched or not.

I walk down the hallway that leads to the stairs to the basement kitchen, and as I pass a heavily curtained window I stop, suddenly desperate for some daylight. The house is well-lit generally, but the fact that I know it's daytime and yet I'm in a building where every window is covered and all the light is electric is already becoming strangely oppressive. I look guiltily around, feeling a little silly as I do so because I know Jack is safely tucked up in bed, then pull one of the curtains back a few inches, blinking as the bright morning sunshine hits my face. I stand there for a few seconds, breathing deeply, letting my eyes adjust, looking out into the pretty courtyard that Jack only uses at night, and thinking what a terrible waste that is, then my eyes drift to the left and I groan inwardly.

Another one to add to the list, I think. There's an outbuilding, a summer house of sorts, that I'd forgotten about. It's a wooden structure, painted sage green, with a small covered veranda on which sit a little bistro-style table and chairs. I've only been inside it a couple of times; unless things have changed, it has a storage cupboard for garden tools, used by the maintenance man Jack employs once a week to keep his outside spaces neat, plus a sofa perfectly positioned by the floor-to-ceiling window to give a good view of the courtyard past the veranda. In front of the sofa, doubling as a coffee table, is an antique chest, used to store cushions for the outdoor furniture. Again, as the gardener clearly has full access to the place and Jack never minded me using it back then, I think it's an unlikely hiding place for sensitive documents, expensive jewellery, or a stash of DVDs, but I can't rule it out.

I sigh, then let the curtain fall back into place and head down to the kitchen. I don't look at it as I walk to the fridge, but I know that the camera in this room is embedded in the face of the large antique clock that hangs on the wall. I have a vague plan in my head for evading it which just might work, but it's going to be tricky, and I don't have time this morning. Instead, I grab some yoghurt and berries from the fridge and then a banana from the fruit bowl and throw them into the blender that sits on the beautiful walnut worktop below the clock. As I wait the minute or so it takes to make the perfect smoothie, I pull my detector out again and do my well-practised drift around the room, carrying out my discreet double-checking, but I can only find the camera I already know about, and I offer up a silent thank-you to the universe.

I slide the gadget back into my pocket and gaze around, taking in the copper sink and dove-grey cabinets with brass door pulls, and then, down a few steps, the slightly sunken dining area with its long wooden table and benches, and a large TV on the wall. I wonder if searching here might be more wasted effort. I know Jack's housekeepers are always under strict instructions to clean floors and surfaces only, and never to open drawers or cupboards, but the kitchen is obviously an exception. Rhona, like all her predecessors, cooks most of Jack's meals for him, which means she has full access to all the cupboards and storage areas. He's not going to hide anything here, is he? Unless there's a secret safe or something somewhere? Still very aware of the camera silently recording me, I switch off the blender and pour the thick, creamy smoothie into a glass. Then I amble around the room once more as I sip my breakfast, surreptitiously checking out the porcelain tiled floor, the island with its built-in wine rack, the two professional-looking ovens, and the integrated coffee machine. All very slick, all very high end and expensive, but also very *ordinary*. Nothing's jumping out at me, nothing striking me as unusual. What about the pantry, though? Is that any more likely? Last time I checked, there was no additional camera inside it, but I pause nonchalantly outside the door, wondering if I dare go in, knowing that if I do I'll be clearly seen by the kitchen camera.

Shall I risk it, really quickly? I think. It's where the freezers are. I could say I wanted to add ice to my smoothie or something, if he ever asks me what I was doing.

I'm going to do it. I take another mouthful from my glass and grimace, pretending it's unpleasantly warm, just in case. Then I push the pantry door open and walk in. The overhead light, clearly sensor-activated, flicks on, and I take a moment to get my bearings. The room is about ten feet long, with neatly arranged shelves of tinned goods, jars of spices, bottles of spirits, glassware, and flower vases filling one wall. Along the opposite wall sit a washing machine, a tumble dryer, a tall wine fridge and two upright freezers. I stare at them, then take a few steps closer, my eyes widening. One of the freezers is large and white, the other slightly smaller and silver in colour. And the smaller freezer has a padlock on it. A shiny stainless-steel padlock, attached to two metal cables, one fixed to each of the two doors, clearly making them impossible to open.

Who locks their freezer?

I feel a little rush of adrenaline.

What was it Johnny said about freezers, when he was listing clever places to hide things?

'If you wrap important stuff in plastic and then aluminium foil, and stash it in your freezer, first of all it just looks like food, but also if your house catches fire, it's going to have a better chance of surviving that too—'

'Can I help you, Heather?'

I jump violently. The voice has come from the doorway behind me, and I whirl around to see Rhona standing there, her eyes narrowed, a litre container of milk in one hand.

'Rhona!' I gasp. 'I-I… Sorry, I thought you'd be in bed by now.'

'Mr Shannon ran out of milk. I just nipped out to get some, in case he wants tea before I start my shift tonight,' she says. There's no hint of warmth in her voice and her steely gaze is fixed on my face. 'Do you need something?'

'No, I'm fine. Well, I just… Well, I made a smoothie, and it didn't taste great – a bit warm, you know? I prefer them cold, so I was going to put some ice in it, but…'

I'm gabbling, sounding suspicious even to my own ears. I wave my glass at her.

Calm down, you idiot! You're dating Jack, and you've stayed the night. You're perfectly entitled to get some ice for your drink. Just ask her.

'But… one of the freezers is locked, for some reason. Do you know why?'

I try to keep the question light and breezy, and her eyes flick to the padlocked doors and back to mine.

'Meat,' she says.

'Er… pardon?'

'Meat,' she says again. 'That's the meat freezer. Mr Shannon likes a good steak, as I'm sure you know. He took delivery of some Japanese A5 Wagyu recently. Couple of hundred quid a pop. He's locked the freezer just in case we have a break-in. He said he doesn't mind a burglar clearing out his wine store but he'd be livid if they got his steak. He keeps the key on his keyring, nice and safe. If he fancies a steak for dinner, he comes down and opens it up himself and chooses one. There's ice in the kitchen fridge, in there. Just press the button.'

She nods her head towards the cream refrigerator in the kitchen and opens the pantry door a little wider. I take the hint, mentally kicking myself as I slink past her.

There's a frigging automatic ice maker in the door of the fridge. How did I forget that?

That was a terrible excuse for snooping in the pantry… but a locked freezer? Just because it has expensive meat in it? Really? How will I be able to check, though, if the key is on Jack's keyring?

Slowly, I help myself to some ice and turn back to Rhona, who's still standing there, the pantry door closed behind her now. I smile.

'Thanks for your help,' I say. 'I'll leave you to it.'

She says nothing, her dark eyes again looking almost black. As I leave the room I feel them following me, and a chill runs up my spine.

Why is she always so unfriendly? Why does she stare at me like that?

This is hard enough without the sinister housekeeper popping up out of nowhere all the time. But at least she's inadvertently given me a useful piece of information. There's a locked freezer, and I know where the key is. It's on Jack's keyring. He only has one, as far as I know – a simple gold ring with about a dozen keys on it. I remember teasing him the first time I saw it, asking why on earth he needed so many keys, and he made a point of going through the entire bunch, tapping each one in turn.

'Car. Front door. Back door. Summer house. Filing cabinet, even though I never bother locking it. Desk drawer, same…'

I definitely don't remember a meat freezer key, though; that must be a new addition.

The question is, where does Jack keep that keyring? As I head back upstairs to get changed and leave, I think hard, but I can't recall seeing it anywhere. Another job, then. I'll need to watch where he puts his keys when we come in from our next date, try to get hold of them, and then somehow open that freezer, and see if there's more than just expensive steak in it. And I also need to start sussing out whether there are any women in his life who could be the female accomplice. But one thing's for sure, whatever I do next, I need to keep away from bloody Rhona.

There's something about her that gives me the absolute creeps.

FIFTEEN

Amber

'I'm mortified, Amber. I'm just disgusted at myself. But at the same time... well, *you* know...'

'Don't. Yes, I know, and... Look, don't think about it. These things happen.'

It's Thursday night, and I'm on the phone to Heather, tucked into the little half-covered phone booth on the landing. I'm keeping my voice low; there are two other women loitering just feet away, impatiently waiting their turn. The phone is bolted to a shiny metal plate on the wall. I can see my reflection in it – it's distorted but even so, clear enough to make it obvious even to me that I look different. I've looked different for a few days now. Brighter of eye, smoother of brow. It's hope, that's done this. The lifting of a layer of despair. Even Stacey's noticed.

'You 'ad bootleg Botox or somethin'?' she said earlier, squinting at my face. 'What's got you all chipper?'

'Dunno,' I replied. 'I think I'm just happy my old mate

Heather's back in my life. She was my best friend for years, since school, and then we fell out, but now… It's just been *so* nice to talk to her again.'

'Good on ya,' Stacey said. 'Long may it last. I was getting sick of lookin' at your miserable mug. You look almost pretty now. Almost, mind.'

She squealed and ducked as I threw a rolled-up sock at her, and we both laughed, and that felt good too. I didn't expect to make friends in here, proper friends. But Stacey's definitely a mate now – for life, I hope. I'm not sure how I'd get through the long days without her.

I need to be careful though. Even with Stacey.

Don't tell her too much.

Watch what you say.

I know my cellmate has no connection with Jack Shannon, but she knows his name and knows what I was found guilty of doing to him. I can't give her the smallest hint about any sort of link between Heather and Jack, and now, on the phone, I'm trying to be ultra-careful too. This talking in code thing, just in case anyone is listening in, is a bit tricky though. So far, Heather's casually told me she's now 'back with her old flame' and slept with him on their second date. She's clearly pretty unimpressed with her own self-control, but I totally get it. He may be a vile person, rotten to the core – he may, in fact, be completely *insane* – but I too remember what it was like to look into his inscrutable eyes and feel his hands caressing my body. It's as if he casts a spell, and it makes him almost irresistible. And Heather *has* to sleep with him, doesn't she, if she's to convince him she's gone back to him for *him*? There's no way around it. She did what she had to do.

'Do you know what?' she says now. 'I can't find my keys. You know that bunch I have? Can you remember where I usually put them when I come in, Amber? I've got a head like a sieve at the moment.'

Keys? For a few moments, I'm flummoxed. Why is she suddenly going on about *keys*? Then I realise. *Jack's* keys. That's what she's asking me about. She needs *Jack's* keys.

'Oh, gosh, let me think,' I say. 'Don't you usually leave them in your jacket pocket, and hang it in the bedroom wardrobe? And then just switch them to the next day's jacket? Have you looked there?'

'No. No, I haven't. I will though. Thanks, Amber. What would I do without you?'

She laughs lightly, and I smile.

I really can be of some use to her, even from here, I think, and feel a rush of pleasure.

'When's your next date?' I ask casually.

'Saturday night. And Sunday night too. It's Easter weekend, and I'm off most of it. I don't have any other plans, so I'm going to hang around all day Sunday and go to work from his on Monday.'

Easter. I'd almost forgotten. One day merges with the next here.

'Sounds lovely,' I say, not meaning it in the slightest, and knowing *she* knows I don't mean it either.

'Oh, and erm… I'd quite like to meet some of his friends, actually,' Heather continues. '*Female* friends, I mean. The first time we dated I met a couple of his lad friends – guys he knew from uni who came and stayed for a weekend. And a few of his colleagues. They popped in once or twice for sort of "social slash business" meetings, drinks and dinner. But he doesn't have *that* many mates, as you know, and I only met blokes. I thought it would be good to meet some of his *women* friends. Any suggestions?'

I've noted the heavy emphasis on *female* and *women*, and I frown. OK, so she needs to meet up with women that Jack might be friendly with? I think for a few moments.

'Well, his personal assistant, maybe? Her name's Naomie. Naomie Anderson. She's been with him for quite a while and he relies on her pretty heavily, I think. He's good to her too, though – bonuses and restaurant vouchers, that sort of thing. I only met her once and she definitely seemed to worship him, although I'm pretty sure he's not interested in her in that way. Other than her, I don't think there's anyone I'd really class as a female friend, to be honest.'

'Naomie. OK, thanks,' she says. 'Maybe I'll give her a call.'

I'm intrigued, but I can't ask her any questions. I know Nathan's given her a checklist, but I don't know everything that's on it, so I'm just going to have to trust her on this one.

'Right, well, I'd better go. I'll call again soon, OK?' she says. 'Be good. Oh, and happy Easter. Do you get any chocolate eggs or anything in there?'

'Maybe. I don't know. I actually forgot it was Easter, to be honest. I hope so. Anyway, you have fun. Eat double chocolate, for me. And take care, please.'

There's a moment of silence on the line, and I know she knows what I'm trying to say.

Take care. Really take care. You're playing Russian roulette here, Heather. One false move, and you're in trouble. Big trouble. But you know that. We both know that. So take care, my old friend.

'I will. I'll be fine,' she says softly.

A moment later, the line goes dead, and I feel unexpected tears pricking my eyelids. I stand there for a moment, trying to compose myself, thinking again about what this woman is doing for me, the risk she's taking. I wonder, not for the first time, how I can ever possibly repay her. How can you thank someone, recompense them, for doing something so huge? All I know is that if she pulls this off, if I get out of here, I'll spend the rest of my days trying to make it up to her.

'Oi! You finished or what?'

A sharp voice from behind reminds me there's a queue of other women waiting to use the phone, and I turn swiftly and apologise. As I walk back to my cell, I wonder again about exactly what evidence Nathan has asked Heather to look for. I tried to explain, when she visited me here, exactly what happened with Jack, but it's so cloudy, so confused in my head now that I'm not even sure myself if I got all the details right. I know I wanted to finish with him for a while, that's for sure. It had all become too much, just as Heather had tried to warn me; the darkness, in more ways than one, had started to become suffocating. I'd begun to pull away, slowly over a period of weeks, and he clearly sensed that. He asked me more than once if I was still happy, and then took me to bed and somehow made me forget my misgivings in the way only he can. Eventually, though, I knew I couldn't do it anymore, and I finally plucked up the courage to tell him it was over. That's when he asked me to come to his house on that final night, the night my life fell apart so spectacularly.

The night everything changed.

He told me he'd gathered up the few belongings I'd left

there, and that there were no hard feelings. He said I should pop in to collect them and have one last drink with him and, relieved he was taking it so well, I drove over there. Jack was between housekeepers at the time, and he'd messaged to say he'd leave the front door on the latch. He'd been upstairs in his office, and even as I walked into the room and he turned to look cooly at me, I could sense something was off. There was a… malevolence in the air that was almost tangible. That's when he told me he knew I'd been plotting against him for weeks; he knew I'd stolen jewellery from his home; he'd seen the emails I'd been sending to potential buyers. He said it was all over, that he was going to the police and my life would be ruined. I'd gaped at him, incredulous.

'What are you talking about? What jewellery? What theft?' I remember spluttering, but he just laughed, and then did something extraordinary. He opened the top drawer of his desk, and pulled out a knife, and then, as I stood there, gawping at him, rooted to the spot in shock and disbelief, he thrust it into my hand, closing my fingers around the handle.

'Stab me. Go on. I know you want to,' he said, in a low, menacing tone, his face just inches from mine, his breath hot against my skin.

'No! *No!* Jack, what are you *doing*? Why are you doing this?' I gasped, and he laughed again, a bitter, high-pitched little laugh that sent a chill through me.

What happened after that is a blur. I don't know if it's down to some sort of post-traumatic amnesia, but I genuinely can't remember the next few minutes. I have a hazy sense of someone else being present, but I have no idea who, or where they suddenly came from. All I know is that, at some point later that evening, I was back outside in my car again, my breathing ragged, fear coursing through my veins and making me lightheaded. I was unsure I'd even be able to drive, but I knew I had to get away, that I couldn't stay anywhere near that house for even a second longer. I drove recklessly and far too fast for those residential London streets, not caring. I remember being desperate to get home, to be safe. I remember wondering why my palms felt so sticky on the steering wheel, and what exactly the dark stain I could see on my pale blue blouse was. I remember my heart beating so hard in my chest that it hurt. When I did get home, my shaking hands fumbling with the door key and tears streaming down my face, I slammed the door behind me and reached for the light switch – *all* the light switches – needing to banish the darkness. Then I caught a glimpse of myself in the hall mirror.

And that's when the screaming started.

Blood. It was blood, very obviously. All over me. Smeared down the front of my top, crusted between my fingers, matted in my hair. Blood. *Whose* blood? Mine? Jack's? Someone else's? I remember falling back against the wall opposite, sliding down it and landing in a crumpled heap on the floor. I remember shaking violently. I remember trying to piece together the events of the past few hours in my head and being unable to make any sense of it. And that's where the police found me, less than half an hour later, when they smashed my front door in.

That's when it all began. That's when it all ended.

How can Heather, however hard she tries, make sense of all that? How can she even believe me, when so much of what I told her is so vague? And yet, the little sliver of hope is still there, keeping me going, giving me a new vision of the future I never dreamed possible, even as recently as a few short weeks ago.

Hope. It's all I have left.

I'm back at my cell. I swallow hard and walk inside.

SIXTEEN

Heather

It's Good Friday evening, and I'm in Spinelli's, an Italian wine bar in Chiswick. There's a large glass of cold Sauvignon Blanc on the table in front of me, and Felicity is sitting opposite me. She chose this place because it's tiny, tucked out of the way down a side street and – crucially, she said when she suggested we meet up – doesn't have any CCTV cameras, something she's again somehow checked out ahead of time. In fact, she told me, the entire street is 'secure'. This obsession with avoiding cameras still seems ludicrously over-the-top to me – OK, so Jack's home may be full of the things, but somehow I don't think he has access to the footage from cafés and bars across London. I pointed this out to Felicity when we were arranging this meet-up, then immediately felt bad when she told me that yes, she *knew* she was being a little ridiculous, but she just couldn't help it.

'It's just what I'm like, Heather. I was a worrier as a kid and I'm still a big worrier now, and it's got worse with all this stuff about Nathan and Lacey's lives being threatened. They're all

I've got, family-wise, and I just don't want *anything* to jeopardise what we're trying to do here, you know? I'm just so bloody *nervous* all the time. I know it's stupid, but it makes me feel so much better if I know we're not being watched or recorded.'

I apologised and told her I understood, but now and again when I think about it, I get a prickle of unease about this whole Nathan and Felicity situation. What risks are *they* taking, after all? None, because they've somehow managed to persuade *me* to do all the dirty work, while they stay safe and anonymous. But I'm involved now, and I do get that Felicity's seriously anxious and scared, so if it makes her feel better to hang out in places where she won't be filmed, fine.

'Thanks for coming,' she says. She's ordered a gin and tonic, and she picks up her glass and takes a sip, then puts it down again and glances over her shoulder. There's only one other couple in the bar, a man and a woman over by the window, and they're holding hands across the table, clearly engrossed in one another. Felicity stares at them for a moment, then turns back to me and smiles. She's wearing a pink wool coat and her hair is loose for a change. I've only ever seen it pulled tightly back, and it's longer than I assumed it was. It flows past her shoulders and gentle waves frame her fine-boned face.

'I don't know how wise it'll be to meet up in person too often, but it seems so impersonal just talking on the phone and on Zoom, and as Nathan's out of the country… We're both so grateful, Heather, for what you're doing,' she says earnestly. 'I just wanted to tell you that again, and buy you a drink, and also, I have some more information for you. Nathan's tracked down the guy he mentioned, the one he suspects might have worked on the email hacking? But first, are you hungry? It's not really a restaurant but they do nibbly stuff – bruschetta and crostini, things like that? Gosh, it's warm in here, isn't it? I need another gin.'

She wriggles out of the pink coat and drapes it over the back of her chair. She smiles at me again, and I smile back.

'Great,' I say. 'To be honest, I had a big lunch at work. Kwee and Milly shut the shop early because it's a bank holiday and they got some sandwiches and cakes in to thank us all for working the shift. But nibbles sounds good.'

We spend a couple of minutes perusing the menu and ordering from the pleasant barman, then chat easily while we wait for the food. Despite the way her endless worrying is starting to grate on me, I've warmed to her a lot recently; we've spoken on the phone numerous times now, and I've realised she has a deliciously dry sense of humour, very like mine, and a slightly cynical attitude to life which again I recognise as being similar to my own. She's single, having come out of a two-year relationship six months ago, and she's a scientist, currently working in Twickenham as a lab technician for a company called ProPowder Global. It's a 'coatings' company, which apparently means things like paints, lacquers, and sealants. I find this strangely fascinating, and she laughs as I bombard her with questions about what she actually does.

'It's not very exciting really,' she says. 'It's just lots of testing and analysis. Checking all the coatings meet environmental standards, doing things like salt spray and humidity testing. I mean, *I* love it, but I'm a bit of a nerd.'

'I too am a nerd, so I totally get it,' I reply. I pick up my glass and clink it against hers.

'Ahh, but being a book nerd is much more exciting,' she says. 'All those glamorous launches and world-famous authors—'

'Bruschetta for two?'

She's interrupted by the arrival of our food, and we decide to order another round of drinks to accompany it. As we eat and drink, I forget for a few minutes that I'm actually here to discuss this strange undercover mission I've somehow found myself embroiled in. Instead, it's just like being out for a fun evening with a friend, and I'm enjoying myself.

Once the plates are empty though, Felicity dabs her mouth with her napkin and clears her throat.

'Right, well, I suppose we should get down to business,' she says. 'What's your plan for the weekend? You said you're staying two nights? Tomorrow and Sunday? That should give you a decent amount of time on your own?'

'I hope so,' I reply. 'Sunday is Rhona's day off this week, so hopefully she won't be lurking around. Her days off vary according to Jack's work schedule, but her not being there on a Sunday is good. I'm going to try and get hold of his keys when he's asleep and get into that meat freezer I told you about. Then I'll carry on searching the house.'

She nods.

'Great. And you're getting on with him OK, generally? You don't get any sense he suspects you have an ulterior motive?'

I shrug.

'I don't think so. He's still a bit… reserved with me. Maybe I'm just hyper aware though, because of the "unfinished business" thing. I can't help worrying he's plotting some grim punishment, and then other times, I think maybe not. He did say on our first date that what happened before was all water under the bridge. And we do get on, in a strange way. We both like books, and... um... physically, it's...'

I can feel myself blushing. I stop talking and take a gulp of wine as Felicity gives me a meaningful look.

'OK, OK, I don't need to know. Whatever it takes, eh?'

'Yes, indeed,' I say, trying to be business-like again, and to stop thinking about Jack's naked body. I can't bear it, sometimes, the mixed emotions that man arouses in me.

'Oh, and I'm going to email Jack's PA, Naomie Anderson, too. I forgot to tell you about her. Amber mentioned her. I'm wondering if she might be a potential female accomplice?' I say.

Felicity nods.

'Strangely, I was going to mention her too. Nathan told me about her. He's struggling to come up with any other options at the moment, but he did say she might be worth chatting to.'

'I think so. Amber says she's pretty devoted to Jack and she's about his only female friend. It's his birthday soon; I thought I might make some excuse about wanting to get him a present but not being sure what to get. I was going to ask if I could pop in for a quick coffee to pick her brains – what do you think? I feel like I need to see her face to face. I thought I'd try asking a few questions and see what her reaction is.'

'You'll need to be so careful though.'

Felicity's face creases into a frown.

'If Jack finds out you've been meeting up with his staff and asking weird questions, that could blow everything.'

'I know, I know. Don't stress,' I say quickly. 'But I need to get on with this, you know? It's already getting to me a bit.'

Felicity nods and reaches across the table to rest her slender hand on mine.

'You are flipping amazing,' she says. 'I still can't believe you're doing this at all. So fine, do what you have to do. Oh, and before I forget, the hacker thing…'

She whispers the last few words, looking furtively over her shoulder again, then reaches for the bag she'd tucked under the table when we sat down.

'Not the same as mine tonight, thank goodness. Got any apples in it?' I say, raising an eyebrow, and she snorts with laughter.

'Not tonight. Hell, where is it?'

She roots around in the depths of the big leather bag then pulls out a sheet of paper with a triumphant, 'Aha! Here it is. This guy worked at Shannon Medical on and off, on a freelance basis, while he was a student. His name's Yiannis. Look.'

She pushes the page across the table to me.

'He was there in the IT department for a while when Nathan worked there, but apparently he'd also worked for them the previous year, which was the summer Rose and Jack were dating. He's super bright, Nathan says. A real tech-head. But the thing that struck Nathan as a bit odd, in retrospect, was that twice when he was over at Jack's for movie nights, Yiannis was around too. This was at a time when he wasn't actually working at the company, and Nathan particularly remembers one little exchange. Yiannis apparently burst into the lounge yelling something about having cracked it, and then sort of stopped dead when he realised Jack wasn't alone. Jack hurried him out of the room and muttered something about Yiannis helping him with some computer program that was playing up, but now Nathan's wondering if it might have been something else. There'd been rumours about the guy having some sort of major family problem while he worked at the company. Maybe he needed extra cash to sort that, whatever it was? Nathan's trying to find out where he's working now, and he said he'll email you. He just thought he might be worth talking to. What do you think?'

I nod, slowly, reading the neatly written details Felicity's given me.

> *Yiannis Pappas*
> *Was studying IT at Middlesex University*
> *Lived in Brentford*

'Maybe,' I say. 'How to approach him, though? Leave it with me.'

We sit and chat for another hour, and again I find myself relaxing, taking pleasure in the wine and the company and the quiet ambience of the bar. When Felicity and I part just after 10pm, we hug, and I'm smiling as I walk home. The evening is mild, the streets busy with good-natured Friday night drinkers and clubbers. As I close my front door behind me though, I think about tomorrow night, and my return to Barnes and to Jack, and my shoulders stiffen. Moments later, my phone pings and there, already, is the email Felicity promised Nathan would send. Yiannis Pappas is now working in cyber security for a company based in north London.

He's essentially an ethical hacker, from what I can make out. They basically assess IT systems and databases for vulnerabilities and advise companies on how to make them safe. And, as far as I know, they do that by doing what a malicious hacker would do: they try to gain access to places they shouldn't in order to expose their weaknesses. Obviously, the companies they're working for give them permission to do that as part of the process. But if Yiannis has the skills to do that with permission, he also has the know-how to do it without permission. I think he could be our man, I really do!

I can almost hear the excitement bubbling from Nathan's written words, and my temples begin to throb. That's two people I need to contact now, and I have so much of Jack's house yet to search…

Suddenly, it all feels overwhelming. I crawl under my duvet and turn off my bedside light. The darkness of my bedroom envelops me, but a few seconds later I spring up again and reach for the switch.

Too much darkness.

I can't, not tonight. I leave the light on and fall into an uneasy sleep.

SEVENTEEN

Jack

Jack is sitting in the back of a sleek black Mercedes E-Class, heading for the office. It's his car, but he rarely drives it himself. He employs a driver who's on call during the hours of darkness to whisk him to Shannon Medical and back again whenever he feels the need to actually visit the premises instead of running it from home. He tries to go in at least once a week, sometimes twice, and he makes himself stay for four or five hours, but he always leaves for home in plenty of time before sunrise. He fears getting stuck in the early morning rush hour, or the car being involved in an accident, meaning he'll be out in the world as the sky lightens and the shadows fade. He hates himself for this fear, and he knows that one day he's going to have to tackle it, to conquer it, but right now he has too many other things going on, and not enough head space to handle everything at once.

And so he keeps his visits to the office brief, walking the floor and chatting to the night-shift team, making sure everyone's happy and everything's running on schedule. The business operates twenty-four-seven, bank holidays and Christmas included, and everyone works rotating day and night shifts at Shannon Medical, from the cleaners to the human resources department. It's unusual, but Jack has it that way so he gets to see every member of his staff in person at some point every few weeks, something that wouldn't happen if some employees only worked nine to five. He likes to think he's a good boss – personable, approachable. Yes, he's sure there's gossip about him, and about his lifestyle; rumours about why he chooses to live as he does. That doesn't really bother him. There's always talk and speculation about management in *any* company. But other than that, he feels like his staff have got his back. When the thing with Amber happened, he was inundated with get-well messages and flowers. Even now, he's constantly asked how he is, whether his recovery is going well, if his ability to use his hand is improving. They care, and it's nice. He likes it. But… it's not enough.

What Jack really wants is a *partner*. A woman to share his life with. Someone who he might, eventually, trust with the truth about why he is the way he is. Someone who might be able to help him. He tries not to think too much about Rose Campbell and Amber Ryan these days. He'd thought, briefly, that both of those women might be 'the one', but clearly he was wrong and, well—

He feels his fists tensing and he flexes his fingers to release them. He leans back in his leather seat, turning his head to stare out of the window as the car moves smoothly through the dark streets, the pavements still busy with Friday night revellers. In the front, his driver, Yuri, has the radio on low.

Jack can hear that some talk show is playing. The car slows and stops at a red light, and a young man steps out unsteadily to cross the road, a woman with long blonde hair looping her arm around his waist and laughing up at him, wobbling on chunky platform shoes that accentuate the curves of her calves. Jack watches the pair for a moment, then looks back through the side window, where a gaggle of people are standing in the pool of light cast by the neon sign of a kebab shop. The girls are in short, tight dresses and the men are jacketless.

It's... what? The 29th of March? Nearly April, he thinks. Summer will be here before he knows it, and the days are growing longer, squeezing out the hours of darkness. He prefers winter now, although he didn't when he was young. Back then, it was all about summer. Those long, hot days of the school holidays that seemed to last forever. Pitching a tent in the back garden with his friends, crawling out of their sleeping bags with the first rays of the morning sun to fry eggs on a camping stove. Sunshine and warmth. Happiness...

'All right, boss? Ten minutes, I reckon.'

Yuri's voice jolts him back to reality. He nods and thanks his driver as the car begins to move again, then slowly pulls his phone from his pocket and scrolls through his apps. He was startled when Heather Harris suddenly appeared back in his life. Actually, startled is an understatement. He was astounded to receive her message and, unusually for him, for several minutes completely unsure how to respond. Why would she want to come back? Nobody comes back. Even now, even though they've already slept together and she seems happy to be back in his bed, he's wary. There's something about this woman; how he felt when they split the first time took him by surprise. He expected to be angry, and he had been at first, but his fury and bitterness dissipated quickly, to be replaced with a low-level and lingering sense of sadness and resignation. He still isn't sure if that was simply due to how frantic his work life was at the time, or for some other reason. He knows he felt very differently when Rose, and later Amber, ended *their* relationships with him. Then, the feelings of rejection and rage were savage as they coursed white-hot through his veins.

But Heather… He's been thinking hard about Heather. She was friends with Amber Ryan once, a long time ago, and he wonders if that's relevant. He watched her carefully when he mentioned Amber's name to her that first night, and there was nothing of note in her reaction, but still. He's been observing her, and he's still unsure. He can't be certain, but he thinks that maybe she knows about his security system, or some of it at least. There was an occasion, the first time around, when he was playing back footage from his living room and he thought she might have spotted the camera concealed inside the spine of a novel on his bookshelf. It had seemed to him at the time that she was doing her best to pretend she hadn't, nonchalantly moving away, and not looking directly at it. He tried to test his theory by asking her to take her clothes off in the lounge on Tuesday evening, but unfortunately Rhona came in at just the wrong moment. So does she know, or not? It's irritating him.

Now, he finds the app he's looking for and taps on the file for Wednesday morning. He's viewed the footage before, and frowned over it before, but he watches again anyway. Each time he does, his suspicions grow.

First, Heather heads into his office, and stays in there for ten minutes or so. Fine – he said she could use his phone charger, and maybe she was working on her phone while it charged. She spends a lot of time on it, posting book 'content' as she calls it on her Instagram page, and sending work-related emails. He understands; he's like that himself, never really switching off. It's what she did next on Wednesday morning that's piqued his interest. He fast forwards as Heather enters the gym and wanders around, still seemingly engrossed in her phone. And then she takes off her hooded sweatshirt and throws it onto the water cooler, directly towards the camera hidden inside it. A second later, the fabric settles, obscuring his view. Music starts pumping, but he can see nothing of Heather or her workout, and he stares at his screen, wondering. Does she know there's a camera there too? But how? Or is it just a coincidence her hoodie landed where it did? Again, he's not certain, and he *really* doesn't like the feeling.

He taps through to the camera in the kitchen, and watches as Heather prepares a smoothie. She sips it, walks around the room, and enters the pantry. His heart skipped a beat the first time he watched her do that, and he felt a surge of relief when Rhona appeared. He can't hear their brief conversation because the sound is low and muffled – there's no camera in the pantry to record it – but seconds later Heather reappears and walks to the big fridge in the kitchen. She helps herself to some ice before thanking the housekeeper and leaving the room again. Ice. She was just looking for ice. Or was she?

'Here you go, boss. Pick you up at four-thirty, yes?'

Yuri again, as the car slows to a halt. Jack looks up from his phone to see the tall brick façade of Shannon Medical looming over them.

'Four-thirty's perfect, thanks Yuri,' he says. 'I'll give you a buzz if I finish any earlier.'

He gets out of the car, reaching back into the footwell to retrieve his briefcase. He raises a hand as Yuri drives away, presumably to park up in a quiet corner of the car park and have a nap. Jack doesn't care what he does, as long as he's ready to take him home again before dawn. Yuri's been with him for over a year now and hasn't let him down yet. Most of his staff are like that; Jack likes to surround himself with people who won't let him down, and if they do, even once, they're out. It doesn't happen often, though.

It's girlfriends who let him down, not his staff.

Jack stands there for several moments, still thinking about Heather. It's a moonless night, the sky a velvety black. The darkness calms him, wrapping itself around him like a comfort blanket.

His phone beeps. It's a message from Naomie, his PA, wondering what time she can expect him because there's some urgent paperwork she needs him to sign. He stares into the inky night for another few moments, then turns and walks towards the building. From somewhere close by, a fox howls a high-pitched scream that sounds eerily human, like a woman in distress.

EIGHTEEN

Heather

Saturday evening, and I'm sitting in Jack's lounge, waiting for him to finish getting ready to go out. It's shortly after 8pm, and it's only just dark. There are faint streaks of daylight still visible in the sky outside, which means, of course, that the curtains are tightly closed, and I already feel trapped and fidgety. It doesn't help that the first person I encountered when I arrived was Rhona, who told me in her usual unsmiling manner that Jack had only been up for an hour and was still in the bathroom.

'He said to wait in there,' she said, gesturing towards the living room. She stood there, silently watching me, as I slipped my jacket off and hung it on the rack in the hall. I glanced at her as I pushed the living-room door open, but her eyes were dead and there was no expression on her face. A shiver ran through me.

What is it with her? I thought, as I quickly closed the door behind me, leaving her outside. *She's… she's scary. I think I'm actually scared of her.*

It was only then that a ghastly thought crept into my head, one that probably should have entered it earlier. Rhona's only just started working for Jack in the last couple of weeks, but what if they know each other from before? Is that why she's so unfriendly? Could *she* be his female accomplice, the one who made the call about the jewellery? Maybe she's even the one he enlisted to stab him; she looks like the type who pulled wings off butterflies when she was a kid. I'm pretty sure Jack has no idea why I've really come back into his life, but what if Rhona's suspicious? Could she be keeping an eye on me? The way she keeps materialising out of nowhere…

I pace the room, too restless and uptight to sit down. Earlier, I sent two carefully worded messages. The first was to Jack's PA, Naomie. Her email address was easy to work out because all his staff are simply firstname.surname@Shannon-Medical.com. The second went to Yiannis Pappas, through a personal contact form on his profile page on the website of the company he now works for. After a chat with Nathan about the best way to approach him, I deliberately kept my message short.

> Hi Yiannis, I've been given your name by someone who suggested you might be able to help me out with a private project. Could you drop me a line at this email address so we can discuss further? Thanks.

As it's a bank holiday weekend, I'm not expecting a response from him until Tuesday at the earliest, but a reply from Naomie to the message I sent her popped into my inbox within minutes. As I'd planned, I told her I'd recently started dating Jack and would be in the area of her office on Wednesday, on my day off.

> I know this is a bit forward as we've never met, but you must know him well. Would there be any chance you'd have time for a quick coffee? I really need some advice about what to get him for his birthday and you seem like the perfect person to ask?

The response had been brief, but positive.

> OK. There's a coffee shop just down the road from our building, Espresso Express. I can meet you for a few minutes at 1.15?

I accepted the offer immediately, but now I'm all over the place, wondering how I'm going to handle this. Do I simply bring up the subject of 'my friend Amber' and see how she reacts? I just don't know, and as I pass the huge antique Baroque French mirror on the wall for the fourth time, I pause, realising my jitteriness is showing on my face.

Calm down, I tell myself. Jack will appear in a minute, and this has to be just another pleasant evening. I can't afford to give him the slightest inkling that I'm stressed or worried about anything.

I hear his footsteps in the hallway and turn to face the door, forcing a smile.

'Hey, you,' I say. 'Happy Easter. You look *good*.'

He does. Putting all my true feelings and fears about this man aside, and viewing him purely from an aesthetic standpoint, it still strikes me every time I see him. He's *stunning*. We're going for cocktails and then dinner in town tonight and he's wearing slim-fitting dark jeans and a tailored navy jacket with a snow-white shirt underneath, the top button open. His hair is still a little damp from the shower and looks artfully tousled, and as he returns my smile and tells me I look good too, I repeat a silent mantra in my head.

Do not let him get under your skin.

Do not let him get under your skin.

Do not let him get under your skin.

You're here to expose him, I think. *He's a bad, bad person…*

But the game must be played, and so as our taxi arrives and we head off into central London to enjoy dirty margaritas followed by a delicious meal at a three-Michelin-star restaurant that's usually booked up for months ahead ('I pulled a few strings,' Jack murmured to me, with a wink), I play it like a pro. I've found myself wondering more and more about what makes Jack tick. Even though I gave up trying to get to the bottom of his strange psyche the first time, now I'm increasingly feeling as though this is incredibly important; that it'll explain not only why he *lives* as he does, but why he's *behaved* as he has, too. I *want* to understand it, I *need* to know why he'd do such terrible things, and I'm trying to be subtle, but every time I ask even a vaguely probing question about his childhood or his family, he quickly shuts the conversation down and changes the subject.

I've always known he has no siblings, and that both of his now-deceased parents were only children too, meaning his family is small – no aunts, uncles, or cousins. And I know, of course, that his dad was a police officer, a Chief

Superintendent, in fact, with the Metropolitan Police. It's his mother I'm more interested in, because she's the one he really won't talk about. I know the business was hers, and that she inherited it as a much smaller concern from her father, growing it significantly before it was passed on to Jack after her death, whereupon he *really* made it take off. I know she died when he was in his teens, but that's all I know. This evening I decide to try again, first casually chatting about my own mum, and about how she's recently taken up taekwondo, to my immense surprise. Then I swallow the final spoonful of my dessert and say:

'What sort of stuff did your mum like to do? Or was she always too busy with the business?'

He glances up from his plate and eyes me silently for a couple of seconds, then shrugs.

'She liked hiking. Didn't have much time for it though,' he says, then looks down at his dessert plate, scooping up another spoonful and putting it in his mouth.

I take a sip of water and decide to plough on.

'It's so sad you lost her so long ago,' I say. 'I'd love to have met her, and I'm sure she'd have been so proud of you. I mean, the company's just exploded, hasn't it? She'd have been amazed. You've never told me... what happened to her? Do you mind talking about it?'

He looks at me again then picks up his napkin and wipes his mouth, holding eye contact. I suddenly feel a little quiver of unease. We've been having a nice enough evening, the conversation light and gently flirtatious, but now I feel a shift in the mood. The atmosphere is suddenly heavy around our candlelit table.

'She died suddenly,' he says tersely. 'I was sixteen. Can we leave it there, please? I'll get the bill.'

Shit.

He barely says a word on the cab journey back to Barnes, and as we walk into the house Rhona is standing in the hallway like a silent statue. My feeling of despondency increases.

God.

This house. These *people.*

'I'm just off to the supermarket,' she says, by way of greeting. 'You're running short of a few things, Mr Shannon, so I thought I'd go now, when it's quiet.'

She reaches for her coat, and Jack mutters: 'Fine. Thanks, Rhona,' and strides past her, me following in his wake. I feel her eyes on me, but I ignore her, unable to deal with a clearly pissed-off Jack and a malign housekeeper simultaneously, and at the same time thinking how batshit crazy it is for her to be heading to the twenty-four-hour Tesco or wherever at midnight, as if that's a totally normal thing to do.

In the bedroom, I grit my teeth and try to appease him.

'I'm so sorry,' I say gently, and reach out tentatively to take his hand. 'I know you don't like talking about your mum, and I shouldn't have asked. It must have been awful to lose her so young, and if you ever want to talk about it, I'm here for you, OK? But I promise I won't ask you again. Forgive me? It's just because I care, you know?'

For a few moments he stands there, his back rigid, his eyes vacant. Then, he slowly slips out of his jacket, dropping it onto the carpet, and my heart rate quickens. Have I pushed it too far? What's he going to do? I open my mouth to say something else, to apologise again, but suddenly, his expression softens, and he entwines his fingers in mine and pulls me towards him.

'It's fine,' he says. 'It's just sometimes the past is best left in the past. Come here.'

I feel a rush of relief, and then we're kissing, his tongue in my mouth, one hand in my hair and the other cupping my breast. We fall onto the bed and Jack pulls at my dress. He peels my underwear off roughly, and then he's inside me, and for the next couple of minutes I'm lost. My body responds to his mouth and his hands and the thrust of his hips; it betrays me.

I shouldn't be enjoying this. I shouldn't even be doing this, I think, even as I moan with pleasure. *But... oh, my God!*

Jack collapses onto his pillow, breathing heavily, and closes his eyes. It's what he always does, this post-coital sleep, but tonight I'm not going to do my usual thing and snuggle up beside him. I heard the gentle clink of the bunch of keys in his pocket when his jacket hit the plush wool carpet, and the jacket is still there, like a dark dozing animal curled up on the floor. And I know Rhona is out, so this is my chance.

I stand up and walk quickly to the bathroom, pulling off my rumpled clothes and putting on one of the two always fresh white towelling robes that hang on the back of the door. Then I return to the bedroom, push my feet into my trainers, pick up my phone, and lean over Jack, who's still lying flat on his back.

'I'm thirsty. I'm just going down to get a drink. Do you want anything?' I whisper. There's no response. His breathing is slow and steady, his left hand limp by his side, the injured one curled protectively against his body.

Good.

I creep to his jacket, cautiously moving the fabric, looking for the pocket. I slide my hand inside, closing it over the irregular metal bundle, and remove it with barely a sound.

The keys. I have the keys. I glance at Jack's inert form once more, then tiptoe to the door and slip out of the room.

NINETEEN

Heather

The house feels eerily quiet as I walk quickly downstairs to the kitchen, but at least Rhona has left the lights on. It's nearly 1am, and if I'd had to do this in the dark, it would be even more nerve-wracking. Even so, adrenaline is making my legs feel shaky, and when I stop at the door to the rear courtyard, my fingers tremble as I fumble with the door handle, trying to open it noiselessly. Jack is, I very much hope, still sound asleep on the floor above, but I don't have much time and I can't risk any interruptions.

I step out into the dimly lit yard, and make my way from planter to planter, picking a few flowers – a couple of daffodils, a crocus, a tulip – and a sprig of foliage. When I have enough to make a small posy, I head back indoors. I need an excuse for going into the pantry again, in case Jack does watch his camera footage back, and I can't use the 'looking for ice' lie a second time. But I saw vases in the pantry, lots of them, and so my plan is to pretend I wanted to surprise Jack with flowers by the bed when he wakes up. He's not really a flowers kind of guy, but it's all I can think of, and I'm hoping he'll appreciate the gesture, especially after our little tiff earlier.

Flowers to say sorry, again, for asking him about his mother, even though in any normal relationship, that really wouldn't be a big flipping deal, I think, as I head down into the kitchen. I dump the flowers beside the sink, open the glassware cupboard and pour myself some sparkling water from the fridge. Then, trying to keep my breathing steady, I go to the pantry and step inside, half closing the door behind me because, although I'm pretty sure the kitchen camera can't see me in here – wrong angle – I'm not going to take any chances. Carefully, very carefully, I ease the bunch of keys from my dressing-gown pocket, trying to avoid a telltale jangle, and study them. There are numerous larger keys and a few smaller ones, some brass, one stainless steel. I step closer to the small silver freezer and peer at the padlock. It must be this key, right?

I stand very still for a few moments, listening, and hear no noise coming from anywhere apart from the gentle hum of the fridge in the kitchen and the freezers next to me. But Rhona's been gone nearly an hour now, and it can't be long before she's back. My hands are shaking again as I insert the key into the padlock. And then…

Yes! YES! I think, as the lock springs open. *I'm in!*

I drop the padlock on the ground, pulling open the two horizontal doors of the freezer. It's full, each shelf neatly stacked with packages, most in plastic wrap, a few in foil.

OK. Be methodical and be quick.

I start at the top right and rapidly work my way down, lifting out each item in turn. It does indeed all appear to be meat, and is labelled as such, most of it clearly visible through transparent wrapping. But I can't be sure about the foil-wrapped pieces, even though they're definitely the shape and size of a steak or a pair of pork chops. Do I need to check? I pause, holding a weighty bundle, thinking about the jewellery Jack accused Amber of stealing. Could *that* be hidden in some of these parcels? Damn. It might be. Quick, *quick*! I start again, hurriedly picking up each item that's in opaque wrapping and carefully peeling back just enough of it to see yet another frozen fleshy ribeye or leg of lamb before smoothing the foil back down again. By the time I'm halfway down the left-hand shelves my hands are aching with cold, my fingertips numb, and I've discovered nothing, other than a new sense of awe at just how much varied and expensive meat one man can have, or need, in his house. But when I finally reach the bottom shelf and remove two large bundles labelled 'venison – butterflied haunch' and 'venison – whole shoulder', I pause. Underneath the butchered deer is another package, but this one doesn't look like the others. It's flat, and rectangular. The size of... A4 paper?

I swallow, glancing nervously over my shoulder. I've been in here for at least two minutes, and my 'choosing a vase' excuse won't wash if I take much longer. I put the two chunks of venison down on the floor and slide the flat packet out. It's foil-wrapped too, and I gently turn back a corner, to see a blue plastic zipper bag underneath.

It's no good, I'm going to have to open it properly, I think. My heart is really hammering now and my chilled fingers are clumsy. I open out the foil covering and unzip the bag.

Holy. Crap.

Paper, documents, dozens of pages. I pull one out and read it, my eyes widening. It's a printout of an email, sender Rose Campbell. Rose. It's from *Rose*. My heart is beating so fast I can feel it banging against the wall of my chest.

> All being well, I'll be depositing the final £10,000 to my Atlantic Central, Belize savings account on Friday. As discussed, can you please then transfer the entire balance to my new instant access account?

An email to an offshore bank. I grab another page, this time from the bottom of the stack. Another email, from Amber this time, to somebody called Robin Knight.

> I have a beautiful selection of family jewellery I'd like to sell, including a pair of rose-gold and diamond earrings, a white-gold Cartier bracelet, and a platinum and emerald ring. If I send photos initially, would it be possible to give me a very rough valuation? These pieces will be in my possession very soon and I can bring them to Hatton Garden…

I gasp. This is one of the emails that was used to build the case against Amber, but Jack shouldn't have it, should he? When he was attacked, the police seized Amber's laptop and work computer and gained access to her email accounts, but there's no way they would then have printed off copies and handed them to Jack, is there? No matter how 'well in' he might be with the police. And there's no way whatsoever he should have *Rose's* private emails. So the only way he could have these copies in his possession is if *he* wrote them in the first place, or got someone else to write them, and then printed them off to keep, just as Nathan said he would. But *why*? Why would you keep them? It's so *stupid*. So incriminating. Then, immediately, I answer my own question.

To relive it. To gloat. To glory in what he's done. He sits and watches the videos and reads the emails and he gets off on it. I feel sweat trickling down my back.

Then I jump violently as a distant *bang* echoes through the house.

The front door. That's the front door closing!

Rhona's back, I think. *Shit. Shit.*

I reach into my dressing gown pocket and pull out my phone, stabbing at the screen to open the camera. I take shots of the two emails I've just read. Then, feeling increasingly panicked, I desperately stuff the pages back into the bag and zip it up, then rewrap it, trying to replace the foil as neatly as possible, to leave it as I found it. I slide it back onto its shelf, dump the venison on top of it, and replace the padlock on the freezer doors, shoving the keys and my phone back into my pocket.

Footsteps. I can hear footsteps on the stairs. I spin around and grab the first vase I see on the shelf behind me. I'm walking out of the pantry when Rhona appears in the kitchen doorway, carrying two shopping bags. She stops abruptly.

'Oh. What are you doing?' she says.

I force a smile, and wave the vase in her direction.

'I picked some flowers from the courtyard for Jack,' I say. 'I thought I'd put them by the bed. He's having a nap but for when he gets up. And I needed a drink. I'll be out of your way in a minute.'

'Right.'

Rhona dumps her bags on the worktop and watches as I hastily arrange the flowers in the vase and pick up my glass. I hate this, the way she silently stares with judgement in her eyes. But now I'm wondering again if there's more to it. If she was part of what Jack did to Amber. If she's keeping an eye on me.

Be nice. Smile. Act normal, I think.

'OK, done. I'm off to bed,' I say cheerfully, as I walk past her. 'Have a good night… Erm, I mean, day. Or whatever. Shift. Have a good shift…'

Aaagh. Stop babbling, woman, I think, and my voice tails off, as Rhona continues to stare at me, although I think I see her mouth give a tiny, amused twitch. She must think I'm a complete idiot. I groan inwardly as I head back upstairs, and once in Jack's room I check that he's still asleep, reassured by his gentle snoring, and put the vase of flowers on his bedside table, where he'll see it when he wakes up, which could be any minute now. Then I crouch down beside his jacket which is still lying on the carpet, and slip the bunch of keys back into the pocket. In the bathroom, I lock the door and quickly save the two photos I've just taken to the cloud, then delete them from my phone. It's one thing ticked off my list, and I agreed with Felicity and Nathan that anything I find I will photograph but leave in situ, for now.

'Put it back exactly as you found it. We can't risk him noticing anything's been disturbed until we have enough to build a decent case,' Nathan said.

Suddenly, I feel exhausted. The adrenaline rush is over, and my head is fuzzy with tiredness, my legs weak. I stumble out of the bathroom and slip under the duvet, but sleep doesn't come easily. Right up until tonight, there were moments when I still wondered if Nathan might be wrong about all this. I do trust him now, and Felicity – or at least I think I do – but there've still been times when I've thought, *Really? Seriously?*

But now, everything's changed. What I've just seen – that's evidence, pure and simple. And now I need more. I need the videos, the jewellery… I need it all.

I *want* it all.

I feel Jack stir beside me, and I squeeze my eyes shut and lie very still. Moments later he's out of bed and then I hear the bathroom door opening and closing. I breathe a sigh of relief when he emerges again and leaves the room. I have a few hours on my own now to rest. And then, hopefully, when he comes back to bed later, I'll have the house to myself for the day. The thought of more creeping around, trying to avoid those blasted cameras, makes me feel sick, but I've come this far, and tonight, finally, I've made progress.

We know where the emails are. It's a start.

TWENTY

Heather

'Jeez, Heather, you look knackered.'

I look up to see Kwee looming above me, looking concerned. I'm sitting on the floor in the shop, rearranging some titles on the bottom rows, and I'm not entirely sure but I *think* I may actually have fallen asleep, just for a few seconds, with my head resting against the edge of the bookshelf. This is *not* good.

'I am, a bit,' I reply. 'I didn't get much sleep last night.'

'Ohhh.'

Kwee's expression changes, her brow puckering.

'Gentleman Jack keeping you up with him, is he? An all-night session? You need to be careful, there, Heather.'

She's looking at me strangely, and I feel a whisper of unease. Does she know more about Jack than she's letting on? More than I've told her (which isn't much)? But how could she? I'm being ridiculous, and I smile wearily.

'Something like that, yes,' I say. 'Actually, do you mind if I go and get a quick coffee? I'm nearly finished here anyway.'

'Of course. Go. I think I'll cope without you for a few minutes. Take a break. It's lovely outside. I'd have it out there if I were you.'

She nods at me and strides off. I watch her go, blinking to clear both my vision and my head of completely unfounded paranoid thoughts, then haul myself to my feet and head upstairs. When I've made my coffee – extra strong – I follow Kwee's advice and take it out to the front of the shop. She's recently put a couple of small tables and chairs out here as somewhere for people to sit and read the new books they've just bought. It is indeed a lovely day, the sun bright in a cloudless, duck-egg blue sky, and I slip my cardigan off my shoulders and enjoy the warmth on my bare skin as I sip my drink slowly. It's Easter Monday, and also, as it's the first of April, April Fool's Day, although I feel so shattered that if anyone did attempt to play a prank on me, I'm not sure I'd even notice. I feel listless, lethargic, although the people walking past me down Chiswick High Road are moving more slowly than they would on a normal Monday too, mostly families and couples sauntering along, enjoying a day off, instead of the usual harassed-looking businessmen and women scurrying to appointments. Jack kept me up most of last night; after sleeping through the day on Sunday, he got up around 7pm and announced that, in honour of Easter, he was taking the 'day' off, and fancied a movie marathon and a takeaway.

'We can take turns choosing the films. It'll be awesome!' he said, pulling me into an embrace, and his face looked so boyish and excited I almost softened, just for a moment. I hugged him back, but I hardened my heart.

'I mean, that's fine, and I can stay up until midnight or so,' I said. 'But I'll have to go to bed at some point, Jack. I'm working tomorrow, remember!'

His expression darkened with disappointment and a hint of annoyance, and I immediately backtracked, telling him I'd stay up as late as I could, and who needed sleep anyway?

'Exactly. You can sleep when you're dead,' he replied, and my stomach flipped.

It's just an expression. Don't overthink it, I thought at the time, but as the evening went on my anxiety began to spiral.

He's doing it again.

Jack did this before, the first time we dated. Initially, he'd been happy to let me sleep at night, but after a few weeks he'd begun persuading me to stay up to match *his* hours, even though he knew I'd been awake all day. He did it repeatedly, feigning upset or offence when I tried to refuse, gaslighting me and making me feel *I* was the one being unreasonable; telling me he just wanted to spend more time with me and that if I cared about him I'd want that too. I'd tried to comply, but eventually I'd become so fatigued I couldn't think properly, and even began to believe him when he told me I was being selfish, and that if I wanted our relationship to work I'd rearrange my hours to fit with his. It was yet another reason I eventually cracked, but this time, I have to play along. It's not going to be easy, though. Last night, I fell asleep on the sofa twice, once just after 1am and again just before three. Both times, he poked me in the stomach until I woke and sat up again, groggy and grumpy, and when I finally insisted on going to bed at 4am, he rolled his eyes and said petulantly, 'Fine. I'll sit here by myself then. I'll see you when I see you.'

Damn, I thought, and I swallowed my annoyance at his childish fractiousness and slipped an arm around him, whispering in his ear the things I'd do to him before I went to sleep, if he cared to join me in the bedroom. It worked, and half an hour later we were in bed and doing anything but sleeping. As a result, when my alarm went off at nine, I'd managed about two hours, and dragged myself back to Chiswick feeling very grateful for today's bank holiday eleven o'clock opening time.

Now, I watch wearily as a golden Labradoodle with a curly coat and big brown eyes bounds eagerly past, a very petite woman clinging to its lead and shouting, 'Jasper! Jasper, slow down!' ineffectually at the dog who completely ignores her.

I can't get those emails out of my mind. When I messaged Nathan and Felicity yesterday to tell them what I'd found and to share my photos, they were both thrilled. I deleted the messages immediately after I sent them, which is another thing we agreed in advance, but I suddenly remember now that I've forgotten to delete their replies. I pull my phone out of my pocket.

Bugger.

I really do need to stay on top of things like this, even though it's *my* messages that would be the much more incriminating ones, should Jack ever happen to see them. Nathan had replied:

> Amazing work. You're a superstar. Fantastic start. Keep going!

And Felicity had been just as excited.

OMG, this is brilliant! We knew it! Go, Heather! Be careful though. Speak soon. Felicity xx

I smiled when I first saw their comments, but now, maybe because I'm so tired and out of sorts, as I read them again I feel a faint sense of disquiet. They said they'd help as much as they could, but what have they done, really? It's *me* that's taking all the risks here, and yes, I agreed to do it, but sometimes…

I give myself a mental shake.

Stop it.

What can they do? Nathan's over a thousand miles away, and it's not as if Felicity can just walk into Jack's house and help me look for stuff. Focus on how well it's going, that's what I need to do.

I haven't told Amber yet, but I'm due to speak to her on Wednesday evening, so I'll let her know then, I think, as I wipe the messages, wishing I had more good news to send. I spent yesterday searching two other areas of Jack's house, taking advantage of Rhona not being around. In the morning, I managed to do the main kitchen, desperately hoping that my cunning plan to cover the camera embedded in the clock face would work. It did. I made another smoothie, using the blender on the worktop directly below the clock, and 'forgot' to click the lid properly into place. The result was instant and fairly epic carnage: a thick, gloopy, fruity mess all the way up the wall, all over the clock, and even on the ceiling. For Jack's benefit, should he watch the footage back, I shrieked convincingly and did a lot of loud muttering and swearing about the massive clean-up job and my own stupidity. Then, after checking the clock face and being as certain as I could be that the camera location was well-covered with a thick, yoghurty coating, I searched the entire kitchen and the dining area on the lower level of the room at top speed, rummaging as quietly as I could through every well-organised drawer and cupboard, before actually having to get to work with cloths and hot water, not wanting to incur the wrath of Rhona when she came back to work. As predicted, I'd found absolutely nothing of interest, and the clean-up was a huge pain in the ass, but it was another area ticked off my list.

In the afternoon, the summer house. It was a nice enough day, a little blustery but with blasts of warm sunshine, and I couldn't bear to spend the entire day in the curtained sealed-up tomb that is the house, too scared to let any light into a room in case Jack should get up unexpectedly and wander in. To be fair, he's always told me to use the garden whenever I like, and so I took my book outside, and sat with a mug of tea on the little covered veranda. After half an hour or so, very aware that the courtyard is under CCTV surveillance, I casually stood up and wandered into the summer house, knowing there's a little fridge in there where bottles of water are kept for the gardener. I took a bottle and then, sipping from it, did a quick, discreet scan of the place, but there was no sign of any cameras, and so I swiftly searched the only two possible hiding places in the small structure: the tool cupboard – nothing – and then the chest on the floor. It was still stuffed full of chair cushions, and although I gave each a good squeeze, wondering if anything might have been sewn inside, they all looked normal and unaltered to me. I headed back out to the veranda with my water, and then a few minutes later, nonchalantly drifted inside again, this time looking closely at the wooden floor.

Could these boards have been lifted, and stuff hidden underneath?

The building is old, and the floorboards look worn and smooth, clearly showing their age but with no sign of having been ripped up and put back again. I studied every inch, then gave up. I still think it's highly unlikely that Jack would stash anything important out there, especially as he doesn't appear to have fitted a camera anywhere. So, for now, that's another one off the list, leaving me with the lounge, dining room, snug, cellar, and attic.

I sigh and stand up. I'm about to push open the door of the shop when I hear the ping of an email and glance down at my phone. My eyes widen as I see the sender's name.

Yiannis Pappas. *Gosh.* On a bank holiday.

> Hi, I've looked you up on social media etc and can't imagine what 'private project' you might need help with but I'm intrigued. I've taken a long weekend to visit family in Oxford but I'll be driving back tomorrow morning. I'd prefer to keep this offline. Could meet you at the Canalside Café in Brentford at 1pm?

Bingo. Perfect, I think, and briskly type a reply, agreeing to meet him there. I'm still working on my cover story, and now that's something else I'll have to apply my weary brain to this evening, but it's more progress. Yiannis tomorrow, Jack's house again tomorrow night for our Tuesday evening date, and Naomie on Wednesday. But now, back to work; I've already been out here too long. As I try to slip my phone back into my jeans pocket I fumble and almost drop it, my fingers sliding across the screen. I look down, and frown. The very last page of apps is visible – I download hundreds, most of which I never use; it's a bad habit of mine – but one has just caught my eye. It's a vaguely familiar icon I know I didn't add myself. I tap on it, and stand very still, staring.

And there we are, I think. I'm surprised it's taken him so long.

It's a tracker app. One of those apps some parents install on their kids' phones so they always know where they are, except I'm no kid and Jack Shannon definitely didn't ask my permission to add it to my phone. *Again.* It's illegal to do this, to put a tracker on someone's phone without asking them, but he clearly doesn't care about that. He did it to Amber too, as I learned when we had our chat in the prison visiting room. He must have done what he did last time – grabbed my phone when I'd just been using it before I nipped to the loo or something, before it had a chance to lock itself, and installing the app quickly before I returned. He wouldn't have even needed to go to the App Store, which would require me to be there to use facial or fingerprint recognition. He'll have simply downloaded the tracker to his own phone first and then 'shared' it with mine. Easy. I still remember how shocked and violated I felt when I discovered it the first time. I confronted him immediately, while I was still angry and upset, and he'd looked stricken, telling me it was for my own safety. He claimed he'd been desperately worried about me 'gallivanting' all over London on my own, going to book launches and author talks. He made me feel, once more, as if *I* was the one who was doing wrong, making him sick with worry.

'I can't focus on work when I know you're out. I'm terrified of something happening to you. Once I know you're back in your flat, I can relax. Surely you can see that? Why would you deny me that peace of mind?' he'd said.

I'd been so confused and so worn out by his behaviour by then that I reluctantly acquiesced, but it had been one of the final nails in the coffin, and our relationship survived only a few more weeks. This time, though, I've been expecting it, and I'll be reacting very differently. I'm going to pretend I haven't even noticed. I'm not going to say a word, because this time I have a Plan B. I have a second phone, a 'burner' phone. A phone that's already been purchased and the number of which Nathan and Felicity already have. I know Felicity has done the same; from the very start of all this, she's been using a separate dedicated phone just for communicating with me and Nathan about our little scheme. From now on though, I'll be juggling. When I'm at work, or at home, or at Jack's, or going somewhere I've told him about, like a book event, I'll use this phone. But when I'm out meeting Yiannis or Naomie or doing anything else I don't want him to know about, it'll be the burner. My new 'safe' phone with no tracker. I just have to remember, and not get them mixed up. Tomorrow, I'll bring both to work. But when I go out to meet Yiannis at lunchtime, I'll leave this one here in the shop and take the burner.

I head back inside with a satisfied smile.

You think you've got one up on me, Shannon, I think. *You think you can control me again. But not this time. This time I'm one step ahead of you.*

And you're going down.

TWENTY-ONE

Heather

On Tuesday lunchtime, the Canalside Café is busy when I arrive just before 1pm. I hesitate in the doorway, scanning the faces at each table, trying to match one of them to the profile photo of Yiannis Pappas I found on his company website. The sun is streaming in through tall windows while outside, the light glistens on the calm water of the Grand Union Canal, which links London to the Midlands. Then I see him, at a table for two on the far side, looking directly at me with a questioning look on his face, and I smile.

Here we go.

I make my way towards him, my stomach twisting with nerves.

Do not screw this up, Heather.

There are so many things that could go wrong. Will he believe the story I've concocted? And what if he goes to the police and tells them about me? What if he tells them he's been asked to get involved in something dodgy?

'If he *is* the one who helped Jack hack those email accounts,

I doubt it will have been the only dodgy thing he's ever done, but who knows?' Nathan said. 'He might have done the job for Jack and then realised the dreadful consequences when Rose died, or when Amber went to prison. He's an ethical hacker now, so he might be a reformed character. But we just don't know; he may still take illegal jobs on the side. We just need to be very careful.'

My other fear is a big one. Is there any way he can find out about my connection with Jack? I don't think so, certainly not from my end. I know he's looked me up on social media, but I never talk about relationships or my social life on Instagram or anywhere else, and I've never posted a photo of me and Jack together – not back then or now. It's just that if he and Jack are still in touch, and Jack's mentioned my name…

I think it's unlikely, as Jack certainly likes his privacy and doesn't shout about his relationships either, especially one as new as ours. It's a chance I have to take, and to complicate matters I don't have much time. Brentford is only ten minutes or so in an Uber from the shop, but I didn't like to ask for an extended lunchbreak, so I need to be out of here again in about half an hour if I'm going to be back by 1.45.

How much, if any, useful information can I wheedle out of this complete stranger in just thirty minutes?

'Yiannis? Hi, I'm Heather. It's so good of you to agree to meet me.'

'Hi. No problem.'

He stands up quickly, in a strangely old-fashioned, chivalrous way, gesturing at the chair opposite, then sits down again. I take a seat and thank him, trying not to let my edginess show. He's slim and dark, and he's looking at me a little warily through small round silver-framed glasses.

'So, where did you get my name?' he asks.

I've prepared for this question, obviously. I discussed it with Felicity and Nathan, and we decided vagueness would be the best approach.

'Well, it's a bit random, but a friend of mine, Chloe, who went to Middlesex Uni, knew someone who knew someone who knew you – I'm sorry, I can't actually remember any of their names,' I say, with a sheepish shrug. 'And when I told her what I want to do, she said maybe you could help. She remembers her friends talking about what a computer genius you were back then. My crowd's all more artsy, you know? I honestly don't know anyone who's any good with technology. I knew it was a longshot, but I thought I'd look you up online and there you were. I know it's very cheeky, but if you can help, I'll pay you well. If you don't ask, you don't get, right?'

He's listening intently, eyes boring into mine. As I finish my spiel my throat tightens. Does he believe me? Then I feel a flood of relief as his face relaxes and he leans back in his chair.

'Oh. Well, I don't know about genius, but I'll take it,' he says. 'So, what's this mysterious project you need help with? Hang on – do you want a drink or something?'

A waitress has just appeared at our table, brandishing a notebook, and we order two flat whites. As she walks away, I say quietly: 'Well, it's a bit sensitive…'

I look around quickly, but there's music playing and everyone else in the place is either chatting to companions or into mobile phones. Even so, I lean across the table towards Yiannis, and he mirrors my action, resting his chin on his hand, a flash of interest in his cocoa-brown eyes. *He's cute,* I think, then mentally rap my own knuckles. For goodness' sake. What's wrong with me? If he *did* help to frame both Rose and Amber, he's just as bad as Jack.

I can feel my muscles tightening. I have to get this right.

'OK, so I have an ex-boyfriend who treated me badly. I mean, *really* badly,' I say. 'I don't want to go into detail – it's too painful, to be honest. But there were times I thought he was actually going to kill me. I went to the police, but he's clever, you know? He talked himself out of it, and no charges were ever brought, and now I don't know what to do. I can't bear to let him get away with it, and I can't stand the thought of him doing it to someone else…'

There's a truthfulness about this story that's making it easier to tell than an outright lie, and suddenly I feel less jumpy. I've been looking at Yiannis while I've been talking, but now I drop my gaze to the table, running a hand across my forehead, as if I'm getting upset.

'The problem is, I don't have any physical evidence against him,' I continue. 'He's too smart for that. He never put anything in writing – his threats were all verbal – but he made my life a misery. I was so, so scared for such a long time. And so… well, I was wondering if there was any way I could sort of… you know, get into his emails, and send myself copies of some of the horrible things he said to me? Maybe even backdate some of them? Is that possible? So I'd have something to use against him… It wouldn't be making things up, not really. It would all be real stuff he said to me. But just, you know, written down, so I could *prove* it.'

I stop, feeling a little nauseated. Is he falling for it? I look up, and to my surprise he's looking at me with sympathy in his eyes.

'Yes, that's possible,' he says slowly. 'Also illegal, though.'

I nod as the waitress reappears with our coffees. She deposits them on the table with a cheery: 'There you go! Pay at the counter on your way out. Thanks guys!' and heads off again.

I watch her go then whisper, 'I know it's illegal. But… have you ever done anything like that before? Could you help me? I'd pay you really well, as I said, and it would be for such a good cause. He's… he's a monster, Yiannis.'

Again, not untrue, I think as I bury my face in my hands and let out a little sob, then wonder if I've gone too far. I'm a decent enough actor – I was a member of the drama society back in uni – but it's been a while, and maybe I'm laying it on too thick. Or maybe not, because suddenly I feel a gentle touch on my forearm, and look up again to see Yiannis's hand. He holds it there for a moment longer, his fingers warm on my skin, then withdraws it, looking a little awkward.

'Please don't cry,' he says. 'Look… OK, yes, technically I could help you. I have… I have some experience with that sort of thing. I'm an ethical hacker, as I think you know, so I have the skillset, obviously. But… I need to think about it. I have a good job, and I don't want to risk my career. But maybe you were sent to me for a reason. Can you give me a day or so? Let me sleep on it?'

I feel a little frisson of excitement.

'What do you mean?' I say. 'Sent to you for a reason?'

It's his turn to stare at the table.

'I got involved… with something a bit similar to what

you're asking about a while back. I needed money at the time, and… I'm sorry, I can't say any more. I regret it, that's all. And maybe if I help you, it'd be like giving something back. Making amends. Doing some good. But I still don't know. It's risky. And I need to go now. But I promise I will seriously think about it, and I'll message you tomorrow, OK?'

Oh my God. He must be talking about Jack, surely? It's too much of a coincidence.

My excitement grows, but I try to keep my expression neutral, my tone passive.

'OK, I totally understand, and thank you. I really, really appreciate it. And let me pay for these. You go,' I reply, gesturing at our mugs. He nods and holds out a hand. We shake, and then he turns and walks briskly out of the café.

In the cab on the way back to work, I think about how much I'll have to tell Amber when we speak. I send Nathan and Felicity a quick update from my burner phone; my normal phone with its new tracker app is sitting safely in the staff kitchen back at the bookshop.

> Guys, I think you were right. He mentioned getting involved in something he implied was shady a while back, and said he regrets it. He's not sure if he wants to help me out because it's risky and might damage his career, but he also said it might sort of help him make amends or something. He's going to let me know tomorrow! Cross everything x

Felicity messages back within seconds.

OMG! That sounds promising. What are you going to do if he says yes? Felicity xx

We're already at Chiswick roundabout, and the shop's just a minute away now, so my response is brief.

Don't worry. I have a plan x

TWENTY-TWO

Jack

'Great. Speak soon. Have a good day!'

Jack ends his video call and reaches for his water bottle. It's shortly after 3am on Wednesday and he's just finished a meeting with a supplier in Hong Kong, where it's a few minutes past ten in the morning. Down the hallway, Heather is asleep in his bed. She came round after work last night and, instead of going out for dinner, they decided to chill in front of the TV and order in a Thai takeaway. It had been an enjoyable enough evening, but Heather seemed a little tense, and he wondered if she'd already discovered the tracker he'd put on her phone. Maybe not. The first time they dated, she found it and challenged him about it; this time, he's hidden it in a folder of random apps he thinks it's unlikely she uses, on the very last page of her app library. If she's found it, she hasn't said anything, but she still didn't seem quite herself last night. She was, he thinks, a little quieter than usual, less affectionate.

When they went to bed though, the sex was still as good as ever, and he wonders now if he imagined her earlier reserve. Maybe it was because they were in the lounge and she knows about the camera. Or perhaps she doesn't… Christ, he fancies her. There's always been something there with this one, something he's never really managed to find with any of the others. His girlfriends are always beautiful, always smart; Jack Shannon doesn't do ugly or dumb. But Heather's got something extra. It's not only their shared love of books and art and good food, although that's great. There's just a feistiness about her, a spirit he craves to tame, while at the same time half hoping he can't. He doesn't like her questions though. When she starts trying to probe into his past, asking about his family. About his *mother*. No, he doesn't like that at all. If he does decide he can trust her enough to talk to her about… about *that*, it will be on his terms, at a time that suits him. But *does* he trust her? He still can't make up his mind. He's watched back the security camera footage from when she stayed at the weekend, and there's nothing there except her pottering around the house and garden, and an amusing incident in the kitchen when she tried to make a smoothie and didn't put the lid on the blender properly. The resultant swearing and banging about as she cleaned up the mess made him first smile, and then pause for thought. Could that have been deliberate? Could the smoothie mix have been deliberately aimed at the clock face to obscure the camera lens for a reason? He thinks it's very unlikely she even knows that camera is there, though, so he's letting it go, for now.

And yet… there's just *something*. It's bothering him. He

stands up and walks to the window, checking there are no tiny gaps through which the light might sneak in. It won't be sunrise for a while yet, but he's felt it getting worse, recently, this aversion to the day. He returns to his desk and picks up a document he needs to work through, but he can't concentrate, so he reaches for his phone and sends Rhona a message, asking her to bring him a strong coffee. It's the system they use when there's someone else in the house, someone who sleeps at night; when they're here alone he just opens his office door and shouts his requests until she hears him. While he waits for his drink, he gives up the attempt to work and stares at the portrait on the wall opposite, thinking about Heather.

He wants to believe she's returned to him because she has feelings for him, but how can he be sure? So far, she's done nothing too out of the ordinary, and now he can keep an even closer eye on her with the tracker. But, as he hears Rhona's soft tap on the door, he suddenly decides to do something else, something that will give him even more reassurance. He'll do it now, this morning. If she passes the test, maybe then he can relax a little. *Maybe.*

'Come in,' he says, and Rhona enters the room, carrying a small tray. She puts it down on the desk and he raises an eyebrow. Next to the requested coffee is a slice of fragrant, rich-looking fruitcake on a white plate.

'I've been baking,' she says. 'I thought you might need an extra little pick-me-up.'

'Wow,' he says. 'That looks delicious. You're a godsend, Rhona. Thank you.'

She smiles and departs, and he breaks a corner off the slice of cake and pops it into his mouth. It's moist and sweet and exactly what he needs. Rhona *is* a godsend. Uncomplicated. Reliable. She makes his life easier. But Heather… the jury's still out. He'll see what happens later, how she reacts. And if she fails to convince him, well…

He sighs and gets back to work.

TWENTY-THREE

Heather

I'm still in bed, dozing, when Jack comes into the room just after eight. I found last night difficult; my meeting with Yiannis unsettled me more than I realised, and I couldn't stop thinking about him. First the emails I found, and now, quite possibly, the man who helped Jack send them. Even if he does regret it now, what would make a man help someone like Jack carry out such a meticulously planned, sustained, and vicious campaign against two innocent women? Why would *anyone* do that? And Yiannis seemed so… nice. He came across as polite and caring. I'll never trust another man again after this.

I'll never trust *anyone* again.

What's *wrong* with people?

I think I've been pretty good at playing the role of contented girlfriend until now, but last night I found it hard to keep smiling. I felt jittery and restless as Jack and I watched TV together, and yet, as always happens, when we went to bed, it was as if my logical mind switched off and my body took over, and I gave in to the sensations his touch somehow awakens in me, despite everything. It's really starting to disturb me, the way I seem to be able to detach from reality when we sleep together; it's as if the man who's done such horrible things and the man who makes me feel physically better than I've ever felt before, with anyone, are two completely separate beings. I *shouldn't* want him like this. I should despise him and fear him, every minute. And now, here he is again, sitting on the edge of the bed, his hand warm on my bare shoulder.

'Hey, sleeping beauty. Come on, get out of bed. I'm horny as hell, and I want to try something…'

He licks my earlobe, his tongue hot and wet, and I'm instantly wide awake, but the sudden heat I can feel low in my belly is tempered by the questions that flash into my brain.

Get out of bed? Try something? What does he mean?

'Aren't you getting in here with me?' I whisper, and turn my head so my lips brush his. He shakes his head.

'No. Come on. Come with me. Just put your dressing gown on. Rhona's busy downstairs. It'll be fine.'

He pulls the duvet off me and I sit up, my heart starting to pound. Suddenly, I know exactly where this is going and know what he's going to do – what he's going to make *me* do – and I want to refuse to go with him. I want to tell him to leave me alone, but he's striding across the room to the bathroom, reaching behind the door to grab a robe, and then slipping it around my shoulders, taking my arms, and putting them into the sleeves.

Moments later, I'm on my feet, and Jack has my hand firmly clasped in his, and is leading me towards the door and out into the corridor.

'Jack! Please, where are we going?' I plead, but he ignores

me. He pulls me along behind him to the gym, opens the door, drags me in, and shuts the door behind us.

'I want to do it in here,' he says.

I stare at him, and his eyes lock onto mine. I can see the challenge in them.

He suspects I know about his cameras. What I did in the kitchen and what I did in here with my hoodie, maybe it was all too obvious and now he wants to check. He's testing me, I realise, and suddenly I want to cry. But what can I do? If I say no, if I refuse to have sex with him here, he'll know that I know, and that would make what I need to do from here on in incredibly difficult. But if I do what he wants me to do… I feel a burning sensation in my chest. The thought of being filmed doing such an intimate act, the thought of that footage existing, to be watched back over and over, and maybe even shown to God knows who…

'OK,' I say.

I have to. I have no choice.

'But are you sure Rhona won't come in here?'

I'm clutching at straws now, because I don't think he would care at all if Rhona walked in on us, but it's all I've got. He shakes his head and reaches for me, pulling at the belt of my dressing gown and slipping it from my shoulders.

'She won't come in,' he says softly, and now I'm naked, the towelling robe at my feet. My body tenses. I'm desperate to cover myself and instinct is screaming at me to put one arm across my breasts and a hand between my legs, but Jack's leading me across the room to the bench in his weights area. He pushes me down gently so I'm sitting on the end of it and then lying on my back, fully exposed. He's wearing jeans and a

T-shirt, and his feet are bare. He unzips the jeans and pulls them down to his thighs, then pulls his boxers down a few inches too. He's ready, I can see that, his breathing becoming ragged. He leans down and kisses me, his tongue probing my mouth. Then he stands up again and lowers his pants further, and as he does so I see his eyes flit to the water cooler, and then back to me. I can't react, I mustn't, and so I stretch my arms up towards him and pull him down until he's on top of me, his body hard and heavy on mine. He groans.

'I want you,' he whispers. It's fast and rough and, for the first time ever with him, it gives me no pleasure at all. All I want is for him to finish. I want him to get away from me and to let me get the hell out of this room. As he stands up and rearranges his clothing, he grins.

'That was fun,' he says. Though it takes an effort, I smile back and agree, rolling off the bench and retrieving my robe. I pull it on with my back to the water cooler and I feel like bursting into tears.

That wasn't fun at all, I want to scream. *I hated it. I hate you, you twisted bastard.*

But I don't say anything. I *can't* say anything. It wasn't rape; I can't say that. I let him have sex with me because I *had* to, not because I wanted to. Whatever label you put on it, I still feel violated. Defiled.

I want to run away, to leave this house and never come back, to abandon this ridiculous mission, and for a moment I actually think I might do it. I could just go upstairs, get dressed, and leave. I could never come back. I could tell Nathan and Felicity I can't do it anymore. It's too much.

And then I think about Amber. My friend, who's facing life in prison. And I know I have to stay. I *have* to see this through.

Get angry, not upset, I tell myself, as I turn back to face Jack. *Get furious. I hate you, Jack. I fucking hate you!*

'What are you doing now?' I ask, and I force myself to smile at him. I make myself slip my arms around his waist and gaze adoringly up at him. He leans down and kisses me on the forehead, and I can tell by the contented expression on his face that it's worked. I've reassured him.

He thinks it's all OK. He thinks I'd never have had sex with him in here if I knew about the cameras. He thinks I'm stupid.

My anger grows hotter.

'I'm going to bed. I'm knackered,' he says. 'What about you?'

I'm going to meet your PA and ask her questions about you, you scumbag.

What I actually do is shrug and say, 'Oh, I'll just chill out for a bit and then head off home. I need to do some laundry and clean the flat – just boring stuff today. I'll call you this evening, OK?'

'Great.'

He kisses me again, and we wander back to the bedroom hand in hand. By the time I've showered and dressed, he's already asleep. I can hear him snoring softly as I creep out of the room. A quick check now to make sure the coast is clear, that Rhona's finished her shift and is out of the way, and then, I'm going for it. Another search before I leave.

Another step closer to getting this job done, getting myself out of this damn house, and getting my life back.

TWENTY-FOUR

Heather

I don't think I've ever been so efficient in my life. I feel fired up, determined, and more furious by the minute.

By ten o'clock I've already searched the lounge and dining room. In the former, I easily block the book camera's view – a little casual bookshelf browsing led to a large hardback 'accidentally' being left leaning against the spine of the book with the hidden lens – and a quick scan of the room reveals, to my relief, no further cameras. *If* this scanner is as reliable as I hope it is, of course. That niggles at me constantly, although the fact that Jack hasn't said anything to me about my searches so far is somewhat reassuring. I'm still completely paranoid that he or Rhona is suddenly going to appear and ask me what on earth I'm doing, though, so as always, I work fast.

As I did in the gym, I turn on some music to mask any noise I might make and then whizz around, opening every cupboard and drawer, lifting rugs, checking picture frames and the hems of the curtains, tapping wood panelling and feeling for any potential secret compartments, even digging my fingers into the soil of the huge pot plant that stands in the corner of the room. Johnny mentioned plant pots as excellent hiding places for small objects, but this one yields nothing, and as I finish and move into the dining room next door, I'm as sure as I can be that the lounge is clean. I do my now well-practised, nonchalant walk around the room, pretending to be engrossed in my phone, but I can't find any cameras at all in here – maybe there are dinner party conversations, business-related or otherwise, of which Jack doesn't want any record. I begin working my way methodically around the space, which would be bright and airy if the flipping blinds were open. There's not much furniture, just a vast oak dining table and chairs, a cabinet full of crystal glasses, silver cutlery, and a huge white dinner service, enough for at least a dozen guests. The table, Jack once told me, is late Victorian Jacobean-style; the chairs, which match each other but not the table, yet somehow work beautifully in the elegant room, are eighteenth-century Georgian mahogany. I look closely at the seats, which are upholstered in deep purple velvet, then decide they're too perfectly finished to be hiding anything and move on to the sideboard. I remember that this is also eighteenth century, this time in walnut, with brass handles and slender, tapered legs. It's so packed with glass and tableware that I can't imagine there being room for anything else, but I check carefully anyway, until once again I'm reasonably happy there's nothing hidden here. Jack will see me coming into this room, of course, if he checks the footage from his hallway camera. But I can easily say I needed to do some social media stuff before I left, and wanted to sit at a table. Nothing too strange about that. It'll be fine, and I'll do a couple of Instagram posts shortly to cover myself, just in case.

So, now what?

I return to the lounge and sit down in the dark, not bothering to turn the lights on. I want, so much, to fling the curtains back and to feast my eyes on the spectacular view of the Thames. I want to sit here for a few minutes in a patch of sunlight and regroup. I can imagine what it looks like out there right now, mid-morning on a bright April day. There'll be boats of course, too numerous to count, passing by constantly; cruisers and canoes, commuter clippers and flat-bottomed sailing barges. Wildlife too, a surprising variety – the Thames is home to more than a hundred species of fish alone. And then there are eels, wild oysters, cormorants, herons, and even the occasional harbour or grey seal; all of them right outside, and yet none visible to anyone in this vast house. I feel the old frustration bubbling up inside me, but I can't think about it, not now. If Jack wants to miss out on all that, to live his weird little life, fine. Fuck him.

So, focus, Heather.

Where else is there left for me to search? The snug, the cellar, and the attic. The snug won't be too hard, I hope, so maybe I'll leave that until the weekend and tackle one of the trickier areas now while the coast is clear? I still have a bit of time before I need to leave – first to pop home to switch phones, and then to go and meet Naomie. I make my decision and stand up, heading for the stairs. The attic it is. I've done some research into both the cellar and attic spaces of a house like this, and I've asked Jack a few casual questions too, knowing he loves talking about his home and the work he's done here. So, although I've never been up to the top floor, I'm pretty sure I understand the general layout, and I have an excuse ready if by chance he should wake up and find me there.

Even so, goose bumps prickle my skin as I creep up the final set of stairs at the end of the bedroom corridor. Jack told me he only uses the space for storage, and when I reach the dark, narrow landing I find it just as I expected, with a ceiling so low it brushes the top of my head. Through the gloom I can see three doors, two slightly ajar, one closed. I push a stray hair back off my forehead, then stand stock still, listening for any sound from below, but the house is silent, and so I tiptoe across uncarpeted floorboards and carefully, terrified it will squeak, push the first door open.

It moves soundlessly, and I step into a tiny windowless space no bigger than an understairs cupboard in a modern semi, the air dank and musty. I run my hand over the nearest wall, trying to find a light switch, but I can't feel one. I don't even know if there's power up here so I give up, pull my phone from my pocket and turn on the torch. The room is empty, with dusty boards underfoot and bare walls, but I walk slowly around it anyway, scanning for cameras – I can't find any, thank goodness – and then running my hands over the peeling paintwork, checking every corner. There's nothing here, so I move on, and find that the second room is almost identical, although it's a little larger, and has a window – curtained of course – but it means the darkness is less absolute, and that steadies me a little. I repeat the process, but find nothing unusual here either, and as I close the door quietly behind me, I frown. If Jack's using this top floor for storage, he clearly doesn't have much to store.

Is it all going to be behind the final door? This is the one that's firmly shut, and I hesitate outside it, suddenly feeling inexplicably nervous.

Come on. Don't be stupid. It's just another empty room.

I reach for the smooth brass doorknob and turn it. I take a cautious step into the room, and then...

OH MY GOD!

I gasp and stop dead, my heart leaping in my chest, as in the far corner something moves. It's a figure, squatting on the floor, and as I stand there frozen with fear, it turns. A person. There's a person in this room, staring right at me.

TWENTY-FIVE

Heather

'Heather! What are you doing up here?'

It's Rhona, crouching next to a small pile of cardboard boxes. I exhale heavily, clutching my chest.

'Rhona! You nearly gave me a heart attack! What are you doing up here? It's nearly eleven o'clock – shouldn't you be in bed?'

She glares at me, her face half in shadow, half lit by the eerie glare from a torch she's propped up on the highest box, angled downwards. I notice that one of the boxes, the one on the floor next to her, is open, and I frown. What's she up to?

'I couldn't sleep, and Mr Shannon told me I could store some stuff up here, so I just brought a couple of boxes up. That OK with you?'

Her voice drips with sarcasm, and I feel a surge of indignation.

Charming, as always, I think, but I swallow my annoyance and force a smile.

'Fine. Nothing to do with me. Good idea. You don't have

much storage room downstairs, do you? I just came up to take a picture of this book, with the river down below in the background. You know, an arty shot for the 'gram,' I say, and pull the book I've carried up here out from under my arm.

'Instagram,' I add, helpfully, in case she's unfamiliar with the abbreviation. She scowls, but I ignore it.

'Do you mind if I open the curtains for a minute?' I say cheerfully.

'Whatever,' she grunts and, sighing inwardly, I walk across the room and pull the curtains back. Instantly, the room is flooded with light, and I have to put a hand over my eyes. As they adjust, Rhona mumbles something incoherent and angry-sounding, which again, I ignore.

I can see the Thames below now, glittering in the sunshine like a sinuous, watery snake. I lift the book to the window and take a few photos. Behind me, I can hear sticky tape being torn from a roll, and after a few moments I turn to see Rhona standing up, her torch in her hand, the open box now taped shut.

'I'm going to bed. I'll leave you to it. Take care of yourself,' she says. Her tone is softer now, her tetchiness seemingly having evaporated.

Maybe I frightened her, walking into the room unexpectedly like that?

Although her words – 'take care of yourself' – sound like some sort of threat.

'OK. Sleep well,' I say, and she nods and leaves the room, pulling the door gently closed behind her. I stare after her for a moment, then remember I'm in a room that may well have a hidden camera in it, and that if it has, the conversation Rhona and I have just had will have been recorded. I let my phone slip from my hand, and as it lands on the floor I swear loudly and squat down to retrieve it, making sure to turn my back to the boxes, which appear to be the only objects in the room. As quickly as I can, I reach into my pocket and slip the camera detector out of it, then pick up my phone and push that into the pocket instead. Seconds later, I'm back on my feet and on the move, the detector doing its thing.

Dammit!

The alert flashes onto the screen. There *is* a camera in here, and… *bugger.* I think it's in the freshly taped-up box, the one Rhona was just fiddling with. I keep my eyes fixed on the device in my hand, feeling a bead of sweat on my forehead.

That's Rhona's stuff, isn't it? Why is there a camera in her box? Did she put it there on Jack's orders? But why today? Even if she is watching me, how could she know I would come up here today? I only decided myself a few minutes ago. This doesn't make sense. What's going on?

I start to feel panicky, but I also know I can't just walk out of here without searching this room. The fact there's a camera here must mean something. It must mean there's something to protect, something worth keeping tabs on. So…

Trying to look relaxed, I mutter: 'Gosh, it's warm in here,' then, still gripping the detector in my hand, I wriggle out of my hoodie, and toss it onto Rhona's box.

Yessssss, I think triumphantly. The old hoodie trick again and, as it did in the gym, my top's landed in just the right position, draped over the top of the small box with the fabric dipping down on all sides, virtually covering it, and therefore surely obscuring any view from the electronic spy inside it.

There are two larger boxes behind the one with the camera, and a few more to the right, plus a small collection of other items leaning against the wall: a battered-looking pogo stick, an old guitar and, randomly, a pair of oars. They're relics from past times, when Jack was a different person. When he was someone who went outdoors and had fun. I stare at them for moment, then turn back to the boxes and stop dead. The camera will still be recording sound, so how can I possibly go through these boxes, opening them and rummaging inside them, without arousing suspicion? There are no speakers up here to play music through, and it would be weird to suddenly start up a playlist on my phone when the purpose of my trip to the attic is, as I've just told Rhona, to take photos.

What can I do? Sing?

There's nothing else for it. Desperately hoping the sound won't reach Jack down in his bedroom, I start to hum loudly and tunelessly. Then I reach for the top box which has 'BOOKS' written on the side in black marker pen. Thankfully, it's unsealed, and I pull the flaps up to find it contains exactly what its label indicates. Books – children's books. *The Velveteen Rabbit*. *Where the Wild Things Are*. Classics. And others, from the 90s: *The Gruffalo*, several from the *Goosebumps* and *Horrible Histories* series, *The Illustrated Mum*, all a little battered, all clearly read and reread innumerable times. These are books from Jack's childhood that he clearly doesn't want to sit alongside the beautiful hardbacks on his lounge shelves, but can't part with. I swallow, feeling strangely touched.

Maybe there are little bits of that man that are good, even if most of him is rotten to the core?

I'm still humming, my throat starting to ache, as I gently

close the box again and, as carefully as possible, lift it to one side so I can get to the next one. This one is also unsealed, and it's labelled 'PHOTOS'. I open it to find a layer of tissue paper, which I remove as quietly as I can, my humming intensifying. I think I'm actually singing a Wurzels song now – where did that come from?

Flippin' heck. I sound like a crazy person, but what else can I do?

Under the tissue paper there are indeed photos, some framed, some loose. Pictures of a little boy, as a baby, a toddler, in school uniform. It's Jack, very obviously. I'd recognise those eyes anywhere. In some of the photos there are adults too: a tall, broad-shouldered, strong-jawed man – presumably his father, as in several pictures he's in police uniform. And a woman, petite and dark, with eyes so like Jack's I feel a shiver run up my back. *So* alike.

It's as if he's looking at me from inside a woman's body, watching me, knowing what I'm doing here, I think, then tell myself to stop being ridiculous. They're just photos, and this is unmistakably his mother, the woman he always refuses to talk about.

What happened to you? I ask silently, staring at her face, and she smiles back. I gaze at her for a few more moments and then go back to the box. I peel back another layer of tissue paper to find more photos. Holiday snaps this time, of Jack and his parents on beaches, in fields, at a theme park. Outside, in the sunshine, with Jack smiling, looking happy and comfortable.

What went wrong? What the hell happened to him, to turn him into what he is now?

There's one more layer of tissue paper. I lift it out, expecting more photographs, and freeze. On the bottom of the box, there's a stack of square flat plastic boxes. DVDs, not photos. I reach in and take one out, and my humming stops abruptly as a little gasp escapes my lips. On the front is a white sticker, and on it are two lines of text, neatly written in blue pen.

A RYAN
June, 2023

TWENTY-SIX

Heather

The route to the coffee shop where I'm due to meet Naomie involves a short Tube journey and a ten-minute walk. As I turn into the road where I'm expecting to find Espresso Express about halfway down on the left-hand side, I mentally pat myself on the back for actually managing to get myself here without missing my stop or walking into a lamppost. My head is so full of what I found in Jack's attic that already I barely remember the journey, and I'm not sure how I'm going to stop myself blurting it out to his PA and asking her what she's doing working for such a flaming psychopath. Obviously that would be a terrible idea and something I *won't* do but… holy cow.

There were a dozen or so DVDs in the box; several were marked with Amber's name, with various dates from throughout the period she and Jack were in a relationship, including the one dated last June, the month she was arrested. Could that one show what actually happened in his office that night? There were several too marked 'R CAMPBELL' – Rose –

again with various dates, including November 2021, the month she died. That, I'm assuming – *hoping* – will be the video Nathan caught Jack watching that triggered his confession about what he did to her. And then, to my horror, there are several others, with dates going back a few years, and with names I didn't recognise.

G BROWNING
A HART
S BAKER

Other women he filmed without their knowledge? There were none there with my name, but after what happened in the gym this morning, I suspect it will only be a matter of time before footage of me is copied onto a disc too, to be added to this sordid little stash. The thought makes me nauseous. The urge to pick up that box, stalk out of the attic with it and take it straight to the police, was almost impossible to resist. The thought of leaving them there for Jack to move and hide elsewhere or even to destroy, terrifies me. But it's what I agreed with Nathan and Felicity. Leave everything where I find it, until I have *all* the evidence we need. The jewellery is still outstanding, and we still need to try to properly confirm the identity of the hacker, and of course find the attacker and the female accomplice… I know this, and yet, when I was safely out of the house an hour or so ago, I rang Felicity and *begged* her to change the plan; to let me steal the box; to end it *now*.

'Those DVDs alone could be all we need,' I said, as I marched to the station, my heart thudding, as breathless as if I'd just climbed ten flights of stairs. 'If they really do show what Jack did to Rose and Amber… I mean, the dates fit… And what about all those other DVDs? It'll be obvious they show women filmed without their consent. And I was amazed there was none with my name, but I'll be starring in one of them any day now, you wait and see…'

I told her then about this morning, and she gasped, and told me with a shaky voice how terribly sorry she was that something like that had happened to me. But on the subject of taking the box to the police now, she was adamant.

'It needs to be properly planned, not done on the spur of the moment. First of all, what if Jack catches you? I mean, you *might* get away with it. But what if he wakes up and there you are, striding down the corridor with all those DVDs on you? He could kill you, Heather. Or at least injure you very badly. I know we don't think he's physically hurt anyone so far, but who knows what he'd do to try to stop that evidence leaving his house? And then there's the possibility that those DVDs are perfectly innocent, just general footage of those women maybe.

'I know the dates on the Rose and Amber ones tally, and we know he definitely has – or *had* – one of the confrontation with Rose, but he may have edited it or even wiped it by now. Who knows? And we're only guessing that he filmed what happened with Amber. We don't know for sure what's on that DVD. Look, I agree with you. I think what you've just found *could* be vital. It could be exactly what we need. It could be actual footage of him confessing. Maybe even footage of the stabbing. But we don't know, do we, not until we can watch them? And if we take them now, and there's nothing of any use on them, he'll know they're gone and that's it. Our chance will be gone forever. They're not enough on their own. We have to hold our nerve, just for a little while longer. Leave the emails in the freezer, leave the DVDs in the box, leave it all undisturbed. It might only be for a few more days. We need it all, Heather. A watertight case.'

And so I acquiesced. I took photos of the DVDs in the box anyway, like I did with the emails, then replaced everything exactly as it was when I found it. A quick glance into the remaining boxes revealed nothing out of the ordinary – childhood sports trophies, a chipped, old-fashioned blue and white dinner service, a few old Christmas decorations that looked as if a child had made them. *Jack?* I wondered.

Two of the boxes were, as she had told me, clearly Rhona's. They were packed with winter coats, knitwear and boots, clothes she presumably felt no need to keep down in her little apartment now the weather was warming up. The only box I didn't dare look inside was the one she'd taped up, the one with the camera, because I couldn't work out any way to do that without being caught. So I simply lifted my hoodie from it and left the room, but doing so was torture. Could the jewellery be in that one? If it is, it's going to have to stay there until we finally, somehow, go back to collect all this stuff, and I leave Jack's house for the last time.

My fear is growing, though, and now I'm not just scared of Jack, I'm properly frightened of Rhona too. I can't get my head round that camera in her box, and why she was putting it there *today*. Was that her own security camera, to protect her belongings? Is she as paranoid as he is? Or did she put it there on his instructions? And if Jack, or both of them, are watching what I do while they sleep, why has neither of them said anything yet? Surely by now they'd be suspicious of why I seem to be blocking the camera lenses so often? Once or twice could be written off as a coincidence, but I've done it so many times: the gym, the kitchen, the lounge, the attic… and Jack's not stupid. Or did what I let him do in the gym this morning convince him that I'm oblivious to the electronic eyes that see my every move? There are so many questions I just don't know the answers to, and the not knowing is agony. But, as Felicity said, this might take no more than a few more days. I only have the snug and the cellar to search now, and if Yiannis does message me today as he said he would, and agrees to help me, well…

I stop dead. Somehow, the tiny bit of my brain that isn't currently obsessing about all this has registered that I've just walked past the café. Expresso Express, there it is. I stand there for a few moments, gathering my thoughts, then take a deep breath and push the door open.

The place is big, thirty or so tables, and is about half-full. I looked up a photo of Naomie Anderson on the Shannon Medical website, and so I spot her immediately. When I reach her, I smile and hold out my hand.

'Naomie? Hi, I'm Heather. It's *so* kind of you to do this, honestly, thank you.'

She looks at me for a few seconds, her eyes flitting from my face to my shoes and back up again, then she holds out a hand too and gives mine a firm shake. She appears to be in her early forties, a curvy woman with wavy black hair, dressed in a smart grey trouser suit, and when she speaks it's with a soft Caribbean lilt.

'Hello. It's no trouble. I usually come here for lunch anyway. Nice to get out of the office for a bit and see the sun when I'm on day shifts. I do more nights than most, because that's when Mr Shannon needs me. You know.'

Her words are pleasant enough, but she's not smiling and there's a coolness in her eyes.

I'm going to have to be very careful here, I think as I sit down.

'Yes, I know. Do you mind it, the nocturnal lifestyle?' I ask.

She shrugs, large gold hoops in her ears swaying gently.

'It's OK. I'm single, no kids. If I had a family, it might be different. Anyway, what can I do for you? I have to leave in about fifteen minutes.'

She's clearly been here for a while already, a half-drunk orange juice and a small crumb-strewn plate on the table in front of her. She hasn't asked if I want anything to eat or drink, and I decide not to bother looking around for a waiter.

'That's fine. I really do appreciate you sparing me even a few minutes,' I say. 'So, as I said in my email, I've recently started dating Jack – Mr Shannon. Well, it's actually the second time we've dated… We were together for a few months a couple of years ago, but I didn't buy him a birthday present that time around. We weren't getting on so well at that point and it didn't seem appropriate, but this time… As I'm sure you know, it's his birthday in a few weeks' time, and I wanted to get him something really nice, you know? But he's the kind of man who has everything. Men are hard to buy for at the best of times, aren't they, and I'm really struggling to think of something he'd like. I mean, I know what his interests are – art and books and stuff like that – but the type of paintings and hardbacks he collects are way out of my budget, so I really need some advice. I don't know any of his friends well enough to ask them, so I thought, well, his PA will know him better than anyone…'

The words are spilling out of me, and Naomie is staring at me with one perfectly shaped eyebrow raised and a detached look on her face.

'So, can you? Help me, I mean? Can you think of anything he'd really like? I'm tearing my hair out.'

A little smirk twists her mouth for a moment, then the passive expression returns.

'I mean, I could come up with several ideas,' she says slowly. 'But don't you think it's a bit impersonal to ask me to select a gift? Surely you should choose something that's meaningful to the two of you, if you're a *couple*?'

She doesn't actually draw air quotes as she says the word 'couple', but she emphasises it in such a way that it's pretty clear she's sceptical.

'I wasn't really asking you to *select* a gift, just maybe give me some ideas,' I say, trying to keep my tone friendly. 'Something he's mentioned at work, maybe? Or, you know…'

I plough on, desperate to get to the real point, conscious that the clock is ticking. Shall I start with Rose?

'Do you have any idea about presents previous girlfriends might have given him?' I say. 'Did he ever date anyone you knew? Anyone who worked for him?'

Naomie stiffens.

'Once. But she was a thief and a drunk,' she says coldly. 'I don't know what he ever saw in her. Clearly just out for what she could get. I doubt *she* ever bought him a thing.'

Wow, I think. If only you knew. My God.

I have a sudden urge to grab her by the shoulders, to hiss

the truth at her, but that would clearly be a terrible idea right now, so I force a surprised expression onto my face.

'Oh gosh,' I say. 'That sounds unfortunate. Other girlfriends then? Amber Ryan, before— Um, well, before what happened? I knew her once, you know, many years ago. We actually went to school together – can you believe that? Bit of a mad coincidence!'

I'm watching her closely, waiting to see how she reacts, and at the mention of Amber's name, Naomie's eyes narrow, her mouth hardening into a tight line. When she replies her words drip with venom.

'I have no idea if *she* ever bought him a gift, but we do not speak her name, OK? Nobody at work does. She nearly destroyed him. She nearly killed him. She disfigured him for life. That wonderful man was traumatised by what happened in that house that night. I'm not sure he'll ever really recover. So please, do not mention her name to me, or to him, *ever*. That's the best advice I can give you. And if you want to buy him a present, just get him some good cologne or a silk tie. He likes to smell good and look good, and he still manages that every single day, despite what he's been through. But honestly, I'm not sure why you're bothering. I mean, you're not really his type. He told me you work in a *shop*. It's not quite… Well, never mind. I'm sorry, I need to go now. Goodbye.'

And with that, she stands up and marches out of the café. Moments later, I see her striding past the window, and then she's gone.

Bloody hell.

I sit back in my chair, feeling a little stunned. I can't work out how useful that was yet, but it's pretty clear Naomie thinks the sun shines out of Jack's pert bottom. Would she really talk about him like that, and be so derogatory about Rose and Amber, if she knew the truth about what Jack had done to them? Surely not. I shake my head as I stand up too and leave the café. As I walk back to the station, I replay the conversation in my mind.

I don't think she knows. I really don't. I don't think she's his accomplice. But if not her, then who? Someone else he works with? A female friend I don't know about? Or… could it be Rhona? The more encounters I have with that woman, the more my gut tells me she's not what she seems. And that camera thing this morning… My stomach swirls, dread starting to grip me again. I'm pretty sure Naomie will tell Jack I've been to see her, but I'm hoping the birthday gift cover story will be enough to convince him, even if she does tell him we talked about Rose and Amber. There's nothing I can do about that now, anyway, and as I stop outside the entrance to the station, fumbling in my bag for my wallet, I run through a mental checklist of my remaining tasks.

I have to search the snug and the cellar. The jewellery could be in that box in the attic, but it might not be. And should I ask Nathan to do some research into Rhona's background? I'm surprised he hasn't suggested doing that before, actually. I'll do some myself too… and then there's Yiannis. If he is our hacker, maybe he knows who did the stabbing too. But how do I ask him?

Please, please let him get back to me and agree to meet up again, because if he doesn't, I have no idea what to do next…

As soon as I get home, I check my real phone, desperately hoping there'll be a message. And – flipping hell! It's as if the universe has actually heard me and responded promptly, for once. It's from Yiannis.

> Hi Heather. I think I can help you. Can we meet after work tomorrow? 8pm at The Weir in Brentford? Y.

TWENTY-SEVEN

Amber

'What'll it be tonight, then, A6868RX? A cosmopolitan? A mojito? A long slow screw against the wall?'

Stacey winks suggestively at me, and we both laugh.

'A cup of tea, I think,' I reply, 'if you're making one?'

'I am,' my cellmate replies, and hauls herself off her bunk to walk the few steps to the kettle that sits on a shelf in the corner. It's odd, but I don't miss cocktails, or alcohol in general, at all. I used to love a good night out – dinner and drinks and on to a club. But when everything's taken away from you, it's much simpler things you really crave. Tea in a fine china cup, a soft sofa to curl up on to watch a film on a wet Sunday afternoon. Not booze. To be honest, there's plenty in here anyway, if I really wanted it. Stacey and I joke about cocktails, but other women are busy making their own alcohol, using the fruit we get with meals, adding sugar and yeast and fermenting it in their cells, somehow managing to conceal it, somehow getting away with it. Again, like the drugs, is it a blind eye being turned? I don't know. I tried it once, this prison brew, and it's disgusting, but I guess it's an acquired taste. Needs must. I can imagine it taking the edge off the boredom, at least. I've come to the conclusion that a lot of the arguments and fights we see here on a daily basis – and I'm talking proper fisticuffs, hair-pulling, punching, rolling-on-the-floor fights – are partly down to people just looking for something to do to pass the time.

'Here you go, luv.'

Stacey hands me a mug of tea, and I thank her and tell her it's perfect, as always. It actually is: just the right depth of colour and the ideal quantity of milk. If I shut my eyes as I sip it, I can imagine just for a few seconds that I'm back in my own apartment, drinking tea at my kitchen table, about to head off to see a friend or go to work. Except, I don't have a job, not a real one, anymore, do I? What would I actually do for work, if I got out of here? Mud sticks, and even if my name were cleared, I know I'd never be able to go back to the events business. I've actually almost finished a car maintenance course in here, and I've really enjoyed it. I like the idea of doing something like that, something practical. Maybe I'll get a job in a little backstreet garage. Who knows? Or work with Heather, in her shop…

'Shit! What time is it? I'm supposed to be calling Heather!'

I remember suddenly, and stand up too quickly, sloshing tea down the front of my sweatshirt and onto the floor. Stacey rolls her eyes.

'Go on, dolly daydream. I'll wipe up your mess,' she says.

'You are an *angel*,' I reply, and I rush to the door and jog down the corridor, hoping the phone will be free. To my relief, it is, and I'm connected to Heather quickly. She's at home, and my heart leaps as she tells me what she did this morning.

'I decided to go up to the attic,' she says. 'I found some old DVDs. There are a few of you, and...'

She hesitates, clearly trying to choose her words prudently.

'And a few of some of the other girls too. You know, Rose, and a few others. I haven't been able to watch them yet but it was great to find them...'

Oh. My. God.

She's found DVDs, hidden in Jack's attic! I want to scream down the phone. Are they actually labelled with our names then? And 'a few others'? More than just me and Rose, then? What's on them? Sex, I presume, on some of them, but what about the others? Jack, telling Rose what he did to her? And... in his office? With me?

My fingers feel slippery on the receiver. That would show what *really* happened that night. Suddenly the thought of such a video existing makes me light-headed and panicky. Heather is still talking, and I push my hair back off my face, trying to concentrate.

'... And at the weekend, I was sorting through some... erm, some stuff and I found some old emails. From you, you know. Interesting reading.'

She falls silent for a few seconds and I clap my hand to my mouth. Emails too? She's found *emails*? The emails I was alleged to have sent about selling the stolen jewellery? Seriously? The woman is a miracle worker. *How?* How has she done this? I'm desperate to ask, but I can't, so I simply say, 'Woah, you've been busy! Lots of... tidying and sorting. Well done, you. Have you been out at all? How's the new boyfriend?'

'Oh, you know,' she says, and I hear an almost imperceptible hardening of her voice.

'He's… It's a bit up and down,' she says, and I feel guilt sweep over me. I wonder how bad it is. Poor Heather. I want to say something sympathetic, something so she knows I care and that I understand what a massive sacrifice she's making for me, but she's still talking. She sounds decisive and business-like now.

'But, apart from that, I've been out a couple of times in the past week,' she says. 'I met up with a… a friend who works in IT, actually. He's got a very interesting job. In fact, you and he know some of the same people, as it happens. He… might be able to help me out with a little project I'm working on. I'm meeting him again tomorrow night, which will be nice.'

I nod, taking in this latest little coded nugget of information. Does she mean she might have a lead on who helped Jack hack my emails? That's what it sounds like.

Blimey.

'Lovely,' I say. 'And did you manage to have a chat with Naomie?'

'I did,' she says. 'I met her in a café. I'm not sure we have much in common, to be honest.'

Oh, I think. *So Naomie wasn't any help.*

This is so frustrating. I *think* I understand what she's telling me, but I'm not a hundred per cent sure, and there's nothing I can do about that. But it all sounds positive, doesn't it? More than positive. It sounds as if she's making real progress, finding things that really might give me half a chance of getting out of here. It's just… a DVD. *God!* My vision blurs, and I lean against the wall for support. I find I have to blink away a bead of sweat.

'Anyway,' I hear her saying, on the other end of the line. 'I need to run. Lovely to talk to you. We'll catch up soon, OK?'

'Great. Thanks for calling, Heather. Thank you *so* much.'

It's not her fault I'm suddenly more anxious than I've been in months, and so I put as much emphasis as I dare on my final words, hoping she'll understand how grateful I am. I can hear the smile in her voice as she replies. We always did understand each other, me and Heather. Well, not *quite* always. Not those times we fell out. But now – she knows.

'That's OK,' she says softly. 'Bye, Amber.'

I put the phone down, and stand there, staring at nothing for a few moments. Then, on wobbly legs, I walk slowly back to my cell.

TWENTY-EIGHT

Heather

It feels like the longest Wednesday in the history of the world. The longest *day* in the history of the world. So far, I've had sex in front of a security camera, searched an attic and found a boxful of (I hope) incriminating evidence, sussed out a potential accomplice to a crime (or maybe not), and spoken to my imprisoned friend in code.

Who am I, and what has my life become?

And it's not over yet. It's after eight o'clock, and all I want to do now is collapse on the sofa, watch some mindless television, and then crawl into bed. But instead, I need to call Nathan, do some research into the life and times of Rhona MacDonald, and nip upstairs to pick Johnny's brain, again.

I messaged Nathan earlier to check that he was free this evening, so I sit down at the dining table and dial his number.

'Hey, you. How's it going?' he says.

'I'm OK. A bit knackered, but OK,' I reply.

'God, yes. Fliss filled me in on everything that's happened

today. I'm so sorry, Heather. About Jack, and… the gym, and all that. He's a wanker. Are you sure you're OK?'

I hesitate. I'm not OK, not really. But I've already decided I'm seeing this through to the bitter end, so what's the point in complaining?

'I'm fine, honestly,' I say. 'And the DVDs, that's a result, isn't it?'

'It really is. It's amazing. We're nearly there, Heather. And Amber? Have you spoken to her?'

I tell him I have, and then move quickly on to Rhona.

'I'm getting more and more uneasy about her, Nathan. I disliked her the very first time I met her but the more I see her, the more I think there's something off about her. And now this thing in the attic… She's *got* to be helping Jack. The way she looks at me, and keeps appearing out of nowhere when I'm around… and now that camera in the box? I know she's only been working at his house for a couple of weeks but I honestly think they've known each other longer. I'm *sure* they're in cahoots. I'm going to check her out, but could you help, do you think? We should have done it before, really.'

Nathan is silent for a few seconds.

Then he says, hesitantly, 'I suppose we *could* do that.' He pauses, then continues. 'But I honestly doubt she's got anything to do with it. I mean, that camera was probably just her own. People do that sort of thing nowadays. And I think if she was someone Jack trusted enough to be involved, I'd have come across her before. I've never met her. I've never even heard of her. I think you're being a bit paranoid, and I totally get that, considering all you're going through. But I'm just not sure—'

I bristle at that.

'Paranoid? I'm *not* paranoid. You don't know what she's like, Nathan. Always creeping around, looking me up and down, popping up when I least expect her. There's something weird about her, and I am *not* imagining it, OK?'

My voice is getting louder and louder, indignation turning to anger.

'OK, OK, I'm sorry.' Nathan's tone is placatory. 'I didn't mean to imply— Look, if you really think that, of *course* I'll help you check her out. I'll get on to it this evening, as soon as I get *somebody* to bed. Somebody who *was* in bed, but who for some reason has decided to get out again…'

I hear a giggle and a rustle on the line, and for some reason the sound makes my anger dissipate. This is why we're doing this, isn't it? For Lacey, to keep her safe, as well as for Rose and Amber. Maybe for those other names on the DVDs too, whoever they are.

'OK, well, thanks. I'd better let you go,' I say, in a slightly friendlier tone. 'Get that little poppet to bed. I'll do my own research later. I just have something else to do first. I'm meeting up with Yiannis Pappas again tomorrow, and I'm going to ask Johnny upstairs about immunity from prosecution, just to get his take on it. If I know what I'm talking about it will help later, if we need to try to persuade Yiannis to give evidence against Jack. I'll be discreet with Johnny, obviously, before you say anything.'

I've told Nathan and Felicity a bit more about Johnny over the past week or so, and although they say they trust my judgement, I can tell they're both a little concerned.

'I'm sure you will, but… you've asked him about a few

things now, haven't you? Are you sure that's safe? Hasn't he asked you why you want to know all this stuff?'

Nathan sounds worried.

'No, he hasn't. Seriously, don't stress. He's a good guy. It's fine. Trust me.'

He doesn't reply for a few seconds, and when he does that note of concern is still audible.

'Well, OK. If you say so. But be careful, Heather.'

'I will. Goodnight, Nathan.'

I end the call, and then, stopping at the fridge to take a nicely chilled bottle of Pinot Grigio from the top shelf, I leave my flat and head upstairs. I messaged Johnny earlier too, suggesting a quick drink and a catch-up, and he opens his front door with a broad grin.

'Well, hello there, young Heather. Come in, come in.'

He's immaculate as always, his grey hair and goatee beard neatly trimmed, his blue T-shirt crease-free, and as I step into his cosy living room, and hear jazz music playing softly, I feel my shoulders drop.

'God, I need this,' I say. 'It's been a hectic couple of weeks, Johnny. I need some of *this* too – have you got a couple of glasses handy?'

I thrust the bottle towards him, and he raises an eyebrow and smiles again.

'I think I can find some,' he says.

Glasses filled and bodies settled in the two comfortable chairs, we spend a few minutes just chit-chatting. Johnny tells me he and Carlos are getting on quite well at the moment – for them – and I tell him I'd guessed as much, having heard no loud, dramatic shouting in Spanish drifting down from upstairs for at least a fortnight now. He asks me about work, and I give him a few new book recommendations, and then he tells me about a new crime thriller he saw at the cinema at the weekend, one he thinks I'll enjoy. Then, finally, I get to the point.

'Johnny, I know I've talked to you about a lot of… strange things recently. But, can I ask you about something else? I need to know how easy it would be to persuade the police, or the Crown Prosecution Service or whoever, to give someone immunity from prosecution. If that person had been paid to do something illegal, but then gave evidence against the person who paid them, if that makes sense?'

Johnny puts his wine glass down carefully on the little round table next to his chair, and leans back, looking at me quizzically.

'What *are* you up to?' he asks. Then he says slowly, 'OK, well, he'd be described – if it *is* a he; let's assume that for now – he'd be described as an assisting offender. And honestly, full immunity's only offered in the most exceptional cases. The CPS would have to consider things like whether justice would be best served by having him as a witness for the Crown rather than as a possible defendant. As in, would it be better for public safety to uncover the information he has rather than convict him for whatever he's done? And whether they can get that information without offering immunity. There are lots of very strict criteria. So, there's no simple answer, I'm afraid. Every case is different.'

'OK.' I take another sip of wine as I think. 'I think he's pretty important, in this particular case,' I say. 'I'm not sure there *are* any more potential witnesses.' An image of Rhona's face flashes into my head, and I hesitate. 'Well, I mean, there might be, but I can't... well, I'm not sure, not right now.'

'Right,' says Johnny. 'If he comes clean about his involvement and then gives evidence against the other party, he could be offered a reduction in sentence, if not full immunity. If he has a previous clean record, that would benefit him. And if he can hand over some sort of proof to corroborate what he's claiming happened, that would be good too. Does that help?'

I nod.

'Yes, it does.'

But, I think, assuming Yiannis is our man, will he really tell the police what he knows if he doesn't get full immunity? If he risks being sent to prison? He should be punished, really, but is it more important that Jack is punished, and that Yiannis helps that happen?

Then another thought strikes me.

'Johnny, what if this person wants to give evidence, but is scared of retaliation? Would the police be able to offer him any protection?'

He shrugs.

'Sometimes, yes. If it's a really serious case, and there's a significant risk of him being hurt by the other party. He might be relocated; he might even get help to change his identity. They can come up with a press strategy too, in some cases. As in, asking the press not to report on his contribution to the case, which might help to keep him safe. It's all possible, but without knowing the details it's kind of hard to really know, love.'

'I get it. Thanks Johnny. You're the best. Honestly, I feel better just sitting here. It's so nice.'

'You can come up here and sit any time you want,' he replies. 'But whatever you're doing, just be careful, OK? I'm getting worried about you.'

'I'm all right, I promise,' I say.

He nods resignedly and picks up his drink again. For a few minutes, we sit in companionable silence, listening to the music – it's Miles Davis, I think – and sipping our wine. I think about how pleasant this is, and how different I feel here compared to how I feel in Jack's house. Grand it may be, but give me Johnny's homely living room any day. I feel my eyelids starting to droop, my tense muscles relaxing, and I desperately wish I could just sit here until bedtime and then stagger back downstairs. I can't though, can I? Things to do. But when this is all over…

'Johnny, I'm going to have to go. But next week, or maybe the week after, can we do this again, and get a takeaway or something? My treat. Make a proper evening of it. Carlos, too, if he's around? You've been so helpful recently, and I'm sorry I'm being so vague about everything, but I'll explain soon, OK?'

'That sounds perfect,' he says.

When we say goodbye at the door, he gives me a warm hug, and for some reason I feel tears welling in my eyes as I trudge back down the stairs.

I just want this to be over, I think, as I let myself back into my own apartment and flick the kettle on for a coffee. *I've had enough now, I really have.*

I'm desperately tired, but I can't sleep yet, so I make some strong coffee and sit down at my laptop with a sigh. I open Google. 'Rhona MacDonald' is my first attempt. There are over seven thousand entries, and although I spend a couple of minutes scrolling through the images pages, I can't see anyone who even vaguely resembles Jack's housekeeper. I need to narrow the search down a bit, but how? I know little to nothing about her.

I try again, entering 'Rhona MacDonald London' and 'Rhona MacDonald Scotland', the first bringing up virtually nothing and the second a vast number of potential results. I try narrowing it down further by throwing the word 'housekeeper' into the mix, but that doesn't help either. When I move on to social media, I scroll through endless Rhonas but none of them look anything like her, and after an hour I slam my laptop shut, feeling exasperated. Nothing. No online presence at all. But why? Everyone's online nowadays in some capacity, aren't they? Well, maybe not everyone. Jack isn't, not on social media anyway. But most people of my age, of *her* age, are. She can't be much older than mid-thirties. It's odd, and now I'm feeling even more suspicious. Is Rhona MacDonald even her real name?

I start getting ready for bed, wearily turning over the facts as I brush my teeth.

Maybe Nathan can get to the bottom of it? Although he didn't seem keen, did he? That accusation of me being paranoid…

Suddenly, the mistrust is back and I stop brushing. I stare at myself in the bathroom mirror, seeing the doubts in my mind reflected in my eyes.

Shut up, I tell myself. He's got a lot on his plate, that's all, trying to make a life for himself and Lacey. Trying to keep her safe. We're all on the same side in this. We are. You're overtired. Go to bed. It'll all seem better in the morning.

As I drift off to sleep, though, my last thought is of Rhona. Who is she really? Why can't I find a trace of her online?

And, the biggest question of all, how frightened of her should I really be?

TWENTY-NINE

Jack

Jack checks the time and sighs. It's just after eleven. He's in the main office tonight, and he has a lot to get through. The company's just about to sign another big contract to supply ophthalmic equipment to a major high street optician, and he needs to double-check every detail, but he's struggling to concentrate. He can't stop thinking about Heather.

In a way, what happened this morning in the gym reassured him. If she willingly had sex with him there, surely she doesn't know about the hidden camera that was silently recording them? He went to bed feeling less agitated, but this evening, when he got up and had a quick scroll through the footage from when he'd been sleeping, the doubts returned. What was she really doing up in the attic?

Although the sound was a little muffled, he could hear her telling Rhona she'd come up to take some photos. But after his housekeeper left, Heather had, just as she'd done in the gym, tossed her sweatshirt over the box containing the camera, blocking its view of what she did next. After that, there'd just been a few minutes of her humming and singing to herself and some indistinct noise, before she picked up her top again and left. He rushed straight up to check, but nothing seemed out of place, and he walked slowly back downstairs with a frown crinkling his brow. He tried to convince himself she probably *was* just taking photos, moving around to get the best vantage point. But then he arrived at work and Naomie – who's working day shifts this week – called in for her handover and told him something that made his jaw drop. Heather had contacted his PA, and asked if they could *meet up*. And that meeting had happened in the coffee shop down the road at lunchtime today.

'When was that arranged? Why on earth didn't you tell me she'd got in touch with you?' he spluttered, but Naomie quickly explained that she hadn't seen any point in bothering him with such trivia when he had so much on his plate with the new contract, and that she'd decided to wait and see exactly what Heather wanted before telling him about the encounter.

'She said in her email she needed advice about what to get you for your birthday, and she thought as I know you better than most, I might be a good person to ask,' she said. Jack felt his irritation and alarm begin to subside and his heart softening.

'Really?' he said. 'And did she ask about anything else when she turned up?'

'Not really,' Naomie replied. 'She said she was struggling for ideas, and asked me if I knew if any previous girlfriends had given you anything you particularly liked. I told her we don't talk about your previous girlfriends.'

Her voice tightened as she said the word 'girlfriends', and Jack who has long suspected his PA has feelings for him he'd rather not encourage, felt his lips curve into a smile. Naomie is generally the politest, most diplomatic employee he has, but on the topic of his exes, she can be vicious.

'And that was it?' he asked.

'Yes,' she said, and he left it there, but he still doesn't really know what to make of it. It does make some sort of sense that Heather might seek advice from another woman about a birthday present for him, and the sweetness of the gesture gives him a warm feeling in his chest. But why not just chat to Naomie on the phone? Why go to all the trouble of travelling to meet her in person? And the fact that she asked, even in a seemingly innocent way, about previous girlfriends…

Jack leans back in his chair and rubs his eyes, then straightens up again and stares at the numbers and words on the screen in front of him, as if they're going to answer the questions spinning round his head.

Then he nods slowly to himself. He knows what he needs to do. And he needs to do it as soon as possible. *This* weekend.

Time to stop these half measures. Time to find out if she's up to something, once and for all.

THIRTY

Heather

It's two minutes past eight on Thursday evening, and I'm pushing open the door of The Weir bar in Brentford. Work was a real struggle today; I slept badly last night, again, and all day I found myself horribly preoccupied and uncharacteristically irritated by the neediness of some of our customers. I spent the afternoon refreshing the window display, and yet even when I was crawling on my hands and knees to prop up a book in the far corner, a woman peered in at me to ask, in an imperious tone, where she might find the latest Philippa Gregory.

I pushed my hair back from my sweaty forehead and told her that as Philippa was a historical novelist, she might care to have a look in the historical section, and she glared at me.

'Well, where's that?' she snapped. I gave an audible sigh and crawled backwards out of the window space, only to be rescued by Milly, who was just passing and had overheard the exchange. Once she'd shown the woman to the appropriate part of the shop, she came back.

'It's not like you to be so cranky in front of customers. What's up?' she said, and I apologised, mumbling something about not sleeping well and having a few 'relationship issues'.

She raised an eyebrow at that, looking at me with a strange expression, and I felt a rush of unease, as I had before when Jack came up in conversation with Kwee. But, thankfully, another customer needing assistance suddenly appeared at her shoulder. She bustled off and didn't mention it, or him, again. I really can't go on like this, though. If I don't get on top of things, I'll lose my job, and that would be unthinkable.

Not much longer. Not much longer.

I repeat the phrase in my head as I walk into the bar, and immediately spot Yiannis at a table on the left, a half-drunk pint of lager in front of him. I smile, and as I approach he smiles back and stands up, like he did the first time, moving around the table to pull out my chair for me.

'Such a gent,' I say, and his smile grows wider.

'Blame my mum,' he says. 'She always insisted on manners.'

'And that's not a bad thing,' I reply.

'I suppose not,' he says. 'Can I get you a drink? I got here early so I've already got one in but I wasn't sure what you'd want.'

'A white wine? Sauvignon Blanc, ideally? Thanks,' I reply, and he nods and heads to the bar. He's served quickly and is soon walking back towards me, glass in hand, but the short interlude gives me time to organise myself, and by the time he sits down again I'm ready. My plan is this: to attempt to get this man to say *something* that makes it obvious it's Jack he's talking about; to record our conversation; and then, when we hand our findings to the police, maybe we can get him to agree to give evidence, my recording of him acting as gentle persuasion. My handbag is on the table, the top slightly open, the voice recorder on my burner phone switched on. I've tried it out in noisy spots a couple of times in the past few days, and I'm confident it's close enough to capture this conversation clearly. I take a few sips of wine, and begin.

'So, you said you think you might be able to help me? What made you decide?' I ask. 'Is it something to do with what you mentioned last time? You said you got involved with something a bit like what I need once before – was it some sort of email hacking? I'm kind of intrigued.'

He stares at me for a moment, his dark eyes fixed on mine, and then nods.

'I was in a bad way. My mum… she hadn't been well, and she got herself into a bit of trouble. A painkiller addiction that got out of control. We tried the NHS, and they did help, but she really needed a good rehab place and they cost money, you know? And we just didn't have it at the time. I was still a student, and my dad's a taxi driver. He does OK but he doesn't have that kind of cash. These places cost a fortune. Other than me, there's just my younger brother who was still at school, and we didn't have any relatives who had any money to spare either, so…'

He shrugs, and I find myself glancing at my bag, hoping the phone is picking this up. Is he about to tell me about Jack? My heart rate quickens.

'So what happened?' I ask quietly. 'You got offered money to do… what?'

He sighs, picks up his pint, and swallows a mouthful of beer.

'It was this company boss... He heard I was good, you know? He was a nice guy – bit strange in some ways – but always friendly, and one day he took me aside and asked me if I could help him out with something. I can't tell you the details, obviously, but...' He pauses, and sighs again. 'He wanted me to send some fake emails, from one of his staff members. He offered me so much money, Heather. I knew I shouldn't do it, but I just kept thinking about my mum, and the difference it could make to her recovery. And so I did. It's not that hard, particularly if you have access to internal mail. People rarely check their work email settings. Anyway, I did it, and something – well, something horrible happened. To the person I'd been sending the fake emails from. It was an accident, but it still made me feel just terrible.'

My heart is beating so hard I wonder if he can actually hear it from across the table.

It was him, wasn't it? He's talking about Rose. There's no way this is a coincidence. No way.

'What happened?' I ask, and I lean a little closer. My voice is low, barely a whisper, but he looks around the bar uneasily, and shakes his head.

'I can't... I can't say any more,' he says. 'But the thing is, my mum still didn't get better. She had one stint in rehab, and when she came out she was great for a while. But a year or so later, she relapsed, and this time she was worse than before. Hard drugs this time. Twice, Dad and I had to trawl the streets in the middle of the night looking for her. The second time, we thought she was going to die. She was lying unconscious in a doorway. It was horrific. My *mum*. The woman who was so law-abiding, the woman who taught me all my lovely manners…'

There is a hint of a smile, and then his expression clouds over again.

'Drugs are evil. They can get hold of *anyone*. Anyway, by spring last year we knew we needed to get her into rehab again, fast, or we'd be organising her funeral. And then… I don't know, it was like fate. Serendipity, whatever. He asked me if I could do it again. Send fake emails from someone's account. I didn't want to, but, you know, the money he dangled in front of me… I just couldn't say no. So I did it. It was a bit trickier that time, because the person didn't work for the company, but again, not that hard if you know what you're doing. And then…'

He shakes his head, and sinks it into his hands, his fingers clawing at his thick, dark hair.

'Again, something really bad happened. I feel sick when I think about it, but I can't do anything about it now. It's too late, and if anyone knew, I'd be in such big trouble. Jeez, I don't know why I'm telling you all this. I barely know you. But I believe in karma, you know? And, as I said before, maybe you were sent to me for a reason. If this guy, this ex of yours, is as bad as you say he is, and I can help you to punish him, it might even the score a bit. Something like that, anyway. Do you understand what I mean?'

I understand perfectly, I want to say. I understand – or at least, I'm almost a hundred per cent certain now – that you played a major role in helping Jack Shannon do the terrible things he did to Rose and Amber. And I hate you for that. I really, really hate you. But you're also one of the very few people, maybe the only person, who can help us to finish this. So…

I take a deep breath.

'Yes, I get it,' I say. 'I do. And I'm so grateful. I just need to make sure this is really what I want to do. I'm a bit scared; I just need to think about it for a little while longer. Can I call you when I'm absolutely sure?'

I reach across the table and touch his sleeve briefly, then whisper, 'Thank you.'

Suddenly it's all too much, and my eyes fill with tears. Embarrassed, I look down and brush them away with the backs of my hands.

'Oh, no!'

Yiannis is fumbling in his pocket. He pulls out a tissue and thrusts it at me.

'Please don't cry. It's OK. Here. Gosh, people will think I've just broken up with you or something.'

'Haha!'

Unexpectedly, I laugh. I know that what he's done is awful, and the consequences are horrendous, but I also get why he did it. Two wrongs definitely don't make a right, but if he's telling the truth, he did it all to save his mother, and the horrified look on his face now is just too comical.

'I'm heartbroken,' I say loudly, and dab theatrically at my face with the tissue. He stares at me for moment then grins.

'Oh, stop it,' he says. 'What are you like?'

I laugh again, then put the tissue down on the table.

'OK, I've stopped,' I say. 'But seriously, thank you. I'm knackered, so I'm going to say thanks for the drink too and call a cab, but I do really appreciate this and if I decide to go ahead I'll get back to you very soon, OK? And don't worry, my lips are sealed about what you've just told me. Not that I know any details, but still.'

He nods.

'Got it. And thanks. You have my number if you need me.'

Fifteen minutes later, I'm in an Uber, heading for home. As soon as I'm back in the privacy of my flat, I call Felicity.

'I've got the recording. And it all fits,' I say. 'There was no mention of anything physical, so I don't think he did the stabbing, but the rest of it, almost definitely. And he really does feel guilty – you can see it in his eyes. I think he might be persuadable, you know? To give evidence against Jack, I mean. Although if he's not given full immunity from prosecution, maybe not. We'll see.'

'Great work, Heather,' Felicity says. 'So, in terms of searches, just the jewellery to find now? Oh, and Nathan mentioned you wanted to look into Rhona's background. Did you… discover anything of interest?'

She asks the question slightly awkwardly, her tone almost too casual. It makes me hesitate for a few seconds before replying. Am I imagining the way her voice changed when she mentioned Rhona?

'No. I couldn't find her online at all, actually,' I say. 'Which is bizarre in itself, don't you think? She's not on any of the social media platforms, she's not on LinkedIn, and there's no mention of her anywhere. It's made me even more suspicious of her. Did Nathan get anywhere, do you know?'

Another slight hesitation.

'No, I don't think he's had time yet. Things are a bit crazy at the factory, apparently. I'll give him a nudge though. Listen, do you want to meet up for a drink on Sunday evening? We can have a proper catch-up then. What do you think? Same place as last time?'

Nathan hasn't had time? I feel a flicker of anger. He and his little girl are in fear of their lives, and he's too busy to do a quick background check on a woman I think might be involved in all this? Seriously?

It's back yet again, that feeling that something isn't quite right here. I don't say it though, because meeting up *is* a good idea, I realise. I want to look Felicity in the eye and ask her about this Rhona thing to her face. I want to see how she reacts. I want to see if I *am* just being paranoid, or if there's something else going on that I haven't worked out yet.

'That'd be great,' I say. 'After dinner? About eight-thirty?'

'Perfect,' she replies. 'I'll see you then. I'll send you a message to confirm. Take care. And call one of us if you need anything, OK?'

'I will. Bye, Felicity.'

I hang up but I sit there for a while, thinking.

I like Felicity, like her a lot; that's the problem. I've become genuinely fond of her, so much so that I really think we could become proper, long-term friends, even when all this is over. But why do I keep getting this nagging feeling?

They can try to shut me down as much as they like, but I am going to get to the bottom of this.

THIRTY-ONE

Heather

'Another movie? I've got *Top Gun,* the original 1986 version, not the remake. Fancy it? We can watch it here if you like, if you can't be bothered to move to the cinema room?'

Jack pokes me in the thigh with his bare toes, and I blink and pick up my phone to check the time. It's nearly 3am on Saturday, and we're sitting one at each end of the sofa in the living room. I'm so tired I can barely keep my eyes open, but Jack, who decided again to 'take the day off', is fully alert and wanting to play. When I arrived at his place after work last night, he was just getting up, and told me he was in the mood for 'a pyjama day'.

'It's been a long week. What do you think?' he said enthusiastically, pulling me close and running his hands from my waist up to my shoulders, beginning to massage them with practised fingers. 'We can crash in the cinema room and get Rhona to sort out some proper movie snacks. Nachos, chicken wings, ice cream?'

'You've just got up and you want ice cream for breakfast?' I asked with a grin, although inside I was screaming, *No! I don't want to stay up all bloody night with you, you freak. I have work tomorrow!*

'Sure, why not? Life's all about balance, after all,' he replied, and kissed my forehead. 'I'll make sure I get you to bed early tomorrow night. You'll be fine. We're doing it, no arguments.'

And so, by eight o'clock we were watching the most recent Spider-Man film and tucking into nachos piled high with refried beans, guacamole, and sour cream, with spicy chicken wings and blue cheese dressing on the side. That was fine; I was tired and hungry, and whatever I might think about Rhona, she's a blooming good cook. After that, Jack wanted a second movie. He rifled through his vast film collection and pulled out *Toy Story 3* with a triumphant whoop; I rolled my eyes and asked him how old he was. He laughed and waved the DVD at me, and my stomach twisted as I thought about his other DVD collection in the attic.

As we reached the end of the second film, we'd drunk a bottle of champagne and he was growing amorous, nuzzling my neck and running his fingers along my collarbone. Normally, that would make me shiver with desire, but tonight when he whispered in my ear, 'Bedroom. Now,' all I wanted to do was punch him in the stomach and tell him to piss right off and never touch me again. Instead, I gritted my teeth and followed him upstairs, grateful at least that he wasn't trying to make me shag him in front of a camera this time.

Now, as we lounge on the sofa, both only half-dressed

despite the fact that Rhona's lurking around somewhere with her vacuum cleaner, I feel the usual hollow ache of shame.

What's wrong with me, still sleeping with a man like this? Yes, I need to keep him happy so I can finish this job, but, *Christ*. It's disgusting.

'So, *Top Gun*?' he says again.

'I'm shattered actually,' I say.

I am. Waves of drowsiness keep washing over me. My head is muzzy, and not just from the alcohol, my limbs like lead weights as I sink into the plump cushions of the sofa. Even speaking is an effort, but I force myself to focus. Jack hates it when I sound tired. When he's wide awake, everyone else has to be too.

'Can you not just watch it yourself?' I continue. Once again, I tap the screen of my phone, which is lying on the cushion next to me. 'It's three in the morning. Look. And I have to be at work in about six hours. I need *some* sleep, Jack.'

He frowns and shakes his head, and my heart sinks. I knew it was pointless to argue. He's in one of *those* moods, and is insistent on me staying up. I know what he's going to say now: it'll be something to try to make me feel guilty, to let me know how hurt he'll be if I leave him down here and go to bed. He really is like a child sometimes – needy and petulant. But it's control he's really after. He wants to bend me to his will, to manipulate me. It's what he does.

'Oh, OK, then. Let's do it. I can catch up on sleep tomorrow,' I say quickly, before he has a chance to say anything. 'Let's watch it in here, though. I'm just going to the loo first. Give me two minutes.'

He smiles.

'Go on then. I'll get it set up.'

With what feels like superhuman effort, I haul myself off the sofa and head for the bathroom. It's only when I walk back into the living room that I realise what I've done, and I freeze in the doorway, aghast.

Oh. My. God.

I've made a terrible mistake. Jack is standing up with a phone in his hand, and I instantly know it's mine – the one I left lying on the sofa cushion. But it's not my *real* phone, the one Jack knows about, the one he put a tracker on. This is my burner, my back-up. I came straight from work so I had both with me, and I shoved them deep into my bag when we went upstairs to have sex earlier. I must have pulled out the wrong one when Jack went to use the bathroom afterwards.

This is my secret phone. The one without a tracker. The one I use to message Nathan and Felicity. The one I take with me when I don't want Jack to know what I'm up to, or where I'm going.

What am I going to do?

The panic is instant. It rises in my chest, making me feel dizzy. Will Jack realise it's a different phone? Oh, shit. *Shit.* I've copied over some apps, but not all of them. Will he notice? And could he have seen anything incriminating? I unlocked the screen to check the time just before I left the room. He could have opened my emails, my WhatsApp, my texts… Have I deleted all the latest messages from Nathan and Felicity? I'm so tired, I don't know, I don't *know*…

'I nearly sat on it,' he says, smiling at me. 'You should probably keep it in your pocket or something. I'm a bit clumsy after a few drinks.'

He tosses the phone to me. I gasp and grab it, my brain trying to unscramble my frantic thoughts. I attempt to reconcile them with his relaxed demeanour. Is it possible that he hasn't even noticed it's a different phone? He has had a few drinks – several more than me… He *is* a bit drunk, I realise, watching him stagger slightly as he bends to pick up the television remote then sinks back down into his seat.

'Come on, it's starting,' he says, and I can hear the slur in his voice.

I sit down slowly, pushing the phone into the pocket of the hoodie I'm wearing over a pair of knickers. If he realised, if he's read any of the messages that might still be on this phone, he'd have said something. If he's noticed it wasn't the one he put the tracker on, he'd have asked me why I have two phones. He *would*. I know Jack. So maybe I've got away with it? But what a stupid, idiotic mistake. It could have ruined everything. And it could have been dangerous, really dangerous. I can't look now, but if I didn't delete all my messages, the most recent was from Felicity. As far as I can remember though, it was just confirming the arrangements for tomorrow night. So, even if he did read it, no big deal, right? I'm just having a drink with a friend. That's allowed…

'Come here. Snuggle up,' he says.

Jack doesn't take his eyes from the screen as he reaches for me, slipping his arm around my shoulders, his face glowing as the familiar soundtrack begins. I feel my heart rate slowing as I let him pull me close.

It's OK. It's fine. I got away with it.

But that was close. Too close.

However tired I am, that can't happen again.

His eyes still glued to the TV, Jack reaches for the whisky glass that's now sitting on the low table in front of us. I think about the weekend ahead, the adrenaline of the past minute or so banishing my weariness. Work tomorrow – well, later today, now – and then Jack wants me to come back tonight because he's booked a table at a new gourmet Indian restaurant in Chelsea.

Then, on Sunday morning, when he goes to bed, I will do one final search.

I need to find that jewellery.

And then I can get out of here, for good.

THIRTY-TWO

Heather

I stand in the kitchen, listening. Except for the soft *tick, tick, tick* of the clock on the wall, I hear nothing. Silence.

Good.

It's just before ten-thirty on Sunday morning, and after – thankfully – a decent night's sleep this time, I'm more than ready to give this search one last go.

Work was hellish yesterday. After Jack pretty much refused to let me have any sleep at all, other than a quick doze on the sofa in front of the TV, I dragged myself through my duties as best I could, putting on my biggest smile and sprightliest appearance whenever Milly or Kwee came into view but secretly wishing all the customers who kept asking me for things would just bugger off. I love my job so much normally. I adore helping people discover new authors or choose books as gifts, and it's starting to really upset me that my stress and exhaustion levels are now so high that my mood and my appreciation of my once very nice life are suffering, badly. I've tried to stop worrying about the major cock-up of leaving my burner phone for Jack to find. When I checked my messages I found, almost to my own surprise, that there was just that one innocuous-sounding message from Felicity, and my reply. I must have deleted all the previous ones after all, and I felt greatly relieved that even in such a frazzled state, I was still with it enough to have done that.

And, I keep telling myself, we're so close now. It's the final push. So, here I go. At least my head is clear this morning and my senses are alert. I didn't even drink very much last night. In the restaurant, I told Jack I was so tired from the night before that alcohol would just send me to sleep right there at the table.

'Fine,' he said. 'But I'm getting a bottle of wine. I'll drink it myself if I have to.'

He seemed out of sorts, more than a little surly, and when I tried to ask him what was wrong, he shut me down with a snappy: 'Business stuff. I don't want to discuss it.'

Fine by me, I thought. I know I still need to maintain this charade, but I'm close to giving up. I don't want to sit and make small talk and flirt and flatter him. I don't want to be with him at all. And maybe I was subconsciously sending out some sort of stay-away-from-me vibes, because, in a rare move for Jack, he didn't try to have sex with me when we got home. Instead, he muttered something about needing to get back to work, gave me a half-hearted kiss on the lips, and retired to his office, letting me go to bed alone for nine blissful, uninterrupted hours, until he slipped in beside me about half an hour ago.

I'm standing in the kitchen now, pretty sure that Jack's sound asleep and that Rhona's back in her apartment. I'm aware of the camera watching me as I flick the kettle on and then stroll casually down the few steps to the lower dining area. Just the snug and the cellar to search this morning, and – major result – now that I've finally done my research, it turns out that my fears about having to search a dark, damp cellar were unfounded. To my deep joy, it seems this house doesn't really have one, other than a former coal hole – a small vault under the pavement at the front of the house. I double-checked with Jack, saying I'd been reading about Georgian properties in a historical crime novel and was intrigued. He confirmed there was no cellar space as such ('a bit of a shame – I'd have liked a wine cellar,' he told me) but was happy to point out the coal hole, with its circular cast-iron cover under the front steps of the building.

'You can see they deliberately made them too small for a person to fit through,' he said. 'The coalman would tip the coal down a chute under that cover. The servants could access it from inside the house via the servants' hall down in the sub-basement. We blocked it up when we did the conversion though. These under-pavement vaults *can* be used for extra living space, but they need waterproofing and I felt it was an unnecessary expense. It's not as if I *need* any extra space, with just me living here. We filled the chute with concrete and just walled the little cellar up.'

I've decided I'm still going to check it out as far as I can though. I didn't have this information when I was searching the kitchen, but now that I do, I just want to see if the coal hole really *is* totally inaccessible now, or whether there's an access point I've missed. What an excellent hiding place a vault deep beneath the house would be for valuables, right? Valuables like jewellery that someone's claimed has been stolen, for example.

I've already checked and there appears to be no camera down here. The dog-leg shape of the room means the kitchen camera can't really see what I'm doing, but even so, I need to be quick. I glance nervously over my shoulder, half-expecting Rhona to suddenly appear, but the room is still empty, and so I quickly walk to the wall that would have separated the dining area and the old cellar and start running my hands over it. It's been wallpapered, which I already think makes it unlikely anything's hidden behind it, but I check every inch anyway, feeling for any unevenness, and any possible secret door or cavity. I can't find anything, so I go back to the end of the wall and start again, this time tapping it very gently. I've been worried about doing this, knowing the watching camera is recording sound too, but when I put the kettle on I filled it to the brim, and I'm hoping the noise it makes as it boils will cover me.

Tap, tap, tap.

I work my way rapidly along, left to right. Suddenly I pause. That last tap sounded different. I repeat it and suppress a yelp of excitement. There's an area at around knee height, a couple of feet across, and it sounds hollow. Speeding up, I tap my way to the end of the wall, but it's solid there and sounds like normal, and so I return to the little patch I paused at and try it again.

Tap, tap.

Definitely, *definitely* different. I stand there for a few moments, the noise of the kettle reaching a crescendo up in the kitchen, and wonder what to do. I can't exactly start ripping the wallpaper off, can I? But how else do I find out what's behind there? Is there a little alcove? A small storage area? An access point into the old coal hole after all? Is something hidden there, something important? Or is this nothing? I don't know, and I don't know how to find out. I stare at the patch of wall, then quickly make up my mind.

I leave it. When we go to the police, I'll tell them about it and they can knock through and see what's there, if anything. There's nothing I can do now.

So, just one more room – the snug, back up on the ground floor. I make myself a cup of coffee to satisfy the security camera then carry it upstairs. The snug is a room I know Jack uses more when he has no visitors. It's a smaller, cosier version of the living room and has walls lined with yet more bookshelves, a small TV, and a vintage tan leather sofa softened with sheepskin throws. In the corner by the window there is – to my great joy – a little reading nook. It's my favourite spot in the house, although I've only sat in here once or twice; there's a button-back armchair that's the perfect size for curling up in, and a side table on which stands a Victorian table lamp which has somehow been adapted to cast the most perfect light in just the right place.

The room also has, as I discovered on a quick wander around it last night while I was waiting for Jack to get ready to go out, no security cameras in it. This surprised me, and it's making me feel nervous now as I walk in and put my coffee mug down carefully on the edge of one of the bookshelves. Why no camera here? Is it because it's a room that Jack uses a lot himself, and rarely invites visitors into? Or *is* there a camera, and I've missed it? My scanner doesn't seem to have let me down so far, though. I hesitate, wondering what to do, then sniff.

Rhona's been cleaning in here fairly recently, I realise. The air smells faintly of furniture polish and the rug in front of the sofa still bears the faint tracks of a vacuum cleaner in its thick pile. I don't remember the room smelling like this last night, so she must have been here in the last few hours. That bloody, bloody woman!

Damn. I'm going to have to scan it again, just in case.

One fake 'engrossed-in-my-phone' stroll around the room later though, there are still no alerts flashing up on the scanner. I start the search, fervently hoping the thing's working properly. I'm really only looking for jewellery now, but I'm very aware that although it would be lovely to find it all together in one big box, if Jack *is* concealing it somewhere in the house the collection may well have been split up and stashed in various locations, although I'm yet to find one. And so I methodically lift every book from its shelf and flick through the pages before replacing it, checking for any hidden compartments as I go, just as I did in the lounge. Then I move on to the rest of the room, checking behind pictures, under the rug, running my hands over the walls, feeling along the hems of the heavy curtains at the windows, and getting glimpses of a bright morning outside that makes me yearn for sunlight on my skin and fresh air in my lungs.

Later, Heather. Later.

As I work, it strikes me yet again how ridiculous this is. I'm sneaking around while the homeowner sleeps, searching his house for secret doors and evidence that could put him in prison. *Me*, who really has no idea what she's doing and could quite easily have missed any number of covert hiding places. And yet, I've done OK, haven't I? I've found emails in the freezer and DVDs in the attic and I'm pretty sure I've made contact with the man who hacked into Rose and Amber's accounts. I'll chat this through with Felicity when I see her this evening, but I don't think there's much more I can do in this house after today. And as long as Jack – or flipping Rhona – hasn't twigged what I'm up to, and destroys the evidence before we get a chance to alert the authorities, we're almost home and dry—

'WOAH!'

I'm standing right next to the door, feeling my way around the frame of the final painting, when someone walks into the room so unexpectedly that I stumble backwards and almost fall over the sofa behind me.

It's Rhona, wearing a black cotton dressing gown, her hair pulled tightly back off her face. She holds out a hand to me, her eyebrows lifting in what looks like a combination of surprise and amusement, and I automatically grab it and haul myself back to an upright position. Her skin feels cool and slightly damp, as if she's just got out of the shower. I glance down at her fingers in mine and stiffen.

What's that?

'Sorry. Didn't mean to give you a fright. Thought you'd have gone home by now,' she says, pulling her hand away.

'What-what are you doing up here?' I splutter. 'It must be nearly midday. I mean, that's midnight for you, isn't it? Why…?'

She shrugs and pulls the belt of her dressing gown into a tighter knot.

'Couldn't sleep,' she says. 'I came up to borrow a book. Mr Shannon said I could, anytime, by the way.'

She sounds defensive, and I back away from her, trying to smile.

'Great. In my job, the more books people read the better. What's your favourite genre?'

She shrugs again and looks around the room, eyes moving from the bookshelves to the curtains. I feel a tingling in my chest. Have I put everything back properly? Is it obvious I've been rooting around in here?

'You've left a gap in the curtain,' Rhona says curtly. 'He won't like that. Never mind, I'll sort it.'

I swallow and watch as she stalks across the room and pulls the curtain firmly back into place, shutting out the tiny sliver of daylight. Then, ignoring me, she starts walking slowly along the shelves, scrutinising the spines of the books. I stand and watch her for a few moments, then clear my throat.

'Right, well, I'll leave you to it,' I say. 'Hope you get some sleep.'

She turns and looks at me with a strange expression.

'Thanks. Take care,' she says.

Take care. That's the second time she's said that to me. I can't decide if her voice is just low and quiet because she's tired, or if there's a touch of menace in it. I suddenly feel a cold sensation on the back of my neck. I need to get out of here, pronto. I don't say anything else; I leave the room and practically run upstairs to collect my things. I was pretty much finished in the snug anyway, and all I want to do now is open the front door and step out into the light and the sunshine.

Two minutes later, that's exactly what I do. I walk quickly

away, feeling strangely unsteady on my feet. When I'm sure I'm out of view of all the windows of Jack's house, I stop and lean gratefully on the railing that edges the path, looking at the river, lucent and serene below me as it flows past on its endless journey. I think about Rhona, and about what I just saw on her hand as she reached out to steady me when I staggered backwards.

A scar.

There's a small scar on the outside of her right hand, just below her little finger. I've never noticed it before. It's a scar that looks as if the cut that put it there was small, but deep; the sort of scar that looks as if it might have been caused by a knife.

I hold my own right hand up in front of me, as if *I* were holding a knife by the handle, and make a stabbing motion in the air. If I *were* holding a knife, sinking it into something – or some*one* – and my hand slipped down the blade, it might well make a cut just like that, on the side of my finger.

Rhona MacDonald. *What are you doing here, really? And how long have you actually known Jack?*

Despite the warm morning, I shiver. Then I walk rapidly away, heading for home.

THIRTY-THREE

Amber

I put the phone down and walk slowly back along the corridor to my cell, foreboding prickling my skin. I've just had my planned Sunday evening phone call from Heather, and although she didn't – *couldn't* – say, not directly, I know there's something wrong. She sounded tense, and didn't stay on the line for long, saying she was heading out for a drink with Felicity, and that she didn't really have any news, other than that she wasn't sure how much longer her relationship with her 'new boyfriend' was going to last. I took that to mean that maybe this thing is close to its conclusion now, and I felt a surge of excitement. But when I asked how the weekend had gone, she became diffident.

It's something to do with Rhona, Jack's housekeeper, that's got her flustered, I think.

'She's a bit… two-faced,' she said, and I frowned, trying to understand what she was telling me.

Two-faced? So, not what she seems? But what does that mean?

We ended the call with me none the wiser. Heather's low mood was contagious. Now I find myself walking more and more slowly, dragging my feet along the grubby, worn floor. I don't want to go back and sit in that dreary cell. I want to go outside. I want to go for a Sunday afternoon stroll on Hampstead Heath. I want to pop into a pub for a steak-and-ale pie. I'm still having moments of sheer panic, but the last couple of weeks have given me too much hope, maybe, that something like that may ever be possible for me again. But now…

I feel tears springing to my eyes. Something's wrong. I can feel it. As I reach my cell door and stumble inside, I feel the old fear rising.

Maybe this is how it's meant to be, because I *do* deserve to be here. A crime is still a crime, even if you don't remember committing it, after all. A hazy memory is no excuse. And yet, what if I *am* innocent? And if what Heather's attempting doesn't work, how can I endure this? How can I stay here, for years to come? *How?*

The cell is empty. Stacey's obviously off doing something she probably told me about earlier but I currently can't remember, and I slump onto my bunk and howl. Suddenly, completely irrationally, I yearn for superhuman strength. I want to rip the bars off the window, barge my way past the guards, and smash through doors.

I want to get. Out. Of. Here.

I let myself cry for several minutes, my shoulders shaking, my breath coming in gasps. Then I stand up and wipe my tears away furiously. *Enough. Enough, now.* It's going to be OK. And if it's not, then, I'll survive, won't I? I've made it this far. One day at a time. One *hour* at a time.

I walk out of my cell again and start pacing up and down the corridor, ignoring the curious glances of some of the other women. If only I could get more exercise, more fresh air. The gym is small, the equipment dated, and it's vastly oversubscribed; if we're lucky, we each get a short session twice a week. I do it, but I'm not a gym bunny; I used to run and go for long walks on the Heath or in Trent Country Park, and I'm increasingly craving the outdoors, even in the coldest, wettest weather. We get an hour a day, and while prison exercise yards look vast on TV, ours certainly is not. It's a small rectangle of cracked concrete and it takes approximately one minute to complete a single slow lap, everyone ambling around it in an anti-clockwise direction.

'Why do we always walk that way? Are we *allowed* to go the other way round?' I asked Stacey, who arrived two months before I did, on one of my first days here. She shrugged.

'Dunno. Just the way it is, mate,' she replied.

I stopped questioning or wondering after a while. There's just a certain way things are done here, I realised. No point in arguing about it, or rebelling against it. We're all just numbers, after all. Well, letters and numbers. A6868RX reporting for duty.

And so now I pace the corridor.

Up and down. Up and down.

I think about Heather, and I pray, to whom or what I have no idea.

Please. Please. *Please.*

THIRTY-FOUR

Heather

I'm sitting at a window table in Spinelli's, a glass of Merlot on the table in front of me, my right leg bobbing up and down and a knot of tension festering in my stomach. I wolfed down half a microwave lasagne for dinner before I left the flat, and now I wish I'd just had a sandwich. I feel a bit sick, and Felicity being late for our drinks isn't helping.

Where is she? It's nearly quarter past nine. We were due to meet at eight-thirty, and I arrived ten minutes late, relieved to see she wasn't yet here and that I hadn't kept her waiting. But now *I've* been waiting for over half an hour, and the message I sent a few minutes ago asking if everything's OK hasn't been read yet. I spoke to her earlier, and she said she was definitely coming. I called her as soon as I got back from Jack's to update her about my final searches of the house, and to tell her about the scar I spotted on Rhona's hand.

'It's made me even more convinced she's involved,' I said. 'I seriously think that scar could have been caused by a slip of the knife when Jack was being stabbed. They've known each other much longer than they're making out, I'm sure of it.'

'I mean, maybe, but maybe not,' Felicity said quickly. 'Anyone can have a scar on their hand. She's a housekeeper; she uses knives all the time. It might just be from chopping vegetables or something. I wouldn't jump to conclusions, honestly, Heather. We really don't think—'

Again, this weirdness about Rhona. I felt a surge of fury.

'Well, I'm sorry, Felicity, but I *do* think. You've never even met her. You don't know what she's like, and I really could do with your support on this. I'm at the end of my—'

'Oh gosh, I'm sorry. You're right. I haven't met her. I apologise, OK?' Felicity sounded contrite. 'I'm sorry, honestly. If she's freaking you out, then I totally get it. But this is *so* nearly over now. I'll talk to Nathan, but I think we should plan to get the stuff out of the house next weekend. One more week, Heather. We can sort out the details later, but I think just see Jack as you tend to do now on Tuesday night, so as not to raise any suspicion, and then at the weekend we go for it. That'll give us time to plan it properly. Look, I need to run now but I'll see you tonight. Eight-thirty, OK?'

But she's still not here, and I stare nervously out of the window, taking the occasional disinterested sip of my wine and wondering what the hell's keeping her. I send a second message, which also doesn't appear to have been read, and then try calling her, but all I get is her voicemail.

At nine-forty, I give up. I've been here for an hour, and I'm bone-tired. I need to sleep. I'm not sure how Felicity was planning to get here – maybe she's on a broken-down Tube with no phone signal; maybe she couldn't get an Uber and her phone battery died. I don't know, and I can't decide whether to be worried or annoyed. Her and Nathan's odd response to my concerns about Rhona is still bugging me, and now Felicity doesn't bother turning up for our meeting? And yet, they've been right about everything so far. Jack *does* have emails and DVDs stashed in his home; they're almost certainly right about Yiannis too. So maybe I am over-reacting about the Rhona thing. I tried to tell Amber about it when I spoke to her earlier, but the necessity of saying as little as possible made it difficult to convey my worries, and I'm not sure she really understood.

I'll tell her everything soon, I think, as I trudge slowly home through the dark streets. When she's out of prison. *When*, not if. Because she has to be released, after this. She has to be. If all this is for nothing…

I've just climbed gratefully into bed when I finally hear from Felicity. But as I read the message that pops up on my phone, I'm not sure whether to feel relieved or even more worried.

> Hi – so sorry I didn't show earlier. Was worried I was being followed this afternoon. All OK though. Let's rearrange? Speak soon.
> Felicity xx

I reply:

> Shit! Followed? Who by?

I have to wait for a couple of minutes before she says:

> I don't know. Probably nobody. Don't worry!

I think for a moment. I know how obsessive Felicity is about security. I can easily imagine a perfectly innocent person who just happens to be walking the same route as she is sending her into a tailspin. And so I reply and tell her OK, that I'm in bed and knackered, and she sends back a thumbs-up emoji followed by a kiss.

I put my phone on charge, and turn off the light, expecting to fall asleep as soon as I snuggle under my duvet. Instead, I lie there wide-eyed in the darkness for a long time. What if someone *was* following Felicity? Rhona, maybe? I might have got away with Jack being in possession of my phone on Friday night, but what if he's looked at it before? Is that possible? I don't think so, but what if someone *is* following Felicity now, and it's all my fault? But no… if Jack had found something that made him suspicious, he'd almost certainly have confronted me immediately, wouldn't he? And he'd go after *me*, not her, surely?

The questions spin round and round, but I have no answers to any of them, and eventually, exhausted, I fall asleep, dreaming of footsteps behind me on a moonlit road, and a scarred hand reaching for me, tightening round my throat.

THIRTY-FIVE

Heather

Tuesday night. It's just after nine, and I'm sitting in Jack's living room with the TV on mute and a gin and tonic in my hand.

'He's having a lie-in,' Rhona announced when I arrived. 'He got up at six and went to the gym and then went back to bed. He said to tell you he's cancelled the table he booked for dinner. He wants to order in instead. And he said help yourself to a drink and he'll be down soon.'

I'd been hoping to get another look at her hand, but she was wearing yellow rubber gloves and had a mop and bucket at her side. She passed on the message from Jack with a resigned look on her face, as if even she despaired slightly of her employer.

'Oh,' I replied, surprised. Jack and I had discussed our plans for tonight, and he'd told me he was looking forward to trying a new floating restaurant on the Thames. I'd heard the buzz about it too, and had been happy for him to make a reservation, hoping the novel surroundings and good food would be a welcome distraction from my compulsive dwelling on the events I know are coming. But now he's apparently cancelled in favour of a takeaway *and* he's still in bed?

Jack's an early riser, generally; he rarely sleeps past six or seven when alone, even if it is *pm* rather than *am*. For him to still be in his room after nine, and to go *back* to bed after his workout, is unheard of and unsettling, and the thought of having to spend the entire evening in this house is not something I relish. I swallow a large mouthful of gin – I made myself a double – and sit, staring at some gameshow on the silent TV screen, and I worry.

I'm still obsessing about Felicity suspecting she was being followed. Rhona and Jack would normally be in bed on a Sunday afternoon, and there's no way Jack's going to go out in daylight, but what about Rhona, on his orders? And yet, how would she *find* Felicity, or know who she was? I've thought hard about this now, and even if Jack *has* somehow accessed my phone messages at some point, there's never been any detail about Felicity's address or even her full name in them. There's no way they could find her. So, is Felicity just imagining things? That wouldn't be too surprising at this stage of the game; I'm pretty stressed myself. But the whole thing's clearly really rattled her. Yesterday afternoon I had a voice message from a troubled-sounding Nathan, saying he'd been trying to get hold of his sister since the previous night but her phone was going straight to voicemail.

She's OK, Nathan – she got paranoid someone was following her yesterday so she pulled out of our drinks last night, but she's fine, don't worry! I think she's just over-anxious at the moment. I'm pretty anxious myself!

He replied to my message a couple of hours later, sounding relieved and saying he'd finally managed to get hold of her and she was indeed fine. But today, Felicity's still clearly worried. She texted me earlier with security obviously very much on her mind.

Hi Heather, just a quickie, the lab's crazy today, but can I just ask something? Have you told anyone else what we're doing? Anyone at all? Or is it just the three of us? Felicity xx

I replied quickly, hoping to reassure her.

Of course I haven't told anyone! Not a soul, I promise. Stop worrying, Felicity. If Jack or Rhona did have any suspicions, don't you think they'd have confronted me, in the house? Rather than following you around? It's not really logical. And it'll all be over in a few days – keep the faith, OK? X

But now that I'm back here, I'm the one feeling rattled. I put my G&T down and stand up, crossing the room to the window and pulling the drapes back. Instantly, the oppressive atmosphere lightens. The night-time view of the river is exhilarating, its surface studded with moving lights as boats plough up and down, the reflections of illuminated buildings rippling and dancing in the pitch-black water.

I stand there, drinking it in, the normality of the outside world soothing me. When Jack suddenly grabs my waist, I jump violently, my heart juddering.

'Jack! I didn't even hear you come in,' I gasp. I turn to face him, and he pulls me towards him. He smells fresh and minty, straight from the bathroom, and he's barefoot, in grey sweatpants and a tight T-shirt.

'Sorry to keep you waiting,' he says.

He dips his head to kiss me and forces his tongue between my lips. His hands roam my hips and bum and his breathing is already quickening. I let him do it, remembering how much I used to love this. I used to love the way he made me feel as if just touching me instantly turned him on, the way he gets immediately hard when he presses his body against mine. But not now, not anymore, and after a few seconds, I pull away.

'Hey tiger,' I say, forcing a smile. 'Can we at least have a drink and some food first? I'm starving, and if we're ordering a delivery we should probably do it soon. It's getting late.'

I'm not hungry at all, in reality, and I know I probably *will* have to have sex with him one final time before this evening is over.

But please, not now, Jack, I think. He frowns, clearly not happy. Tonight, I definitely need a few large drinks first…

'You're not going off me, are you?' he says, and there's an edge to his voice, a sharpness. 'We can eat later. It's London, Heather. Round-the-clock food delivery. But if you're hungry, we don't have to waste time going upstairs. We can do it right here.'

He pushes me backwards, and I stumble over my feet, but he steadies me and makes me keep walking until I feel the edge of the sofa at my knees. A moment later I'm on my back on the soft cushions, and Jack's looming over me, pushing my maxi dress up to my thighs and fumbling at my pants. His clawed right hand seems stiffer than usual, and he growls with frustration as he gropes at the silky fabric, trying to get a grip.

'No! No, we can't!'

I feel panic beginning to grip me. He wants to have sex here? In front of the uncurtained window, *and* the security camera? I glance automatically towards the bookshelf, and then back at him, my eyes wide. He's got hold of my underwear now and is pulling it down to my knees. I grab his injured hand and squeeze it a little too hard.

He winces, breathing heavily, his face inches from mine. His eyes are narrowed and his left hand is already pulling his sweatpants down.

'Jack! Please! What about… what about Rhona?' I plead, and he laughs.

'She's mopping the kitchen, as far as I know,' he says. 'But even if she does walk in, so what? Makes it a bit more exciting, don't you think? Come on, Heather. Where's your sense of adventure?'

His mouth clamps onto mine again, and I give up. I let him kiss me. I let him push inside me. I let him do it all. It's nasty, rough sex, and it hurts me, and so I let my mind float away. I separate it from my body and what's happening to it, even as I yearn for him to stop. Even as I desperately wish he would get off me and just *leave. Me. Alone.*

I try not to think about the camera because, I realise, as Jack groans in my ear, it doesn't even matter that this is being recorded now.

I'll never have to do this again. This is the very last time.

And you're going to be punished, Jack Shannon. You're going to get what you deserve, for what you did to Amber, and Rose, and all of us…

He grunts loudly as he collapses on top of me, his head sweaty against my neck. He lies there for a couple of seconds, panting, then rolls off me onto the floor.

'Jesus. I need a drink now too,' he says, his eyes closed and his chest heaving. 'Any chance you can give Rhona a shout and ask her to grab me a cold beer?'

'Sure,' I say quietly. He ignores me as I rearrange my clothing and go to do his bidding, but when I return to the living room he's up and fully dressed, standing by the window in the same spot I was in when he grabbed me.

'It's beautiful, isn't it?' he says softly, not turning around.

'It is,' I reply. 'Rhona's on her way with the beer.'

'Thank you.'

He turns to look at me, and I'm not sure what I expect to see in his expression after what's just happened, but it's not this. I stare at him. He looks… devastated. There's a haunted look on his face, a sadness in his eyes I've never seen before.

Is he actually about to cry?

'Jack? Are you OK?' I ask, in spite of myself.

His eyes hold mine for several seconds, and then he nods.

'Fine. It's just sometimes… Oh, it doesn't matter.'

He turns back to the window and holds out both hands to steady himself against the frame.

'I wish I could see it in daylight. I wish I could go for a walk along the river. I wish I could… could be fucking *normal*.'

He hisses the last few words, and I stare at the back of his head.

You'll never be normal, I think, but I can't say that, so I reach out and put a hand on his shoulder.

'You will be, one day,' I whisper. 'You can do it, Jack. You *can*.'

He doesn't reply, and a few moments later Rhona walks into the room with a tray of beer and roasted nuts, and he's instantly back to his usual self, thanking her jovially before flinging himself onto the sofa. We order Chinese food, and although there's little conversation – episodes of the remake of *Frasier* play back-to-back on the TV – it's comfortable enough, considering how the evening began. Well, maybe comfortable is an exaggeration, but it's… *tolerable*. It's tolerable.

Just after midnight, Jack tells me he has to go to his office.

'Breakfast meeting with Tokyo. Eight hours ahead there,' he says, as he pecks me on the cheek and leaves the room. Relief sweeps over me and I go to bed alone. For some reason I don't understand, I find myself crying silently for a long time, before I eventually fall into a dreamless sleep.

THIRTY-SIX

Jack

Jack stares at his computer. The figures on the spreadsheet jump and judder before his eyes. He blinks, and the numbers steady and settle back into their rows and columns, but it's no use. He can't concentrate; his mind refuses to stay in work mode. Tonight, what happened with Heather… None of that was good. And then, that moment of weakness he showed, when he just… blurted it out, that thing about wishing he was *normal*. Why did he do that? Where did that come from?

Sometimes, he can convince himself he *is* normal; that the way he lives is a perfectly valid choice for someone who runs an international business. But it's not, is it? Not really. He knows that, and everyone else does too. And yet, most of the time, he gets on with life and the job and it's fine. Except now…

Jack stands up and starts to pace the room. It's just before three in the morning, and he knows Rhona will be up shortly with what, if he lived in the daytime world, would be his afternoon coffee, maybe with a slice of her delicious homemade cake on the side. He's needed that more than ever over the past few days, that little touch of—

There's the word again.

Normality.

He's not feeling good. His mental health is spiralling downwards and he hates himself for it. He hates feeling weak and unable to control his emotions.

He hates *her*.

He hates her more every day, even though it's been more than twenty years since he last saw her. Since the day she left him.

His mother. The woman who made him what he is today, both good and bad. The woman who destroyed his life – and who gave him everything at the same time.

Carol Shannon was an extraordinarily successful businesswoman. She started Shannon Medical in the 80s and grew it rapidly. While her husband climbed the ranks of the Metropolitan Police, Carol managed to have a baby and carry on working full-time, taking a young Jack into the office with her and teaching him about the company he would later inherit from the minute he could talk.

But Carol had her demons too. When he was a child, he knew only that his mother would have days when she didn't go to work but instead stayed in bed, sobbing, while his father wandered helplessly in and out of the bedroom, telling a fretful young Jack that Mummy was tired and needed to be left alone. As a teenager, he slowly began to understand a little more, hearing the words 'depression' and 'bipolar' for the first time. He looked them up and realised his mother was ill rather than just sad or angry. And then, came the day everything changed.

Jack was sixteen. It was summertime and they were a week into a heatwave, the soil in the carefully tended beds in their large garden cracked and dry. Jack loved the outdoors, and he'd spent the morning cycling through the local woods with a group of school mates. On their way back, they stopped for a dip in the lake, where they splashed and laughed, loving the freedom from school and rules. He arrived home just after two, expecting the house to be empty. Both his parents should have been at work, but his mother's car was in the driveway. Although he made a quick tour of the house, calling her name, there was no response, the rooms silent and empty.

Dread began to creep over him then, starting low in his stomach and crawling upwards. It tightened his chest, making his hands tingle. He knew, somehow, what he would find when he forced himself to walk on stiff, reluctant legs down to the bottom of the garden and through the archway that led into what was always known as 'Mum's bit', a quiet seating area with a gently bubbling water feature, and a timber pergola covered in jasmine and honeysuckle. He saw her as soon as he passed under the arch. She was swaying gently, the sun so bright that for a few moments it looked as if a spotlight were shining on her, turning her blonde hair into a glimmering halo. He ran to the pergola and pulled frantically at her clothes, her body; he tried desperately to free her, to stop what was happening, but he knew even as he screamed and begged that it was pointless. She was gone. She'd left them. She'd left *him*.

Slowly, over the next few years, Jack's life changed. When he turned eighteen he inherited the business, although he didn't fully take over until he'd completed his business degree at university. By then, an initial shying away from sunshine had begun to develop into a reluctance to venture out in daylight at all, and soon he began to realise he no longer needed to. It was *his* business, *his* life, and he could behave exactly as he wanted. And so he did. His father noticed, of course, and tried to understand, but he and Jack had never been as close as Jack and Carol, and although he offered help more than once, Jack's angry refusals soon made him back off. When he got sick and died, there was no longer anyone to care what hours Jack kept, and as for the women in his life…

Jack stops pacing, and stands still, eyes fixed on the landscape on his wall. His mother had been his everything, and although logically he's always known that she didn't want to leave, that she didn't reject *him*, it's as if something in his brain won't let that logic win. The sense of abandonment, of not being enough for his mother to stay alive for, haunts him, day and night. He tried, for a while, to separate these feelings from what happened with his girlfriends. He tried to understand when relationships didn't work out. He tried to blame himself and not them. But he can't seem to do it anymore.

He can't seem to handle the betrayal, the feeling of being discarded, of being spurned and deserted. And that means he's behaved badly, very badly. He's hurt people who've hurt him. He's hurt them in a way that's so out of proportion to their perceived crimes that it's shocked even him. He needs help, he knows that, but he also knows he's not ready to ask for it; may never be ready to ask for it.

And then Heather came back into his life. She's the only

one who's ever come back, and he thought, he really thought for a while—

Stop it. STOP! he thinks fiercely.

He slumps back down onto his chair and sinks his head into his hands.

Maybe after this, things can change. But not yet. Not until this latest chain of events comes to its conclusion, because it's too late to stop it now, isn't it? He has to see this through, and there can only be one outcome.

And it's not going to be a good one.

Certainly not for Heather, anyway.

THIRTY-SEVEN

Heather

'Right. I think we have a plan.'

'I think we do.'

It's Thursday evening, and I've been chatting to Nathan on a Zoom call for the past hour. Felicity hasn't been able to join us; there's been a sickness bug at the lab, apparently, and although she hasn't succumbed, Sod's Law has come into play and she's been put on night shifts for a few days to cover a colleague who's unwell. We tried to find a time that would work for all of us to chat in person, but it wasn't possible.

Felicity messaged:

> I'm so sorry! Such awful timing. But honestly, I'm happy to leave the final plans to you guys. Just send me the details when you've nailed everything down, OK? Xx

Briefly, I felt annoyed that she seems to be opting out of this final crucial stage a little. Could she not have claimed to be sick too, when there are such important discussions to be had? Surely the safety of her brother and her niece should take priority over everything else right now? And then, as quickly as my indignation rose, it subsided again. Felicity *is* still going to be very much involved, and with her rapidly growing fears and suspicions about everything from CCTV to mystery stalkers, maybe it *is* better if Nathan and I are the ones to fine-tune exactly how this weekend's going to play out. And so that's what we've been talking about for the past sixty minutes or so, both of us sitting at our dining tables with a glass of red wine in hand, very much as if we're chatting in a bar, despite actually being hundreds of miles apart – him in his Spanish living room and me in my Chiswick kitchen.

'OK, so let's double-check all the timings. Shout if what you've written down is any different to this, OK?' Nathan says, and I nod.

'Shoot,' I say.

'Right, so you'll spend Saturday evening with Jack as planned. When he goes back to bed on Sunday morning, you'll wait until midday, when you can be pretty sure both he and Rhona are asleep, and then you'll take Jack's keys and whizz around the house and collect everything. The emails from the freezer and the DVDs from the attic.'

'If they're all still there,' I say. I'd hoped to have a chance to check ahead of Saturday, but I was too nervous in the end. Taking Jack's keys again would be too risky, and I've done enough sneaking around that house to last me a lifetime.

'They will be. I'm quite sure we'd know about it by now if he knew you'd found them. OK, so, Felicity will be waiting outside, parked a discreet distance up the road, from eleven-thirty, and as soon as you have the stuff you get the hell out of the house and you both take the whole lot to the police. You tell them Jack has raped you…'

I look down at the floor, trying not to react. This is the story we've decided on to persuade the police to act quickly and arrest Jack on Sunday. Our great fear is that he'll wake and realise his stuff is missing and try to run. We're deliberately planning our raid to happen in daylight, instead of under cover of darkness, for this very reason, but even so, we can't rely on Jack's phobia entirely. And, after all, it's not a complete lie, is it, to say he raped me? He forced me to have sex when I didn't want to, and although I lay there and let it happen, was it really fully consensual?

I don't know. I can't go there in my head, and even though I despise Jack now, I can't decide if saying this to the police is right or fair. And yet, was any of what Jack did to Rose or Amber right or fair? No, it wasn't.

So fuck you, Jack Shannon.

'You say he's raped you more than once,' Nathan is saying. 'And you tell them you think he's making plans to do a runner that day and they need to get round there fast. If you ask to speak to a female officer, I'm hoping that'll help. He's got friends at the Met, we know that. But he doesn't know everyone, and they can't ignore an accusation of rape. Once he's in custody, hopefully the evidence we're bringing them will be enough to keep him there.'

'And if he wakes up and catches me in the act and destroys the stuff *then*?'

It's my greatest fear right now. I had nightmares last night, his heavy hand on my shoulder, our precious evidence being wrenched from my grasp.

'He won't. And if the worst does come to the worst, you've taken a few photos, haven't you? That might help a bit. And we have Yiannis now, remember. Our secret weapon.'

'If we're right about him. And if he'll talk,' I say.

Our plan is that once the evidence has been safely handed over to the police, I'm going to message Yiannis and ask if we can meet urgently. Felicity and I will then go and see him and come clean. We'll tell him the truth about who we are and what we've been doing. We'll tell him I recorded my last conversation with him, and beg him to tell the police what he knows about Jack. Yes, it will implicate him too, and we can't guarantee he won't be prosecuted, but I'm hoping that if we find a sympathetic police officer, and tell them we have a witness who can divulge exactly what Jack did, and how, they just might be able to give Yiannis some assurances. Nathan, however, seems to be taking a rather harder line on this one.

'If he won't talk, we'll dob him in anyway,' he says. 'Your recording might be enough for them to at least bring him in for questioning. You seem to have a soft spot for him, Heather. But think about what he did. Without his help, Jack probably couldn't have done half of what he did to Rose and Amber. He's just as guilty. So seriously, don't be too sympathetic.'

'I know, I know.' I sigh. 'OK, I'll worry about that on Sunday. I've got to get everything out of the house before we even think about talking to Yiannis. What about Rhona?'

Nathan picks up his glass and swallows the last of his wine.

'What about her?' he says.

'The fact that she's probably another accomplice, obviously,' I say.

What, this, again? I think. *Come on, Nathan…*

'Let's worry about that afterwards, too,' Nathan says. 'Getting Jack into custody is the most important thing. We can worry about her and Yiannis once that's done.'

'But what if she does a runner when the police arrive to pick up Jack?' I say. I feel myself getting angry again. '*She's* not afraid to go outside in daylight. If she *is* involved, she'll be out of there and we'll never find her again. I'm sorry, but we're going to have to agree to disagree on this one. I know her and you don't, OK? And I'm afraid I don't care what you think. I'm telling the police she's been in on everything he's done, and that they need to arrest her too. If she's innocent, she'll have nothing to worry about, will she?'

'But… well… Oh, OK, you're right.' Nathan wipes a hand over his face. 'Sorry. Of course you're right. Yes, do that. It makes sense. Sorry, Heather. I'm just a bit obsessed with Jack, for obvious reasons. But you do what you think's best.'

He looks and sounds remorseful and, feeling somewhat mollified, I reply: 'OK. I will.'

'Good. So, that's it then? We're happy?'

He gives me a tentative smile.

'Happy isn't quite the right word but yes, the plan sounds fine. If it works,' I say.

The room is warm, but suddenly I feel a chill. There's *so* much riding on this. It's been less than three weeks since that first date with Jack at The Bridge Arms, but it's been the longest three weeks of my life. All the lies, the deceit, and the worst anxiety I think I've ever experienced. And now the success of this entire venture hangs on my shoulders, just three days from now. If I screw up, if Jack's moved or destroyed the evidence, if he or Rhona catch me trying to take it out of the house…

There are so many ifs, so many things that could go wrong.

'It *will* work,' Nathan says firmly, leaning forwards towards his laptop camera so his face appears almost comically oversized on the screen.

'You've got this, Heather. And you're going to finish it in style, OK? Don't doubt it for a second.'

'Ha! Well, that's nice of you. Let's hope so, eh?'

We end the call a minute or so later, agreeing that Nathan will update Felicity, and we'll liaise on Saturday evening before I arrive at Jack's, just to confirm everything's still good to go for Sunday. Alone again, I move to the sofa, turning the TV on and trying to breathe slowly and deeply. I need to stay calm – I have to – but I can't stop terror gripping me every time I think about the weekend. And even though Nathan backed down over Rhona, finally, I still can't shake this feeling that something isn't right there.

And yet, I have to trust him, don't I? I have to trust both of them. It's too late to pull out now…

I pick up my wine glass and take a long drink, the alcohol warming my throat. But I can't turn off my thoughts, and the questions keep multiplying and bouncing around my head.

Will it really be worth it? Will Amber be freed? Will Rose's death be avenged? Will Jack get what he deserves, at last? And what if the answer's no? What if all of this has been a massive waste of time? What then?

I have a sense of foreboding I can't shake off, a feeling of impending doom. Is it just the weight of responsibility that lies so heavily on my shoulders? Or is it a warning, from deep in my subconscious?

All I know is that I've never been so scared in my life.

THIRTY-EIGHT

Heather

'Drink! Drink! Drink!'

There are squeals of laughter from around the table as Milly grimaces, glugs down the contents of her glass, then slams it down.

'Urgh!' she says, shuddering.

It's Friday, and we're on a work night out; Milly and Kwee like to host one a few times a year. This time, we're having Mexican in a lively restaurant with a Mariachi band that's been playing for the past hour. The tequila's just appeared and I can tell things are about to get messy. I wasn't going to come tonight because my fears about the weekend have taken such a hold of me that I had to excuse myself from till duty today at one point, with the excuse that I felt light-headed and needed some air. I told Jack I was going out with the team tonight though, and later, when I weighed up the options, I decided that an evening of food, wine, and company was a vastly better choice than sitting on my own at home and fretting. And so here I am, with Kwee and Milly, plus Hannah, Gavin, and Abdul, our three part-timers, and Gregory, who cleans the shop so beautifully every morning before we open.

'Come on, Heather! Your turn. Truth or drink!'

Gavin elbows me in the ribs. We're playing a silly game, taking turns to ask slightly risqué questions and knocking back a shot as the punishment for those who decline to answer. Milly's tequila was her penalty for snorting with laughter but saying nothing when Hannah asked, 'Have you ever faked an orgasm?'

'Well, not with me, I should bloody hope!' Kwee said indignantly, and Milly pecked her on the cheek reassuringly then picked up her glass.

'Go on, then. Truth,' I say, reluctantly.

'Right! I've got one,' says Gregory. 'Have you ever made a sex tape?'

'Ooooooh!'

There's a chorus of approval from around the table, and I'm about to reply with a resolute *NO!* when I hesitate. I've never *willingly* made a sex tape, but now there's Jack's gym and his living room. I'm probably on a sex tape *now*, aren't I? Almost certainly more than one. I might already sit alongside the others in that box in the attic. Can I remove them, if I find some with my name on them on Sunday, before I take them to the police? The thought of anyone watching them…

Suddenly, I feel mortified and my cheeks start to burn.

'OH! Now this is interesting!'

Across the table, Hannah beams with delight, and the others are all smiling too, a couple of them sniggering.

'Heather, you dark horse,' says Kwee. She's looking at me

strangely, and I feel a shiver run up my back. Is she being odd about Jack, again? She looks at Milly and the two of them exchange glances with expressions I can't quite define.

There's something they're not telling me. I'm sure there is. But what?

Then I give myself a mental slap.

What's wrong with me? I'm turning into someone who doesn't trust *anyone*. This is Kwee and Milly, my friends. And this is only a stupid game. I don't have to tell the truth, but I really, really can't be bothered to make up an excuse for my hesitation or to try to explain.

Sod it.

I pick up the nearest shot glass and down the spicy contents, to a cacophony of whoops and hoots from my colleagues.

'Well, well, well. Who'd have thought it?' says Kwee, and I feel again that she's eyeing me curiously as I smack the glass back down onto the table and wipe my mouth with the back of my hand.

'Good on ya, girl,' says Milly quickly.

I give her a wink, but inside I feel shrivelled and ashamed. How is it easier to lie to my friends and imply I've been a willing participant in a sex video than to tell them the truth? And yet the truth sounds so far-fetched that I can't imagine who would believe it.

'Oh yes, my boyfriend, who's a complete freak, who never goes out in daylight, and who has hidden cameras all over his house, bullied me into having sex in front of them. He has a whole stash of sex tapes in his attic. Oh, and he probably drove one woman to her

death and sent another one to prison for a completely staged crime too… And yes, I'm still seeing him…'

Ridiculous. Insane. This whole thing is fucking insane. No wonder I'm going completely off my rocker, and starting to imagine suspicious behaviour in even my closest friends.

I don't stay much longer after that. I'm working tomorrow anyway, so I have a good excuse, and just after eleven, I plead tiredness and say my goodbyes.

Back home, I strip off my clothes, give my face a cursory wash, and slap on a bit of moisturiser, then fall into bed without even brushing my teeth. I crave the oblivion of sleep, but my brain is whirring with a mixture of dread about what's ahead and relief that, whatever happens, the end is in sight. After nearly an hour of lying on my back, staring rigidly into the darkness, I give up. I sit up in bed and switch the TV on, flicking through the channels until I reach Sky News. I haven't read or watched any current affairs in days, I realise, and so I lie back on my pillows as the 1am bulletin starts, wondering what tales of death and destruction are about to unfold on the screen. Is a good news story too much to ask for?

'BONG!

Horror crash on M6 – five people die in motorway pile-up.

BONG!

Police release photofit of woman found murdered in Chiswick alleyway – can you identify her?

BONG!'

There's another story, something about a by-election, but I'm frozen, my mouth open.

What was that? That story about a murdered woman? The

one with the photo that flashed up briefly on the screen? That looked like… But, no, it can't be…

Hand shaking, I reach for the remote control and hit rewind, then pause the screen as the picture reappears. It's a woman with blonde hair and high cheekbones.

It's Felicity.

It's Felicity, but it can't be Felicity. Because this is, apparently, a photo of a dead woman.

My heart is beating so fast I feel breathless, my fingers trembling so much now that I can barely work the remote. I fast forward, back to the live news show, but they're talking about the lead story of the motorway crash.

What's going on? I really start to panic now, and at the same time I wonder if I'm dreaming. Maybe I did fall asleep after all, because this can't be real. I don't feel like I'm asleep though – I can feel the adrenaline coursing through my body and I can feel my phone in my hand as, panting, I open the London News website. There it is, on the front page with the same photo.

Felicity.

It's her. It is. But *how*?

Police have issued an image of the woman found dead in an alleyway in Chiswick, West London, on Wednesday evening. The woman, who officers say appears to be in her early thirties, had been beaten and strangled before being dumped in a wheelie bin. She was wearing a pink coat with a white jumper and dark blue jeans, but there were no personal belongings or identification on the body, which was discovered when the resident of the flat above Bearside Alley went to add some refuse to the bin ahead of the usual Thursday morning collection. Police say they believe the body had been there for at least two to three days before it was discovered, and are asking anyone who recognises the woman to contact them on…

The words blur in front of my eyes. This is a photo of Felicity. The age is right, and Bearside Alley? That's near Spinelli's, the wine bar Felicity and I last had a drink in together. The bar we were supposed to meet in on Sunday evening, the night she didn't show up. And…

'*… She was wearing a pink coat with a white jumper and dark blue jeans…*'

I think I'm going to throw up. A pink coat. Felicity was wearing a pink coat the last time we met. I remember it clearly. It fits. Everything fits, but it doesn't make *sense*. I read back through the news article again.

'*… The woman found dead in an alleyway in Chiswick, West London, on Wednesday evening…*'

'*… Police say they believe the body had been there for at least two to three days before it was discovered…*'

Found on Wednesday. Dead for two to three days. So that means this woman was killed on Sunday or Monday. And therefore, how *can* she be Felicity? OK, so I haven't actually spoken to her, but we've been chatting all week, haven't we? All those messages about being frightened she was being followed, the sickness bug at the lab, working late shifts, making plans for the big showdown this weekend. And Nathan's been talking to her too. He'd know if something was wrong. Felicity is alive; she has to be. And yet…

I scroll back to the photo, and Felicity stares back at me.

Her hair, her eyes, her face.

Felicity is dead, according to this.

Which means I've been messaging a dead woman.

And she's been messaging back.

THIRTY-NINE

Heather

'It's her. Heather, it's her. How? It can't be…'

Nathan sounds, unsurprisingly, completely shellshocked. It's after 2am in Spain, and I had to call him three times before he finally answered. Now he's seen the online news articles too, and my heart is breaking for him. This is his sister.

'Nathan, I'm so sorry. I just can't get my head round it. You told me you spoke to her, didn't you? Did you *actually* speak to her or was it just texts and WhatsApps? Because look at the dates—'

'No, no, I just said I'd got *hold* of her. I haven't… I can't think… No, I haven't actually spoken to her since last weekend. Since Saturday maybe? It's just been messages… How? How can she be dead?'

'I don't know.'

I'm feeling properly sick now. The Mexican food and tequila of earlier are swirling in my stomach and threatening to make a violent reappearance.

'I don't understand. How did we not know? I mean, I assume there was a news report about it on Thursday, but I didn't see it. I probably wouldn't even have seen it tonight if it wasn't for my bloody insomnia. I'm so sorry, Nathan.'

'I haven't seen any news for days,' he says. His voice sounds thick with tears now. 'Too busy, too distracted, you know… Oh Jesus. Poor Fliss. But who's been messaging us from her phone, then? What the *hell*? And why would someone kill her? What has she ever done to anyone? And to put her in a *wheelie* bin! To throw her away like… rubbish. In a stinking *bin*! I swear to God, if Jack Shannon is behind this, I'll kill him myself…'

He's weeping now, big gulping sobs, and so am I, tears streaming down my face.

'Nathan, what do we do?' I say, when I can speak again. I can still hear him crying on the other end of the line, and I desperately wish he was here with me so I could offer some comfort. What terrible news to receive when you're alone, hundreds of miles away. Alone except for a small child, of course. How can he possibly tell Lacey about this unthinkable thing that appears to have happened to her aunt?

'We need to call the police. We need to tell them what we know. I mean, maybe one of her friends or colleagues has already done that by now, because her photo's out there. Maybe they already reported her missing too, when she didn't show up at work? But you're her next of kin. It needs to be you, doesn't it? If a body… If she needs to be formally identified…'

I hear him gulp, then take a breath.

'Yes, I'll do that, I'll call… but Heather, I ask again, who's been messaging us both, if it wasn't Felicity? Who's been pretending to be her all week? Fuck. Fucking hell. It *must* be Jack. Who else can it be? But *how*?'

'I don't know. When she first told me – when *somebody* sent a message to tell me – that she thought she was being followed, my first thought was Jack or Rhona. But I'm just so confused. Why would they go to all the trouble of killing Felicity and not me? I've been right there in the house. I'm the one who's doing all the snooping around and lying to them. Why not attack *me*? It doesn't make sense, does it?'

There's a few seconds of silence.

Then Nathan says slowly, 'No. No, it doesn't. Could it have been a random killing, then? A mugging gone wrong? The news article says there were no personal belongings with… with the body. So did the person who did it take her bag and everything else? But why start pretending to *be* her? And whoever it is, they clearly know everything we're up to now, if they didn't already. Not quite all of it because we were always very careful with what we said in written messages, but still, there's been enough to give them a good idea. I still don't *get* it though.'

'N-nor do I,' I stammer. 'I'm so scared. What do we do?'

'Right. OK. Hang on, just give me a minute.'

I can hear Nathan breathing heavily, obviously trying to clear his head. I wait in silence, my stomach churning.

'Let's think logically,' he says. 'If this really is my sister, we don't know if Jack's behind it or not. But for Felicity's sake, we have to carry on. We have to finish it. So, this is what I'm thinking. It's Saturday now, isn't it? You're supposed to be seeing Jack this evening, and staying the night. Make an excuse. Tell him you've got food poisoning or something. We need to be certain about whether Felicity's alive or dead, and if she really is then we need a plan B, and I'm not in a fit state to work out what that is yet, so just stall, OK? I'm going to ring the police in London now, and then I'm going to book myself on the first flight from Valencia to Heathrow. I'll go and ID the body—'

His voice breaks again, and my heart twists.

'Sorry. And then I'll come to yours, and we'll talk. We'll decide what to do. Even if it's her, there's no point in telling the cops anything about Jack yet. We need to bring them the evidence we do have against him, as we planned. But we still need to do it quickly, in case he does a runner. I think it still has to be Sunday. We just need to work out how. Look, I need to go and make arrangements. I'll leave Lacey with a friend, somewhere secure. I'll see you in a few hours, OK?'

'OK. I'll see you in a bit, then. Take care, Nathan. Safe flight.'

'Thanks. And Heather? You stay safe too. Stay in your flat. Don't go to work, just in case. Call in sick and stay home. And lock the doors. Don't let anyone in except me. Promise me. Please.'

My throat tightens, but he's right. I might not be safe either, now. Neither of us are.

'I promise,' I whisper.

FORTY

Heather

'I actually don't know what to say. I think I might need a minute… Heather, I can't believe you've left it 'til now to tell me about this. What were you thinking?'

Johnny is sitting on my sofa, a stunned expression on his face. Next to him is Nathan, pale and drained, after a dawn flight to Heathrow and a harrowing trip to the police mortuary where, deeply distressed, he was able to confirm that the body under the sheet is indeed that of his sister Felicity.

When he arrived at my door in a cab early this afternoon, he simply dropped his bag and held out his arms. Without hesitation, I wrapped myself around him, both of us immediately bursting into floods of tears. On the face of it, it was a bizarre first encounter, because of course Nathan and I have never met before in the flesh. But strangely, being with him in person doesn't seem odd or uncomfortable at all. He's incredibly attractive – even more so than I thought when we first met on Zoom, but it's so much more than that now. Before, despite my regular misgivings, we were united in a common cause; now, we're united by grief too. I'm sadder and sadder with every passing hour. It's surprised me, how bereft I feel. Nathan is, of course, distraught at the loss of his only sibling. It was him, to my surprise, who suggested bringing Johnny into this, after we'd sat and talked for an hour about what to do next and made very little progress.

'I know I've been a bit reticent about you asking his advice, but you really do trust him, don't you?' he said. '*And* he's an ex-cop. I just think we need help, Heather. My head's too mashed to come up with a sensible plan, and we can't risk getting this wrong. It's too important.'

And so I called Johnny who was, fortunately, at home with few plans for the weekend, having apparently fallen out with Carlos yet again last night. He came downstairs almost immediately, a bemused look on his face, and now he's sitting wide-eyed, looking from me to Nathan and back again.

I get up and go to refill the kettle, flicking it on for our umpteenth coffee of the afternoon. As Nathan suggested, I called both Kwee and Milly at the shop and Jack first thing this morning, telling them I'd been throwing up since the early hours.

'That's weird. Nobody else has reported being sick after that Mexican last night,' Kwee said. 'Maybe you have a tummy bug? But of course, stay home until you feel better. Don't worry.'

I thanked her and then, *genuinely* feeling like throwing up, rang Jack. It was after eight, and I was half hoping he'd have gone to bed early so I could just leave a message, but he answered on the second ring.

'Oh, Heather. I'm seriously pissed off about this. I was

really looking forward to seeing you tonight,' he said. He sounded stressed, and I tried not to think about what that might mean. I apologised, and told him I was sure it would just be a twenty-four-hour thing and that I should be able to come round tomorrow.

'OK,' he replied with a heavy sigh. 'I'll be here. I can leave a key somewhere outside for you, in case you get here before we get up? Get well soon.'

Felicity Dixon has now been officially named as the murder victim, and her name was released to the media shortly after Nathan's formal identification of her body. We assume that means the messages from her phone will now stop; it also means whoever killed her will know we know those messages haven't actually been from her for days. We turned the TV on before Johnny's arrival and Nathan's eyes filled with tears when her face flashed up on the screen, especially when the newsreader told us that police still had no leads in the hunt for her killer. They told Nathan this morning that they had little to go on so far. There are of course no CCTV cameras in the immediate area, as I already knew. They are, however, still going through footage from a few private doorbell cameras and the like, although no eye-witnesses have as yet come forward to say they saw anything of the attack. As far as forensics go, they're still hoping they may get something from the body or the bin it was stuffed into.

'But the guy said they've got a backlog at the lab at the moment,' Nathan told me. 'Seven murders in London in the past two weeks. He said it usually averages 110 to 120 a year, so about two a fortnight. The lab's struggling to cope with this "little surge", as he put it. He's hoping to have some results by Monday though.'

And by then, we both hope, we'll have our own evidence to present to the police too.

I refill the coffee pot and carry it back to Johnny and Nathan. As I top up their mugs, Johnny finally speaks.

'Well, first, Nathan, I'm so sorry about your sister,' he says. 'I saw that story on the news earlier in the week and I had no idea it would land so close to home.'

'Thanks,' says Nathan quietly.

'As for your next step… Seriously, guys, can you really not just go to the police with this now? If you even *suspect* that Jack, or this Rhona woman, might have had a hand in murdering Felicity, then it's far too dangerous to send you back in to liberate that evidence, Heather. You say he's never been violent before, but if he's done this then his behaviour's clearly escalating. This is a job for the professionals now. Surely you can see that?'

'No.'

Nathan is shaking his head and the *no* is vehement.

'I understand why you might think that, Johnny, but Jack is much too in with the Met, I promise you. If we report him now, one of them will tip him off, I'm sure of it. He'll destroy every bit of evidence in that house before the cops even knock on the door. I mean, he could have done that already, but that's the chance we have to take. This is the only way. I wish it wasn't. But honestly, even if he did… *did* kill my sister – and I still can't work out how that would have happened, so maybe we have that wrong – but even if he did, I still think if he wanted to hurt Heather, he'd have done it by now. For some reason, she seems to be special to him. Heather, I know you've gone through some stuff with Jack this time, and I know it's been horrible. I'm not trying to minimise that. It's just…'

I'm sitting on a chair opposite him, and he holds out a hand to me. I take it and discover that his skin is warm and his grip is firm and comforting. I shake my head.

'Shhhh, it's fine,' I say. 'You're right. He's never hit me, never attacked me. As for the rest, I don't want to go there right now, OK? I'm all right.'

It's not something I want to talk about today, especially with Johnny here. We've told him most of it, but not everything. Out of the corner of my eye I can see him watching us curiously, but he doesn't ask, and a moment later Nathan releases my hand. I turn to look at Johnny properly.

'It has to be me,' I say. 'I have to go back and end this. It shouldn't take me long, provided Jack and Rhona don't get in the way. Whoever's been pretending to be Felicity in those recent messages knows some of our plans, but do they actually know who we are? I'm really hoping not; I know Felicity just had us in her phone as "H" and "N". No full names or other details. And we didn't talk about days or times or anything specific until Nathan and I had our Zoom call, Johnny, so that's something.'

Nathan nods.

'We nearly always used just initials in our messages, although Felicity does… *did*… have a habit of signing her full first name sometimes. No surnames or anything else though. And I told her I'd wait to send her the full details for the weekend this morning when she came off her run of night shifts, just in case we decided to change anything. Which I didn't do in the end, for obvious reasons. So, that's good, I hope.'

He rubs a hand across his eyes, and I reach over to squeeze his arm.

'I'm still terrified though, to be honest,' I say. 'I feel like we need a few extra security measures or… something. Any ideas, Johnny?'

I'm even more frightened now. The fact that Felicity is dead, actually dead, is finally starting to sink in, and although I know that now, more than ever, I want to finish what we started, I'm definitely starting to feel shaky.

Can I really do it?

Johnny stares at me in silence for a few moments, then leans forward, elbows on his knees.

'Yes, I do have some ideas. First, you getting those emails out of the locked freezer relies on you accessing Jack's keys again, right? Far too risky at this point. I'll give you something – it's a locksmith's tool. I'll show you how to use it. And I'm coming with you both – no arguments. If you're going to take on Felicity's role, Nathan, and wait outside, I'll wait with you. You might need two of us for back-up, Heather, if anything goes wrong, heaven forbid. I'm going to give you a little listening device too. It's very discreet, don't worry. You can slip it in your pocket, or… in your bra, or anywhere. It'll mean we'll be able to hear what's going on inside the house, and if you have any trouble, we can be straight there. Does that sound helpful?'

'Wow, yes. That would be amazing.'

Suddenly, I feel a little better.

We should have confided in Johnny sooner.

Then, something occurs to me.

'Nathan, we were going to wait until afterwards to contact Yiannis. But do you think we should check on him? I mean, if Jack *is* behind Felicity's death, Yiannis might be at risk too. He's the only other person we know of who knows what Jack did, right?'

Nathan and Johnny exchange glances.

'Yes,' Johnny says. 'Give him a quick call. If he replies, say you dialled him accidentally. Would you definitely recognise his voice?'

'I would. OK, good idea.'

I dial the number stored in my main phone, and when the call is answered I know it's him immediately, and feel relief wash over me.

'Oh, gosh, Yiannis, it's Heather here,' I say. 'Heather Harris. I'm so sorry – I didn't mean to call you. I must have hit the wrong entry in my contacts. I'm an idiot! How are you, anyway?'

He laughs, sounding relaxed.

'No worries. All good thanks. Call me if you need me though, OK? I'm still up for helping you out.'

'Ahh, thanks. I will. Sorry to disturb you. Talk soon, maybe.'

I end the call, and Nathan says, 'All OK?'

'I think so. He sounded fine, thank goodness. We can't afford to lose him as a possible witness. So now I just need to message Jack and tell him I'm feeling better and will definitely come round tomorrow. What if I lie, and say I'll get there around six? Might be safer?'

We're actually thinking of more like 3pm – the middle of

the night for Jack and Rhona – but there's no need to tell Jack that.

'Perfect,' says Johnny.

I send the message, not expecting a reply for several hours, but Jack is clearly either up very early today – it's just coming up to five o'clock – or has left his phone switched on while he sleeps, because he answers within minutes.

> Great, glad to hear that. I'll try to be up by about 6.30. I'll leave a key under the big rock next to the yucca at the front. See you then x

'All systems go,' I say, and I feel a shiver of fear. Nathan and Johnny both nod slowly.

'Time for a glass of wine?' Johnny says. 'I have a nice red upstairs. I'll go and get it.'

'Sounds good to me,' Nathan replies. 'It's been a hell of a day.'

I nod and agree, but inside the fear is growing again, gnawing at my stomach.

I don't want to do this. I will do it. I have to. But I have such a bad feeling about it now, a bad, bad feeling…

'You OK?'

Nathan is looking at me with a concerned expression, and I realise I'm gripping the arms of my chair and my body is rigid.

'It's going to be all right, you know? Especially with Johnny on board now. We can do it, Heather. Together. OK?'

I take a breath. He's right. We've got this. We don't have a choice.

'Of course we can,' I say. 'Bring it on.'

FORTY-ONE

Heather

It's Sunday. 2.55pm. I walk with leaden legs towards Jack's house, having just left Nathan and Johnny in Johnny's car about a hundred metres down the road. Nathan slept on my sofa last night. As I made up his makeshift bed, I felt a swell of gratitude that I wouldn't be alone, and a sense of security I realised I hadn't felt for days.

I might actually get some sleep tonight, I thought, and to my surprise I did. A full eight hours. The sadness and anxiety hit again as soon as I opened my eyes though, and worsened an hour later when Nathan had a call from the family liaison officer assigned to him by the police. He told him that one of the private doorbell cameras across the street from the alley Felicity was found in had provided some footage of a figure dressed in black walking into the alleyway with her and then marching briskly away again a few minutes later.

'He said it's not clear enough to make out if it's a man or a woman,' Nathan told me. 'But Felicity seemed to be walking willingly, as in they weren't dragging her or anything. So does that mean she knew her attacker? It's doing my head in, Heather. Let's just hope the forensics report is more helpful, eh?'

That was a few hours ago, and now I'm breathing deeply as I walk. I go over the plan in my head, envisioning each step I need to take once I'm inside that front door. I don't have much with me: an empty backpack to carry what I find, leaving my hands free… in case; I'm wearing combat trousers and a jacket and everything else I need is stashed in my pockets. In one is a small but powerful listening device, about the size and shape of a matchbox. It's voice-activated, so will start recording as soon as there's any conversation or indeed any significant noise, and can record constantly for up to two hours. It's linked to an app on Johnny's phone, which is well within range no matter where I go in the house. I can't receive any communication *back* from Johnny and Nathan, but it's reassuring to know they can hear me, and that they're a quick sprint away, should I need them.

God, I hope I won't, I think, as I approach the house. I look up. As usual at this time of day, the curtains are closed at every window and the sun reflects off the river behind me making the glass gleam. I wipe my hands on my jacket then climb the few steps to the arrangement of rocks and potted trees that frame the front door. After a quick check over my shoulder – the street is deserted – I bend down and lift the rock next to the yucca plant, as per Jack's instructions.

There it is – a clear plastic bag, the key visible inside. I pick it up, and moments later the key is turning smoothly in the lock and I'm closing the front door behind me. I stand completely still for a few seconds, listening. Nothing. The house is dark and silent, and as I reach for the light switch on the wall I say softly, for the benefit of Nathan and Johnny, 'I'm in.'

Right. First, the easier bit. I'm wearing trainers – no heels to clack on the wooden floors – and I walk quickly and quietly along the hallway and up, up, turning lights on and off as I go, until I'm on the attic floor. I ignore all the cameras now because they don't matter anymore. If this all goes to plan, Jack's soon going to be very aware of what I've done today anyway, so the fact that my every move in this house is being recorded, is irrelevant. And so far, so good; there's still no noise from any part of the house, and I hope this means Jack and Rhona are sleeping soundly, unaware of my presence.

'In the attic,' I say, once I'm inside the room with the boxes. I scan the pile, which appears to be unchanged since I was last here, and bend down to open the box of DVDs. My heart rate speeds up.

Please, please let them still be here, I think, as I push aside the layers of old photographs and tissue paper. *Please, don't have moved them, or destroyed them…*

'They're here!'

I say it out loud. There it is, that sordid little pile of DVDs. My hands are shaking a little now as I slip my backpack off my shoulders and toss them in, my breathing quickening as I notice a new one, a disc in a cardboard sleeve that definitely wasn't there before.

H HARRIS
April, 2024

You bastard, I think, but there's no time to dwell on it now. I lick my lips and realise how dry my mouth is, then zip up the backpack. I wriggle it back onto my shoulders and say, 'Got them. Heading back down now. All quiet.'

This is the bit I'm most nervous about.

I creep downstairs, horribly conscious of every creak of a floorboard. I can feel fear coiling in my stomach. And then—

BANG!

I stop dead, and gasp.

What was that? I'm on the middle landing, the one where Jack's bedroom is, and I deliberately didn't turn the light on, not wanting to take the slightest risk of waking him. But was that his door closing? Is he up? Is he about to walk around the corner and find me here?

Oh shit, shit…

My heart's beating so fast I think I might faint. Black spots float across my vision and I reach out a hand, trying to find something to lean on, then jump in terror as I hear another noise. It's a fluttering sound, and it's coming from right behind me. I whip my head around, but there's nobody there. The landing is dark and empty. I hear the sound again and sweat beads on my upper lip. The sound is coming from behind the heavy damask curtains at the window.

Is somebody there, hiding? No, no, please…

And then I hear a familiar crooning sound, and I almost laugh out loud. I take the few steps to the window and pull one of the curtains aside. Relief washes over me. A pigeon. A *pigeon*! They're outside Jack's place all the time, perching on the roof and the ledges and, particularly on sunny days when the glare from the river bounces off the windows, there's the odd casualty; a bird that gets dazzled, misjudges its descent, and crashes into a windowpane. It's clearly just happened again as I can see the slightly greasy, feathery imprint on the glass, but thankfully the pigeon merely looks a little stunned. It's sitting on the sill outside, ruffling its feathers and cooing indignantly.

Fuck's sake, I think, and let the curtain drop back into place. I take a breath and gather myself. I wonder if Johnny and Nathan heard me gasp; I'm not sure if the listening device is sensitive enough to pick up a sound like that, but I don't want them to panic and race up here, so as I finally reach the kitchen I say in a low voice, 'Heading into the utility room now. Not sure if you heard that but I got a little fright on the way down. False alarm. Idiot pigeon flew into one of the windows. All good.'

Right. Focus.

I'm highly aware that I'm very close to Rhona's apartment down here in the basement, so I need to work quickly. I go into the utility room and look at the padlocked freezer. It's the same lock, as far as I can tell. I described it to Johnny last night, and he disappeared upstairs for a few minutes and came back down with a similar one, then spent half an hour showing me how to open it without a key. He made me practise over and over until I could do it in less than a minute.

I slip the backpack off, dump it on the floor, and reach into the left-hand leg pocket of my combats for the small plastic case I put there earlier. This is, apparently, called a comb pick set – nine small double-ended lock picks, so eighteen in total, all slightly different shapes and sizes. Inserted into the key aperture at the base of a padlock, they're designed to allow both pins inside the lock to be pushed out. Just in case that doesn't work, Johnny also gave me a set of skeleton keys which is currently secreted in my right trouser pocket.

'Skeleton keys? Johnny, are you a secret housebreaker or something? Where do you get these things? And why do you have them?' I asked him last night, a little shocked.

He laughed and winked.

'There are whole websites devoted to them, if you look online – anyone can buy them. They're just something I held onto when I left the force. Yes, maybe not strictly legal for a police officer to use, but I often found them handy in house searches. I'm saying no more; ask me no questions and I'll tell you no lies.'

Nathan and I both raised our eyebrows, but right now I'm more than grateful for Johnny's help, legal or not. If this works, it's going to be a hundred times safer and easier than an attempt to steal Jack's keys again. I inhale slowly, let the breath out, and wriggle my fingers, surprised to see they're steady now, the trembling of earlier gone.

I can do this. I can, I think, as I examine the base of the padlock, then select a pick. I insert it carefully, moving it around and up and down, as Johnny showed me, trying to feel it connect, but it doesn't work. There's no click.

Come on!

OK, plenty more to try. Don't panic.

I select another, and try again. Then another, and another. When I'm on to the fifth, I pause. What was that? Did I just hear something upstairs? A soft thud? I open the pantry door a few inches, listening hard, but other than the ticking of the clock, I can't hear anything.

I'm imagining things now, I think, as I lift the padlock again, and bend to choose another pick from the little case on the floor. I wiggle it in the lock and—

Woah! I'm in!

The padlock springs open with a small clunk and, my hands quivering again, I drop it on the ground and yank the freezer door open. I have another moment of dread – will the package I need still be here? But then I see it, still there on the bottom shelf, and I exhale, realising I've been holding my breath. I reach for it, ripping the wrapping off just to check, and see the stack of printed pages inside.

I've got them. I've got the emails, *and* the DVDs.

I feel a bubble of elation in my chest and a sudden, faintly ridiculous urge to do a little happy dance around the room. I've done it. I've *done* it. But there's no time for dancing, so I crouch to stuff the package into my backpack, then push the comb picks into my pocket. I straighten up again, switch off the utility room light and say:

'Got the emails. We're done, guys. I'm on my way out.'

Hoping fervently that they really have been hearing me – this is the signal for Johnny to move his car – I walk back out into the kitchen. I pause to listen again, then sprint across the tiled floor and up the stairs. The hallway is dark, but there's a chink of daylight around the front door frame, and I walk briskly towards it, hoisting the backpack higher on my shoulders. I allow a little smile to play on my lips.

This is it, I think, as I reach for the door handle. *The last time I'll ever have to walk through this door. The last time I'll ever set foot in this damn house…*

Shit.

The door handle won't work. I jiggle it. I didn't lock this door behind me when I came in, I know that, so I should be able to just walk out. I twist the knob again, harder this time, but although it moves, the door still doesn't open.

What the...?

I try once more, but it's locked. The door is *locked*. How can it be locked? My stomach heaves, but I don't want to think about what that might mean, and anyway, I have a key, don't I? Where did I put it? I start to fumble in my pockets, first the exterior ones on my jacket, then the inside breast pockets. No key. Where is it? I reach down to check the leg pockets of my trousers, remembering that if all else fails and I've somehow lost it, I have Johnny's bunch of skeleton keys. And then:

CLICK.

I freeze as the hall light comes on.

'Hello, Heather.'

The familiar voice is terrifyingly close, and I blink, dazzled by the glare. And then it's as if I can feel the ground falling away beneath my feet and my head begins to spin.

It's Jack.

Jack, fully dressed, is standing right beside me.

FORTY-TWO

Jack

'Jack! You-you scared me! Why...? Why are you up so early? I wasn't expecting—'

Heather looks up at Jack with wide, frightened eyes, and he stares back at her, trying to harden his heart. He can't let her get to him, because however he may feel about her, she's failed him, just like all the others. Like his mother did, like Rose did, like Amber did. All of them, all the same. Except, in many ways, Heather's worse, isn't she? Because she never had any feelings for him at all. She came back to him purely to sell him down the river – no pun intended. He can see the bulging backpack, full of what he strongly suspects are the DVDs from his attic and the emails from his freezer and who knows what else. He can see the terrified look in her eyes that's intensifying every second. He can smell her sweat, light but acrid, as if fear is oozing from her pores. And yet she's still pretending, isn't she? Still pretending that she's just here for a date, a chilled-out Sunday. She's even trying to smile at him now. She's pretending she's not afraid. She's lying to him, with every word and every gesture.

Bitch.

'Give it up, Heather. I know exactly why you're here, and what you've been doing.'

His voice is cold, hard, and she visibly recoils, backing away from him, her body pressing against the locked front door.

'Jack, please…'

Her reply is feeble, her voice wavering. He moves a step closer, expecting her to carry on begging. He wonders how long he can put off the moment when he grabs her and ends this. But then, to his surprise, she suddenly moves, fast, swerving around him and darting down the hallway, heading for the stairs that lead down to the basement.

'Help!' she screams. 'Help me!'

Jack watches her go for a moment, then follows at a more leisurely pace. She's obviously heading for one of the other external doors – there's one that leads out of the basement – but it doesn't matter which door she goes for now. They're all locked and bolted, and all she's doing is running herself into an even more confined space.

'Playing hide and seek?' he calls out, as he saunters down the stairs. He can't see her yet, but he can hear her panting. He flexes his fingers, then reaches into his jeans pocket and pulls out a long turquoise silk scarf. It was his mother's, one of the few reminders of her he's kept all these years. That and the business, of course. He doesn't want to kill Heather. He doesn't want to hurt her at all, but he has no choice now, does he? If she leaves this house with what's in that bag, he's finished.

Even with his friends in the Met, there's no way he'll walk away from this one.

He stands still, listening to her breathing.

She's over there, he thinks, in the little lobby next to the back door. *She can't get out, so what's the hurry?*

He thinks about how best to do this. He's only killed someone once before – the other day in that stinking alleyway – and he doesn't relish having to do it again. What he did to Rose Campbell wasn't nice, making out that she stole so much money from the company, but he wasn't really responsible for her death. OK, he made sure she was drunk when she left, and he didn't stop her getting into her car. But it was her decision to drive. Rose killed herself. Not his fault.

And as for Amber… When she started to pull away from him, his plan was already in place. It had been for a long time. He still can't quite believe how well it worked. She got a life sentence. *Life!* For a crime that didn't even happen. A crime he staged. A crime he faked. It's incredible. What's a few little stab wounds and one hand that doesn't work quite as well as it used to, to get that sort of result?

Felicity Dixon, though. That was… unexpected. That night when Heather left her phone unattended and unlocked when she went to the bathroom, giving him the chance he'd been waiting for… that was the day he knew for certain. He spotted immediately that it wasn't her usual phone, the one on which he'd installed the tracker app. This was a cheap model, disposable. He quickly scrolled through her recent messages and noticed that there were very few, making him wonder if she was deleting them as they came in. Why would she do that? But the few that were there, from the previous twenty-four hours, made his heartbeat pound in his ears. Messages from someone listed only as 'N' about 'it' being 'nearly over now'. One message told her how well she'd done over the past few weeks. And one was from somebody she was clearly planning to meet, last Sunday night, at Spinelli's. Somebody called Felicity.

He thought, fast. Then, he took a chance and deleted all but the most recent message from Heather's inbox. He had no idea who 'N' or 'Felicity' were, but his gut told him this was not good and it was probably best that Heather didn't realise he'd read several of her messages. The look on her face when she re-entered the room and saw her phone in his hand confirmed it. She tried to play it cool, but he could see she was horrified and that she knew she'd slipped up. He casually handed the phone back to her, saying nothing at all about what he'd just seen, but he knew right then that he needed to go to this wine bar and try to find out what they were up to. What *Heather* was up to. He saw her again the next night, and it was hard to hide his suspicions and to act normally with her. They went out for an Indian meal, but when they returned home he didn't trust himself not to give himself away, and brusquely bid her goodnight and retired to his office.

The next evening, he made sure to arrive at the place she had scheduled to meet Felicity just before eight. He dressed carefully in a dark hooded jacket, jeans, and black leather gloves. He kept his head down, and stayed in the shadows and away from streetlamps as much as possible. When he got there, he spotted a narrow alleyway between two buildings, just a hundred metres or so from Spinelli's. He stood at its entrance for a minute, trying to decide what to do next. And that's when he saw her, the young woman, walking quickly along the pavement towards him. She paused under a streetlight to check her watch, and then looked over her shoulder, as if checking whether she was being followed, and that's when it struck him. He knew he'd never met her before, but she looked familiar. There was something about her jawline, her bone structure. Did she look like someone he knew, maybe? Was she *related* to someone he knew?

He didn't even stop to think, then. He took a chance. He stepped out of the alleyway, and called out the name he'd seen on Heather's phone.

'Felicity?'

She stopped dead, and he moved closer, smiling in what he hoped was a disarming manner.

'Hey. Heather's here, with me. Change of plan,' he said, gesturing towards the alley, and Felicity's eyes widened and she gasped.

'*You!*' she said. 'But... but...'

'It's OK,' he replied, soothingly. 'Nothing to worry about, I promise. I'm not going to hurt you. I just need you to come and see Heather for a moment. If you don't, well, *she* might get hurt...'

His fingers twitched, and he knew that if she tried to run, he'd easily be able to grab her, but it didn't come to that. She hesitated for a couple of seconds, looking around the empty street, and then called out, 'Heather? Heather? Are you there? Are you OK?'

There was no reply, obviously, but Jack began to feel agitated then, conscious that the clock was ticking, that Heather could walk past at any minute, heading for her wine bar rendezvous with this woman, and so he said quickly, 'She's OK, but you need to follow me *now*. Or she won't be. Do you understand? You're not going to get hurt, either of you, if you do as I say. This is just going to be a chat.'

To his surprise, Felicity looked around once more, a panicked look on her face, and then nodded.

'Um… OK.'

He stood back and pointed to the alleyway entrance, and she meekly walked in. And then… he's not really sure *what* happened then. He genuinely intended just to question her, to make her tell him what was going on, and what those cryptic message were about. Instead, as soon as she walked into that dark enclosed space with him, something clicked inside his head. It was as if a door closed, the door to the rational, sensible side of his brain.

He just… lost it.

Lost it big time.

He bent down and picked up a short, thick piece of metal that was lying on the ground – a broken pipe or something, he doesn't even know exactly what it was – and he simply swung his arm and smashed it into the side of her skull. She didn't make a sound, just slumped to the ground. He stood over her for a few moments, breathing heavily, and then he crouched down and put his gloved hands to her soft, pale throat and began to squeeze. His bad hand ached and throbbed, but even so, it wasn't hard; he knew she was dead less than a minute later, her eyes open and blank, her body limp. He grabbed her small handbag and pulled out her phone, using her unresisting finger to unlock it, then tapped his way into the menus and changed her security settings, removing fingerprint recognition and setting a pin code instead. Then he pushed the bag inside the front of his jacket, lifted her lifeless form – she was light as a feather – and threw it into one of the big double wheelie bins that lined the side wall of the alley. He pulled a few black rubbish bags from the adjacent bin and piled them on top of her. A strange, relaxed feeling crept over him, as if what he'd just done was cathartic, healing almost. He retrieved the thing he'd used to crack her skull and stuffed that inside his jacket too, and then he just walked away. On the way home, he stopped on an unlit section of the Thames towpath and threw the weapon, his jacket, and his gloves into the river.

Felicity's phone beeped twice with texts and rang once while he was busy; the messages were from 'H', very obviously Heather, from a number which must belong to her secret phone. He ignored the messages, and when he was back home, he went through the phone, finding only one other number listed in the address book – the mysterious 'N' again. There was nothing else on it at all, and that made Jack even angrier and more suspicious. This was clearly a burner phone too, just like Heather's second phone, because who only has two contact numbers in their phone? And everyone gets messages all day long – who deletes every single one?

He stared at the phone for a while, thinking, and then, remembering the way Felicity had looked anxiously over her shoulder, he sent Heather a message to explain why Felicity didn't show.

Heather had replied promptly, and his follow-up message seemed to reassure her. It bothered him greatly that he still didn't know who Felicity was. The only thing of any interest in her handbag was what looked like a work rota – a grid showing a timetable for the next two weeks. The company name at the top was ProPowder Global, and the timetable mentioned three laboratories, Labs A, B, and C, with names and times filled in for each day. To Jack's frustration though, only first names were used.

Felicity, Lab C, 8am – 4pm
Helen, Lab A, 4pm – 12am
Amir, Lab B, 12am – 8am

He looked up ProPowder Global online, but there were no employees' names listed on the website, and he couldn't think of any way he could contact the company and ask for the surname of one of their staff without raising suspicion. He even tried googling 'Felicity ProPowder Global', but nothing came up, so he'd had to admit defeat. The only other items in her bag were an unmarked door key, a lipstick, and thirty pounds in cash. Not wanting anything in his home to have both his and her fingerprints on it, just in case, he threw the whole lot in the river, even the money. Over the next few days though, what she and his so-called girlfriend had been doing slowly became all too clear.

He saw Heather again on the Tuesday night. He was obsessively checking the news websites, expecting at any moment to see a story about a body being found, but there'd been nothing, and it made him tense and irritable. They were due to go out for a meal again, but he couldn't face it and cancelled the table, and then, desperately trying to make himself feel better, he forced her to have sex with him on the sofa in the lounge. He knew, as he'd pinned her down on the sofa, that she didn't want it – that she didn't want *him* – and yet he carried on. Despite everything she's done, he's not proud of that. He actually felt a little remorseful afterwards. It left him feeling pathetic and weak, especially after he admitted that he wished he could be 'normal' again.

Jesus.

Oh, he put on a good act. He pretended everything was OK, pretended he hadn't seen any of the messages that flew back and forth between her and Felicity. There was 'N', too, who messaged on Monday.

> Hey – Heather told me you didn't show last night. What's this about being followed? You OK, Fliss? Can your big bruv help with anything? x

Her brother, then. Jack had replied:

> Yes, all OK, don't worry! x

There were a couple of other messages after that, expressing relief that Felicity was all right and telling her that they all needed to chat soon. But 'N' only signed his messages with a kiss, no name, and Jack puzzled over it for hours, trying to work it out. A brother and a sister, working with Heather? Because they were all working together, that became very obvious as other messages from both Heather and 'N' trickled in. They talked about 'getting the stuff' out of the house and made plans for a video call to sort out the final details. And then, suddenly, it clicked.

Nathan Dixon.

'N' was Nathan Dixon, it had to be.

The man Jack had once let his guard down with, one night when he'd had far too much to drink. The man he'd told about his delicious revenge on Rose Campbell, and his future plans. The man who'd threatened to go to the police, forcing Jack in return to threaten his life, and that of his young daughter. Dixon had left his job and, presumably, the country, not long after that, and Jack had never heard from him again. But now… it *had* to be. There was nobody else it could be.

He screamed out loud in rage when he worked it out, causing Rhona to come running into his office, looking alarmed. He told her he'd just stubbed his toe on the leg of his desk, but inside the fury was white hot. The Dixons had recruited Heather and Heather was an old friend of Amber Ryan's… It all made sense, and he couldn't believe it had taken him so long to put it together.

But he had the upper hand, and so Jack played along as the messages continued to arrive. There was talk of 'finishing this', of Felicity waiting outside the house for Heather, about going straight to the police. Heather played her part well, he thought bitterly. It sounded like she hadn't found everything, but she'd found enough. He considered carefully whether to destroy it all before she came for it; all the things he enjoyed taking out on days when he felt particularly low to reread and rewatch, to relive what he'd done until the buzz came back. He needed to feel the satisfaction, the joy, of such perfectly executed revenge. He probably should have destroyed it all as soon as he had the slightest suspicion that Heather was not back in his life for the reasons she claimed to be. But, after careful thought, he decided there was no point, when she and at least one other person still knew about it. He needed to get rid of the *people*, not just the evidence, and he thought he knew exactly how to do that. He worried about whether anyone else knew, though, and decided to risk asking Heather in another message from 'Felicity'.

Her reply reassured him, but it also made him even more angry.

> Of course I haven't told anyone! Not a soul, I promise. Stop worrying, Felicity. If Jack or Rhona did have any suspicions, don't you think they'd have confronted me, in the house? Rather than following you around? It's not really logical. And it'll all be over in a few days – keep the faith, OK? x

You think I'm stupid, Heather, he thought viciously. *But you're the stupid little bitch. And yes, it really will be over in a few days. Over for you, anyway.*

He obviously couldn't pretend to be Felicity in the Zoom call they were planning, so he concocted the story about the bug sweeping the lab, and Felicity's night shifts, and had told them to just send on the final details. Then, of course, the body was found, and on Friday night the woman's photo was all over the TV news. The messages to Felicity's phone stopped then, unsurprisingly, and Jack allowed himself a little giggle, imagining how shocked and confused Heather and her co-conspirator must be, realising they've been exchanging messages with a dead woman. When the name of the victim was released yesterday, he knew he'd guessed right.

Felicity *Dixon*.

The downside, of course, was that he was no longer

receiving any messages so he didn't know exactly when to expect them, or what they were going to do now one of them was dead. But then Heather got in touch, claiming to be ill and changing their weekend plans, and saying she'd come round on Sunday afternoon instead.

So – still going ahead, he thought, and decided to make it easy for her, even telling her he'd leave a key out. He had a feeling he knew exactly how it was going to play out. He remembered that both of Nathan's parents are dead; common sense told him the man would, therefore, have come back from wherever he'd run off to when he left Shannon Medical, to identify his sister's body. And, as it did appear there were only the three of them involved in all of this, it was highly likely that Nathan would take Felicity's place on Sunday afternoon and be outside waiting for Heather.

He's out there right now, he thinks.

But Jack knows that Nathan will never willingly step inside this house again. And going outside to try to find him, particularly in daylight? No. So, his plan is simple: kill Heather, and then use her phone to send Nathan a message. He's going to say that Jack walked in and found her in the pantry, but that she managed to grab a vase and swing it at his head. He's going to write that Jack is currently unconscious, but that she's struggling to open the freezer to access the emails and needs his help, now. And then, when Nathan appears, well…

He'll have to dispose of two bodies, which is not something he ever dreamt he'd have to do, but he has a plan for that too. He's told Rhona to take a couple of days off, saying he's got friends coming to stay and wants the house to himself. She said she'd take the opportunity to head home to Scotland to visit her mother, and he stood in the hallway and watched her leave, bag in hand, when her shift ended this morning, smiling with satisfaction as he headed to bed to get a few hours of rest before Heather's arrival this afternoon. He told his driver, Yuri, that he doesn't need him for a day or two either, and the Mercedes is parked out back, the boot space plenty large enough to accommodate two bodies. He'll have to haul them up from the basement kitchen and out through the rear courtyard to the car, but he's fit and strong and the house and garden aren't overlooked by any neighbours. He's already turned off all the security cameras inside and outside the house; he'll do a thorough clean-up afterwards too, but he's not planning on any blood. He'll strangle them both, which is nice and tidy. And he'll make sure the bodies are never found, or not for years anyway, by which time any forensic evidence on them will, he hopes, be long gone. Tonight, he's going to drive to the lake he used to swim in with his friends as a teenager. He's been there relatively recently. One night, a year or so ago, he made the two-hour journey just to sit in the dark and gaze at it, reminiscing, remembering brighter, happier days. It's deserted at night, but there are always boats moored there at a little jetty, and as luck would have it, he still has a pair of oars, from a childhood dinghy, stashed in his attic. All he has to do is liberate one of the boats and take the bodies out to the middle of the lake. It's one of the deepest in the UK outside the Lake District, so if he weighs the bodies down with rocks from the shoreline, he's pretty sure they'll stay down there for a long, long time. He'll have time to do it and get back before sunrise too, if he gets a move on.

Right, let's do this, he thinks.

It'll be a shame for Lacey, Nathan's little girl. Her mum died when she was just a baby, he remembers. How old would she be now? Five? Six? To lose her father too… but she'll survive. Kids are resilient, aren't they? He survived, when his mother died. Lacey will be just fine.

There are a couple of other minor issues. Amber Ryan is one. No doubt she knows what her old mate Heather's been up to. But he's not too worried about her. Even if, when Heather and Nathan are reported missing, she kicks up a fuss and tries to blame him, who'll believe her? Nobody believed her at her trial, did they? They locked her up and threw away the key. So, who's going to believe her now? Her friends disappearing will change nothing. She's not a problem, and she'll rot in jail.

Just in case, once Nathan and Heather are dead, Jack will – reluctantly, but needs must – destroy all the evidence in Heather's backpack himself. And then, just one more loose end to tie up.

Yiannis Pappas.

The man without whom he couldn't have done any of this. But could Yiannis have been compromised too? Did Nathan, Felicity, and Heather find out about him? Was it too risky after all, to let him go about his life, knowing what he knows? Yiannis will go to prison too, of course, if anything happens to Jack. Jack won't hesitate to give the police all the details about clever young Yiannis, and his role in all this. But if Jack's getting away with it – and he's pretty confident he is now – then Yiannis is that final outstanding detail. So he'll have to be dealt with too, and as soon as possible.

Jack never intended to become a killer. But, as he stands in his kitchen, listening to the rapid, frightened breaths coming from just metres away and the frantic scrabbling at a door he knows is firmly locked, he realises with a small shiver of shock that he likes it. He *likes* this sense of power over life and death. He was powerless to breathe life back into his dead mother, but now he can control whether someone lives or dies, and he *likes* it. He's *enjoying* himself.

'Coming, Heather,' he says in a singsong voice. 'Ready or not.'

FORTY-THREE

Heather

He's close, so close, and I'm just waiting now for him to pounce. He's going to hurt me, maybe even kill me – I can feel it. I could see it in his eyes when he looked at me up in the hall, that mix of resignation and cold fury. That expression told me everything I need to know, everything I've feared this whole time.

He knows, but how much does he know? *Was* it him, who killed Felicity? Was it him who's been messaging us, pretending to be her? If so, he's even more dangerous now because he knows everything. He knows exactly what we're doing here today.

It's finished. It's over.

I press my body against the back door and listen to him breathing, and then I jump as he speaks again in the same weird, singsong voice he used a few moments ago.

'Didn't you hear me, Heather? I'm coming for you. Ready or not. Better hide. Better hide *good*.'

I look around frantically, but I'm trapped. There's nowhere

to run. Why did I run in here? *Why?* Why did I run myself into a dead end? Unless this door magically springs open, I'm in serious trouble. I start to panic – my chest heaves and my heartbeat is banging in my ears. I can hear another banging sound too, a repetitive *thud, thud, thud,* and I don't know what it is, but I need to think.

Think, Heather!

And then, suddenly, my head clears.

Even if he's been pretending to be Felicity, he doesn't know everything, does he? We stopped including her in our messages as soon as her body was found. So Jack might assume that Nathan's out there waiting for me, but he doesn't know about Johnny. He doesn't know there are two of them. And he definitely doesn't know I'm wearing a voice transmitter…

'The back door!' I scream. 'Back. Door. Now!'

Nathan and Johnny will already have heard me running and they will have heard the conversation with Jack upstairs. But what if they've raced to the front door? Is that what that noise upstairs is? Them trying to break it down? Abruptly, the noise stops, and I know I'm right. But how long will it take them to get round to the rear of the house, and to find this door? And then to get through it? Is it even possible? It's old, made of solid wood…

'And, there she is. Not a very good hiding place, Heather. Two out of ten, I'd say.'

Jack.

He steps into the lobby, and I see that he's got something in his hands, something blue-green and silky. He stops and looks around with a quizzical expression.

'And who were you talking to?' he asks. 'Yourself? Nobody will hear you down here, you know.'

Stall him. I need to stall him, I think desperately. *I need to get him talking. I need to buy some time.*

Come on, guys. Hurry!

'Jack, please. Just… just tell me why. Why did you do it all? Rose and Amber, what did they ever do to deserve that?'

A sneering smile curls the corner of his mouth.

'I had my reasons,' he says. 'It's too complicated to explain now. There's no time. There are other things to be doing. But you, Heather, I thought you were different. It could have worked with you. You could have—'

His voice cracks, and to my surprise I see the sheen of tears in his eyes. He takes another step towards me, and lifts his hands. I see that the silky thing is a scarf, and I know exactly what he intends to do.

He's going to strangle me.

'You could have saved me,' he says. 'I actually thought for a while I could get back to living… to living a normal life. But it turns out you're not different after all. You're the same as all the others. That Felicity bitch got what she deserved too. I didn't know who she was, you know, when I went to meet her. I just knew the two of you were up to something, when I read the messages on your phone. I guess you were supposed to delete those, weren't you? I helped you out there, but I read them first. And it turns out she's a Dixon, isn't she? My old mate Nathan, back to piss me off again. The three of you, plotting together. She deserved to die. So do you, and so does he. You all deserve what you're going to get. You're all the *fucking same!*'

It was him. He killed Felicity. It was him, and I led him to her. And now…

I scream again, as loud and long as I can, and he lunges for me.

'Nooooo!' I roar, and I duck, but he lunges again, ramming the full weight of his body against mine. He pins me against the wall, and when I look up I see that he's winding the scarf around his hands, preparing to wrap it around my neck. I cry for help again, frantically fighting to free myself, but I can't… I can't move…

And then there are another pair of hands grabbing my hair. There's another voice shouting something I'm too panic-stricken to understand.

Rhona!

It's Rhona. She reaches around Jack, her hands entwined in my hair as she painfully yanks my head to the side. Out of nowhere, Rhona's joined the party, and now it's two against one.

And just like that I know it's over and all the fight drains out of me. My legs start to shake and my body slides slowly down the wall, my scalp burning as Rhona's hands maintain their vice-like grip on my hair.

I'm going to die. They're going to kill me, and there's nothing I can do to stop them.

FORTY-FOUR

Heather

I scream, loud and long and desperate, as panic paralyses everything but my vocal cords. But it's no use. It's too late now. This is how it ends. This really is where I'm going to die, crumpled on the floor in this dark basement, at the hands of a man who's already done so much damage and hurt so many people. How stupid was I – how stupid were we all – to think that we could stop him? All we've done is *more* damage; all we've done is cause *more* loss of life.

Stupid, stupid, stupid.

I writhe helplessly, my eyes squeezed tightly shut and my skull exploding with pain, as Rhona and Jack grab at me with hands like vices, both of them bawling unintelligibly. A buzzing starts in my ears and my head begins to swim. I think I might be losing consciousness, and maybe that's a good thing.

'I told you to take a few days off! You're supposed to be off!' I hear Jack screech, and even as I groan as his hands claw at my throat, trying to wrap his silky weapon around it, I find myself wondering why the hell he's scolding his housekeeper about not sticking to her shift pattern at a time like this. Why isn't he thanking her for her help? After all, when you're in the process of murdering someone, two pairs of hands are surely better than one. Especially when one hand doesn't work properly.

And then, quite suddenly, there are two more people in that cramped hallway. I've been vaguely aware of a new banging sound, close by this time, but now there's an almighty CRASH and the back door slams inwards, bouncing off the wall. Two more bodies pile on, and I'm aware of yelling and punching, but mostly that the hands that were mauling my body melt away.

I open my eyes, terrified, and press my back against the wall. For a few moments I can't make any sense of what's happening here, or who these new people are. I blink, gasping for breath and trying to shrink away from the noise and the flailing limbs. My body is rigid with fear and my head whips from left to right.

'What…? Who…?' I stutter.

And then, as quickly as it began, it just… stops. There's Jack, somehow lying on the floor, holding his stomach and moaning. Nathan and Johnny – *Nathan and Johnny!* – stand over him, breathing hard. And there's Rhona, who reaches out a hand to grab my arm and pulls me gently up from where I'm still crouching on the stone floor, trembling. I can feel a fine trickle of something warm running down my face, and I shrink away from her.

'It's OK,' she says in a soft voice. 'I'm on your side, Heather. It's all over. You're safe now.'

'What? What are you...? What do you mean?' I whimper, but she slips an arm round me and leads me into the kitchen, lowering me carefully onto a chair.

'Later,' she says.

Some time passes – I have no idea how much. Minutes? An hour? Time ceases to have any meaning. I still can't take all this in. I can't seem to put events in any sort of logical order in my head. I know, vaguely, that things are still happening around me, but I feel as if I'm dipping in and out of awareness, my world taking on a dreamlike quality.

I see Johnny *sitting* on top of a thrashing, cursing Jack, hissing at him to 'Keep still, you tosser!' I see the police arrive, and I see Jack being led away in handcuffs, howling about the daylight he's being forced to go out into. The officers on either side of him wear puzzled expressions, and I start to try to explain, then sink back into my chair again. I hear Rhona and Nathan speaking to other bemused-looking officers and handing them my backpack, telling them that not only has this man just admitted to killing Felicity Dixon, we also believe he's guilty of at least two other serious historic crimes. Plus, today's attempted murder, of course.

That'll be me then, I think idly. *A victim of attempted murder. Holy shit.*

Jack yells something about Yiannis, too, as he's manhandled out of the house.

'You need to arrest him,' he bellows. 'Pappas. If I'm going down, so is he. So is *fucking* he!'

I don't know if any of these officers know Jack, or knew his father, but they take him anyway. I suppose they have to, given the allegations the three of us are making. They don't arrest

Rhona though. Jack doesn't shout for her to be taken in too, as another of his accomplices.

Because she's not, apparently.

No, Rhona's one of the good guys. Nathan knows her. He even hugged her earlier, when everything had calmed down, and I stared in astonishment.

Have I somehow slipped into a parallel universe?

The day goes on, and now it's later, much later, and finally I'm starting to come to. The shock – for that's what it is, I suppose – fades and my mind sharpens again, and it fills with so many questions. I remember this afternoon in a series of flashbacks, like watching the recap at the start of a new episode of a TV drama. There's an ambulance outside, and yellow police tape flapping. A paramedic peers at my scalp where a clump of hair was ripped out as Rhona tried to haul me away from Jack. She tried to stop him from strangling me, it seems.

'I'm so sorry,' she whispers, hovering behind the ambulance crew. 'It was the only bit I could grab. I'm sorry I hurt you.'

I shake my head, still shell-shocked. Rhona, the creepy housekeeper. Not creepy at all, as it turns out. Nice, even. *Amazing.* Saved my life, probably. I have so many questions, but no time to ask them, because my scalp is being patched up, and then we're being split up and taken into different rooms to answer questions.

Initial statements, they said. Full statements would be required later – tomorrow maybe. And then, finally, I am in the back of a police car, on my way home. I want to sleep. I want to close my eyes for a long, long time, but then I remember that when my backpack was handed over I didn't remove the new DVD, the one with my name on it. I sit bolt upright, feeling a hot flush of embarrassment.

People will watch that now, I think. *They'll see my naked body. They'll see Jack screwing me…*

But really, does that matter, in the grand scheme of things? It's over. Jack's in custody. We did it after all. We did it for Rose, for Amber, and for Felicity now too. It *was* worth it, all of it. And they won't let him go, will they, not when they see the evidence? Even with his contacts.

And he *admitted* killing Felicity. There, in that sweaty little hallway, next to the back door that now hangs, splintered and broken, from its hinges. He told me he actually murdered a woman. They can't let him go, not after this.

We bloody *did* it.

FORTY-FIVE

Heather

Home. A long, hot shower. I try to wash it all away. Will I ever be able to?

It's late evening, and we're all back together again, at my flat. I feel almost myself again – a little fragile, but OK, considering what I now think of as my near-death experience. And there are four of us this time, sitting in my living room, all still wired, all needing to talk, to share our accounts of the past few hours. Yes, Rhona's here too. She can't go back to her apartment at Jack's; the house is, we've been told, likely to be sealed off as a crime scene for several days, and so I've said she can stay here, on my sofa. Johnny's offered to have Nathan upstairs at his place. I can't quite believe I've offered Rhona a bed, but I know I'm about to hear her story, and I know that I owe her, and so I sink down on the sofa next to her and reach for my glass. Somebody – Johnny probably – has opened a bottle of wine, and there's pizza too, although we've barely picked at that. The boxes are open but still almost full, and the smell of cheese is heavy in the air.

'Right,' I say, and touch the plaster on my head gingerly. 'Ouch,' I add, and Rhona grimaces.

'Sorry, again,' she says. 'Anyway, shall I start? Or maybe you should, Nathan, as it was you who got me involved in all this in the first place.'

They've already told me, a little earlier, that Rhona MacDonald is actually Rhona Ross, a private detective Nathan hired to 'help you out and keep an eye on you'. I glared at him, astounded and instantly furious.

'Erm, wasn't that exactly what I suggested? Right back at the beginning?' I spluttered. 'And you said Jack would suss it immediately if we did that? That he was too clever? And… and what? You go and do it anyway, and put me in there as well? Why the hell couldn't Rhona have done it alone? Why did you even need me?'

We were waiting in Jack's hallway, about to get in the cars that were taking us home, and Nathan told me he was 'so, so sorry' for not being honest from the start and that they'd explain all later. Now, I look expectantly at him.

'It was a two-person job,' he says. 'When I first met Rhona, we discussed her doing it by herself, but we quickly realised how risky that would be. As his housekeeper, Rhona obviously had access to most of the house, but we needed someone he'd let his guard down with, someone who could be in spaces that maybe Rhona couldn't easily hang out in without raising suspicion. And we needed backup in case he did happen to realise quickly that she wasn't who she said she was. You probably didn't realise it, but Rhona helped you out quite a bit.'

'Did you?' I turn to Rhona, surprised. I was only aware of

her lurking around, and the fact that she was always popping up out of nowhere.

'I did, actually,' she says. 'I sized you up when you first appeared on the scene, and I thought you looked reasonably fit but probably not strong enough to put up a decent fight if Shannon turned nasty.'

That explains the way she was always looking me up and down, then.

'I wasn't very nice to you, but that was deliberate,' she continues. 'I couldn't risk Jack overhearing or recording any sort of suspicious conversation between us, and I needed him to think I was on his side, a loyal employee, especially as I wasn't on the scene much longer than you. I was too scared to do much searching of the house, either, for the same reason. Nathan and I decided it was better if you knew nothing at all about the real me. One of us could so easily have given it away with just a word or a look. But I helped you as much as I could. I stayed up as late as I could in the mornings when you were there, to make sure you were OK. And I think... I think I stopped Jack... making you have sex with him in front of a camera at least once. I used to listen at doors, sometimes, when you were together, and walk in on the pretence of wanting to clean the room if I thought you were in danger.'

I remember the night Jack suddenly ordered me to take my clothes off in the living room and then Rhona walked in, stopping him in his tracks. I meet her eyes and nod.

'Thank you,' I whisper, and she nods back. Out of the corner of my eye I see Johnny and Nathan exchange glances.

Rhona clears her throat.

'I was basically there to facilitate you, as surreptitiously as possible. When I found you downstairs by the locked freezer, I told you the key was on Jack's keyring, so you'd know where to look. I disabled a few cameras for you too. The dining room – I managed to smash that while I was dusting. I located it and dropped a heavy ornament on it. Jack never said anything because I made sure it looked like an accident, and I guess he didn't want me to know he had cameras everywhere either. I did the same in the snug, and I tried to knock out the one in the attic too, but you walked in just as I opened the box. I pretended it was my own box, and just taped it up again, but it wasn't. I blocked the camera when I put my own box down.'

I nod again, remembering the scene in the attic, and how I assumed Jack hadn't bothered fitting cameras in the dining room or snug.

'I kept her updated on what you were up to so she knew what you'd found and which rooms were next on your list to search,' Nathan says. 'And obviously, you now get why I wasn't very helpful when you started wanting to look into Rhona's background. I'm really sorry you're only finding out about this now, but I hope you understand our reasons for keeping you in the dark?' He pauses, a small smile briefly appearing. 'No pun intended,' he says, then his expression becomes serious again. 'It would have taken twice as long and been twice as difficult if there hadn't been two of you,' he says.

'And you were good,' adds Rhona. 'I was seriously impressed at how well you avoided the cameras and how thoroughly you were able to search the place. You'd make a good private detective.'

'I think I'll stick to books, thanks,' I say quickly, but secretly I feel a little rush of pride. I *did* do well, didn't I?

Except for Felicity, a little voice in my head says, and my stomach contracts. My gaze drops to the floor. Then I realise Rhona is talking to me again.

'Well, if you change your mind,' she's saying, and she picks up her wine glass, raising it in the air before taking a drink. As she puts it down again, I see the scar on her hand and frown.

'That scar,' I say, pointing at it. 'I'd actually begun to think you were colluding with Jack, that *you* were the female accomplice. That it might even have been you he got to stab him. That didn't help.'

She looks down at her hand, and smiles.

'Old gardening injury,' she says. 'That's a good point though. We never did find out who the stabber was. Or find the jewellery, or work out who made the phone call to that jeweller's for him. Maybe he'll tell the cops, now he's in custody.'

'I wonder if it was Naomie, his assistant, after all?' I say, and Rhona shrugs.

'He must have had suspicions about us much earlier than we thought he would,' says Nathan. 'That's obviously why he felt the need to check your phone messages, Heather. Because now we know that *is* what led him to Felicity, and—'

He stops talking, looking stricken. I feel a wave of nausea.

'Nathan, I'm so, so sorry. I'll never forgive myself, never.'

I can make excuses now. I can say that the way Jack was behaving meant I was so debilitated and confused through lack of sleep that I screwed up, and forgot to delete messages, and briefly left my phone unattended. But I won't, I *can't* make excuses. This *is* my fault, and the thought is almost unbearable. It's my fault she's dead, my fault she died an unspeakable death in a seedy alleyway, my fault she was dumped in a bin and left there alone in the dark. Felicity would still be alive if it weren't for me. Tears fill my eyes, but immediately Nathan is there, crouching on the carpet in front of me. He takes both of my hands in his and squeezes them gently.

'*Don't,*' he says fiercely. 'We all knew the risks of getting involved in this. I will miss my sister forever. But look how much good has come out of it. Jack's been arrested. Hopefully, he'll go away for a very long time, and Lacey and I can feel safe again. Rose's family will learn the truth about her death, and Amber will… hopefully she'll be out of prison soon, and be able to live her life again. *So* much good, Heather. And I know, I *know,* that Felicity knows this too, and that she's celebrating with us. It's not your fault. Never think that, please. It's Jack's fault. All of this is down to Jack.'

'Let's take a break for a few minutes. This is a lot to deal with, and we haven't eaten since breakfast. Come on guys, I'll grab some plates.'

Johnny hasn't said much for a while, sitting there listening quietly to the conversation, but now his murmured suggestion suddenly seems like an excellent idea.

I nod and wipe my eyes, and for a few minutes we nibble on the chorizo and mozzarella slices and drink our wine.

When the food has almost gone, I say, 'I wonder what will happen to Yiannis? Do you think they've arrested him too? I guess he'll realise now that the story I came to him with was totally made up. I sort of wish I'd had a chance to tell him myself.'

'Once more, don't feel sorry for him,' Nathan says, a grim edge to his tone. 'He deserves everything he gets.'

'I suppose so.'

'I *know* so,' he says. 'There's a lot we still don't know, guys. But I'm hoping the police will answer our remaining questions over the coming days. We've got this far, and it's further than I ever dared to dream we might get. It's just so…'

He has tears in his eyes suddenly, and he swallows hard, then wipes the back of his hand across his face.

'Sorry. For now, can we just raise a glass? To my sister, who started this with us, and didn't make it to the end. Fliss, I owe you everything, and I'll never forget you. To Felicity.'

I'm crying now too, and I raise a shaky arm in the air, holding my glass aloft. Rhona and Johnny, both looking stricken, do the same.

'To Felicity,' we chorus.

FORTY-SIX

Yiannis

Yiannis Pappas sits on the narrow bench in the tiny cell he's spent the night in and wonders why he feels so strangely calm. Maybe it's because he's always known, deep down, that this day would come, and now that the waiting is over it's as if a weight has been lifted from his back, the weight of guilt and regret that's been crushing him for such a long time. He thinks he can guess why the day has finally arrived; he thinks he might have known it as soon as he met her, that pretty woman who told him the story about her ex-boyfriend, and what she wanted to do to him. He thinks she knew all about him, from the beginning. He thinks she's the reason Jack Shannon is now apparently in custody, and why late last night the police came to his door too. He holds no grudge, if it was down to her. He deserves this. They both do.

He wonders if she knows everything though. She knows about the IT side of it, the emails. But does she know how far he went, to help Jack? Does she know he did something so terrible, so far out of his comfort zone, that he still has nightmares about it, wakes drenched in sweat with tears running down his cheeks?

He watched Amber Ryan's trial unfold with horror. It seemed at times as if even *she* wasn't sure what happened that night; as if she thought that, somehow, she might actually have done what she was accused of. On the morning the jury were due to be sent out to begin their deliberations, he went to the court. He stood outside and stared up at the imposing building, his heart thudding, wondering if he could pluck up the courage to barge his way into the courtroom and scream the truth into the faces of the judge and the lawyers. Was he brave enough to tell them all what really happened, to tell them that the entire crime had been staged, that Amber was innocent? They'd *have* to let her go then, wouldn't they? They'd *have* to put him, and Jack, on trial instead? He didn't do it though. He stood there for a full hour, and then he turned and slunk away. He was a coward, and the shame of that is nearly the worst thing. But now, his day of reckoning has arrived, at last, and he's almost looking forward to it.

He remembers it all so clearly. Every second of that night is seared into his memory. He still isn't sure why he agreed to do the 'stabbing'; he likes to think of the word in inverted commas, as if it wasn't real, but of course it was horrifically real. Staged, but not fake. He still had to plunge that knife in, over and over again. He still had to experience the sensation of sharp metal cutting into soft flesh. It was *horrendous*. But the money… It was so much money. More than he ever dreamed of earning in one day, in one hour. It was enough to save his mother. And so, he agreed, and the plans had been laid.

Jack had recently fired his housekeeper, and hadn't got

round to hiring a new one yet – deliberately, Yiannis later suspected. The fewer people in the house that night, the better. A few days before, Jack disabled the security cameras that covered the rear courtyard, later telling the police he'd noticed they'd stopped working but hadn't had time to fix them. It meant that Yiannis could get in and out of the house without being filmed; they simply propped a ladder against the wall below Jack's office window, and at an agreed time, after dark, Yiannis shinned up it and slipped into the empty room, hence also avoiding the cameras in all the hallways and corridors. Jack told Yiannis there were no cameras in his own office, so he secreted himself behind the open door and waited.

When Amber arrived, he heard the conversation, her shock and confusion, and Jack's cruel laughter. He felt sick, revulsion coiling in his guts. But it was far, far too late to change his mind, and when he heard Jack use the code word they'd prearranged, he sprang into action. Loud music, switched on by the remote control Jack had left behind the door for him. Lights off. Confusion and panic, fumbling for Amber in the dark, grabbing the knife Jack had just put in her hand. Jack guiding Yiannis's hand, indicating the right spots. Then he did it. Slash, slash. He wrapped Amber's hand around the bloodied knife again and ran for the window, hitting the light switch again before he flung himself back onto the ladder and melted into the darkness. He heard her horrified gasps, her terrified sobs. He still hears them now, in the dead of night, in his tortured dreams.

Amber was the only one seen on CCTV entering and leaving the house that night. But now, it turns out, Jack lied about having no cameras in his office. He fitted one just for the occasion, apparently. He recorded everything. He watches it back from time to time. He *enjoys* it. That's what the police told Yiannis last night. They know exactly what happened in that room now, and so today, he's going to tell them the rest. Every detail. How he quickly put the ladder back in its usual place in the summer house. How he flung the knife in the river, and later burned his bloodied clothes. How much Jack paid him, and why he agreed to take the job. How he promised Jack he'd never tell, and Jack promised him that his role in what happened would forever remain a secret.

Everything's changed now though, hasn't it? The secret's out, and it's a good thing. Not many in his position would think so, but today is a *good* day.

He's finally free.

Yiannis leans back on his bench, feeling the cold hard wall behind him, and smiles.

FORTY-SEVEN

Heather

Today's the day. It's taken a few weeks, a mountain of red tape, statements, questions, and analysis of evidence, but finally, it's happening. Amber's being released from prison, and I'm the one who gets to go and meet her at the gate. I'm on the train now, in a window seat, my eyes fixed on a blur of buildings and fields and people and trees outside as we speed towards Downhall. I feel simultaneously horribly anxious and also happier than I have in ages.

It's been a whirlwind since that Sunday in April when it all came to an end; it was, in fact, actually the start of a whole new period of shocks and uncertainties. The family liaison officer assigned to our case brought us jaw-dropping updates almost daily. One mystery was quickly solved: Naomie Anderson wasn't involved in any of it, after all. To our surprise, it turns out the so-called 'female accomplice' doesn't actually exist.

'He had a voice changer app on his phone. Can you believe that?' I said to Johnny, as we sat in the garden together after I'd been given that little nugget of information. It was one of those balmy spring afternoons, the few clouds like tiny fluffy marshmallows in a baby-blue sky.

'He made that call to the jeweller himself, pretending to be Amber. Why would anyone make a voice changer app? Surely it'd only ever be used by criminals?'

Johnny shrugged.

'I think a lot of people who are up to no good do use them, yes. But they can be quite handy too. Rhona would probably tell you that they're used a lot in her game. Good for making discreet enquiries. And people who call in to radio shows to voice controversial opinions, and don't want their mates or employers to know it's them? They use them sometimes. Good for women who live alone and worry about nuisance callers too – we used to recommend a voice changer app sometimes when I was in the force to make it sound like there's a bloke answering the phone. Or, you know, just for playing tricks on your friends. They're legal for all that kind of stuff. But if you use one as part of committing a crime, it's very much illegal.'

Poor Naomie is, by all accounts, utterly devastated to discover the truth about her beloved boss. The entire staff of Shannon Medical are said to be in shock, and at the moment nobody seems to know what will become of it, or of them. We know what became of the jewellery Amber was accused of stealing though; to our great surprise, and probably because he's hoping it will get him a lighter sentence, once he'd calmed down, Jack apparently admitted absolutely everything, pleading guilty to all the charges against him. On a return visit to his house with police, he showed them exactly where he'd hidden the half a million pounds' worth of gemstones, and it was precisely where I'd thought it might be when I searched the lower dining area off the kitchen: concealed inside the wall that blocked off the old coal hole.

Go, me, I thought, when I heard. Maybe Rhona's right about me making a good private detective.

There was forensic evidence too, eventually, from the scene of Felicity's murder – traces of Jack's DNA sealed the deal and confirmed his guilt. Voyeurism has also been added to his list of crimes. Most of the other women on the DVDs in the attic have now been identified. Two of them were sex workers, recognised by a couple of local officers; others were women he had brief relationships with. Yiannis has admitted everything too, and it turns out that not only did he help Jack hack the emails, he also carried out the staged stabbing. I was a little shocked at that. He's been charged with a number of things, including perverting the course of justice, and he's likely to receive a custodial sentence, although his full disclosures about Jack's crimes will, we've been told, reduce the duration a little. We're OK with that. It's Jack we really want to see punished, and while at first we were euphoric that he'd been taken into custody, now we're getting edgy. Despite his full confession, things on that front are not developing quite as we'd like them to.

Rhona, who's taking a month or so off before starting her next undercover job, is on the phone to me every second day, worrying, as is Nathan. He's now back in Spain, but planning to return to the UK to pick up his life with Lacey again in the coming months, which is something I'm quite looking forward to. We've kept Amber informed, and I know she's scared too, but we've vowed that we won't discuss it today. Whatever happens in the coming weeks, Jack Shannon is *not* going to ruin today. Kwee and Milly have given me the day off, and when Amber walks out of those prison gates we're going to go back to Chiswick and then go out for a late lunch. And we're going to make plans. Amber, with her criminal record wiped clean, is hoping for a complete career change. Her face will be hugely recognizable, she knows this; there's been wall-to-wall publicity about the case since Jack's arrest. The crimes he's now been charged with and the story of Amber's innocence are front page news. It's been almost amusing, the way the journalists who pilloried her at the time for her 'shocking, money-grabbing behaviour' are now backtracking furiously, writing sympathetic opinion pieces about women in coercive relationships and bombarding her with interview requests, all desperate to be the first to sit down with her and hear her story.

She's turned them all down. She could make a fortune out of this, but she's not interested. There'll be compensation money coming her way at some point, and she just wants her life back. She wants a job where she can keep a low profile and a little flat somewhere near mine in west London. She's going to stay with me for now though. She'll see her mum too – Mrs Ryan is planning to travel to London to be reunited with her daughter this weekend, in fact – but Amber is struggling to forgive her mother for thinking she was really capable of such heinous acts. I thought that too, of course, but that's all in the past now; I hope I've redeemed myself and even Amber herself wasn't quite sure what had happened in Jack's office. We all know the truth now. It's over, and we're moving on.

The train slows down and I realise we're almost there. I straighten my jacket and push my hair back off my face.

It's time.

Amber's coming home.

FORTY-EIGHT

Amber

'Five minutes, Ryan, and I'll be back to walk you out.'

Lisa, the prison officer who'll be escorting me, taps on the open cell door, and I grin and nod. I'm almost ready – I'm just shoving the last of my belongings into a black holdall. My books, including those from the course I've just finished, my toiletries, a few clothes. There's not much, but it feels strangely liberating to be leaving here with so little, to be given the opportunity to start afresh. A new career, a new life, a new me.

I can't quite believe the events of the past few weeks. I can't believe I'm minutes away from leaving this place, from walking away and never coming back. They did it. They really did it. In the end it was much, much worse for Heather than I feared it would be – she's told me everything now, including the things Jack made her do. He nearly killed her, on that last day, and I will never be able to thank her enough. All of them. Heather and Nathan and Johnny and… I feel a twinge of sadness, even though I never met the woman. Felicity. Jack's final victim.

I've already said my goodbyes to the friends I've made here. It was particularly hard taking my leave of Stacey. She sobbed as she hugged me, and I promised I'd be back to visit as soon as I could. She's gone to the gym now; she told me she doesn't want to be here when I walk out of 'our gaff', as she calls it, for the last time. As I close my bag, pushing with one hand on a trainer that's protruding from the opening as I yank on the zip with the other, I smile as I remember some of our silliness in this grim little space. I'll miss her, I really will. But I need to go now, because I have things I need to do. Urgent things.

The relief of my conviction being quashed is still overwhelming. Even *I* had doubts; there were moments when I was feeling very, very low, and even I wondered. I wondered if I might be capable of doing what they said I did, if there was something deeply wrong with me. And then, a few days ago, the relief was tempered with distress and fury when Heather finally told me something she'd been keeping from me for a little while now, aghast about it herself and fearful of my reaction.

Jack Shannon has been released on bail.

Heather told me the FLO assigned to the case came round to her flat looking very ill at ease, and tried to explain that it didn't often happen when someone's been charged with murder, but that now and again, in exceptional circumstances, bail *is* granted.

'Exceptional frigging circumstances of having friends in high places,' she spat into the phone when she told me. His legal team are, it seems, citing his daylight phobia, saying that as the prison he was being held on remand in after his initial Magistrate's Court appearance didn't seem to be able to accommodate his need to stay up all night and sleep all day, his being there was 'too damaging for his mental health', and there was a danger of him becoming too unwell to appear in court for his sentencing, unless he was allowed to return home until that date.

'Apparently, if the court's satisfied there's no significant risk he'll cause physical or mental injury to anyone, and he can meet various other conditions, off he goes, and so he did,' Heather told me, the anger in her voice vibrating in my ear. 'His passport's been taken from him, he's wearing a tag, and he's got to stay at his home address, but seriously, I can't believe this. He's a murderer, and he can go *out*! I mean, only to the office to wrap things up there and to visit his solicitors, who I presume must be giving him night-time appointments, but still. Normally criminals who are tagged have a curfew and have to stay at home from 7pm to 7am, or something like that. They've reversed it for him. You couldn't make it up. It's a *joke*!'

We know now why Jack lives in the dark. In what I'm sure is an attempt to go for the sympathy vote, he told the police about a childhood trauma he experienced on a sunny day, and they passed the information on to us. We don't know how to feel about that, but we're still angry that he seems to be getting preferential treatment. Heather tried to put on a brave face, telling me it sucked but it won't be for long, and that everyone's pretty sure he's going to get a long, long prison sentence – a life sentence, like the one I got. Only, I'm not so certain about that. He'll milk it all in mitigation; his childhood, his phobia. He'll use all his charm and all his wiles. Jack Shannon is smart, *so* smart, and that, combined with the people he knows, the contacts he has… I think he might get away with it, or at least some of it. And that can't happen. It *can't*.

'Ready? Let's get you out of here!'

Lisa's back at my door, gesturing towards the corridor. I smile, and bend to pick up my bag, shrugging it onto my shoulder. I take one last slow look around the cell. Time to leave. Time to get back into the real world. Time to see Heather's smiling face out there in the sunshine.

'Ready,' I say. 'Prisoner number A6868RX is leaving the building.'

FORTY-NINE

Heather

It's Friday afternoon, just half an hour from closing, and I'm tidying the display tables at the front of the shop, waiting for Amber to come and meet me for an after-work drink. She had a job interview this afternoon, and she called earlier to say it had gone well, and she was hopeful.

'They're going to let me know on Monday, but we got on great,' she said happily. 'It's a really busy little garage, and so well organised, and they're all women too. Isn't that cool? I'd love it, I think. Cross everything for me!'

She's going to be an apprentice car mechanic. She did a car maintenance course in prison, apparently, and she loved it. Who'd have thought it? It's a world away from her glamorous former life in events, but it's what she needs now, she says. She finds it fascinating, understanding how engines work, taking things apart, putting them back together, fixing them.

'A bit like what's happened in my life,' she said the other day. 'I was taken apart, but I'm back together now, and I'm starting to work properly again. It feels so good, Heather.'

Jack's due to be sentenced very soon, and that's the one dark cloud on our sunny horizon. We've made a pact not to talk about it; it's out of our hands after all, and we just have to hope that justice will prevail. But we're nervous, jittery. Amber and I, and Rhona and Nathan and Johnny. We're all so close now, and Kwee and Milly have been an incredible support too; I can't quite believe that, briefly, I had doubts about them, when all they were doing was worrying about me being back with Jack. We'll get through this together, this little gang of ours, whatever happens. Of course we will. But the waiting isn't fun. That's why Amber and I are going out tonight, to distract ourselves. We're going to a Cuban bar, with a live band, and we're going to drink and dance and laugh, and Jack Shannon is *not* going to spoil it. We're done with him, for good. In fact, the police FLO has tried to call me twice in the past hour, and has left messages both times asking me to phone her back as soon as I can, but I've ignored her. It'll be something about the case, and I just don't want to know. Not today. It can wait until tomorrow, or Monday even. Tonight, I just want to relax. I want to have some fun and forget about it all.

'Holy *crap*!'

I spin around. It's Kwee, over at the counter, staring at her iPad, her mouth open. She looks over at me, waving a hand in a 'come here, quickly!' gesture. I frown, putting down the couple of books I'm still trying to find the right spot for and walking briskly across the shop floor. It's virtually empty in here now, just a couple of people down the back in sci-fi, and I slip behind the counter and peer over her shoulder.

'What's up?' I say.

I don't see it at first. Kwee has the ITV news website open

on her tablet, a photo of Madonna dominating the page. She's on tour at the moment, and last night had a sell-out show at the O2. But Kwee is pointing to another article on the left-hand side, and to my surprise I see her hand is quivering. I lean a little closer, and then I see it. For a few moments I think my heart actually stops beating.

'What? *What?*'

I gasp the words, trying to read the news piece, but the letters dance before my eyes. I can't make any sense of it. Is this true?

'Hey guys, what's going on?'

There's a waft of familiar musk-scented perfume. It's Amber, at my elbow, looking smart in a canary-yellow jacket.

'Look, Amber. *Look,*' I whisper, and she squeezes into the small space beside me, her chin lightly resting on my shoulder as I read it again. First, the headline.

FELICITY DIXON KILLER DIES IN HORROR SMASH

And then, the paragraphs below it.

Jack Shannon, the man who confessed to killing thirty-three-year-old Felicity Dixon in Chiswick last month, and who also admitted the attempted murder of thirty-four-year-old Heather Harris at his home on the fourteenth of April, died in hospital early this morning after the car he was travelling in was involved in an accident.

Shannon (38), who was on bail awaiting sentencing, had also confessed to faking two other crimes, including one which resulted in thirty-four-year-old Amber Ryan being erroneously given a life sentence in prison. He died alongside his driver, Yuri Markovic, after their Mercedes swerved off Upper Richmond Road in Barnes and smashed into a tree. No other vehicle was involved, and initial investigations suggest the accident may be the result of a mechanical fault…

A mechanical fault?

I feel Amber lift her head slowly from my shoulder and I turn sharply to look at her, my mind whirring. She didn't, did she? She wouldn't. She couldn't have…

'Amber?' I say softly. Kwee is still staring at the article, shaking her head.

'Wow,' she's muttering. 'Wow. That's *insane*…'

Amber stares at me, expressionless, for a few moments.

Then she smiles.

It's a small, satisfied smirk.

'Wow indeed,' she says. 'What a shock, eh? Oh, well. Come on, Heather. Let's go and get that drink, shall we?'

As I said right at the very beginning of all this, you don't expect your life to change in a bookshop. But sometimes, just like that, one chapter ends and a new one begins.

I stare at Amber for another few seconds, letting it sink in, allowing my thoughts to settle. Then I smile back.

'Let's do that,' I say.

Acknowledgments

My sixth psychological thriller (and ninth book!), completed. With each novel, the list of people to thank grows longer, and this time I want to begin by saying a *huge* thank you to booksellers. The thrill of seeing my books on actual shelves in actual shops will never, ever fade, whether it's in the big supermarkets like Tesco and Asda, on the High Street in Waterstones, The Works, or charity shops, or in the brilliant small independent bookshops (with a particular mention for my favourite in Gloucestershire, The Cleeve Bookshop, run by the wonderful Will Williams – thank you so much Will, for all you do for local authors).

And while I'm talking about bookshops, I must also mention Foster Books, the oldest shop on Chiswick High Road in London, which inspired the fictional Meadow Bookshop, Heather's workplace in this novel.

One of the joys of being an author is being invited to appear at literature festivals, the organisation of which is a huge task; in the past year I've had the pleasure of appearing at several, so special thanks to Crimefest, Evesham Festival of Words, Sandon Literature Festival, and Repton Literary Festival, among many others, for all you do to bring readers and writers together.

Back to this novel now, and thank you so much to IT expert

Iran Burdine for the very useful advice about email hacking (for legal reasons I must stress that, obviously, he's never done it himself!), and to my friend and colleague Stacey Lottes, who is such a big supporter of my novels and who appears in this one as Amber's prison cellmate. (Sorry to make you a criminal, Stace, but she's a nice criminal!) And on the theme of prisons, I'm also very grateful to the authors of a number of guides to life 'inside', which were invaluable for research, including 'Prison for Newbies' by prisonguide.co.uk.

And then, of course, there are all the people without whom I simply couldn't produce my books. My brilliant literary agent, Clare Hulton – thank you for continuing to grow my writing career in ways I could never even have imagined. The amazing team at HarperCollins One More Chapter – I am so proud to be one of your authors. The fabulous Jennie Rothwell, who signed off the idea for this book, and came up with the title, before handing me back to my lovely editor, Kathryn Cheshire, now returned from maternity leave – I'm so happy to be working with you again. My copyeditor Lydia Mason – thank you as always for spotting those little (or sometimes very big) errors and always making me smile with your notes. My proofreader Simon Fox, for that final careful check that's so very important. My super-talented cover designer, Lucy Bennett. The HarperCollins teams in the USA, Canada, and Australia, and the fantastic people at ILA who handle my other foreign rights. At the time of writing this novel, I also now have publishers in Spain, Italy, Germany, Hungary, Latvia, Russia, Sri Lanka, and South Korea, something that still blows my mind.

The organisers of the Nielsen Awards – I am still stunned to have won a bestseller award last year, for sales of over a quarter of a million copies of my novel *The Perfect Couple* in the UK alone. Thank you so much. The award hangs in my downstairs loo, and I often go in there and just stare at it in amazement.

The book bloggers and reviewers who work so hard and give authors so much support – you are the best! And, of course, my readers. Your lovely messages and enthusiasm for my books are incredible, and I appreciate each and every one of you.

My husband, family, and friends – thank you so very, very much. Your genuine excitement and joy when good things happen in my book world means everything to me.

And finally, of course, my friend and colleague, Míceál Murphy, the man to whom this book is dedicated. You've had far, far more than your share of curveballs in this life – another huge one while I was writing this book – but your strength, positivity, and sense of humour are awe-inspiring; you are extraordinary. And reader, if you hate swearing, look away now, because I'm popping one more in, for Míceál.

F*** you, cancer.

The author and One More Chapter would like to thank everyone who contributed to the publication of this story...

Analytics
Abigail Fryer
Maria Osa

Audio
Fionnuala Barrett
Ciara Briggs

Contracts
Sasha Duszynska Lewis

Design
Lucy Bennett
Fiona Greenway
Liane Payne
Dean Russell

Digital Sales
Hannah Lismore
Emily Scorer

Editorial
Kathryn Cheshire
Kate Elton
Simon Fox
Arsalan Isa
Charlotte Ledger
Bonnie Macleod
Lydia Mason
Jennie Rothwell

Harper360
Emily Gerbner
Jean Marie Kelly
Emma Sullivan
Sophia Walker

International Sales
Bethan Moore

Marketing & Publicity
Chloe Cummings
Emma Petfield

Operations
Melissa Okusanya
Hannah Stamp

Production
Emily Chan
Denis Manson
Simon Moore
Francesca Tuzzeo

Rights
Rachel McCarron
Hany Sheikh
Mohamed
Zoe Shine

The HarperCollins Distribution Team

The HarperCollins Finance & Royalties Team

The HarperCollins Legal Team

The HarperCollins Technology Team

Trade Marketing
Ben Hurd

UK Sales
Laura Carpenter
Isabel Coburn
Jay Cochrane
Sabina Lewis
Holly Martin
Erin White
Harriet Williams
Leah Woods

And every other essential link in the chain from delivery drivers to booksellers to librarians and beyond!

The Jackie Kabler Thriller Collection

All titles available now in paperback, ebook and audio

The
PERFECT
COUPLE
...OR THE PERFECT LIE?
JACKIE KABLER

USA TODAY BESTSELLER
JACKIE KABLER
THEIR LIFE
SEEMS PERFECT...
BUT IS IT?
The PERFECT COUPLE
The
HAPPY
FAMILY
'Suspense, intrigue and engaging characters. Fabulous!'
Lucy Clarke, bestselling author of The Castaways

JACKIE KABLER
USA TODAY BESTSELLER
The
MURDER
LIST
Your name
is next

The
VANISHING
OF CLASS
3B
What happens
when your worst
nightmare
comes true?
JACKIE KABLER
USA TODAY BESTSELLER

YOUR NUMBER ONE STOP
ONE MORE CHAPTER
FOR PAGETURNING BOOKS